DAVID RENNER defu... a living. Once he was the top bomb cop in England, directing the toughest security squad this side of Tel Aviv. Now he's L.A.'s only hope. Deliberate, sardonic, and stubborn, he will risk his life, his honor, and his heart to stop the daring madman who has become his obsession.

SIMON CAUTE is a bomber for hire, a free-lance killer loyal only to his own destructive impulses. Nothing turns him on like a full-scale blast of TNT—except the possibilities in an ounce of nitro, a stick of plastique, or a blond bombshell named Jilly.

JILLIAN SPEIRS has been linked to at least one bombing. But is the disarming British beauty an actress playing a part . . . or a desperate woman caught between two brilliant and utterly ruthless men?

LIEUTENANT MUSSO of the LAPD is shrewd, gruff . . . and wary of a man who sees a link between six separate bombings with no pattern of victims, no signature, and no common MO. While Homicide, the Bomb Squad, and the FBI compete to make the first arrest, Musso must decide whether to trust Renner or his own instincts—before the next bomb goes off.

FUSE TIME

Bantam Crime Line Books offer the finest in classic and modern American mysteries
Ask your bookseller for the books you have missed

Rex Stout

The Black Mountain
Broken Vase
Death of a Dude
Death Times Three
Fer-de-Lance
The Final Deduction
Gambit
Plot It Yourself
The Rubber Band
Some Buried Caesar
Three for the Chair
Too Many Cooks
And Be a Villain

Max Allan Collins

The Dark City
Bullet Proof
Butcher's Dozen

Loren Estleman

Peeper
Whiskey River

Dick Lupoff

The Comic Book Killer

Virginia Anderson

Blood Lies
King of the Roses

William Murray

When the Fat Man Sings
The King of the Nightcap
The Getaway Blues

Eugene Izzi

King of the Hustlers
The Prime Roll
Invasions

Jeffery Deaver

Manhattan is My Beat
Death of a Blue Movie Star

David Lindsey

In the Lake of the Moon

Randall Wallace

Blood of the Lamb

Rob Kantner

Dirty Work
The Back-Door Man
Hell's Only Half Full
Made in Detroit

Robert Crais

The Monkey's Raincoat
Stalking the Angel

Keith Peterson

The Trapdoor
There Fell a Shadow
The Rain
Rough Justice
The Scarred Man

David Handler

The Man Who Died Laughing
The Man Who Lived by Night
The Man Who Would Be
   F. Scott Fitzgerald

Jerry Oster

Club Dead
Internal Affairs
Final Cut

Benjamin M. Schutz

A Tax in Blood
Embrace the Wolf
The Things We Do for Love

Monroe Thompson

The Blue Room

Paul Levine

To Speak for the Dead

Stephen Greenleaf

Impact

Max Byrd

Fuse Time
Target of Opportunity

MAX BYRD

FUSE TIME

BANTAM BOOKS

NEW YORK · TORONTO · LONDON · SYDNEY · AUCKLAND

FUSE TIME

A BANTAM CRIME LINE BOOK / MARCH 1991

CRIME LINE and the portrayal of a boxed "cl" are trademarks of Bantam Books,
a division of Bantam Doubleday Dell Publishing Group, Inc.

Grateful acknowledgment is made for permission to reprint lyric from
"The Lady is a Tramp" (Lorenz Hart, Richard Rodgers) copyright 1937
CHAPPELL & CO. (Renewed) All rights reserved. Used by permission.

ISBN 0-553-28816-4

PUBLISHED SIMULTANEOUSLY IN THE UNITED STATES AND CANADA

Bantam Books are published by Bantam Books, a division of Bantam Doubleday
Dell Publishing Group, Inc. Its trademark, consisting of the words "Bantam Books"
and the portrayal of a rooster, is Registered in U.S. Patent and Trademark Office
and in other countries. Marca Registrada. Bantam Books, 666 Fifth Avenue, New
York, New York 10103.

PRINTED IN THE UNITED STATES OF AMERICA

RAD   0 9 8 7 6 5 4 3 2 1

For my mother and father

ONE

1

June 7

"THAT ONE," KESTLER'S DATE SAID. SHE BENT OVER THE COUNTER, flattening her breasts against the glass. Kestler stood with his legs apart and watched first her breasts, then the clerk's pudgy, dimpled hand as it moved back and forth over the guns.

"Back up one," she said. "There."

For a moment of sheer panic Kestler couldn't remember her name. Susan? Cindy? The last girl he'd brought here had been named Cindy, and now he could think of nothing but Cindy, his mind otherwise blank and white as the fat clerk's T-shirt.

"I dunno," the clerk said. "That's a very tough guy there for a beginner." He raised his voice slightly over the crack of rifle shots in the back gallery. "What we call a virgin sometimes. You think it's OK to start out with that, Mr. Kestler?"

Kestler grunted and made an impatient gesture with one hand, and his date turned to grin at him. Little bit of a moon-face, he thought. And mascara stuck on like it was

pine tar, but the body wouldn't quit, the body was taller
lying down than standing up, the boobs were so good.

"This is what we call an Uzi," the fat clerk said, holding
up the submachine gun. Kestler's date was reaching for it
before the stock was clear of the counter, putting her hands
all over. The clerk glanced sideways at Kestler, smiled
again, and wiped sweat from his face.

"They still walking down at your plant, Mr. Kestler?"
he asked while Kestler's date turned the gun over and
poked the trigger guard with a tentative finger.

"They're getting tired," Kestler said. "Six weeks on
strike anybody gets sick of it, even those goons. Six weeks
on strike it stops being a free vacation."

"Guys on a picket line," the clerk said. "Some of those
guys would steal the paint off your car." Both of them
watched Kestler's date as she swung abruptly to her right
and fired an imaginary round from the Uzi at the giant
plastic ferns that stood in planter boxes along the far wall.
The fat clerk winked at Kestler.

"You really want to try that one, miss," he said, "I need
to show you how to load the clip, how we switch the
safety lever on and off." Reluctantly, she allowed him to
pull the gun from her hands. "The Uzi," he said, clearing
his throat, "is the official weapon of the Israeli Army.
Israeli assault teams carry nothing else, like when they
raided the Entebbe airport. It fires clips of thirty-two
rounds each, nine-millimeter Parabellum bullets, that's
very big, highly accurate, *very* powerful. You got a folding
metal stock, that's what these holes are for. You got a
muzzle velocity here, miss, of just over twelve hundred
feet per *second*." He clicked the safety and she took the gun
as he handed it back. Still talking, he leaned forward to
adjust the stock against her right shoulder.

"We're talking little *bombs* here," the clerk said. "We're
talking one of the most powerful weapons in the world
you can actually pick up and hold in your hands."

Earning his tip, Kestler thought. The fat man knew
what turned them on, knew exactly what Kestler liked to
hear him say. Since he'd discovered the place eight months
ago, just driving down Santa Monica Boulevard, moping,

looking for something to do, since then he'd brought half a dozen girls downstairs to the basement gallery and let them fly. The world's best aphrodisiac, he told anybody who would listen. He especially told his ex-brother-in-law in the next office, who grimaced in liberal disgust and was certain to call Kestler's ex-wife and tell her, every time. You let them wrap their hands around an automatic rifle or a submachine gun or a big magnum pistol, let them put on the holster, whip it out, and pump eight rounds into a target, they practically go down on you right there in the shooting gallery, they're so hot. He wished to hell he could remember whether it was Cindy or Susan or what. He wished he knew why he couldn't remember.

"And you got to wear these safety flaps too," the clerk said, "as soon as you go through that door there. Los Angeles city law." He pulled out two pairs of oversize gray plastic ear protectors and stretched one set over the woman's stiff Madonna hair job. She turned, laughing, and made a face at Kestler, who kept his hands in his pockets and rocked on his heels. "Most girls look really cute in these things," the clerk said, still fussing with the metal band. "Like Minnie Mouse."

"You think I look cute, Ernie?" She posed with the Uzi in one hand and held the gray ear covers in place with the other.

Kestler looked at the breasts stretching tight against the shirt, the nipples already dark and protruding under her bra. Nipples like fucking bullets, he thought.

"You look like Wonder Woman," he told her, licking saliva from his lips. Cindy, Susan, whatever. "You look like a goddamn storm trooper from Venus. Let's take that thing in the back room and crank it up before I bust."

It was two hours later, long past midnight, before they returned to Kestler's apartment and Kestler stood, stripped to the waist, in the center of his bathroom, staring through the open door. In the next room Kestler's date knelt on the bed, jeans already off, shoes off, panties off. From the bathroom Kestler could just see a thin sliver of mirror, a bare arm flashing, one white hip. While he watched the arm lifted and the bed squeaked and she moved out of

sight. He heard her muffled voice say she was pulling her
shirt over her head, she was cupping both hands around
her bra.

Kestler stepped backward, still watching, and groped
behind his shoulder for the cabinet over the sink. He hated
the goddamn things, but he knew he had a pack somewhere in there with the soap and shaving gear. And she
had only one rule, she'd told him, chewing his ear and
practically shoving her hand down his crotch as they came
up the stairs. No glove, no love.

Kestler pulled the cabinet door open, watching the
mirror, hoping to catch a glimpse as the bra came off. His
ears still rang from the sound of the Uzi, earmuffs or no
earmuffs, so he failed to notice the first odd click as the
catch on the door released. In the last half instant of his
life he suddenly remembered his date's name. Gina. He
snapped his fingers, missing the second click of the cabinet
door. Then the wall of the bathroom exploded in a
thunderous roar he never heard and his skull flew apart like
eggshell under a hammer.

2

RENNER'S SLEEPY MIND CAME UP WITH A WORD: AUBADE.

It darted unexpectedly in and out of his head like a seabird, and he sat up heavily, slick with sweat, blinking the dark room into focus. Automatically his legs swung from under the blankets and his feet felt for the floor. His left hand fumbled on the nightstand for the digital watch his daughter had given him. You can buy little airline bottles of vodka in six-packs now, he had discovered, pocket-size cartons of oblivion to carry out. Drunk for a penny, dead drunk for tuppence. His hand groped over empties until it bumped against the watch and he swayed to his feet, feeling the motel carpet crinkle, hearing a motor far away under the floor throb and change speeds. It was dawn, or nearly dawn, and he wasn't drunk and he wasn't hung over, but the six-pack of Smirnoff bottles he had bought after dinner was empty nonetheless.

I should buy a leather bandolier for them, Renner thought as he crossed the carpet to the window and pulled the curtain. *I should go into the goddamn Parker Center wearing a bandolier of little vodka bottles strapped across my chest like an alcoholic*

Pancho Villa. The sky beyond the curtain was still black, but flecked with patches of floating white light which must have been gulls. An aubade, he remembered, was a song that a poet sang to his lover as they watched the sun rise.

After a moment he turned to the bureau beside the window, hastily dressed in his old madras sports jacket, slacks, and loafers, and walked downstairs to look at the ocean.

In the parking lot the air was cool, light, cotton-damp with mist. He hunched his shoulders against the chill and crossed Ocean Avenue in the middle of the block. When he had come down from Sacramento two weeks ago, the one thing he had insisted on was a motel by the water. He believed, he had told himself rather grandly, in the healing power of the huge gray ocean, of all huge, endless, impersonal things.

He stepped down onto the beach and paused to scrape his shoe. All the time in the world. In London six months ago, a year ago, he would wake up like a human jack-in-the-box, his hands flexing and rehearsing before his feet hit the floor. Instinctively now his wrists spread out, and he stretched his fingers in the chilly air as if he were practicing scales. When he built his famous bomb for the Royal Army Bomb School, he had worked for three days straight, without bothering to sleep, oblivious.

He shook his head and began to walk, holding up the watch again as he went. Five-thirty in the morning. Another hour at least before he could reasonably show up at the soulless little office the Los Angeles police had given him and start back to work. He would write an aubade to work. Work and vodka. Without work and vodka, he thought, he was all out of oblivion.

Behind him the neon lights of the pier swung slowly in tired pinwheels against the sky. To his left, thirty yards away, the trooping waves came solemnly forward one by one, knelt, hissed, and exploded.

Renner veered around a lifeguard's tall chair, and listened to the sand squeak under his shoes. A young couple carrying sleeping bags emerged briefly from the shadowy retaining wall to his right. A man in a red sweat suit came jogging toward him, panting, a bicyclist's safety light pinned to one sleeve and bouncing up and down like a star on a yo-yo string.

California, Renner thought. Ineluctable modality of the flaky. They were going to jog in their sweat suits right up the steps on doomsday morning. They were going to stitch the San Andreas Fault back together with bean sprouts and beads. Back in the late fifties, when Renner was eight or nine, his father had lasted not quite a year in California before yanking his family home to Virginia, where the sky was blue and the grass was green and the children all said 'yes, sir.' What little of Los Angeles Renner remembered had been obliterated by now, transformed into one continuous coiling valley of asphalt from Santa Monica to Riverside. Everything had changed, nothing was what he remembered. He felt like an immigrant into his own past.

A wave's tongue out of nowhere licked at his heels and he moved quickly away, walking uphill. A man wrapped in five or six filthy padded jackets stood swaying under a light stanchion. He called out something to Renner and Renner paused, fumbling in his pocket for change.

When he reached the stairs up to the street, he paused once more to watch the waves. A sober man would be afraid of muggers, he thought. On the other hand, a sober man wouldn't have a demagnetized bomb squad tool kit in one pocket either, or an unloaded government-issue Llama .32 automatic in his belt. At the edge of the water sunlight was just striking through the mist, turning it pale white. Whatever his father thought of it, California was beautiful, a pool of light, mountains and valleys and oceans of spreading light; even now, before full dawn, there was light in every direction—dark buildings, hillsides, trees, all the familiar unconnected fragments of landscape seemed to float together on a shimmering surface of light. Not far away a woman in a running suit stood looking out to sea. When she turned she all but disappeared in the light, her face was entirely lost. From where Renner stood it was hard to tell if she was rising out of the ocean, or disappearing into it.

The light covered the fragments, Renner thought; it held them together. What was left over from the South, what he had decided he really believed in was holding things together, patching them up, embracing the light. A second odd thought veered across his mind: If you knew how to do it, you could use light to set off a bomb.

He shook his head and rested his hand on the tools in his jacket pocket. A car swished past. Over the eastern hills the rim of the sun appeared with the incredible speed of dawn, an orange fireball rising.

3

"WHERE'S RENNER?" MUSSO ASKED.

The sergeant wore the open-collared blue military jumpsuit of the bomb squad and his face was disdainful of the question. He put a gloved hand on his tool belt and looked contemptuously at Musso. "Who the fuck knows where Renner is?"

Musso rubbed his ear and worked his jaw. Wonderful. Six o'clock in the morning. A dozen blaring radios and twenty cops jammed into one tiny blown-to-shit room, not to mention the black smoke everywhere and the guy's blood splattered on the walls. And like all the bomb squad people, this one in front of him, this Gretzsky, had to talk to you as if half your brains were in the toilet. Where the hell was Renner? Renner was supposed to check out every bomb call.

"Musso," Gretzsky said loudly. "Let me educate you to something, you and Echeverria." He motioned to include the yawning plainclothes detective standing crowded against Musso. "This is your whole bomb right here," he said. "This is all it took." He opened his canvas glove and held out his palm to show them a dozen or more shards of curved, blackened metal.

"That's a pipe bomb," Echeverria said.

"Right. That's a pipe bomb the way a 747 is an airplane," Gretzsky said. "The way Farrah Fawcett is a piece of ass. That pipe bomb took out the guy, blew the bathroom to hell, and knocked down half the fucking bedroom wall. But it didn't touch the *back* of the bathroom wall. It didn't even blow out the bathroom mirror. The guy had a pack of Trojans on the shelf over the sink, ten inches over the bomb. Echeverria could still put one on and drive down to Hollywood, never spill a drop."

"You going to write a testimonial to the company?" Musso said. He was leaning forward, over the protruding dome of his belly, and looking skeptically at the pieces of metal. Gretzsky was an idiot.

"I'm going to tell you how good this bomb was," Gretzsky said. He started to pick up one of the pieces of metal, then stepped to one side and let the man with the video camera go by. Musso lifted his gaze for a moment. After they search the wreck for a second bomb, he thought—routine since the sixties, when the radical students would set off the first bomb just to lure in the cops—after that the mob scene starts.

"What happened," Gretzsky began, and he waved impatiently for two more owl-faced bomb technicians to go the other way. Musso rubbed his ear again and squinted through the dust and smoke. A bomb tended to shake out a building like a rug, even a little bomb. Musso had been at bomb sites where the air was still black with dust a week after the explosion.

"What happened," Gretzsky said, coming back and holding out the glove again. "The guy opens the bathroom cabinet door to get something, the lock pulls a trip mechanism that's got to be unbelievably short—the guy must of heard it, two loud clicks. That completes a circuit to a little nine-volt battery, which is attached to a blasting cap—we didn't find that yet. The blasting cap detonates the charge in the piece of pipe, just about face high."

"Like a hand grenade," Musso said.

"Like a *cannon*. Let me show you something else." He knelt to the floor and arranged the metal shards on a green plastic sheet spread across the bathroom floor. The video man stopped to watch and his spotlight cut through the smoke to highlight Gretzsky's hands, now sweeping bits of gritty plaster, wood, and charred junk to one side and fitting a heavy ten-inch square of blackened metal neatly against the reconstructed pipe.

"C-four," Echeverria said, leaning forward to interrupt. "C-four plastic, right?"

Gretzsky didn't bother to look up. "The smoke from a C-four explosion is pure white," he said. "You see any white smoke here, Echeverria? Let me just do my fucking job, OK?"

Echeverria looked at Musso, then took a step backward and crossed his arms.

"The guy started with an explosive charge that was probably TNT or starch nitrate, OK?" Gretzsky shifted the steel square a few inches. "That's genuine high explosive, you don't find that in a hardware store. You got to know how to pack it. With a pipe this short you got to know how to calculate the blast wave and the stand-off distance exactly. Not only does the guy do all this, he *indents* the end of the pipe. Look at this, like the cone at the bottom of a rocket. That's what you call a 'shaped charge,' and it's very tricky. He had a fuse time of maybe two seconds."

"Why a 'shaped charge'?" Musso asked. The jargon was worse than the dust. 'Fuse time.'

"It focuses the goddamn blast," Gretzsky told him, sneering, a sneering teacher talking to his class. He slapped his hands together and made his fingers into a little steeple. "Basic high school physics, right, Musso? An ordinary explosion, the blast wave goes off at a ninety degree angle to the surface. Always. But you make the cone angle thirty, forty degrees like this, you concentrate the blast waves into a jet of hot gas, like a blow torch. That's why a rocket goes up instead of blowing apart. In this case the jet happened to come out about level with the back of young Kestler's head."

"Like a little bazooka," Musso said to Echeverria, twisting to look again at the far wall. Musso had seen two thousand homicides in his life and they had all made him sick and angry. "Like he shot a blimp full of blood."

Gretzsky hitched his belt over his stomach and spread his feet.

"You didn't call him, did you?" Musso said. He came back around and studied Gretzsky's sneer. "You just froze Renner out, right?"

"This bomb," Gretzsky said, pulling his big canvas glove down so slowly, so arrogantly that Musso wanted to yank it off and grind it into his face, "this bomb belongs to the bomb squad. There's no mad bomber, I don't care what Renner says. There's no 'one guy' doing this. Every fucking bomb in this series is different. That's why the task force is a waste of time."

"You didn't call him."

"I did my fucking job."

Musso stared at him for a moment, then turned pointedly away and spoke to Echeverria. "You check for drugs?"

"We didn't find a thing," Echeverria said. He stepped out of the way for a new team of sleepy-eyed video people. "The lady across the hall swears he was clean. I took a quickie statement before the TV got here."

"Television," Musso said flatly. Gretzsky had started toward the two technicians in a corner by the bedroom window, who were stooping and looking for pieces of primary fragmentation to put in their evidence bags. Musso surveyed the wrecked bathroom doorway one more time and began navigating toward the living room. "How old is the neighbor?"

"Sixty-five, seventy," Echeverria said, blowing out his moustache and following. "Lived here six years. Except for being divorced and liking to party, she thought he was straight."

Without breaking stride Musso accepted a clipboard full of paper from the officer nearest the front door and stepped out into the relative calm of the hallway. "Wonderful," he said. "Seventy-year-old L.A. lady tells you he's

straight. Come *on*, Echeverria. Run the medicine you
found through the lab, tell downtown to pull the narc files.
Start the door-to-door on the rest of the neighbors. You
need to be told?"

"You think it was drugs?"

"I think one guy bombs another guy that carefully,"
Musso said, and stopped. The one thing he didn't want it
to be was drugs, Musso thought with distaste. Drugs
meant informers, scumballs, goonies. Drugs meant deals
for names, deals for more drugs; drugs meant you traded
nickels for quarters and never got the quarter anyway. He
slapped dust from one sleeve and looked down at his big
belly, outlined by the high sodium lights from the parking
lot below. *If I get any fatter*, he thought irrelevantly, *they'll
have to bury me in something with a curved lid, like a casserole
dish.*

"That bomb was not a homemade bomb," Echeverria
said, following Musso down the stairs toward the ground
floor.

"I know that."

"That bomb was so simple, it was brilliant."

Musso grunted and turned into the courtyard of the
apartment building. Two blocks away, the lights on the
San Diego Freeway were creeping past, flickering angrily.
The Miramar, Musso had decided after one glance, was
like every other cheap apartment complex in L.A., your
basic army barracks in stucco, built around a too-small
pool and ringed with dying palm trees that landscapers
uprooted in the Mojave Desert and carried back to the city
on flatbed trucks. Who lived here except secretaries and
singles and divorced gray-collar workers like Ernie Kestler? The Alimony Arms.

"Which means," Echeverria said, "that this is not going
to be our case until Gretzsky writes his report and then
Renner writes *his*."

Musso stopped in front of an auxiliary building on one
side of the pool and studied his clipboard. To his left were
a janitor's closet, locked, and a red Coke machine the size
of an upended truck. To his right the window of a brightly
lit laundry room reflected his yellow tie and his Mexican

boots. If it were a drug hit, he thought, Kestler would have been living some place much crummier, either some roach pit in Culver City, or else down by the beach, where the money and the sewage drain.

"This girl you found, the one in the parking lot—" Musso snapped one finger on the clipboard. Against the revolving red and blue lights of the squad cars his pale face seemed to be a moon swimming upstream. "You put her where?"

"Gretzsky said hold any witnesses in the laundry room, he's too busy right now, he'll see them later." Echeverria's voice grew heavily sarcastic. "But hey, I'm only a homicide dick. I got mixed up. The first black-and-white coming in spotted her halfway out of the lot, driving away. I figured, keep her in the manager's office, save Gretzsky the trouble."

Musso smiled. He considered himself a student of human nature, not bombs; he took extension courses in psychology at USC and played tournament blackjack, and he thought Gretzsky had brought it down on himself. Screw the fucking bomb squad.

"You're going to want to see her, Lieutenant."

Musso nodded. "You did the right thing, Echeverria." He led the way and Echeverria followed two steps behind. On the other side of the auxiliary building they walked under an open concrete staircase toward a yellow insect bulb and the sign for the manager's office.

At the door Musso barely paused to knock. On a chair inside a uniformed policeman, still wearing his hat, recognized him and started to rise. To the patrolman's right, just turning on her heel so that her hair shook out in a blond cloud and her skirt whirled high around the curve of one hip, the witness lifted her face toward Musso.

"Fuse time," Echeverria said behind him. "Instantaneous."

4

"GODDAMNIT, MUSSO, WE WANT *DECISIONS! RESULTS! ARRESTS!*"

The Deputy Chief for Special Operations was known himself for decisiveness. E. B. Linacre liked to pace up and down at meetings, chopping the air with the side of his hand. In recent months he had developed a manner of jabbing his finger and stopping abruptly in midstride that department wags said was modeled on George C. Scott in *Patton.* Although he was born and reared in Bangor, Maine, for as long as anyone could remember Chief Linacre had talked with the flat-voweled semisouthern accent favored in California by drill sergeants and Orange County politicians. He was short, dog-faced, and overweight, and nobody in the room thought he was anything less than brilliant at his job.

He stopped at one end of the long mahogany conference table, glaring, and hitched his belt.

"Well, Musso?"

"Round up the usual suspects," Musso muttered. The man on his left visibly pulled his shoulder away. Across the table, in a gesture Musso couldn't stand, the black woman from the attorney general's office slid her glasses down her nose and peered at Musso over the rims.

"You making a joke for us, Musso?"

Musso looked down at his empty legal pad.

"No, sir."

The deputy chief leaned forward on the table bulldog fashion, fists compressed into lumpy white knobs. "You read all the reports we been talking about for twenty minutes, Musso? You read Gretzsky's report?"

"I read them."

"You read Mr. Renner's summary—what do we call you anyway, Renner? I can't remember. Mr. Renner? Dr. Renner? Colonel Renner?"

"How about 'your highness'?" Gretzsky said, shifting in his chair and fingering the breast badge on his blue bomb squad jumpsuit. "How about 'Harvard asshole'?" Musso watched Renner flush.

"You got a problem too, Gretzsky?"

"No, sir." Gretzsky repeated Musso's gesture of interest in his empty tablet.

"You know what our problem is in here?" the deputy chief said. He stalked halfway down the room and stopped suddenly at midtable. There were perhaps two dozen people crowded in front of him, only half of whom Musso knew by sight. There were bomb squad people, homicide people, city lawyers, public relations flacks, stenographers, and two or three police psychologists who made little speeches to each other, then sat back and cleaned their glasses. Circus-circus. The room itself was the least comfortable meeting room in the Parker Center, jammed with surplus filing cabinets and chairs, looking out on nothing but freeway pillars and a covered parking lot.

"Our problem," the deputy chief said, "is that we don't have community here. We got fifteen little Balkan nations, every one of them terrified somebody else is going to get a prize. We got homicide sulking when they don't have first call on every goddamn crime in Los Angeles. We got Gretzsky here in a snit if somebody decides to call in a little outside help for the bomb squad like Dr. Renner—don't worry if the bombs keep popping off the citizens, right, Gretzsky? Just don't upstage your fine blue suit. And we got the attorney general's office counting minorities and TV cameras, right, Ms. Watson?" The black woman stared straight back at him. "God forbid," the deputy chief said, "that this task force should not have the exact statistical configurations of minorities spelled out in the Constitution and the U.S. census for L.A. County."

He strode back to the end of the table and around to a bookcase where a stenographer was desperately pulling at wires running out of a touch-tone telephone. With another jab of his finger he hit a button on the side of the amplifier box and speaker attached to the telephone. "You still there, Huntsville?"

The box squawked something unintelligible to Musso.

"Fine," the deputy chief said. "Sorry to keep you waiting. We're just having a little friendly pep talk here—you butt in whenever you want." He turned his back on the box and walked toward the window. "I was in Washington, D.C. last week," he said to the room at large. "And I went into the office of a man who used to be number five or six in the White House security chain. Before he quit in disgust and went to work for himself. He had just two books on his desk. He had Robert Frost's poems and he had a paperback copy of Tocqueville's *Democracy in America*. Now every schoolboy in America used to read Tocqueville—pardon me, Ms. Watson, I should say school person—and this distinguished officer and patriot told me he was rereading Tocqueville because it was still right on the money. We don't have a democracy in this country, he said. We have a continental-size bump-car ring of special interests. Nobody gives a shit about any other group. We've got office politics on a national scale. We've got a community of greed. And I look at L.A. County and the LAPD and this miserable goddamn task force on bombs and I think I'm about ready to quit in disgust too. The FBI got anything to say, Huntsville?"

The voice on the box was as semisouthern as the deputy chief's, but younger, milder; to Musso's ear its tone was rather scholarly. "We had one of our analysts go over the three reports you sent us."

"We sent you four," Linacre said. "There've been four goddamn bombings."

There was static on the box, then long scratches that Musso took to be the sound of shuffled papers.

"Number one," the deputy chief said impatiently. "Number one was a car bomb two months ago—a married guy sitting in the driveway of his girlfriend's house. Number two was a five-gallon can of kerosene with sticks of dynamite taped around it—we're not sure who the victim was supposed to be. It took out three teenage boys in a crack house, not to mention a guy happened to be walking his dog outside. Number three was a thyratron tube and a blasting cap in the restroom of a Greyhound bus. Again, motive unknown."

"It killed a woman and two men," the voice said. "Right. And number four was a booby trap in an office, some kind of electronic timer you think was connected to a radio. Killed four people."

"That's thirteen people dead," the deputy chief said flatly. "Counting last night."

"Thirteen," the voice agreed. "We studied all of the reports, everything you sent us. But our analyst here is inclined to be cautious. He doesn't see how he can agree with Dr. Renner—is it doctor, or what?"

The deputy chief raised his head to scowl at Gretzsky. "You're saying you don't agree that these bombs were all set by one person?"

"These bombs are so different," the voice said. "You have four entirely different types of bombs there."

"Five now," Gretzsky said. "The one last night was a shaped charge EOD rigged with a trip wire and starch nitrate." He paused and then added with coarse irony, "Of course we don't have Dr. Renner's report on that yet."

"We don't see where you have a serial bomber yet," the voice said. "No pattern of victims, no signature, no common MO. Somebody back here just said Los Angeles is a big city. These things can just happen in bunches, like a statistical blip."

"You mean Los Angeles is a big fruit salad," the deputy chief said. "You got that right."

"You don't see a racial profile?" the black lawyer asked, tapping her pencil on the table. "One of the victims was black. One of them was Korean."

"And eight of them were white males," Musso grumbled.

"No, ma'am, we don't."

"Terrorists?" the deputy chief asked.

The voice was slower still as it answered. "Terrorists," it said, "generally have one of two objectives—one of them is assassination, somebody symbolic or crucial to whatever their cause is. The other objective is really anarchism. To show the citizens that their government is so inept and weak and incoherent that it can't guarantee anybody's safety anymore. That's what terror is really all about. We had a threat two weeks ago in England, some Indian extremist group wanted to blow up the case with the Magna Carta in it at the British Museum. But we don't see any pattern like that in your bombs."

"The last victim worked for a defense plant on strike," a uniformed cop near the chief volunteered. "Kestler."

"We saw that."

"All right, thanks, Huntsville. We'll wait for your written report on the technical end." Linacre hooked his watch in front of his face, then picked up a stack of manila folders and rapped them sharply against the table, his invariable signal that a meeting was over. Around the narrow room men and women began to push back their chairs and stand.

"There was one thing," the box said, almost inaudible behind the scrape of chair legs. "We got a guy here who said you might want to look into one scenario. It's very rare, but it's all he could think of."

"Yeah." Linacre continued to arrange his folders.

"He said maybe what you got in Los Angeles is some kind of bomber-for-hire, a free lance."

Linacre straightened his back and glowered at the bookcase. "You know what, Huntsville?" he said. For a syllable or two, Musso thought, his accent had slipped and you could hear cold, bleak Bangor, Maine rising to the surface. "You know what, that's exactly what Dr. Renner told me when he came down here from Sacramento two weeks ago."

"It's just a thought," the box apologized.

5

"IT'S A DUMB-ASS THOUGHT," MUSSO SAID. "WITH ALL DUE respect."

He tilted back in his chair and watched David Renner make coffee.

Renner stood behind the desk in his shirtsleeves. White shirt, cuffs turned back, tie sawed loose from his button-down collar. Preppy madras jacket hung on the chair. He dug a plastic spoon into a jar of Brim, stuck it in a white ceramic mug with "Ski Lake Tahoe" printed in blue across the side, poured in boiling water from the hot plate by the desk, then drank it, without stirring, with the spoon still in the mug. While he drank he stood and turned the pages of Musso's report.

"Stranger things have happened," he said as he studied a page.

"Free-lance bombers don't exist," Musso said. "Contract bombers all work for the mob, for organized crime."

Renner squinted or frowned at the page he was reading. It was hard to tell which, Musso thought.

"You know the guy who has this office regularly?"

Renner shook his head and turned over a sheet of flimsy.

"Named Riboud. A Stanford grad—the Harvard of the West, right? Make you feel right at home." He paused but Renner didn't rise to the bait. He never did. "This Riboud's on leave now, but when he's here he keeps a jar of pure Kona coffee beans in the desk. He's got three kinds of filter paper in the stationery drawer. He buys Sierra spring water in special glass jugs and uses it to make the coffee *and* wash the pot."

Renner slapped the report on the desk and walked his mug and plastic spoon to the window.

Musso put his hands on his knees. "So is it?" he asked. Stupid meeting. Walk in, twirl your hat on your finger, ask the guy to vote. "You gonna count it or not?"

"I think it's the same person," Renner said with his back still turned. He drank from the mug and stuck the plastic spoon in his pocket. "Two months, five bombings, whether it's free-lance or not I still think it's the same person."

"A crock," Musso said comfortably. Renner was forty, forty-one, dark-haired, sardonic, *skinny*, which was funny because in or out of the police bomb experts tended to be massively confident men, heavy-set, Dutch, built like food lockers. But Renner was lean and underfed. Tired. His clothes in the morning had the disheveled look of a man who had stopped taking care of himself. His thin face when he turned back around had a wounded, little-boy look. Sad, not tired.

"A crock," Musso repeated. "There's not a guy on the bomb squad that agrees with you, or on homicide either. Am I right? Five different victims, absolutely nothing in common. Five different kinds of bombs. Where's the pattern? Where's the signature?"

It was Musso's turn to shake his head. He was generally scornful of technology in police work, but he knew enough about bombs to know that a bomb maker always left a signature—the way you looped your extra wire and cut it could give you away, or the length of time you liked to set a fuse; one guy would always use Atlas powder that came in the ten-inch sticks; somebody else had to have a

pencil cap or a Timex windup alarm clock or a suitcase
from Sears. That was human nature too. Whether you
were bagging groceries or building bombs, you always
developed habits, you always started to repeat yourself.
But these bombs were all random, all different. There
wasn't any pattern and there wasn't any series.

Renner put the coffee mug down on the desk and stuck
his hands in the back pockets of his trousers. When you
saw it straight on, Musso thought, his face looked like a
long block of ice.

"I still say yes," Renner told him in a harder voice,
harder and colder. Gretzsky and the others treated bombs
like mechanical puzzles, something to figure out. You
listened to Renner, looked at his face—Renner *hated*
bombs. "I vote count it in the series," Renner said.

Musso rocked back and forth in his chair. The man was
stubborn. The man was likeable, but he was too cool and
too goddamn stubborn and unless Musso didn't know
human nature at all Gretzsky had already made sure it was
his last week on the task force.

"You want me to be honest?" Musso said. "Whatever
you were doing back in Europe, Renner, this is Los
Angeles, this is America. In Los Angeles when the television expert says you got a problem you start a task force.
You hire nineteen different kinds of ethnics and a P.R. man
and a tame consultant and two months later you give it
back to the police force. A task force is the opium of the
people."

"You made your point."

"No, I didn't. My point is this is life in the nineties, this
is life in a drugged-out, half-assed septic tank of a city. We
take three, four hundred bomb calls a year in Los Angeles.
People blow each other up because they don't speak the
same language anymore, they speak Spanish or Vietnamese
or Farsi or Mandarin or Chicano/Lesbian/Vampire, teenage boys blow up Porta-Johns and winos, dopeheads blow
up each other's Beemers. Gretzsky's right about one thing.
Without a signature there's no free-lance bomber out there,
there's just Los Angeles, there's just turds that won't
flush."

Renner closed his eyes and drummed his fingers on the desk.

"You take your consulting check is my advice," Musso said, "and enjoy it all to hell back in Sacramento. Because after a while the task force always winds down and homicide takes over from the bomb squad the way God meant us to do, and we start to handle these things one by one. That's how these things are solved, one at a time, slow and steady. Echeverria already checked out the guy's wife from last night, for instance, Kestler's wife."

"Ex-wife," Renner corrected, his eyes still closed.

"No, they were just divorced ten months ago. Nobody gets over a divorce that fast. Echeverria says he walked out on her for some little Smurfette, a waitress at Denny's someplace, which didn't last, of course. Most cases like that, a year later the wife would still cheerfully top the guy's prick with a chainsaw."

"The ex-wife can set a shaped charge bomb with a trip fuse?"

"The ex-wife hangs out in bars," Musso said. "Maybe she meets a redneck with a tool box. People first, gimmicks later. What you always start with is the motive, my friend."

Renner picked up the report lying on his desk. "The brother-in-law works as an accountant three doors down the hall from Kestler and hates his guts. You're going to check him out too?"

Musso listened to the sarcasm in Renner's voice and decided he'd talked too much, he should unruffle the feathers. He scratched one of his Mexican boots thoughtfully and then reached into his coat pocket for the palm-size clear plastic flask. Sliding to the edge of the chair, he leaned forward and poured from the flask into Renner's Tahoe mug. Renner raised one black eyebrow.

"Holistic bourbon," Musso said, taking a long swig from the flask himself. "Better than Kona coffee. Yeah, he had a brother-in-law in the same building." Musso screwed the cap back on the flask and thought that Renner's memory was truly phenomenal. There were already seven pounds of reports on Kestler, manila folders

on the desk and the floor, carbons and plastic binders and
flimsies, and he sucks it all in like a sponge. The brother-
in-law was mentioned just once, where Musso had made
sure he would be, in Echeverria's report. The receptionist
said Renner had glanced at the phone list the first day and
after that dialed all the extensions from memory.

"We're gonna look," Musso said.

"And he had one son already out of high school,"
Renner said. He drank the bourbon and Brim slowly.

"A born-again surfer. Lives in a commune by Venice
Beach. Boys do bomb dads once in a while. We're looking
at him too."

"You're wasting your time," Renner said. "To make a
bomb like that you need incredibly steady hands, experience." He thrust one of his own hands toward the window
and Musso watched it tremble in the pale light. "Accoun-
tants can't do it, kids can't do it, redneck guys an ex-wife
meets in a bar can't do it. That was a brilliant, sophisticated
bomb, and the same guy that built it built the other five. I
know it." He smacked his hand suddenly against the desk
like a gunshot. "You want a signature, Musso, it's com-
petence. Ninety percent of the people who make a bomb
blow off their hands or their legs the first try. Ninety-*nine*
percent couldn't make a bomb like that."

Musso pushed his chair back. Somebody in the mayor's
office had hired Renner, not the police department—he
was down on his luck, they said, he used to work for the
State Department in England, but now apparently he just
sat in some rinky-dink office in Sacramento, "coordinat-
ing." Before that, Musso had heard, sifting rumors, he had
a Ph.D. in engineering from Harvard, he was married or
divorced or gay, he knew Dan Rather, he knew Ed Meese,
he was a mole for the Sierra Club. For the hell of it Musso
had sent Echeverria to toss his motel room one day—
nothing but empty vodka bottles, a sleep mask from a
Dracula movie, a book about Henri Matisse, three books
about Thomas Jefferson. Nothing.

"You just stick with that idea, my friend." What he
should have been, Musso thought; with his memory and
concentration, what he should have been was an Ivy

League professor somewhere, teaching freshmen how to bandage their split infinitives. "The trouble is, out in the real world they still like to see a little evidence. I got junkies to interview down by Kestler's apartment, in case it's drugs. I got junkies and scumbags stacked up and circling like airplanes at LAX. You want to sit there and read bomb squad stories or you want to let Echeverria and me show you around the part of California where the sun don't shine?"

Renner glanced at his watch, blinked it into focus and glanced at it again. Then shook his head.

Musso grunted and walked through the doorway. He was thirty pounds overweight, Renner thought as Musso left, and he dressed like a circus bear. But he was an excellent homicide cop. Shrewd, wary, gruff. Renner watched him turn a corner in the corridor.

What the hell was he lying about?

Because he *was* lying.

If you worked with diplomats for ten years you developed a built-in seismograph, you registered precisely when somebody changed the subject and narrowed his eyes and reached in his pocket for a flask of distraction. You also knew when a series of bombs was set by one guy or twenty.

And proof?

Renner rubbed the back of his neck and smiled ironically to the wall, transforming his face for an instant. Who was the mad astronomer in the story who thought he was in charge of the weather? 'It is sufficient that I *feel* it to be true.'

No proof.

He pulled the telephone toward him, picked it up, put it down again. A beige push-button phone with enough extra buttons and gadgets to pilot a jet. The absent Riboud would have chosen the color—café au lait, maybe; cappuccino; the Kona-Phona. He glanced at his watch and picked up the telephone again and dialed his wife in San Francisco.

The message machine snapped on with the third ring
and he heard his wife's voice speaking with the odd, nearly
rude abruptness that he had never let himself notice when
they were together. Then the shrill warning beep for
messages. What messages? It was the day their daughter
was due home from camp. He had left unlatched the doors
he ought to have latched. And there was no vodka in him.
The machine whirred. He pictured his wife when she
listened to her calls later, standing straight by the phone,
one arm cradled as usual high under her breasts, her eyes
assessing her figure in the mirror: thirty-nine years old and
still slim, unpadded, unrelaxed, a defiant figure. She's
good-looking, his father had said at the wedding. Not
perky but good-looking. She's darling, his mother had
said.

Was there a mirror by the phone? He had never noticed
the phone in his wife's lover's house.

When the beep sounded again he hung up soundlessly,
softly.

Two minutes later he walked out into the corridor. At
the point where Musso had turned, he stopped and stood
rubbing his chin with the palm of his hand. Musso, he
thought. What am I doing? Tailing Musso? Sherlock
Holmes is tailing Watson? He saw with surprise that he had
carried the mug of bourbon and Brim out into the
corridor. Ecumenical bourbon, holistic bourbon. Strong
enough for a good old-fashioned commode-hugging
drunk. Lethal enough to make a bomb with.

Lying about what?

"You gonna stand there till somebody calls the cops,
Renner?"

Renner blinked and looked up.

"This is David Renner," the man stopping in front of
him said. His voice was loud, his eyes were feral and
unfriendly. Vincent Brodie, Renner remembered automatically. Hair you couldn't dent with a hammer. Nostrils the
size of black olives. One cop that looks like a pig. Brodie
joined his fists across his belt buckle and jerked his head
toward his companion.

"Santora," the man said obediently and extended his

hand. He was an obvious ten years older than Brodie, fifty at least, and he wore a blue polyester suit and a sad-sack face. "Ray Santora, bunco squad." Through the nearest doorway Renner could see homicide detectives in shirtsleeves, standing around a television set and watching *Barney Miller*. Like every other open space in the Parker Center, the corridor itself was overflowing with clutter—lockers and tables and spare filing cabinets; the near side was lined entirely by wooden benches stacked shoulder-high with evidence boxes. From another door farther up voices rose, then, bellying his big body past two grinning secretaries, Musso headed for the elevator rank.

"Your David Renner," Brodie said with careful scorn, "is a kind of a federal cop. They sent him down from Sacra-tomato to help out the poor old LAPD."

"Not a real cop, Vinnie." Renner forced himself to smile and made a motion as if to go around Santora. At the end of the corridor, a hundred feet away, Musso was punching the elevator button with one hand and scratching his belly with the other.

"You got *that* right, my man." Brodie was a public relations specialist in the deputy chief's office. With all the innate hostility of the breed, Renner thought. And although he never went out of the building, like everybody except the typists he wore a holster the size of a phone booth on his hip.

"Nobody can figure it out," Brodie said. "Renner's got a colonel's rating, but he's not in the air force. He runs the California Explosives Group, but nobody ever heard of that till he got here. On the sixth floor they just told me to introduce him around as an EOD expert."

"Labor unions," Santora said with a sad shake of his head. "All the bombs I ever saw were set by labor unions."

"Renner's a Harvard man," Brodie smirked. "Wears a preppy jacket and looks down on the peons. His old man worked carnivals in Virginia, his mother waitressed, but Renner went all the way to Harvard."

The elevator doors opened and Musso stepped in and said something that made the other passengers laugh.

"I don't hear much about your wife, though, Renner."

"Fuck yourself, Vinnie," Renner said and turned on his heel.

Behind his desk again Renner paused and stared at the smog and the blurred afternoon sun in the west. The smog looked worse than ever; it looked like God's own green snot, he thought, remembering one of his father's milder expressions.

He let his hand make a little circle just above the telephone. So who should he call? Musso must have known when he walked in the door that Gretzsky had already had him fired. Nicely. Bureaucratically. 'Nonrenewed consultancy.' The check was in the mail. Nobody would listen to his phone calls now. The wise course would be to go back to the motel and pack. Pull out another baby bandolier of vodka. Get bombed. He closed his eyes and made Los Angeles vanish. He considered himself a rational man, distrustful of impulse. Why would Musso be lying?

He moved his hand away from the telephone and picked up his sport coat from the back of the chair. In the corridor again, unsmiling again, he worked his way through the clutter toward the squad room.

Musso was a senior-grade lieutenant, he thought. Musso came and went as he pleased. You couldn't quiz him and you couldn't tail him. On the big roster board behind the television set, where the homicide detectives checked in and out, Musso had chalked "Dunkin Donuts" permanently next to his name. If you leaned on Musso, he would growl; if you tried to follow him he would raise one huge paw.

But Echeverria, his shadow, Echeverria was younger. You could lean hard on Echeverria.

In the squad room nobody had seen Echeverria for hours. On the board he had simply written "field" next to his name, which could mean anything from a nap in the patrol car to a shoot-out at La Brea Tar Pits. Renner walked out into the corridor once more, stopped, then turned left toward the elevators.

On the ground floor he exited with the usual crowd of

men in dark suits and uniforms, the usual feeling of being out of place among cops. A cop and not a cop, just as Brodie had said.

Outside the main door he stopped again, hands stuck in his back pockets, a stubborn rock in the flow of pedestrians. There had to be a signature, he thought, they just hadn't seen it yet. Wires, timers. Victims. A signature meant you wrote your name, who you were. He found himself glancing instinctively left and right along the street for things that would blow up, people who would break into a run. He was distrustful of more than impulse, he reminded himself. Where he came from, city streets were dangerous. In Jerusalem a loaf of bread dropped by accident to the sidewalk contained a grenade in its center. In Belfast the tubular frames of bicycles were packed with plastic explosive.

He crossed in the middle of the block to City Hall East, a big new ten-story building the bluish color of drugstore sunglasses, and descended to a sunken lobby. The Parker Center behind him was an aging youth of a structure, nearly thirty years old, with a complexion of gritty concrete and graying glass and an overcrowded interior in constant, chaotic renovation. The supermodern Communications Department was four stories down in City Hall East, at an unmarked stop on the elevator. To reach it from the elevator landing you still had to show your ID badge to a guard in a glass booth, then let another guard open an armor-plated door and lead you down a hallway to a double door labeled "EOC" in small black type. Renner waved his badge again to the duty officer inside the second door and stepped past his cubicle into the Communications Room itself.

The safest place in Los Angeles, they had announced proudly when he received his briefing tour the first day, the safest place in the imperial state of California—four full stories underground, capped and double-walled with reinforced concrete and steel, equipped with *two* emergency generators, oxygen pumps and tanks, storerooms of food, vats of water, a six-bed clinic, a two-room armory. Bombs would bounce off it, earthquakes zigzag around it.

Renner moved straight ahead. Under a low, mysteriously glowing ceiling he could see nothing but row after row of white and blue computer consoles. At each console sat a woman in a dark blue skirt, dark coat, starched white blouse, working the keyboard. Thirty yards away, beyond the last console, stretched a line of low modernistic desks, a wall of tinted glass, a starship's panel of flashing lights. There a dozen more women in uniform were speaking soundlessly into telephones. A movie set, like everything else in California: "*Space Amazons in Blazers.*" The feminine voice is more soothing in an emergency, Renner's male guide had earnestly assured him, that's why most of the operators are women. The feminine psyche handles distress better, gets facts clearer, people *trust* a woman. "It's raining pig shit, sisters," the nearest woman had muttered.

Renner glanced at the left-hand rows of consoles, three deep, where all routine police calls and dispatches were relayed. If you knew the ropes, he thought, and you had a good reason, this was where you could ask to trace Echeverria. A supervisor looked up curiously from his work station, under a sound-absorbent baffle. If you were a stranger, on the other hand, winging it—Renner stepped right, between two consoles, and headed down the farthest aisle, where the click of nails on keys was faster, the muffled voices more on edge. Halfway along he stopped at an empty console and scribbled a sentence on a notepad. Then he folded the sheet of paper, moved three consoles down, and slipped it over the shoulder of a mountainous black woman who wore a shiny tiara of plastic headphones and coiling wires and spoke in a musical singsong into her mike. Without looking up she took the note and continued to type. On the pale screen in front of her face green numbers rose and fell and surged like starlings. "There's an ambulance coming," she said calmly. "Just leaving Van Nuys. Now try to hang on." Still typing with one hand she opened the sheet of paper: *For a good time call 911.*

She let out a huge whoop of pleasure and swiveled her great bulk around, grinning.

"Colonel Renner—always looking for *action*!"

"Sergeant Garbutt—always where it *is*!"

She laughed again, made a mock salute with one finger, and started to stand up. Then dove suddenly back like a mother on a child.

"Nine one one Emergency, Los Angeles Police."

Her fingers slapped out at the keyboard. Automatically Renner leaned close. But without headphones or a special speaker, an observer could hear only the operator's voice. He squinted at the left-hand side of the screen, where the caller's data had appeared: phone number, street address, city map reference.

"That's all, a strange car in your driveway?" Sergeant Garbutt said and waited.

"And your wife's nervous?"

Waited.

"I'll let you talk to the West Covina precinct," she said firmly and the screen went blank.

"Nervous is *not* an emergency," she told Renner as she swiveled back around. "We *all* nervous. You remember that bomb in the embassy toilets in London? You never saw so many nervous ladies after that—every break time we all marched up Oxford Street to Marks and Spencer just to use the john."

"We fixed that bomb," Renner protested. At the next console two women in uniform had gathered around the operator, the external speaker was on, and a distant, unreal sound of gunshots could be heard.

"*You* fixed it, Colonel. Everybody else was running for the doors, you walked right in like a crazy man and took it out. I'll never forget it. Nine one one Emergency, Los Angeles Police."

Renner straightened his back and drummed his fingers on the console.

"How much blood?" Sergeant Garbutt asked.

When Rosalie Garbutt had worked a switchboard in the American Embassy in London, Renner thought, he himself had worked two buildings down and around the corner, directing with unquestioned authority what was supposed to be the toughest security squad that side of Tel Aviv. Now he was tailing smart-aleck cops on two-bit hunches. Musso. He licked his lips in distaste. He glanced around and registered with surprise, as he always did, that there was not a book to be seen, not even a phone book, in the Communications Center.

"I switched my calls over," Sergeant Garbutt said, turning around again. Her face was broad and black, West African flat, her accent off the phone was pure Georgia honey. "'Cause I know you want a favor."

"This guy," Renner said and wrote Echeverria's name on her notepad. "I need to find him."

She frowned as she read. "You want the ATO," she said, indicating the row of consoles nearest the main door. "Auxiliary Telephone girls do all the routine calls." Then she slowly grinned at him, a pink tongue poked between white teeth. "But *you* knew that. My old husband used to say, 'Colonel Renner knows the rules, but he just does things his own cool way, cool and double cool.' He said, 'Colonel Renner hates bombs so much he might defuse one with his own teeth.' How's your pretty wife?"

"I just need to know where he is right now, nothing else."

"I'm gonna be in deep yogurt," she said, punching symbols on her keyboard. "Ring-a-ding-ding." Light green numbers marched out across the screen like ghosts. An outline logo of Los Angeles City Hall flew by, more numbers, green lines on a green sky, grid after grid of city blocks, coordinates—the computer map tilted, the city spun like a ball.

"Here's your boy." Echeverria's name floated out, trailing a kite's tail of blinking digits. "He's on a code six," she read. "Officer out of car, on location. Been there four hours." She printed the address on a sheet of paper and presented it with a flourish.

"Rosalie!" her supervisor called sharply.

Renner held the paper stiffly while she swiveled back once more.

Why would Musso be lying?

Blood moved in his face. Go home, David, fly away home. He folded the paper twice. Climb into a dry martini. Pack your bags, hurry back to another four walls, another stretch in the flat, hot Central Valley, the ironing board of California.

Rosalie looked up, questioning.

Abruptly, feeling a sensation of ice in his stomach, he unfolded the paper again and read it.

7

SIMON CAUTE WOKE INSTANTLY.

Before his eyes were fully open he was standing on the carpet, knees bent, hands spread wide. He had learned the knack in the air force, when he would doze for hours alone in a radar trailer, then suddenly stiffen and jump at the slightest change in the rhythm of the sweeping dial, as a man jumps back from a loud noise or a snake.

Without hesitation he crossed the room to the worktable he had set up next to the television set. The television itself was running as usual, with the volume turned off, the electronic fireplace he glanced at while he worked. At the moment it was showing a soft-porn movie from the cable's adult "menu." Caute grimaced at the thought of the jargonish word, but paused to look because the action seemed to be taking place in London. A lantern-jawed actress with huge breasts was leaning her elbow against a gray brick wall and speaking to an older woman. He watched the camera float across familiar landmarks—Parliament Square, the curving balustrade of Westminster Bridge, a sweeping shot of the white County Council building on the Southwark side of the Thames. Then the camera returned silently to the actress's face. He had the volume turned off because he disliked intensely the sound of most American accents now, especially the childlike vowels and slurred diction of California girls; and who else, he thought, was going to act in a simpleminded dickless soft-porn movie? The camera shifted to the back seat of a car, where the younger actress was now slowly unbuttoning her blouse. Caute watched until both breasts were free of clothing, riding sensuously in the young woman's hands. Then he sat down at the worktable.

It would be late afternoon outside. He could tell from the quality of light filtered behind the drawn curtains, from the faint hiss of surf receding with the tide. In an hour or so he would walk out on the deck and watch the sun go mushrooming into the water. And an hour or so after that little Colin and/or his fairy friends would arrive with envelopes of money, fresh tirades, heads full of unthinking thought. Then he would have to count their money and sooner or later read their little list.

Meanwhile he pulled out the new box of tools he had bought from the architectural supply specialist on Melrose, beautiful Swiss blades, graduated in size and sharpness, each one perfectly mounted on tubular stainless steel handles with black crosshatched grips. A surgeon might envy such tools. He chose the largest blade, not quite two inches long, and used it to cut the tape on the plastic wrapper to his right. From the wrapper he brought out a thick chunk of reddish putty, about the bulk of a delicatessen ball of cheese. With the Swiss blade he sliced a long curling strip, then brought it carefully up to his nostrils and inhaled.

There was no smell at all, just as promised. He stretched the putty with his fingertips into a string. Polish technology. Let them make fun of Poland over here. American culture with its spike-haired goony-headed teenagers. It was Polish explosives that the Syrians had brought through a circuitous route all over Europe, including England of course, before reaching Beirut, where a single truck-bomb had blown away half the Marines in the

American barracks. It was Polish technology that had
developed a plastic explosive that was, for the first time,
totally odorless. No dog could smell it. No airport security
system could distinguish it from soap, shampoo, or Silly
Putty. He pressed the strip back into the ball and rolled it
between his palms. It was the consistency, he thought, of
California breasts.

For a moment he held his tongue out, the tip quivering
just millimeters from the surface of the plastic. In the
Second World War the Americans had developed an explosive called cyclonite so inert that, without a detonator
attached, a man could actually swallow and digest it. The
OSS had served it in flapjacks, code-named Aunt Jemima,
to a group of volunteers in Walpole State Prison in
Massachusetts. Caute thought of them, walking around
for half a day or more with their bellies literally full of
bombs, their whole inner bodies aglow with the possibility
of brilliant, flashing, total explosion. Human bombs.
Human fireballs. His face grew slick with sweat at the
thought. His tongue flickered almost to the skin of the
plastic. Slowly, deliberately he placed the explosive down
on the table and lowered his hand to his crotch.

8

AT THE SOUTH EXIT OF THE PARKER CENTER, GOING INTO THE garage, Renner stopped and let a crowd of uniformed officers hurry past him.

The dumbest mistake he had ever made following his hunches, he thought, was the day in London he had ordered the embassy evacuated because of the beeping box.

A huge suspicious cardboard package, granted, with an illegible return address and faint, irregular electronic sounds coming from deep inside, like the timers on a microwave or a sophisticated bomb. The X rays had been inconclusive, the noise absolutely terrifying. He had requisitioned a water cannon from Scotland Yard, blasted the box into soggy smithereens, and then, wrapped in his bomb suit, delicately extracted one by one a charity school shipment from the Salvation Army, beeping softballs for the blind.

He went through a turnstile after the uniforms and found his rented Ford, parked next to the exit gate on North Los Angeles Street. And there, as usual, he waited, drumming his fingers on the dashboard while the rush hour traffic stalled in front of him, lines of bright-shelled cars in every direction, creeping forward on all fours.

He snapped the radio on, off, glanced above the traffic to the row of palm trees lining the street.

His mother would love the palm trees, he thought. One more flicker of incompatibility: she had found the West Coast romantic, exotic, tropical, and hated to leave it. On the other hand, his father refused now to stir anywhere out of the South. Put a fence around Virginia, he said. Lock me in. Renner looked in the rearview mirror and saw his mother's eyes, his father's thinning hair. They told a story about his otherwise supercautious, superconservative father. When he was twenty-two he had charged up a hill on the coast of Normandy, firing an M1 rifle into a German machine gun nest that had pinned his squadron on the beach. He was hit five times and bleeding like a pig before he reached them and he never slowed a step. He shot two Germans point-blank in the chest, lost his rifle, and took another bullet himself in the face. The third German he lifted screaming over his head and carried him twenty yards through a hail of crossfire to the edge of the cliff, where he simply threw him head over heels into the sea. But his father thought anybody who defused live bombs was a certifiable lunatic.

With a blare of horns the traffic suddenly broke. Renner turned left and drove down North Los Angeles Street, first through the bomb sites and construction fences of urban renewal, then through a bleak skid row of Reagan's homeless. Palm trees vanished. Block after block rolled by and he saw nothing but dilapidated storefronts and warehouses, twisted spaces. The buildings dropped and he glimpsed for a moment Chavez Ravine and the brown knuckles of the Pasadena hills. Then the Santa Monica Freeway catapulted him above the city, and along with a hundred thousand other cars he drove into a taut gray twilight sky, where the sun was falling through the clouds like a smoking match. When he exited onto La Brea his eyes blinked and strained to adjust to the shadows. Echeverria had called in from a cross street just over the line into Beverly Hills. At Wilshire, Renner jogged right, turned again, turned right on Santa Monica. Precisely where he had said, Echeverria sat in his dusty unmarked Plymouth, eating a taco from a wrapper and watching intently the entrance lobby to something called the Pinero Theater.

Renner pulled into a space at the end of the block, switched off his engine, and levered the rearview mirror down. From there he could see that it was a neighborhood movie house, now converted into a legitimate theater. Black plastic letters on the marquee said "Opening Soon," and a battered signboard angled in the middle of the sidewalk held a poster that he couldn't read. Renner popped the handle of his door and hesitated. From the other direction, his belly two steps ahead of the rest of him, Musso was advancing slowly. Under the lights of the marquee his cowboy boots glowed red and green like a trainman's lantern. Echeverria materialized out of the darkness and they stopped to confer just in front of the empty ticket window. They pushed open the lobby door and entered, and Renner got out.

It was a Sam Shepard play, the angled signboard announced, opening next week, performed by a new international company. The signboard itself was decorated with two ribbonlike black masks, one for comedy, one for tragedy. Renner smiled grimly at the title: *A Lie of the Mind*.

Inside the lobby he could hear indistinct voices through a shabby plasterboard partition. He groped up a dark rampway, fumbled for a door. A lie about what?

Musso and Echeverria were seated far below him, in the first row of the theater, but Renner's gaze skipped over them at once to the stage itself.

On the left stood a young man in striped pajamas, a rumpled bed, a gray-haired woman wearing a housedress. Both of them were looking to their own left, where the stage was divided by a line of white paint. On that side was a hospital bed and in front of it, her hands clasped just beneath her chin, a young woman was speaking to another man. Her accent was rich and Southern, halting, a syrupy stammer. Her skin was white, luminously white, her hair blond. In the pale blue silk of her negligee she seemed utterly naked, bathed in light. Renner stood rooted to the floor. Somewhere he heard dogs barking, coming closer. He made no movement. She spoke first to one man. Then the other, as if choosing between them. Her face shed light. He had seen a thousand naked woman; he had never seen anyone whose face was so white, so sharply cut. His blood lit and burned in his cheeks. He felt ashamed, felt that he had blundered into disaster. Even when she stopped speaking and stared up in his direction he made no movement. When Musso grunted and craned his head to see, Renner was still transfixed, outlined against the open door.

9

"This is Jillian Speirs," Musso said finally from his end of the table.

"Jilly," she corrected him with a glower. "My name is Jilly."

Musso shrugged.

"It rhymes with 'chilly,'" Echeverria said.

"You're English," Renner said automatically. To his ears his voice sounded hopelessly stupid. He glanced at Musso to see if he was sneering, but Musso was busily emptying packets of sugar into his coffee, unconcerned. Beside him, staring hard at the woman, Echeverria held his thin body tense and sideways, like the blade of a knife.

"From the north of England," Renner added. "Manchester, Lancashire."

She looked up from her Styrofoam plate with an expression of bemused surprise. "Learned your accents, did you?" she said, exaggerating the North Country twang. On stage she had sounded more southern than southern, more Georgian than Rosalie Garbutt.

"I was living in England," Renner said, "until six or eight months ago."

"London, then?"

Renner nodded.

"London's not England." She dismissed the subject and began cracking the slivers of eggshell on her plate into even tinier fragments. Her fingertips were yellow with nicotine stains, her nails were ragged from biting. Renner thought that she was twenty-seven or eight, that her streaky blond hair needed washing, that her breasts were too small and flat. He couldn't take his eyes off her.

"You two gonna name the kings and queens of England now?" Musso rumbled. "Or guess Fergie's weight?"

"What happened to all the goddamn junkies, Musso?" Renner took off his sunglasses and leaned back in the plastic chair, jamming his hands into his trouser pockets. Getting a grip on himself, he thought. "You and Echeverria had them stacked up like airplanes over LAX, remember? But Echeverria's been here all day long. He was obviously watching the theater door. When I walked in the two of you were ready to pounce from the front row."

Musso tore open the corner of another packet and let a white stream of sugar drain into his cup. Behind him, just past the diner's neon sign, Renner saw headlights moving smoothly up and down Santa Monica Boulevard, schools of white-eyed fish cruising.

"You had her staked out, right?"

Renner drummed his fingers, but neither Musso nor Echeverria answered. He pushed his chair noisily back from the table.

"She was at the scene." Echeverria leaned forward and without asking tore a cigarette loose from the pack lying beside Jillian's purse.

"What scene?"

"The bombing scene. Where Kestler bought it." Echeverria looked back to Musso, and Musso nodded his big head. "She was walking out of the parking lot," Echeverria said, "two minutes after the goddamn bomb went off. A black-and-white was pulling in and saw her."

"I *live* there."

"She wasn't in your report."

"She was also seen talking to a man in the apartment complex an hour *before* the bomb went off," Echeverria said. He clicked his lighter and stared fiercely at Jillian through cigarette smoke.

Him too, Renner thought. He can't keep his hands to himself, he keeps reaching toward her: anything, her cigarettes, her water glass.

Jillian splintered more fragments of eggshell on the plate, ignored them all, ignored the single loose strand of blond hair stretched across her brow and eye. After he had looked back and seen Renner, Musso had broken up the rehearsal with his badge and led them across the street to the diner, arms spread, a placating official bully. "Let us reason together," he had said pompously, spooning himself into one of the orange plastic chairs and holding up four arrogant fingers as a signal for coffee. Jillian had tossed her head, an actress's instant summation of bad American coffee and bullying men. Every gesture she made was theatrical, brilliant, somehow under a spotlight. When Musso held up his fingers, she had overridden him with her British voice, loudly ordering a hard-boiled egg and Coca-Cola in a big cup and holding them in embarrassed silence until the order came. This is Jillian. Renner strained to place her face in a category of faces he knew. Her cheekbones were like two small hard balls under taut white skin. The mouth was long, wide-lipped, English; the face itself was a pale oval straight out of a medieval painting, a centuries-old combination of bone structure and color. He thought of women he had turned to see in the streets of London, just vanishing.

"Two different neighbors *saw* her," Echeverria said. "Talking to this guy for five minutes at least."

"A man I used to know," Jillian said wearily. Her accent had changed again, to pure BBC. "I can't even think of his name."

"You were *arguing*."

She shrugged.

"Arguing," Musso repeated. He shifted in the under-sized chair and leaned his bulk forward, as if to dismiss

Echeverria and take over himself. He held one palm out level, then tilted it slowly, pouring sarcasm onto the table. In her presence, Renner thought, they were all becoming actors. "Human nature," Musso said condescendingly. "It's human nature for people to have reasons for arguing. Not me, of course, I'm a sweet-tempered guy all the time. Not Echeverria, he's a fiery Spaniard. Not Renner, he's a bomb expert and bomb experts are wacko by definition. But a man and a woman standing outside an apartment, shouting—there's reasons, there's names."

"I've forgotten his name."

"Bullshit."

"I told you. He lived in the apartment building where I stayed the first week I got here, six weeks ago." She raised her eyes from the plate of eggshells and glared at Musso. Bullied, but not without a sense of power. Where was power? Renner thought. Her neck was long and fragile, like a young girl's. She was poor. The sleeves of the shabby macintosh she wore over her stage costume were too short and showed her skinny wrists. "He *came on* to me," she said. "You understand that? He was a sex fiend like all you bloody Americans and I gave him the brush-off. He just happened to be standing there in the new place when I walked out to go to rehearsal, a *total* accident. He said he was visiting somebody and I didn't ask who. I didn't want to know. I told you all that before. I told your sergeant here a dozen times."

"I want brother Renner to hear," Musso said. "Before brother Renner gets the idea he should go storming back downtown and tell the mayor and the bomb squad that Musso and Echeverria got secret witnesses stashed all over L.A."

"They're afraid of you," Jillian said, moving her huge eyes to Renner.

"We're not a..id of anybody," Echeverria began. Jillian pushed back her chair and stood up. With deliberate, exaggerated gestures she took her cigarettes and dropped them into her open purse. Renner felt it before he saw it, a skewed, unfriendly smile that stayed in place as she backed two slow steps away from the table.

"You're some kind of supercop, right?"

Renner shook his head.

"A bomb expert." Her eyes were bright, two green-and-white targets. Catlike, they seemed to be lit from within. "I found a bomb once. At the High Holborn tube stop, you know it? The one with all the escalators?"

Renner nodded.

"It was a parcel," Jillian said. "A brown paper parcel tied with white string and it was about six steps ahead of me on the escalator going down and when I looked over The News of the World and saw it the first thing I thought was bloody fucking IRA."

"Sit down," Musso growled.

"So I called a cop. Cop, bobby, I don't know which one to use anymore. A cop like Moby Musso here. And all bloody hell broke loose—they pulled me off to one side, they roped off the platform, closed down the station. Sirens, guns—I thought the London police didn't have guns, but all of a sudden it was like downtown Texas—the next thing I know this special car is coming up the track out of nowhere *bristling* with spotlights and soldiers, and some man in a deep-sea diver's suit is waddling out on the platform."

"The bomb suit," Echeverria said.

Jillian ignored him and continued to stare at Renner. He felt as if his face were opaque, a mirror; she was studying herself in his reflection.

"Was it a bomb?"

"No," she said, "it wasn't a bomb. It was a box addressed to Joseph Picton, Esquire, of Lincoln's Inn Fields and when they opened it it was full of women's under-clothes that Joseph Picton probably wished they hadn't found. The man in the bomb suit stood there draping huge red bras over his helmet. Listen. Musso here kept me prisoner for three hours asking questions, then he told me if I complained he'd take away my green card and I couldn't work. Can he do that?"

Renner shook his head. Musso's big face had gone smooth and blank, a disc of white dough. Jillian lifted the paper cup shoulder-high and slowly poured Coca-Cola into Musso's lap. "If thou were a *sore*," she said to him in a ringing mock-theatrical voice, "and I had the scratching, I'd make thee the loathesomest *scab* in all Greece."

Musso's face was a burst tomato. Echeverria was looking straight down at the floor, between his shoes. She whirled and walked. At the door of the restaurant she whirled toward them again. The macintosh came open in front. Renner watched himself watching the soft curve of her breast against the blue silk, the nipple hard with excitement.

"Y'all bugger off now," she said in her stage southern accent.

Musso was brushing his lap and struggling to get up. Renner studied the stream of lights against the restaurant window. To the clear part of his mind, the pinpoint that defused bombs, it seemed that she was not walking back across the street to the theater now, but getting into a car at the curb.

TWO

10

June 11

"I DON'T BELIEVE YOU DID THIS."

"I don't believe you said that for the three hundredth fucking time."

"Look at it."

Keith Kassabian didn't look at it. He looked up toward the ceiling. He rolled his eyes and looked toward the farthest corner of the salesroom. He took three impatient steps away from the desk and looked down the row of dull green filing cabinets toward the glass double doors that led to the parking lot.

"No bill of lading," his brother said from the desk, and Keith knew it was going to be another one of his lists. For as long as he could remember his brother liked to talk in lists, like a politician making a speech. "No bank reference, no Indian customs number." Sure enough, when he looked back his brother was slapping the papers one by one on the desk as he recited. *Not in the goddamn desk,* Keith thought. Too obvious, too dangerous. "No laundering certificate from India." Slap. "No guaranteed rate of exchange." Slap. "I can't believe you did this. It's not enough you commission the worst designs in the history of the world, a fast-talking con man you knew nothing about—"

"His stuff was good," Keith muttered to the wall.

"Sheep shit," George sneered, and he squared the papers together on his desk. "His stuff was sheep shit." Under his breath he hissed words Keith couldn't understand. Armenian curses. The older George got the more Armenian he got.

"It was two hundred knots per square inch, the sample was." Keith knew he should shut up, he shouldn't even try to defend himself. Because it wouldn't do a fucking bit of good, it never had. "The sample had good, hard colors. It was quality work."

"You didn't think about checking to make sure that was the work he was actually going to deliver, did you, Kay?"

Keith shrugged and started to look around the room again. He knew what his face looked like, how red it was, and fat-cheeked. And gullible. He didn't care. The room was a hundred and twenty feet long, almost half a football field. Seventy feet wide. Two stories high in the back addition, open all the way to the ceiling, windows open, showing the night sky. In the center, in six long rows of neat piles, stacked according to size and country of origin, there were maybe four million dollars worth of rugs, not counting the ones he had bought, which were still piled in the front near the doors. It was his old man's plan of arrangement for the rugs, his father's personal system for how oriental carpets should be laid out and moved around, and George had learned it in practically one month, could walk to any pile blindfolded and tell you what kind of rug it was, what the quality was, the age, the size. Keith still got lost. *Not in there either,* he thought. In the course of a day his brother and the three black stockmen probably shifted a quarter of the piles in the room, showing rugs to customers, pulling out rugs for shipping.

"And because you didn't make them launder before they shipped from India," George said, "we got moths. Right now we got moth larvae stacked six feet high right in front of your eyes."

Keith worked his mouth and said nothing. He had seen

warehouses where Indian moths were fluttering in a brown haze over the rugs, like a cloud of smog. A classic boner. Fumigation cost thousands of dollars. Fumigation made you a laughingstock in the rug business.

"What you are going to do, my friend," George said. He had come around from the desk and was facing Keith now, arms folded across his chest, face stern, unsmiling. He doesn't look a thing like the old man, Keith thought.

"What you are going to do now, brother Kay, is take every one of these sheepshit rugs and peddle them up and down the goddamn Central Valley. You're going to go from motel to motel with the rug liquidation sales, you're going to bust your sorry ass selling this crap, and you're going to come up with two hundred thousand dollars of cost or you're going to sign over shares until you make up the difference."

"I sign over that many shares," Keith said, flushing angrily, remembering again why the fuck he had gone to Venice Beach in the first place, "I'm broke. That's it, that's all I got."

"You wrote out three hundred and twenty thousand dollars worth of debt to buy those fucking rugs," his brother said. "You did it all by yourself. You're going to pay it back all by yourself. You're twenty-eight years old, you're fucking old enough to know what you're doing."

And you're forty-five, Keith thought. And that's where the fucking train stops.

George stood and stared at him for ten seconds, then shook his head, turned his back, and went back to the desk.

Big brother act number one, Keith thought. Ignore the kid, maybe he'll go away. George was nineteen years older than he was. Their mother had been forty-seven when Keith was born—menopausal, they thought, fat and getting fatter, just the way their father liked women. Until two weeks before Keith's birth she hadn't even known she was pregnant. When Keith was born, George was away from home, a sophomore at Berkeley. *It could be any place in the goddamn room.*

"You're staying here tonight, then?" Keith asked.

"I'm staying till I get these invoices straight and I can cook up something to show the bank."

"You told Sally?"

"I told Sally. I told Emma I'd have to miss her Little League game. I told everybody I'd be here till midnight cleaning up after you."

"Well, I'm not staying."

"No shit." George sat down heavily and leaned his elbows on the desk. The picture of weariness, Keith thought. Big brother as martyr.

"What is it?" George asked without looking up. "AA tonight? Or drug rehab? Or you got another hot date down at Venice Beach with all the other screwup studs?"

Keith didn't bother to answer. He wouldn't bother to answer anymore. He picked up his briefcase from the floor and started for the big double doors. There was iron grillwork on the doors, and on every other door and window in the building. Downtown Los Angeles was worse every year for breakins, vandalism, malicious theft. In addition to the iron grilles, George had characteristically put in the finest electronic burglar alarm system you could buy, laser beams and state-of-the-art sensors at every possible entrance. *Just leave them off for one hour,* the guy had said. That's all it would take. With his funny accent, that's all it would *tike.*

At the door Keith broke his resolution and spoke again. "I worked late last night, you know," he said. "I was here till eleven o'clock. I closed the place up."

George raised his eyes from the desk and forced a half-smile onto his mouth. "And you opened it up this morning, too, before me even. So there's always hope, I guess."

"I'm sorry," Keith said, looking straight ahead, into the night that seemed to go on forever beyond the grilled doors.

"Yeah. OK." George shuffled his papers and cleared his throat, as if he were about to say something else. Then he repeated himself. "OK." After a moment he lowered his head again and started to read the first sheet of paper.

Keith slammed the door without glancing back.

Forty minutes later he was parking his car on Pico Boulevard, half a block down from the salmon-colored Holiday Inn of Santa Monica. On second thought, he pulled the car out into traffic again and circled up to the front door of the hotel, where the valet parking attendant took the key, smiled broadly at the five dollar tip, and drove off with a minimum of squealing. The bar was upstairs, on the second floor, and it was a good bar, respectable, nothing at all like the dumps in Venice Beach. In Venice Beach, of course, people knew you, people could be met, but tonight the Holiday Inn was the right place to be. He took a stool and ordered something that would be remembered, something unusual, a brandy Alexander, and listened to the band. At intermission he struck up a conversation with the businessman on the next stool, a fat good-natured salesman from Seattle who resembled his father and gave him his business card. But older than his father. His father had fallen over dead one afternoon five years ago, in a tomato field near Modesto, age sixty-two, looking for land to buy, to get the hell out of L.A. and the rug business. He would probably fall over dead the same way, Keith thought. He was wired like his old man, he was wired for a country life, farms, fat women, black dirt. If he got out of this he would use the money to buy land in Modesto himself, but not a lot of it at first, not enough to draw attention. He would sit in some Armenian farmers' café, drinking thick coffee, cursing the Turks, watching his tomatoes grow. Now he knew what he was wired for. It had just taken time, that was all, everybody was wired for something.

At ten-forty he walked into the corridor by the staircase and dialed the number he wanted. When his brother answered he didn't even hear his voice, didn't hear a sound except the pip of the button in his hand, the sharp click of something on the line, then a distant, menacing *whump*, like the sound of a gas range when it suddenly ignites.

11

"I DON'T KNOW WHERE FEMINISTS GOT THE IDEA LITTLE BOYS ARE taught not to cry," Renner said. He picked up his coffee cup and thought he must have drunk a tank car of the stuff in the three days since he had come back from Los Angeles. But no booze. "One of my earliest memories," he said, putting the cup down again. He couldn't take another drop of coffee or his hands would shake off his arms. He looked across the room at his daughter, sitting with her legs folded under her bottom in the amazing storklike contortion that came naturally to teenage girls. His baby in diapers, his eight-pound-three-ounce life-grabbing marriage-saving guide into the future. How the hell had he started talking to her about feminism?

"One of my earliest memories," he said, "is of my father crying when the radio announced Roosevelt had died. I was what, two years old?" He paused and tried to remember if he had actually seen his father then or simply invented the story. "There was a famous newsreel of Lou Gehrig crying at Yankee Stadium. And I had an uncle— your great-uncle Daniel—who used to cry every time he heard Bach's B-minor Mass." Now she would ask who was Roosevelt, and who was Lou Gehrig? His daughter tugged at something in the hem of her skirt and kept her head down.

"But you don't cry," she said.

Renner picked up the coffee cup once more, put it down, got out of the absurd canvas sling chair. "No."

"When Mother told you she was in love with Edward and was moving to San Francisco, you didn't cry, did you?"

"No."

His ex-wife crossed the room, bent to inspect the empty cup on the little table, then poured more coffee from the bright red enamel pot she was carrying. "Your father doesn't let things out, Casey," she said sardonically. "He leads a life of cool, efficient, masterful control. You want to remember, his main job used to be to stop bombs from exploding."

"Vicki—" Renner turned in exasperation.

"He just *intimidates* his poor little old emotions." Her mock Texas accent, sweet as barbed wire.

"Thank you both *very* much," their daughter said, coming instantly to her feet. "I'll be downstairs cleaning my room."

They watched her stride to the door and disappear through it with a loud slam.

"Thirteen," his ex-wife said.

Renner walked to the edge of the rug, his back to her, his hands in his back trouser pockets. In front of him elegant French doors opened onto a graveled rooftop patio and a panoramic view of San Francisco Bay. To the north the Golden Gate Bridge arched its back out of fog like a golden dolphin. All order requires repetition, he thought. San Francisco was orderly, coherent—water, land, water alternating, rhythmical; great plates of ocean floor sliding under the coast, raising the hills, forming the bay and the inlets. Not a goddamn thing like Los Angeles.

He placed one hand on the doorjamb. The house itself was built precariously on a stone path rather than a street, straight up a hillside, and despite that, according to the story, had survived the great earthquake of 1906. To his left and right there were floor-to-ceiling bookcases overflowing with the leatherbound antiquarian books Vicki's lover collected.

"I poured you some more coffee," she said in a neutral voice behind him.

Renner turned and saw that she was now kneeling by the elaborate stereo system on the far wall, choosing a tape. As he watched, she shifted her weight and her skirt rode six inches up her legs, showing a pale white flash of thigh, spaces, shadows. Under the fabric the line of her panties made a clear, sexy ridge. *And how is it fair that she still turns me on?* Renner thought. *And knows it.* She punched two buttons on the tape deck and stood slowly, smoothing the skirt down over the soft mound of her belly, then reaching back with both hands to tuck in the white blouse, so that her breasts lifted for a moment and Renner remembered fifteen years of easy intimacy, of white slips, soft breasts, legs opening. She shook out her hair and stared back at him.

You're wired for frizzy-haired blondes, a drunken English friend in London had told him one night, watching him watch Vicki cross the floor of the pub. Just like a fucking bomb, go off every time you see a blonde.

She cocked her head to listen to the music coming out of the speakers—something woodwindish, Renner thought, something faint and slow, long-faced clarinets in a mournful dance. His ex-wife was tall—their daughter already had her height—with thin cords of muscle now becoming visible in her neck and arms. In another ten years she would be a lean, stringy middle-aged woman, and turn him on just the same.

"Edward is going to be back here in a minute," she said finally, voice flat and cold again, our lady of the folded arms, "if you want to avoid another explosion."

Renner nodded. "Dear Edward," he said.

She almost smiled, but instead worked her mouth and then pulled a cigarette from a handmade ceramic box on her writing table. Scattered across the table were other jars and bottles of various sizes, with big scripted labels like

"Guilt" or "Logic" or "Answers." Victoria Dalkin-Renner was still insufficiently Californian, Renner thought, with her cigarettes, her books, her incorrigible habits of irony. She had gone to Radcliffe College on a scholarship just like him, and she still had traces of a Texas accent, like lard on a crumpet, she said. She hated her parents, she hated Texas. Renner's first reaction when they had met twenty years ago at a Radcliffe jolly-up was that they hated the same things, so it must be love. They had gone on an impulsive date the next night to hear Joan Baez sing in a coffeehouse off Harvard Square, before she was famous, before they were middle-aged, before their little family had blown apart into fragments. Standing by the table, the Golden Gate Bridge behind her, framed by two shaggy eucalyptus trees in another window, she looked like an older, angrier version of the actress Jillian.

"So you're not going back to England," she said, exhaling smoke. "You're going to stay in Sacramento?"

"She needs her father around."

"She needs a happy father, doing his work," Vicki said. "We're managing just fine."

Renner walked back across the rug and stooped by the canvas sling chair. Without looking at her, he began to fold newspapers and real estate brochures into his briefcase.

"They won't take you back in England, is that it?"

He carefully refolded the AAA map of San Francisco he had been using. He could sit down in front of a homemade bomb and pull the electric wires away with tweezers, one by one, but he couldn't refold a map.

Downstairs a door opened and closed and Vicki glanced at her watch.

"No. They won't take me back. If you quit, you quit."

Vicki shook her head. Then she pointed the tip of her cigarette toward the last of the papers he was folding. Kool menthol filter, Renner thought, in the kelly green pack. Like smoking a deodorant stick. He didn't know they even sold them anymore.

"You told Casey you were looking for an apartment in San Francisco, but what you've got open there is the

Chronicle's theater listing." He looked down and saw with
surprise that she was right.

"Did they fire you from Los Angeles too?"

Renner nodded slowly. "Two out of two." He had the
Chronicle open to the theater listings instead of real estate,
and the Examiner as well. "They didn't much like what I
had to tell them," he said, and looked up. For a moment
her expression showed interest, even sympathy. Married
and not married. What was stranger than marriage? Emo-
tional superglue. Fifteen years in the same bed, six months
of glacial civility, and here they were talking about his
work again, pouring each other rivers of coffee. "They
don't have much range of experience," he said, leaning
back, ready to be domestic, to be comforted. "The bomb
squad sees the same monotonous kind of thing over and
over—pipe bombs and car bombs, kids with blasting
caps—they don't have any idea of what goes on in Europe
or the Middle East."

"And they don't let you show them?"

"Federal, state, and local law." Renner quoted: "'No
federal law enforcement agent from any bureau whatsoever is permitted to disarm or remove an explosive device.'
Only the local bomb squad of the local police. A very strict
rule, which leaves me fifty yards out of the scene."

"But you're not federal any more."

"Federal dollars pay my salary, out of a grant. I'm
prohibited. I can look but not touch." He paused. "Just like
here."

Abruptly her face changed. "Poor David," she said with
mock commiseration. "Two years ago you were running a
team of God knows how many spooks in London, flying
all over the world at a moment's notice, and now thanks to
me you don't even have a real office, just a beat-up desk in
Sacramento."

"It's a reasonable job," he said. He should keep his
mouth shut. He should keep it shut with vodka, and he
knew by the tone of his voice and the bands of tension in
his shoulders that he was pulling into the first bar he saw
on Lombard Street. "And it's actually none of your
business now."

She did something to the treble on the tape machine and the clarinets whinnied, then soared. When she turned back her features were taut and gray in the shadows of the speakers and the books. A mask of slate. *Even fighting is a domestic comfort,* he thought. *Pour me a glass of "Answers."*

"Did you know that Edward pulled every string he could think of in London?" she said, her voice oddly proud. Of Edward or of him? "And he still couldn't find out what you really did?"

"Wonderful," Renner said, thinking he sounded exactly like Musso.

"They didn't even *call* you about the new bombing, did they?" she said.

Renner stiffened.

"Did they?"

Renner snapped open the front page.

"It's not in there, but it was all over the radio this morning," she told him. "A 'mystery device.' Somebody bombed a rug store in L.A. last night—number six—and the fatheaded cops can't even find the timer or the gizmo on the bomb."

"The detonator," Edward said from the doorway. He stood for a long moment staring at them both, then nodded his head once to Renner.

Renner shoved the papers under his arm, clicked the briefcase shut, and picked up his raincoat from the back of the chair. "I didn't know a thing about it."

"At least they could have telephoned," Vicki said. She looked back and forth, from one blank male face to the other.

"It doesn't hurt to telephone," she said.

From Edward's house Renner drove straight to the Bay Bridge, without stopping on Lombard Street. When he reached the Oakland side, he bought every afternoon paper he could find and read them in a Denny's corner booth, over an untouched cup of oil-slick coffee. A 'mystery bomb.' An Armenian rug merchant killed. No evidence. No explanation. In his pocket notebook Renner wrote down names, times, sketched the floor plan of the build-

ing. Twice he walked to the pay phone and started to dial
Musso. Then on impulse he left the restaurant and turned
south, toward the Coliseum, where he watched eight
innings of a baseball game he couldn't remember eight
minutes later. At midnight he pulled into the parking lot of
the apartment complex in Sacramento, turned off the
engine, and sat.

There were only three basic ways of detonating a bomb.
He lifted his stack of newspapers and dropped them into
his lap. Despite ten thousand variations it always came
down to motion, or timed control, or remote control. And
the chemistry at bottom was no more complicated than the
chemistry of a log fire in a fireplace: oxygen, fuel, initiation. Flame from a match initiated a fire. Sparks from a
blasting cap initiated the TNT in Charlie Kestler's bathroom cabinet, sparks set off by an electric current that
Kestler himself connected when he opened the cabinet
door. But a man in a rug store, all by himself at night,
sitting at a desk—motion from something like a booby
trap was unlikely. In a busy store somebody would have
set it off by accident hours earlier. Rule out motion.

A timed control bomb always used some physical
device for delay, either a slow-burning fuse or a corrosive
acid, an impeded electrical circuit or a mechanical clock.
Every one of them left evidence. Even when they blew up
an airplane fifty thousand feet in the sky they left evidence.
In a land explosion, any good bomb squad could find
charred boards or bits of a radio or a clock face almost at
once; any good lab could find microscopic shreds of
electrical wire or traces of acid. He had once seen an Israeli
lab find traces of a melted cough drop that the bomber had
used to delay a fuse. Rule out timed control.

He turned the headlights of the car on, off. A cat's green
eyes appeared, vanished.

There was no such thing as a mystery bomb, he
thought. A bomb was a highly logical, orderly construction. Not like marriage. A bomb followed inevitable,
irreversible laws of science. When it blew up it didn't leave
two people standing in front of a judge. The mystery was
what kind of person would set a bomb in the first place.

Because once the mechanism was started, there was no stopping it, there was no control—you killed or maimed or destroyed whoever happened to be there: cops, politicians, airplane passengers, soldiers, mailmen, unfaithful wives, unlucky people strolling by with their dogs, their children. What kind of mind would blow a life into fragments, blow up somebody's world at random?

He opened the car door into the cool night and listened for a moment to the ticking of metal under the hood. A bomb was the most abstract, impersonal kind of violence he could imagine. The most modern. The most characteristic of a collapsing culture.

At five o'clock, having slept no more than an hour, he fixed instant coffee and sat down at his stack of papers again. He wrote the word "signature" twice on the message pad. Then "remote control." At five-thirty he drove to the airport and twenty minutes later stepped onto the first PSA flight to Los Angeles.

In Los Angeles the sleepy Avis clerk rummaged through her computer, grumbling, and finally came up with a battered Honda, which Renner took and coaxed under the San Diego Freeway and into the flat, hot grid of suburban Inglewood. On Century Boulevard he bought doughnuts in an airless Vietnamese deli and waited, drinking watery coffee, until the rush hour traffic had eased. Then he checked the address he had copied from the papers, and at nine forty-five left the Pasadena freeway near Alvarado and pulled into the parking lot of Kassabian Brothers Fine Wholesale Rugs.

"You could have a letter from Jack Webb, buddy," the bullet-headed cop told him. He handed back Renner's expired task force credentials. "But you can't cross the fucking police line till Lieutenant Gretzsky says you can."

"Where is he?" There was no other cop in sight.

"He's either on a break or on a call. They all split twenty minutes ago."

Renner stared at two versions of his own face, dark and alien reflections in the curved silver lenses of the cop's glasses.

"You got to wait," the cop said.

Two feet behind him was a waist-high line of the phosphorescent yellow tape they used to mark off the scene of a crime. In this case it had been stretched on wooden stakes across the full length of the lot to keep people back. Behind it, thirty yards away, stood a cinder-block building in a state of arrested collapse. The entire front of it had simply been blown away, obliterated, leaving the walls open to the street, the roof tilting rakishly forward and down like a giant tar-covered hat on a skull. Even twenty-four hours after the explosion the interior shell was filled with smoke and gritty dust. The parking lot where they stood was littered ankle-deep with toothy chunks of concrete and swampy with ashes and mud, potholes of water from broken sprinklers and pipes, and firehoses.

Renner walked six steps to his right, along the tape. The cop swiveled, hitched his gun belt, and watched. A brown-ribbed hillside abutted the building, shaggy with ice plant and as high as the roof. Curiosity seekers stood in knots lower down on the sidewalk. Where the sunlight cut through the shadows and smoke, Renner could see big charred lumps in irregular rows—rugs, he guessed, stacked for display. Whoever had placed the bomb had been smart enough not to blast the rugs themselves, but let the sprinklers and collapsing walls do the damage. At the street end of the tape Renner squinted to study the little piles of office fragments that the bomb technicians were collecting on the pavement and sorting through. He could recognize sheets of blackened and warped metal—desk drawers, parts of filing cabinets—other burned plastic shards that might have been anything at all. The cop followed slowly and tapped his fingers on his holster. Renner sniffed the air, but the fire hoses had left everything soaked through and smelling like wet socks; exhaust from the freeway came over the hill and made his eyes burn.

At the curb he looked back again, past the hood of his little Honda car, to the punched-out windows and bulging cheeks of the devastated walls. 'Chaotic and senseless' was what the newspapers always said about a bombing. But no. What a bomb really was, Renner thought, was anger. Murderous, convulsive anger, the sudden explosive release of an unbearable inward emotion. He had never seen a bomb site that didn't look to him like a human face.

12

"BULLSHIT," GRETZSKY SAID.

Renner folded his arms, thought of walls, unfolded them again.

"Bullshit," Gretzsky repeated.

"I love it when bomb guys talk technical," Musso said. He had stepped out of his squad car two minutes behind Gretzsky, at a quarter to twelve, carrying a carton of sugared crullers. While Renner spoke he had eaten two of them, then pulled a little tin box of Dutch cigars from his pocket.

Gretzsky looked at him, looked back at Renner. He snorted and walked in a circle six feet away, kicking at scraps of debris. Farther on, under the Kassabian brothers' shattered roof, another jumpsuited cop was now sifting through rubble with an evidence bag. On the other side of the yellow tape the cop in sunglasses caught his eye and splayed his white palms in a gesture of professional indifference.

"Remote control," Renner said.

Gretzsky walked around a cardboard box of plastic and

metal fragments and stopped in front of him, a hulking shape, buttocks and legs bulging in the jumpsuit like tree trunks.

"If you can't find a timer on site after two full days, what's left except remote control?"

"This bomb was a two-stage mother-fucker," Gretzsky said. "The first charge went off over there, in the middle of the fucking room. The second charge went off sixty feet past that, by the retaining wall. You set it off by remote control, two stages, you're gonna have connecting wire between the charges, a relay switch to number two, a receiver, and an antenna as tall as Musso there. They didn't teach you that at Harvard? This was a *warehouse*, Renner. You got eighteen-inch cinderblock walls, you got a roof full of insulation, you got no windows on the freeway side, no windows on the street side, one fucking door. Somebody's going to drive by with his model airplane radio and get through that?"

"You find the timer?" Musso asked mildly.

Gretzsky lifted his jaw and glowered at him. "I'm going to find the fucking timer the same time you find the fucking arsonist," he said.

Renner knelt on the muddy concrete to replace a burned plastic tube in the cardboard box.

"That looks like something a black dog shat over a cliff," Musso said.

Renner adjusted it in the box. "It's part of a typewriter platen," he said. "From a desk." He looked past Gretzsky's trousers to the big jagged hole in the floor where the first charge had exploded.

"And it was blown over here by Torpex," Gretzsky said. "Which is a mixture of RDX explosive, TNT, and aluminum. The navy uses it in depth charges and it's fucking hard to get."

"Wonderful."

"And it's also inert," Renner said. He straightened and stood up stiffly, hearing the backs of his knees crack. His hands were already stained light brown from the scorched plastic and oils of the platen. In the smoky noonday light they were shivering like frightened birds. "It's inert, so it needs a booster to make it explode, and before that a blasting cap to initiate the booster. So in fact what you have is a three-stage explosive train."

Gretzsky hitched his belt and stared at Renner.

"What kind of arsonist makes three-stage bombs?" Renner said. "With navy ordnance?"

"Get the fuck out of here, Renner."

Renner looked away, at the smoke, the twisted, blackened cinder block walls. Telekinesis, he thought. The force of anger, hate. In his mind's eye he saw a face, not only the ruined face of the building, but another face rising behind it. One face. If he groped toward it, it moved away, dark and silent. He remembered the image that Vicki had once told him Virginia Woolf saw in her dreams, a shark's fin breaking through water.

"It's the *same guy*," Renner said slowly. "He likes gadgets, jokes. A timer would be too simple. But a three-stage explosion without wires—remember the first bomb in the series? It was rigged to go off when the guy started the car, the fuel line was crimped so the engine would stall. The driver had to turn the key a *second* time, he had to *work* at blowing himself to pieces. The bomb in Kestler's bathroom was placed under a box of Trojans." Renner stopped and tried for a moment to remember the details on Kestler—was he dressed when the bomb went off? What was he wearing?

He stooped again to look at the platen. The charges were placed in the middle of the rugs and by the retaining wall. Why would the desk be wrecked?

"Renner, Renner." Musso wagged his big head from side to side. To Renner kneeling on the ground it looked like a pink moon wobbling in a yellow sky, and one part of his mind registered the fleeting thought that California was like Mars; compared to London, California was like another world, with the wrong colors, the wrong alien inhabitants.

"Renner, who gives a shit?"

Gretzsky had started to walk away. Now he stopped and studied the smirk on Musso's face. "You picked somebody up," he said flatly.

"We picked up the victim's kid brother. He's downtown right now."

"On what?"

"On *motive,* Gretzsky. On human nature."

Renner stood slowly up and shielded his eyes against the glare. The sun made the black roof of his Honda into an arc of light and he moved to the right one step in order to see Musso's face.

"Classic straight arson," Musso said. "The deputy chief called it. Right in front of the whirring cameras. Here's a kid in deep money shit, and his half of the insurance comes to seven, eight hundred thousand. This is a guy that's putting a whole drugstore up his nose."

"And the brother?" Gretzsky said.

"He hated the brother. People worked there said the two of them fought all the time, cats and dogs."

"He can make a bomb?"

"He can make a bomb. Two months ago he bought some bootleg cordite over in Venice Beach. We don't know what the hell he did with it."

"Where was he when it went off?" Renner said.

Musso hesitated, then flicked his lighter under the little cigar. "I asked the deputy chief the same thing," he said. "The kid was in a Holiday Inn in Santa Monica. Drinking brandy Alexanders."

"Ten miles away," Gretzsky said.

"Ten miles away."

Gretzsky stuck out his combat boot and shoved the cardboard box violently away from Renner. "There's no fucking radio control in the world that's going to work ten miles away in a city. He had to set it up with a timer."

Renner shook his head once and squinted into the sun.

"Get him the fuck out of here," Gretzsky said.

13

RENNER HAD BACKED THE LITTLE HONDA HALFWAY AROUND AND started turning the wheels toward the street when Musso put down the carton of crullers and walked to the driver's side.

"You going back to Sacramento?" he said.

"No."

"I didn't think so. You drop your job to come down here, you push your way in—you think it's one guy, you think it's *your* guy. Nothing's gonna stop you, is it, Renner? You hate this fucking bomber."

Renner knocked the car into neutral, looked away. His mind flickered through practicalities. He had come down without a suitcase—how much cash was in his wallet? Where would he stay?

"You didn't go to see the deputy chief, did you?" Musso leaned in the window and studied the dashboard panel.

"What about?" Up close, Renner thought, Musso's face was less pink and round, more mottled, a big lion's face, flat, completely circled with thick gray hair that stormed back from his temples and brow, a heavy shadow of beard reaching well down his neck. Beneath his shirt he would be all hair, all fur.

"The blond girl, the actress, Jillian."

Renner bumped the car into drive. "I'm not a cop, Musso."

"Echeverria bet you would. He thought you'd have our asses up for intimidating a witness."

"What I saw looked like the other way around. You ever get the Coke out of your pants?"

"What you saw was a horny dago going crazy for blondes. Your little Jillian had Echeverria's socks rolling up and down."

To Renner it seemed as if Musso's face was hanging suspended in the window, a sunburst of hair and pink flesh. "You know what?" Renner said, jerking his head. "That's a bad arrest. No junkie kid brother could make a bomb like that, three-stage explosive train, no wires, no sign of cordite anywhere."

Musso nodded. "Actresses," he said. "You want to know a strange fact, Renner? In the Dark Ages the Catholic Church used to not bury actors and actresses around the church. You want to know why? Because they were phonies, like the devil. They got rid of their God-given identity and put on disguises. Acting was sinful." He straightened and stood back, working his shoulders. "This car is a fucking rice bucket," he said.

Renner clicked the gear shift from drive to neutral and back again. What people knew never ceased to amaze him. Wrinkles of useless information on the cortex, suddenly and inexplicably connected in memory with other wrinkles, making gossamer patterns of thought. One of the things he had learned in middle age was how little he knew, how much other people could surprise him. Humility, Vicki had said, in other words.

"Jillian," Musso said, "the one more down-and-out actress this town needed. We cleared Jillian, did I tell you that? What it looks like now is that this young Kestler was set up in a labor dispute over where he worked. The plant was on strike, he was kind of terminally unpopular as a foreman. We can't even talk to Jillian now."

Renner started the car forward at a crawl. Musso walked easily alongside, one hand resting on the roof.

"If you cleared her, what do you want to talk to her about?"

"I'm a cop, Renner. I got curiosity the way bomb experts got ice balls. I thought I might ask her again how come she was back out in the parking lot when the fucking bomb went off instead of rehearsing at her roachbag theater." Musso stopped walking and let his hand fall casually away.

"That's all?"

"Echeverria wants to ask her if she's wearing a bra."

He shrank in the mirror as Renner drove forward, past the corner of the yellow tape, and turned right. At the end of the block Renner stopped for a light and stared at his hands. When the light changed he turned right again and wound under the freeway, through a clutter of stolen supermarket carts, brown tarpaulins, stacked sleeping bags blotchy with mud. Reagan's homeless. A family of women and children sat on the curb and watched him with hooded red eyes as he climbed on to the freeway entrance ramp.

Bomb experts too. Blow a country apart.

In the hazy afternoon light California began to roll under him like a ball.

Signatures of bombers. Something—a quotation from James Joyce—hovered in his mind, then flickered away. His memory was a junkyard of phrases and bits that Vicki had shoved at him over the years. He wasn't interested in quarreling with Gretzsky. There was a signature in the bombs, psychological not technical, waiting there to be read. The mind that set them was rhythmical, sexual. He felt its tug. He glanced to his left and saw that the freeway was arcing through a park of new office buildings, horrible precast concrete boxes dotted with hundreds of overlarge silvery windows, like the eyes of a giant fly. On the grass there were slag heaps of modern sculpture, dry palm trees rattling in the breeze. In London Vicki had dragged him to a lecture by a fat literature professor from Penn, fatter even than Musso. The critical mass, Renner had called him and Vicki had hissed him into respectful silence. The professor's topic was literary theory, his question, could a person forge his own signature?

At National Boulevard he exited down into the littered checkerboard streets and headed west toward the ocean-front motels. He was tired from no sleep, hungry, but his mind kept turning like the needle of a compass back to the bombs.

Obsessive, Vicki had said. You are a classical, obsessive workaholic. A burnt-out case, obsessed with bombs. I married one man but I live with another. In London Vicki had met Edward one day at the British Museum and fucked him in his hotel the next afternoon. A life can change that quickly. Every day for a month Edward had waited around the corner and called her as soon as Renner had left for work.

Fuse time, fifteen years.

When he awoke in his bleak, antiseptic motel room, smelling salt air, it was past six o'clock. He drove again, and ate while he drove. At a little past seven he pulled the car over at the Pinero Theater and turned off the engine. Who knew actors' schedules? They could have been rehearsing for hours, they could all be just waking up in their scattered bedrooms, yawning and scratching. He locked the car and walked past the empty ticket window to the row of glass doors. All locked. Everything growing dark.

He walked to one end of the theater and peered down an alley. The streetlights had just come on, but the alley was still a swamp of soft black shadows.

He took two steps into it and almost missed her coming out of the other end of the building. As before, it was voice he registered first, not the accent, which was drowned in the rush of traffic, but a quality of timbre. She was nearly to the curbside, calling good-bye to someone inside and at the same time turning to scan the street.

"Jillian?"

No part of her turned toward him, not even her face.

"You're Jillian Speirs. I met you the other day—with the two cops." He had started to say "bobbies"—she looked so unmistakably English as she waited under the marquee, blond, pale, wrapped in her shabby macintosh. He had forgotten the macintosh. What he had remembered was the intense quality of light in her face. He had remembered the small breasts, the green eyes, the too-wide mouth. Her face seemed to be absorbing the lights of the passing cars, bringing them to a single white focus.

"The show-stopping scene," he said, blinking. "We went across to that diner over there, and you quoted *Hamlet*."

"*Troilus and Cressida*," she said briskly. "Americans are all theater-illiterate. You were the supercop who tried to guess my accent."

Renner nodded. Now that he was here he had no idea what to say. Up close the macintosh was dirty, the cuffs frayed into whiskers of brown thread. She wore it loosely open, revealing a print blouse of small blue and white flowers and a short, tight blue denim skirt. Obsessions bred obsessions. All he was really conscious of was the long-legged body under the clothes.

"Your people said you would bloody leave me alone. Your Sergeant Echeverria called me to say so."

"I'm not a cop," Renner said. "I'm not even super."

She gave him a wry smile of amusement. With a dismissive, theatrical turn of her chin she faced the street in profile. As if on summons a car pulled out of the line of traffic and crossed two lanes toward them. When he held the door for her, Renner saw that the driver was another woman, also unmistakably English in her fair paleness. Jillian got in and tugged at a reluctant seat belt, making it like every other motion into a little drama. "You have a queer accent," she said, without looking up, tugging again. "I'm good at accents and I can't place it."

"My mother was from tidewater Virginia," Renner said. He leaned in, suddenly conscious that he was repeating Musso's posture. "The local dialect there is the nearest thing in the world to Elizabethan English. You probably hear that."

"You keep it well hidden," she said coolly, lifting her eyes.

"I admire the chameleon," Renner said.

She snapped the seat belt into place and the mocking edge returned to her British voice, sharper, lighter. "So you were just in the neighborhood, right? Walking your beat? Looking for bombs?"

He kept the car door open. He could feel the tension of her hand on the inside handle, pulling against him. The driver was lowering her head and peering curiously at them.

"I think you lied about Joseph Picton, for one thing," he said. The line of tension seemed to jump through the metal like a spark, from his arm to hers. His hand was shaking. He let go of the door. A throwaway line. "And I wanted to see you act again, for another."

"Come to the play then," she said, slamming it. "Buy a bloody ticket."

14

KEITH KASSABIAN STAYED IN CUSTODY NOT QUITE TWELVE hours.

Just before six in the evening his lawyer escorted him down the gritty back steps of New City Hall and into the civil service basement garage where a car was illegally waiting. Despite the publicity given to the bombing and arrest, the lawyer observed with dour satisfaction that there were no reporters and no cameras in sight—thirty years' practice in the Los Angeles courts had taught him at least which staircases and which bail officers to use—but he said nothing at all about the small victory to his client; he pointedly said nothing about anything, in fact, as they drove grimly across the twilight and into Pasadena. He was a silver-haired man of sixty-five, a second-generation Armenian the age of Keith's father, wrinkled like a cob nut, and he was getting the boy out on bail as a family favor. But he didn't approve. He drove with both brown hands clasped tight at the apex of the steering wheel, eyes straight ahead, pushing his lips in and out in a stern pantomine of rebuke.

At the curbside of Keith's condominium he relaxed sufficiently to reach in the back seat and hand over a thick burgundy red folder of legal documents. One of his younger associates would call in the morning, he told Keith brusquely. They would have to set up a time for a conference to discuss pretrial motions, in the Pasadena building of course, where all of the Armenian lawyers still kept their offices. But the first thing he should do, the first thing he should do after he thanked God his father wasn't alive to see this—guilty or not guilty, it was a disgraceful charge, a disgrace they could even think of it—the first thing he should do is telephone his brother's widow.

Keith listened from the curb, head bent and parallel to the passenger's window, nodding, gazing down at the sidewalk. When the lawyer had finally driven off, he walked up the flight of outside stairs and let himself into his condo. His first stop was the bathroom, whose Jacuzzi-side oak cabinet yielded a red Right Guard deodorant can with a false bottom. He shook half a gram of cocaine into his palm and licked it off instantly with his tongue, a big, skinny cat. Then he went into the kitchen and poured a beer, drank it, swallowed two amphetamines from a tiny pill jar kept under a row of coffee cups. For a long moment he stood at the sink with the pill jar in his hand, feeling his veins stretch and curl in his neck and arms, so many coils of wire heating up, beginning to glow. From the outside, he thought, his body must look like one of those cartoon-ish outline drawings in a medical textbook, totally trans-parent except for the dozens of red and blue lines that carried his blood. A funny thought. But Keith walked into the living room not smiling. Not smiling he rooted through old papers on his stereo case until he found the address book he wanted. When he reached the front door he stopped, hand on handle, and realized that he had been home nearly half an hour and no one had called. He hadn't thought to turn on the lights, the radio, anything. This was *not being*. This was like death.

Outside he found his car, checked the gas, and pulled onto San Gabriel Boulevard. He drove with exaggerated caution down to the freeway, radio off, hearing nothing

but the swish of his tires and the tattoo of blood in his ears.
It took an hour and forty minutes to reach Venice Beach—
past nine o'clock—twice his normal time at this hour of the
night. Once he left the freeway completely and simply sat
with the motor running, off to one side in a closed Exxon
station. Once he pulled into a Quik Stop Store and bought
a single beer to drink in the parking lot. He had seventy-
four dollars in his pocket. He had eyes that blurred
continuously with tears of fright, a mouth that felt like hot
dry gravel, no matter how much beer he poured on it. His
wrists, he noticed, were unnaturally rigid, he could hardly
bend them. For an instant he allowed himself to remember
why—he saw himself standing at the far end of the holding
cell all through the day, gripping the iron bars as though he
were Superman and they were rubber—then he finished
the beer in one long chug and threw the can rattling out the
window. When he was seven or eight the three men of the
family had gone camping near Fallen Leaf Lake at Tahoe,
a rare occasion, his father, his big brother, himself. At
some point in the night he had awakened in the black tent
alone and started to cry. When his father and brother came
back from their walk he was trembling bolt upright in his
sleeping bag, silently hysterical, *abandoned*. There was no
fear like it.

At Washington Boulevard in Santa Monica he left the
San Diego Freeway and, more quickly now, drove straight
to Venice Beach. You could find commercial parking lots
six or seven blocks up from the beachwalk, crammed in
among all the little brown houses and funky apartment
buildings from the forties, but he worked past them all, left
the car in front of somebody's garage door, and walked,
dimly aware that he was staggering, to the intersection of
Galway and Washington. From this point on the street
waves could be heard faintly, much more clearly the
metallic ringing of weights and barbells as the muscle-boys
worked out on the beach in their special platformed
enclosure. Skaters flashed by, in and out of the street
lamps, first their huge spinning boots, then orange hair,
torsos, radios the size of trash cans. Black teenagers
squatted and laughed around a bongo. Keith hurried past a

closed art gallery, a bagel house, a T-shirt store. Down the
next shingle-crowded alley was a bar called the "Horse/
Cow," which was submarine jargon for something. The
nearest submarine base was actually four hundred miles
north, at Mare's Island in San Francisco Bay. One of the
bartenders had told him. But the sailors from Long Beach
liked it; the faggots liked it; the motorcycle gangs liked the
little periscopes over the bar and the big air horn that
whoop-whoop-whooped in a dive command whenever
the bartenders felt like it.

Keith entered quickly, blinking at the smoke and thunderous noise of the jukebox. The drugs had done nothing,
he thought, worse than useless; they had dried his mouth
out and stung his eyes red—his eyeballs must look like
cigarette tips, he thought—but his mind was clear as glass.
He could read the labels on the bottles back of the bar, he
could pick out the regulars at their tables, the ones he had
seen on earlier trips, mountainous bearded men in T-shirts
and leather vests, tub-bellied and booming. The faggots
were moving around the outskirts of the bar, behind
smoky curtains, most in too-short denim cutoffs, one in a
jockstrap only, one in a white bathing suit called a marble
sack. King Billy bomb balls, Keith suddenly thought, the
phrase squirting into his mind. Some poem his brother. He
leaned woozily between two black men and ordered a
Coors. The three of them watched in apparent surprise as
his hand continued to smack the bar over and over like a
flat wooden paddle. When the beer came he asked for
Francis.

Francis was right there in the corner, one of the black
men shouted, punching Keith's shoulder hard.

"I want to buy Francis a drink," Keith told the bartender.

"Stone!" the black man shouted. His fingers ran like
mice over Keith's shirt, scurrying into his pocket, nibbling
for cigarettes. Close up his breath rolled out in clouds of
peppermint and saliva. Keith turned his head away, chin
buried in shoulder. The bartender thumped a full, unopened bottle of Stolichnaya vodka in front of him on the
bar and took the twenty Keith peeled for him. *Fifty*-four.

Behind the jukebox, down a crate-littered hallway no
wider than a coat hanger, he found the door to the
storeroom he had used before. Inside he waited five, ten
minutes—his watch was blurred under a film of sweat—
until the door opened and Francis came in. Keith held up
his right hand, ready for a high five, a forearm salute,
whatever, but Francis simply took the vodka bottle from
his other hand and walked without speaking to the one
chair in the room.

"Hey, man," Keith said.

Francis was anywhere from thirty to forty-five, not big
as bikers went; acne had left his cheeks, his neck, and even
his forehead covered with fine pits, like scarred sandstone.
His arms were thin and sinewy; out of the leather vest,
down to the knobs of the wrist, they were covered with
illegible purple drawings, writhing.

"So, man," Keith said.

Francis nodded once in acknowledgment, then twisted
the cap off the vodka bottle and swallowed.

"I need to see that guy again," Keith said. He watched
Francis's adam's apple bob like a cork. The drugs had
worked all wrong, he thought. Instead of warming his
blood, heating his wires, they had carved open a vast
nauseous space in his belly, a cavernous hollow; his
stomach felt like an ice house, his eyes like running sores.

"What guy?" Francis said.

"That guy, you know. You fixed me up. In here. You
know the guy. You fixed it. Hey, you saw the papers, the
TV, you know what I'm talking about. I gotta see him,
man."

Francis steadied the bottle on his knee, slapped the cap
back on, and stood up. At the door he hitched his belt
one-handed and stared back at Keith with an expression so
dead and contemptuous that Keith knew suddenly that he
had been wrong, that he had no idea in the universe yet of
fear, abandonment, *not-being*.

"What guy?" Francis said.

15

RENNER WALKED THREE STEPS TO HIS LEFT, DEEPER INTO THE shadows, and coughed. There was vodka in his system. He imagined his face: vodka burning with an orange flame behind his eyes, in his cheeks, a bright jack-o'-lantern of a head, moving silently, six feet up in the air on a column of darkness. But he wasn't drunk. His steps were precise, careful. He lifted his feet over the rubble and debris and made no noise at all.

He walked around the nearest pile of rugs, inhaled, and smelled the pungent aroma of burned, water-sodden wool. At the far end of the wrecked building, under the single streetlight, the cop on duty stood with his arms folded and stared up at the black hilltop, where the cars on the freeway hummed past like bullets.

Renner reached in his sport jacket and fumbled for the tiny Tigar flashlight he had brought to California from London. Purchased from an Abwehr agent in Germany, used in seven countries, shone on who knew how many bombs and wires. A lens face less than two centimeters across, three undying lithium batteries. If the cop saw him, he thought, and this time he heard the vodka sloshing in the bowl of his skull, felt it pulling the mother skirts of his words as they tried to come free—if the cop saw him he would probably shoot. Renner shrugged. He would dodge the bullets.

Gretzsky had moved all of the cardboard boxes and turned them upside down. Gretzsky, he thought, was a sock full of shit.

Renner crouched and played the little beam of light down, across. Brown mud appeared, wrinkled cardboard, the gleaming edge of a puddle. What light and thought had in common, he told himself, was that they both brought objects into existence, and made them coherent, unified. Then let them vanish in a flash. In his mind's eye the girl's body glowed with warmth.

His hands were well trained. When they had to stop shaking, they darted forward confidently, they came back obediently, carrying bits of desks, cords, knobs of melted black plastic.

He gripped the last piece of metal for a long moment, thinking. Overhead the warped roof of the building groaned in the night air, shifting its weight. Invisible smoke rubbed its muzzle against him. Directly ahead, but also out of the cop's line of vision, a shadow seemed to move, black on black. Not a cop. Not a cat. As softly as Renner moved, it moved. As hard as he squeezed his eyes and squinted, it resisted light. When he turned off the tiny Tigar he heard nothing but the sound of his own breath.

Renner's new motel was by the beach in Santa Monica, not half a mile from the old one. At five he woke again, fumbled again through little vodka bottles for his watch, then stood slowly. On the other side of the bed was the black sleep mask he had taken to wearing lately, to keep out the morning light. It had slipped off during the night and now lay on top of a crumpled white pillow, grinning up at him like the skull of the Lone Ranger. He should have worn it to the Parker Center, he thought sardonically, black mask and bandolier, and somebody would have said he was still too formal for California. He reached for his

slacks, jacket, old shoes. What he could do, he could dig up
another six-pack of little vodka bottles somewhere. In the
great tradition of American men alone in motels, he could
get bombed.

On the beach north of the pier he walked quickly,
squinting up at the black sky and feeling the lump of metal
in his pocket that he had taken from the bomb site. This
morning there were only wisps of fog, thin white stream-
ers close to the water. Over the gray line of surf to his left
he could see clearly the lower spiral of the Milky Way,
dipping like a silver bird's wing into the water.

At the lifeguard's chair he stopped and exhaled white
dots of breath. If he remembered his high school science,
the gas in the Milky Way was mostly hydrogen molecules,
but some of it was also pure ethyl alcohol: vodka. Millions
of bottles of vodka floating in the void. *Man overboard.*

When he started to walk again, the Tigar flashlight
bumped against his hip, sand poured over his shoes. The
bomb at Kassabian Brothers was remote control. The
trouble was, Renner thought, people in this country didn't
make remote control bombs. In Europe, yes. In Europe
they bring down airplanes, they blow up prime ministers.
In London and Paris hot-eyed, steady-handed Iranian
students came to study advanced electronics and electrical
engineering. Fanaticism 101. In Belfast the IRA had better
equipped labs than Harvard and Yale. In Europe govern-
ments spent more on antiterrorism equipment than con-
ventional arms. But America was in another world,
innocent, twenty years behind in terror. He'd looked up
the figures in the Parker Center. Last year the FBI reported
just eleven remote control bombs out of more than two
thousand incidents—and those were all in New York City,
a single group of Puerto Rican nationalists whose leader
worked in a quarry and stole a radio blaster—range of five
hundred yards at most.

He stepped over a dark line of ropelike kelp, washed up
by the tide. The same guy built all the bombs. Renner
inhaled smells that had nothing to do with his childhood,
no sense at all of loss attached to them. Cold, fishy air,

damp foreign sand. The jogger grunted toward him, his light bouncing.

Renner jammed his hands in his jacket pockets. As he walked he hunched his shoulders and raised his eyes again. So gas floating in the Milky Way was cold, unattached hydrogen. Keep vodka cold enough, he thought, and it won't explode.

"I think you're fucking nuts, Renner. I should of stayed in bed."

Renner pushed through the damp air another few paces until he reached the waist-high pile of splintered wood and warped black metal which was all that was left of the office furniture. It was six-thirty in the morning and there was no cop on duty at the Kassabian brothers' ruined building, no cop at all except for wet-haired, bleary-eyed Musso standing ten feet away and glowering over the rim of a white Styrofoam cup.

"It was a remote control bomb," Renner said. To his right, some fifty yards away, the sleepy demolition crew was gathering around a trio of rusty dumpsters, drinking coffee, and over their heads the inexhaustible freeway traffic was cutting through luminous morning haze. "Not a booby trap," Renner said. "Not a timed fuse. Gretzsky's right about one thing. NASA might have a gadget for space satellites, but there's no radio triggering device your punk kid could use that works reliably ten miles away. Not in a city, with radio waves coming out of every car and window."

"He had a timer."

"Nobody's found it."

"He had a helper."

"Like Kestler's ex-wife. Like the guy with the self-starting car."

Musso said nothing.

"Look at this," Renner said. From his jacket pocket he pulled out a coil of thin grayish metal, scorched and warped by heat. "I think this is from the brother's desk who was killed. From *inside* the desk. Gretzsky labeled the boxes but not the parts, so I can't be sure."

"You're not supposed to touch bomb evidence, Renner."

"Did you hear me, Musso? Did you hear where I found it?"

"Inside," Musso said. He held the metal strip in one hand and squinted while the other hand raised his cup to his mouth.

"There were at least eight electrical wires running into the desk—he had a new computer, a printer, two telephones—but Gretzsky didn't send any of it to the lab."

"The desk was a hundred feet from the nearest charge," Musso said. He half-swiveled to look through the haze.

"You can put a radio transmitter on the desk, or in the desk drawer, and if you drive by you can radio *it* to act like a relay and detonate a charge up to a thousand yards off, no problem."

"And that's how it was done?"

"That's one way. There're two or three other ways I'm still thinking about. The first question is why this metal got zapped, on the desk or inside it. Gretzsky was sloppy."

"If it was the desk," Musso said. He scratched the rim of the Styrofoam cup against his chin. "You're not in the CIA, Renner. People asked."

"No."

"But you know about shit like this."

"Some."

"Gretzsky was sloppy," Musso said half to himself. After a moment he shoved the metal coil into his jacket pocket, then he pulled the tin of little Dutch cigars from another pocket, extracted one without looking, and lit it. When it was going he exhaled smoke and rotated his head slowly to look at the demolition crew. Some of them were standing and stretching. Others were putting on saucer-shaped hard hats and stiff orange vests. A man with black hair down to his shoulders was positioning a ghetto blaster on a truck gate and turning up the volume. In the thin gray haze, Renner thought, Musso's head looked today like a balloon balanced on the collar of a shirt. Touch it with a cigar tip and watch it explode.

"Nobody looked at the utility closet yet," Musso said finally.

"That's what I want to do right now. That's why I want you as a witness."

When Musso didn't say anything, Renner started to pick his way through the building. Slowly Musso pocketed the tin of cigars and began to follow. At the rear, next to the hillside and directly under the freeway, they stepped across more debris and lumber to an outside utility closet, eight feet high, made of cinder block, just wide enough for two men. The door was wooden, painted green, and half off its hinges. A crossbar latch still hung in place, held firmly at one end by a round Yale padlock. Musso stood with one foot in the hillside ice plant while Renner selected a blade from the tool ring in his jacket.

"I noticed you didn't call Gretzsky for this little charade," Musso said and puffed cigar smoke upward. "The guy that might actually know what you're talking about."

Renner twisted the blade in the padlock and it jumped open with a snap. He pushed at the tilted door.

"On the other hand," Musso said, "Gretzsky can't stand the sight of you. Which maybe you noticed. You're so fucking obsessive, you intimidate people, Renner."

The door came open no more than six inches and jammed, and Renner braced it with his shoulder while he loosened the hinge.

"I play blackjack with Gretzsky sometimes," Musso said. He raised his voice as a truck changed gears overhead. From the front of the building they heard the workmen's radio booming unrecognizable music. "It's like heart surgeons on their day off. They go scuba diving with sharks or they walk into some stockbroker's office and buy an option on pork bellies. When they're working they're not allowed to take risks, when they stop working there's nothing wild enough for them. Gretzsky sits there all afternoon with a bomb and a Timex on his crotch; he finishes that, he wants to be hit on soft twenty-one."

Renner held the door wide enough for Musso to squeeze in, then it shut with a bang behind them. In the musty dark of the closet Renner pulled out his tiny flashlight and played it across the aluminum door of the telephone wiring cabinet.

"We're gonna see wires crossed and twisted, right, Renner? And this little break-in is supposed to show me you didn't come here last night in between vodkas and jimmy it up yourself."

Renner bent forward to examine the cabinet. The thin beam caught the unlatched metal door, the black wires exiting neatly from the bottom into drilled holes in the cinder block. He inhaled the smell of smoke, burnt paint, wood, Musso's cigar, Musso's coffee. He stopped.

"Come on, Renner." Musso turned restlessly in the tight space. His coat made rustling sounds in the dark as he brushed against wood, concrete.

The flashlight found a bright drop of something liquid at the bottom of the cabinet door. Renner extended one finger into the beam and touched it.

"Water."

"You hose down a burning building for two days," Musso growled, "you may find water around."

Renner worked the flashlight up the left side of the cabinet door, pausing at the hinges. The only part of bomb school that anybody ever really enjoyed was the three-day section called IED, Improvised Explosive Devices. There the instructors traditionally amused themselves after the first lesson break by planting little bomb caps in every conceivable part of the classroom. In the time it took the students to go to the john and return they would have rigged desks, briefcases, chairs, even books to go off like firecrackers when you touched them. After the first couple of explosions nobody reached for anything without looking, nobody turned his back, nobody escaped being bombed. In the evening the students tricked each other, improvising their own bomblets for their car doors, their radios, toilets, ballpoint pens. Anything on earth could be made to explode, or look as if it would. On the third day, Renner had taken a short line of black electrical wire and simply draped it under the instructor's car grille, so that it hung down an inch or so in the air, and the whole class had gathered at the classroom window to watch the instructor stop, curse, walk around the car, get down on his knees, crawl underneath on his back.

"Renner," Musso said in disgust. "I'm a size fifty man, you hadn't noticed, and this is a size forty outhouse. Open the fucking door. Show me." Impatiently he lifted one invisible hand in the dark and yanked the cabinet door open.

For a split second neither man spoke. The flashlight beam had jumped with Musso's motion and illuminated for an instant a row of blue and red fuse tabs, next to them a line of telephone wires, two of them twisted and clipped with plastic snaps. On the ledge of the cabinet just below the wires was a thin wooden mousetrap. Where the bait would go was a capsule, a drugstore cold-remedy capsule, gummy with moisture where somebody had sprayed it with water to make it slowly dissolve. Underneath the capsule was a wire that led to a battery, a blasting cap, and two upright sticks of red dynamite. When the capsule fully dissolved, the trap bar would snap over on its spring and complete the circuit to a blasting cap.

"Oh, shit," Musso said. He tumbled backwards, bumped the wall, the door, bumped Renner. His elbow jostled the cabinet. The trap bar, already coming free, started to lift in slow motion, pulling free of the melted capsule. Musso turned again, knocking the flashlight down.

"Oh, shit."

The bar strained out of the capsule, rising.

Renner thrust one trembling hand straight ahead and as Musso closed his eyes to die he heard the mousetrap spring, fly, fall, smack harmlessly onto Renner's knuckles.

16

"It's the same guy."

Francis looked to his left, his right, hitched his belt buckle and walked three steps into the room. Straight ahead, right through the enormous picture window, was the beach.

"It's the same fucking guy," he said. "Six one maybe, black hair, forty. Dresses out of a trash can. Squints at his watch all the time."

"You're sure?"

Francis looked at the beach again before answering. Once, maybe the first time he had ever been allowed to come out here, some teenage girl had gone by on a horse, bouncing in the waves, totally topless, tits like two white eggs.

"Do I look like I'm not sure? The same guy that was in the diner with the fat cop but he's not a cop. Now he's with him again at the rug store and he goes around in the back, right into the outside meter closet, where he shouldn't ever come out again, right? Only, five minutes later him and the fat cop come out jumping and five minutes after *that* we

got a parking lot full of cops and the big guy Gretzsky
from the bomb squad's lining up his dogs, his metal
detectors, there's a bomb truck with one of those metal
balls, the whole fucking works."

"You saw all this, Francis, you were there?"

Francis picked up a ceramic figure from the coffee table
to his left, a glazed shepherdess with long white sleeves,
red dress, brown shepherd's crook in her hand. The colors
were bright and glossy, but it was hard to know if the
figurine was good art or else some piece of junk that Caute
would keep around for one of his whims. Francis lifted his
eyes. Like the television set he kept running in the corner,
always with the sound off.

"I got a construction guy," Francis said, "like on the
demolition crew."

"Construction," Simon Caute said, "is nine-tenths
demolition." His face was deadpan, but his voice was thin
with irony, condescension. Francis stared at him.

What's he's wondering, Caute thought, *is whether to drop
the goddamn figurine casually on the floor, smash it to pieces, and
show me he's his own man, I can go to hell, or whether to stay
cool and aloof. Whether to be like me.* Francis twisted his neck
and appeared to take in the rest of the room, the rattan
furniture with its burgundy cushions, the leather recliner
chair, the framed mirrors reflecting the waves down on the
beach. Next to the television Caute had set up the little
portable worktable, spread over with a white towel and
lined with two bright rows of stainless steel blades.
Carefully, looking past Caute's head, Francis lowered the
figurine to the coffee table.

"This guy called me, what, an hour and a half ago."

Caute looked at his watch.

"I drove by and checked it myself—young kid, crams
shit up his nose with both hands, who knows what he can
really see? But there they are, two hundred cops, TV, the
fat cop right in the middle, the guy I saw at the theater and
at the diner. He looks tired but he moves fast."

Francis stopped and cocked his head and listened to the
patter of a shower running somewhere in the little house,
in another room, beyond the stool at the wet bar where

Simon Caute sat holding his drink, crossing his legs, staring right back.

And what he's wondering now, Caute thought, *is how far to go with me. Too pushy, too familiar, and maybe I decide he doesn't fit in after all, there goes the money. Too humble, on the other hand, too docile and his leather-studded macho dignity can't handle it.* Caute sipped the drink and watched Francis continue his tour of the room. Dignity, he thought contemptuously. An aging biker with a torn-up face, pathetic, washed-out tattoos, holding up Meissen figurines like a connoisseur.

"I want you to find out the man's name," Caute said.

Francis looked down at the row of blades as if he were about to buy one.

"Where he lives. Who employs him."

Caute saw Francis's lip curl at the word. *Employs.* Pompous vocabulary, English accent. This was a man, Caute thought, who knew two words, *got* and *guy.* This was a quintessential Californian. If he were twenty years younger he'd say *dude* and *rad* with an adenoidal gulp and he wouldn't hesitate to pick up one of Caute's knives or turn up the television volume and leave it. Wouldn't hesitate to do whatever he wanted because his California brain wouldn't amount to a handful of hot sand. But Francis was almost forty, old for a biker; his anxieties had crept out into the open and showed their claws. In this place he was off balance, self-conscious, glancing down at his dirty boots to see if he'd left a trail of mud on the white rug.

The shower stopped abruptly. Then started again. Like the father in Faulkner's story, Caute thought, walking into the mansion and smearing dirt on the rug to impress his son. But Francis was too old for bravado, too greedy. And in the story the son killed the father.

"So what about the kid?" Francis was saying. "Kassabian. He's gonna be back every night till he finds you or they lock him up again. We're talking a flake. We're talking a flake in panic city."

Caute eased himself off the stool. What he himself was not good at, Caute thought, feeling unusually up today,

unusually sharp and lucid, not horny for once, not tense—
what he was not good at, as he knew, was handling people.
His insight into them was excellent. He analyzed people
like Francis very well, and he got what he wanted out of
them. But always there was this sense of distance, this *space*
between him and other people. He wondered if he felt
regret. *In my world,* he thought, *there are always spaces
between people; people are always held rigidly apart by some
invisible, icy force, like stars.*

"Go ride your bike now, Francis," he said. "Company's
coming."

When Francis had gone, Caute looked at his watch,
calculated that he had half an hour, then walked down the
wooden steps from his deck to the beach. Always there
were people on the beach, Caute thought. Joggers, riders,
old men with wrinkled pear bellies, kids with their Mach
Two radios. From the water line he could look back to his
house and the red-brown cliffs rising just behind it, brow
of a skull. To the left other beach shacks stretched north in
a crowded, winding row, miles of rickety little houses,
brown-faced and weathered; but on the right, where the
state park began, there was nothing except hard fill, then a
service drive, then the beach. Farther on, they were
building an asphalt bicycle path, wide enough for a car,
right in the midst of the sand, as if the city fathers had
looked out one day and said, This beach is beautiful, how
can we fuck it up?

Inside, the English kid had already let himself in.
    Caute wiped his shoes on the deck mat and walked past
him, into the living room, without speaking, rude just the
way the English like it. His back to the kid, he poured
himself another drink, listened for sounds from the bedroom, turned around finally, slowly.
    "Colin," Caute said and raised his glass.
    The kid mirrored his blank look. Caute walked past him
and sat down in one of the two rattan chairs facing the
ocean, silent television to one side, worktable spread to the
other. MayDay Group, he thought. What an idiotic name.

What a pathetic collection of little English boys, little Cambridge communists straight out of the thirties—which was where Colin got his style, his fair-haired, willowy, aristocratic, lounge-lizard air, his baggy tweed jacket from Bodger's the Tailor, his white-collared burgundy shirt. Caute admired him as Colin poured his own drink and then coolly crossed the white rug and took the opposite chair. Twenty-seven, twenty-eight? But for poise, coolness, *deportment*, he could stare down a duke.

Now he was turning his head and looking at the beach, the sun going down hissing into the water. They were all still bloody Druids at heart.

"I passed your biker friend, leaving," Colin said finally.

"You come earlier than your appointment, you run into people," Caute told him. "Freud was always early too. Snooping."

"We're not paying you to set bombs on the side."

"Hey, you liked Kestler?" Caute said.

Colin's expression never changed. "We liked Kestler very much."

Caute nodded. He could be the chairman of Royal Doulton, inspecting a new line of fine china. But they were talking bombs and human life and for sheer goony savagery nothing could approach the Brits.

"But we don't like the rug store," Colin said.

Caute sipped his drink and watched a boy with a radio the size of a truck's dashboard stroll by on the sand.

"The test was supposed to be Kestler, nothing else," Colin said. "The rug store was gratuitous. We have no interest whatsoever in being caught because of your indiscipline."

The boy's head was jerking forward and back to the music like a chicken's. From one of the other beachfront houses a thin girl in a sweatshirt and Day-Glo bikini bottom was emerging to join him.

"You remind me about your interests," Caute said sarcastically, watching the muscles of her buttocks shiver with each step in the sand, half-moons of white jelly. What the MayDay Group said they wanted was one thing— Caute couldn't even remember their slogans, he had dealt

with so many, ignored so many. But what they liked at
bottom was the thrill of betrayal, destruction—just like
their heroes from the thirties, Anthony Blunt and Michael
Straight. Blunt and Straight. Caute smiled at the sexual
image.

In front of him Colin had taken him literally, was
talking forcefully, repeating in his intense, beautifully
articulate way something about Thatcherism, something
about econo-socio-racial justice, the decay of the West.
More bullshit. When Caute had been stationed at Mildenhall Air Force Base outside of Cambridge, Soviet agents
had naturally approached him. They approached every GI
in Europe who worked EOD security. They figured a kid
makes nine hundred or a thousand a month, the air force
leaves him alone in a radar trailer half the week, makes him
live in a rathole barracks—why not? When Caute said no
thanks, the IRA had followed a few weeks later, Burger
King moving in after McDonald's. Caute had like the IRA
better, they were piss-angry instead of bureaucratic, and
he'd even built a few bombs for them, studying their
technology, £2000 apiece, half down, half if the bomb
actually exploded. But he liked Colin's little group best,
swimming up next, after the bigger fish lost interest; he
liked their style, their elegance, learning, hypocrisy. He
liked the idea of helping them get famous.

"On that condition, no more side bombs, we deposited
the first check," Colin was saying. "Yesterday."

"Barclays Bank."

"Barclays Bank, Little England Street branch, London
NW Three."

"So where do you get your money, Colin?" Caute
couldn't tell in the fading light if Colin was watching the
girl in the bikini bottom or the boy. "Family trust funds?
Some more of those public-spirited bank robberies? Maybe
I shouldn't keep my money in the bank."

"We want it done inside a month, inside three weeks if
possible," Colin said. "If there are any more gratuitous
bombings we reserve the right to stop the second payment."

"You do that, you reserve that right."

Colin stood up and looked at his oyster watch and Caute rose with him. Colin had never stayed anywhere with him for more than half an hour, one of his rules. Caute wondered if Colin liked him, wondered if he respected his work. The English were as good as he was at keeping people distant—better; they never wondered.

"The factory Kestler worked at is still out of production," Colin said. He had left his glass on the table, Caute noticed, with typical English bad manners.

"Right. You can't build your gyroscopes without a foreman."

"So perhaps," Colin said almost coyly, "we get our money from people who like to see factories like that slow down."

Caute tried out several replies in his mind, listened to the lengthening silence, liked that best. Match them for haughtiness, match them for distance. In the twilight now Colin was standing half obscured by shadow. To Caute's left the waves were crashing closer to the pilings of the next house, long white bones of surf, flung up, dragged back. The boy and girl were gone. The bedroom door behind Colin was cracked open six inches, revealing a mirror. Colin pulled a fat brown wallet from the back of his trousers, found unerringly a single folded slip of paper.

"Tomorrow for your answer," he said. "Between seven and eight. In the usual manner."

When he had let himself out, Caute unfolded the slip of paper and held it up to the fading light. There were four targets to choose from, written in Colin's spidery English hand.

> LAX air control.
> Chevron refinery at Long Beach.
> Federal Reserve central office.
> Parker Center, L.A. police.

17

WHEN AN UNEXPLODED BOMB IS FOUND, A LITTLE LAB GOES UP around it. A portable X-ray machine is wheeled into place and a technician in a huge padded bomb suit waddles up to insert the film. What happens next depends on what the film shows. A simple timer bomb made of a clock, blasting cap, and explosive charge can be sprayed with chemical foam, inhibiting all electrical connections. A technician can smother a motion-fuse or booby-trap bomb with a special high density blanket, woven out of fiberglass and metal, which absorbs the blast wave. A small squat radio-controlled robot on wheels, guided by the man crouching in the bomb suit many yards away, can also be sent to the bomb and ordered to extend its dual pincers. If the bomb is straightforward enough the pincers can disarm it on the spot. If it's too complex and dangerous the pincers can sometimes lift the whole device into the air, balancing it while the bomb carrier is rolled underneath, a fiberglass and metal vat shaped like a cement mixer. Then the pincers lower it, the top goes on, and the bomb explodes like a rocket in a bell.

If the bomb is in a place where the machines can't work, people go in.

Renner watched from the sidelines while Gretzsky went through the long procedure of examining the mousetrap bomb. First, the utility closet and the immediate area had to be searched for a second bomb—or even a third—that might have been set as a delayed trap for the police. In the clutter and debris of the Kassabian Brothers building, Gretzsky's people worked very slowly, pausing often, using their robots, standing and sweating for long minutes at a time in the bright sun. Then Gretzsky himself put on the bomb suit and went in the closet. The device there was no longer live—Renner's fingers had automatically pulled the circuit wire—but certain kinds of commercial dynamite and all dynamite sticks more than a few years old are likely to explode when touched, or even to blow up spontaneously. Nobody knew for sure what was in the closet.

After fifteen minutes Gretzsky came out again, waded stiff-armed to the truck, and started to take off the suit.

Musso stood up. Renner put out a hand. Because of its weight and heat a man could wear a bomb suit for only fifteen or twenty minutes at a time. While Gretzsky slumped on a pile of charred rugs and glowered in their direction, a second technician put on the suit.

At three o'clock an FBI expert on terrorism arrived and went into the unmarked van that Gretzsky used as headquarters. Behind the yellow tape the deputy chief marched up and down, dragging a train of reporters. At four the chief left. A police video cameraman followed Gretzsky into the closet again. At five-thirty, as Renner walked back and forth along the tape line, Gretzsky's people loaded their evidence bags into the van and Musso emerged from somewhere in the crowd of cops and cameras to drive Renner to the Parker Center.

The third floor elevator opened directly into a corridor, which in turn led to administrative offices on the left, conference rooms and squad rooms on the right. Renner emerged with a group of sweating bomb squad technicians and started down the corridor toward the task force's usual room. Musso had somehow disappeared in the rush.

Twenty yards ahead the deputy chief was just passing through the double doors, grim-faced, hand on his pistol butt, followed by a man and woman marching in unmistakable FBI cadence.

"Get the fuck out of here, Renner!"

Gretzsky was still in his field uniform, his hair almost black with sweat, his face a car wreck of deep rusty lines and brown greasy streaks. He jabbed Renner once in the chest with the heel of his hand, hard, before Musso appeared out of nowhere, shoving them both to one side and back down the corridor, talking in a high voice over Gretzsky's furious warnings.

"You're not on the task force, Renner," Gretzsky said, pushing, moving.

"Leave him alone, Mikey."

"Get him out of here!"

Two secretaries were squeezing past them, craning their heads to look, somebody else was rolling an overhead projector down the center of the hall.

"I *found* the bomb, Gretzsky."

"You're off the task force, Renner. You tampered with evidence. You disarmed a bomb out of jurisdiction—you know the law. You're out of here, you're out of this goddamn building."

Renner was wedged between Musso and the wall, staring in disbelief at Gretzsky's red face, his red-knuckled fist.

"I *found* it," he said helplessly.

"For all I know," Gretzsky hissed, leaning forward, coming closer, "you want back on the task force so bad—for all I fucking know you *set* the goddamn bomb."

Even as he said it Musso was bumping Renner with his big belly, pushing him away.

"*What?*"

"That was a crude little mousetrap bomb, Renner—you could have set it, you knew what to do the minute you saw it."

Musso stretched past him and shoved open a stairway door. Renner was still turning, spreading his hands and pushing back, but they were already moving fast down the stairs two at a time.

"Let me go, Musso!"

Musso bumped him farther down the stairs, not answering, pushing. They passed a fire door, a landing.

"Did you hear what he said? You don't think I set that bomb?"

Musso was hustling him backward down the steps, passing the second landing, nearing the exit door into the police garage.

"Where you staying, Renner?"

Renner stopped suddenly, digging in his heels, his back flush against the door.

"You ever set a bomb in Europe, Renner?"

"No."

"Never?"

"I don't set bombs," Renner said through clenched teeth. His mind was racing through names, flicking them aside. "People who know about bombs never set them, Musso—they *hate* bombs."

And as he said it he knew he was wrong. In Jerusalem there was an anti-Arab bomber so good the sappers had long ago concluded he was one of them. In Paris—

Musso kicked the door open and pulled him into the garage. "Nobody here knows why you got fired in London, Renner."

"I *quit*. I wasn't fired."

Musso planted himself, feet wide apart, hands jammed in his jacket pockets. On the garage ramp a car slowly circled, raking its headlights over them twice.

"You calming down?" Musso asked. He pulled his tin of little cigars from a pocket and lit one with a match.

"No!"

"You go back in there and bust up the chief's meeting you'll never see south of Sacramento again."

"Gretzsky can't do this."

"Gretzsky can do whatever the fuck he wants. He's a cop and you're not and you're in the fucking Parker Center, you hadn't noticed. And he's right, you broke the rule. This is a holy war for you, Renner. You're a fanatic.

You don't give a damn what other people think. But Gretzsky's on the spot. Gretzsky can't do his job, he can't turn up one ant's turd of evidence against anybody, and now you're gonna go in there and say it's your solo bomber again and make him look like shit. Isn't that right? Isn't that what you're thinking?"

Renner made a motion to go around him and Musso moved easily to block him.

"Where's your car, Renner?"

"You don't say that about a bomb guy, Musso, cop or no cop. I pick up after bombs, I *stop* them."

"This is all talk, Renner. Don't worry about talk."

Renner stood for a long moment, feeling the anger spin through his belly, drain. He worked his shoulders hard like a boxer under the thin fabric of his jacket. He raised his hand and rubbed his chin with his palm, smelling vodka on his skin. When had he had time to drink vodka?

"Go get something to eat, Renner."

Renner lowered his hand and looked to one side, toward the moving lights of the freeway. Musso studied him a moment longer, then nodded, as if confirming some inner opinion. He turned and pulled the door halfway open.

"So what else do I owe you, Renner?" he said.

"You don't owe me a goddamn thing."

Renner drove, stopped, drove again. On the strip along Sunset Boulevard he looked up and saw the floodlit "Hollywood" sign spelled out in white wooden letters on a hillside. Off Sunset, under a street sign for Wilcot Way, still trembling with anger he pulled over to the curb and watched the whores, pimps, and dealers emerge warily from the shadows. Signs. Signatures. The minimart across the street had little rag voodoo dolls lining the window and over the doors separate signs in English, Korean, and Spanish. An incoherent culture, an ethnic pinball machine, a melting pot ready to boil over. He got out of the car and returned five minutes later with a fistful of little vodka bottles. In the car again he lined them up on the dashboard like silver bullets and pushed his mind away from bombs, let it snag and whirl on ironies. Back in the 1880's the

Wilcot family had founded Hollywood as a temperance village, no saloons, free lands for Protestant churches. How the hell did he remember that?

He shifted in the seat and watched a gasoline truck that had backed into an Exxon station, where the driver was spilling a small river of gasoline as he wrestled with a connecting hose. In Paris, in the eighth arrondissment by the embassy, Marines would have inspected the cab and the tank chassis first, gendarmes in blue bullet-proof vests would have stood by with Uzis unslung. In Jerusalem there would have been motionless soldiers stationed along the sidewalk. In Beirut a truck that size, detonated from half a mile away by remote control, would level a full city block and send up an orange fireball ten stories high, belching death.

It was coming to this country, he thought. Reality could explode anywhere, even in a city of actors.

He started the car again. In Europe he had seen one plane come down from the sky in pieces, half a dozen more take off with explosive devices that either malfunctioned or somebody found. In London a year ago they had stopped three vengeance-mad Iranians bound for San Diego.

He hated bombs. He hated the fanaticism, the passion. As he U-turned on Wilshire and headed south again, huge billboards advertising new movies swam across the windshield, giant breasts, explosions of blond hair, red mouths gaping open, wide enough to drive through. His mind jumped, shook, released him for an instant. Who hated passion?

Abruptly he turned east again and found Santa Monica Boulevard, wider than any street in London, lined with palm trees and blue sodium streetlights, split by a grassy jogger's mall. He drove ten minutes, slowed to the right-hand lane, and finally stopped where he had been intending to go all along. He retrieved one of the little bottles of vodka that had fallen to the floor and opened it. His watch said five minutes till ten. The sandwich board sign on the sidewalk said Pinero Theater.

The box office was lit but empty. Renner pushed open the nearest glass door and went in. This time, instead of climbing the stairs to the back of the theater, he moved to the right, down a ramp, following voices.

"'The character?'" somebody asked loudly, uncertainly, an artificial "acting" voice.

Renner slipped in through a curtained doorway and took the first seat he found, five or six rows back from the stage.

"'I couldn't believe it,'" an actor on the far left side of the stage was saying in a thick, implausible southern accent. "'Changed her hair and everything. Put a wig on. Changed her clothes. Everything changed.'"

Renner blinked and adjusted his eyes to the dark theater and half-lit stage. The actor who was speaking was a hulking, pretty-faced jock in his early thirties, with dots of red makeup painted on his cheeks. He wore a checked lumberjack shirt and floppy chino trousers, incongruously cinched up by a length of rope rather than a belt, and he was walking back and forth in front of a shapeless brown couch. Behind it another actor, shorter, pudgy, held a script shoulder-high and looked on stiffly.

"'I didn't even know who I was with anymore,'" the first actor said.

On the darkened right half of the stage, in a single spotlight, Jillian stood motionless. Just to her left Renner could see a man's body, face lost to the darkness. But Jillian's face was clear of makeup, bright, a white oval, and she was staring out toward the back rows with a look of blank, untouchable boredom.

"'You know what she tells me?'" the first actor said.

The man with the script looked up. "'What?'"

"'She tells me this is the real world. This acting shit is more real than the real world to her. Can you believe that?'"

"OK, OK." From somewhere in the dark seats to Renner's left a man obviously the director was stamping down the aisle. As he reached the first row the stage lights splashed onto him like paint and Renner could see shiny patches of scalp, pink skin, corduroy jacket, one hand smoothing back thin brown hair, clamping his neck at the end of the motion.

"This is the *crux*, Ron," he shouted half angrily. "So *play* it, *punch* your words, set up a *rhythm*. He's talking about the theater, you got that? That's what this whole fucking play is about, the theater, the theater's a *lie of the mind*. Got that?"

He bobbed his head to see more clearly the actors who had frozen in midaction on the stage. Jillian crossed her arms. The director scooped air vigorously toward his chest with one hand, a pantomime of pulling his actors closer.

"Listen up, Ron, listen up all of you," the director said. He paced along the first row of seats, impatient, sawing his tie loose with one hand, a round-shouldered bearlike body, a miniature Musso. To Renner's ear his voice was hard and sarcastic, a bully's, Gretzky's. "Forget about trying to *feel* these lines, people," the director said. "You try to get by on just feeling, you're gonna blow your character apart. The best actor doesn't *feel* a thing. He *imitates* emotion, right? He *controls*. He controls his gestures, his accent, walk, pitch. You got to *think* about it, Ron."

"He or she," Jillian said. "He or she controls."

The director barely glanced in her direction.

"Give me a break, doll, all right?"

"You're saying I'm not—what? What are you saying?" The actor in the lumberjack shirt had stepped forward pugnaciously. The director let his head drop, his arm drop.

"I mean, my character's in conflict, right?" The actor jerked his chin toward Jillian, who had emerged in half-light now, dressed in a pale green hospital gown, no shoes, arms still folded under her breasts. "Yesterday," he said loudly, looking at the rest of the cast as if to appeal, "yesterday you're telling us every good character is always in inner conflict, right? All this Chekhov crap. So I want her, I don't want her." He tucked his chin into his chest and made an effeminate little paw in the air, in Jillian's direction. "I *don't* want her," he said. And Renner realized with a shock that the actor was gay, that he was speaking in his normal voice.

The other actors were laughing. Jillian had pulled a cigarette out of somewhere and was lighting it, blowing smoke down her nostrils, and suddenly looking and seeing him.

The director followed her eyes.

"Who the hell are you?" he said.

Renner stayed in his seat.

"This is a closed rehearsal, buddy. I'm telling you to pick up your butt and walk."

"He's a bloody cop," Jillian said from the stage.

When she came out twenty minutes later, Renner was standing on the sidewalk, leaning against his car. She jammed her hands into the pockets of her macintosh and stared at him with the same blank, unreadable expression she had worn on the stage.

"You didn't get me fired, supercop," she said. "Better luck next time."

"Joseph Picton," Renner said.

She turned and started to walk down the street, in and out of the fluorescent lights of shop windows.

"Joseph Picton," Renner said, falling in behind her. "He wasn't in the Holborn tube stop bomb."

"Wasn't he?" She kept on walking, fumbling in her purse.

"No."

Twenty yards ahead of them Renner saw two tarts waiting under a streetlight, wrapped like great pieces of candy.

"Joseph Picton," he said, "was a left-wing Cambridge student who tried to set a bomb in the restrooms of the American embassy in London."

"Lavatories," she said, shaking her hair but not looking at him. "'Two nations divided by a common language.'"

"What was notable about the bombs," Renner said, "was that Picton set them up to go off with a proximity fuse, which is something the Germans invented back in the Second World War. It goes off when a person gets too close, it works by body heat."

The two streetwalkers stepped back to let them pass, flashes of red miniskirts, chocolate thighs. The nearer one giggled and called after Renner in high chattering Spanish and the other one screeched with laughter.

"You speak Spanish?" Jillian said.

Renner shook his head.

"She said you're too skinny but she bets you're built like a horse."

"Tell her she's right."

For an instant she smiled, her face was lifted toward him, the wide, unhappy mouth, the actress's mobile features, wary, interested, mocking, showing her art.

Unaware that he had moved, Renner looked down and saw his right hand stretched forward to touch her upper arm. He dropped his hand as if it were burnt. They stopped in the middle of the sidewalk, under the awning of a drugstore. *I want her*, he thought, *I don't want her*.

"So I read about it in the paper," Jillian said. "So what? I'm an actress, I make up stories. Weren't you listening in there? Half the time actors live in a fantasy world."

"It wasn't in the paper," Renner said. "I know. I defused it."

She shrugged and looked away, right, left. And then before he could speak again she had turned toward the store. From the sidewalk he watched her bottom swing in the wretched macintosh. A photoelectric cell blinked, the glass doors folded open with a hiss. She jerked a shopping cart from a line and disappeared down an aisle.

When he caught up again she was pushing the cart down an aisle of contraceptives and condoms.

"For your proximity fuses," she said without looking back.

"I'm not a cop, Jillian."

"You should wear a big button, like Nixon. 'I am not a cop.'" She pushed the cart around a corner, into a double aisle of shampoo and toiletries. As she moved her head her hair flashed gold, like light caught in water.

"You went to Cambridge," Renner said, a guess.

This time when she turned and looked at him, the blank, distant expression was back; when she spoke her voice was flat, without inflection. Renner stopped. He couldn't keep up with her moods, changes.

"When I was two years old," she said tonelessly, "my bloody father walked out on us, he took a stroll. I was brought up by my mother, but she was a little crazy after that. She used to go up to coppers on their beat and ask them if they'd seen Leonard today. As soon as I could talk she taught me to go up to them too, a little girl. You know what she taught me to say whenever I saw a policeman?"

Renner shook his head.

"'Help,'" she said.

18

"THIS ONE," CAUTE SAID.

He smoothed the folded sheet of paper and spread it out between their coffee cups, on the table. Then he reached inside his jacket pocket and pulled out the twenty-four carat Mount Blanc pen he had bought only a few days earlier. Eyes still on their faces, he drew a fine black line of ink under the last name on Colin's list. Parker Center.

Smiling now, he leaned back in the chair and waited for their reaction. Colin first, on the left, in the same fussy imperial tweed jacket, the duck trousers, the long bony face of a British horse. The other man Caute didn't care for, hadn't expected. He watched their faces for a moment, then glanced away at the rest of the room. Just beyond the glass enclosure of the porch, out on the double-width sidewalk where even in the early morning fog the freaks gathered, Francis leaned casually against a cyclone fence, smothering a yawn, while a boy polished his boots.

"No," Colin's companion said.

Caute turned back to them with a slow, deliberate motion controlled by dislike. An Arab, he thought. Syrian

or Iranian probably, dark-skinned as a walnut, with short
black hair and handsome black eyes. 'Fadhil' was all that
Colin had given by way of introduction—no last name, of
course. Just one more playmate for Colin's little rag-gang
of radicals.

"You gave me a choice," Caute said, addressing himself
to Colin. If he blocked out Fadhil's face it was the same
kind of meeting they had held three times before, in the
same broken-down café by the beach that Colin had
chosen.

But Fadhil was persistent, emphatic, with the little Arab
shit-eating smile that always meant he would sit there
forever without hearing a word you said.

"Yes," Fadhil said. "But we had a further discussion.
After Colin delivered you the list. A *conference*," he said
with odd, illogical emphasis, now turning the smile on
Colin, who looked straight ahead, ignoring it, and crum-
bled a little breakfast roll of flakey whatever between his
fingers. *The Arabs are an easy people to love.* What horseshit,
Caute thought. The first guy in England he had ever done
bomb business with had said that, taking him to some
horrible fly-smeared kebab restaurant in Ely and sitting
him down in the back with three young Lebanese. They
wore white *kaffieyehs* over denim overalls, served him
sweet tea in a little swampy glass, and asked him to put a
bomb in the office of a British dentist who had proposed a
vacation trip to their sister.

This one wore L.A. clothes. He wore a pale red polo
shirt under a silver windbreaker, pleated white trousers a
size too big, sandals over thin black socks. Now he was
telling Caute how seriously they had discussed the list at
their conference, how much they respected his expertise,
pronounced to rhyme with 'pert-hiss,' while Caute paid no
attention at all and wondered instead, sourly, if he were
queer, in the great tradition. In Ely the Lebanese had taken
him afterward in the yard behind the restaurant where they
all pissed tea and dangled their cocks like long brown ropes
in front of him.

"No, we still owe it to him to listen to his reasons,"
Colin finally told Fadhil, lowering his head and hunching

his shoulders. A horse looking over a stall. Caute was a short man himself, or he thought of himself as short, five nine and a half, and one of the things he admired about Colin was his aristocratic height.

"My reasons," Caute said. "I love it. Listen. You people don't understand America. You sure as fuck don't understand California. Vandenberg, the Federal Reserve—give me a break. The Parker Center is the only place on your list where *anybody* can go *anytime*. A police station's like a hotel lobby. You got half the city driving up to the front door every day to see about their brother-in-law that just got busted. You got people wandering around in so many different uniforms, suits, hotshot disguises, nobody knows who's a cop, who's a lawyer, who's in there to clean out the john. All it needs is a fuse. You want a microcosm of America, Colin sweetheart, take the fucking Parker Center. I can walk in there any day I want to and leave a bomb."

"Excuse me," Fadhil said, frowning and smiling at once. Politest people on earth, Caute's friend had said. They think that lets them do anything they want to do. "Security at the Parker Center is *very* tight. I have friends who are stopped at the security desk every day, never given passes."

"Your friends are brown, right? Your friends want to go right up to the sixth floor and park their camels in the chief's office, right?" Fadhil's smile was a little smaller now, two hundred miles farther away. Good. "I'm not talking about upstairs. There's other parts, better parts."

"Metal detectors," Colin said.

"I make bombs out of metal, Colin?"

Both men stared at him for a long time. Caute shifted in his chair and watched a beefy waitress pass sideways between tables. Out on the sidewalk Francis had finished getting his boots polished. Now he was watching the same kid shine another man's shoes, an Asian with gleaming black biker's shorts and no shirt on.

"The Federal Reserve office has a *massive* computer," Colin said.

"I'm talking about *downstairs* at the Parker Center,"

Caute told him. He looked at Fadhil. "You ever call nine one one? You know what that is?"

"This computer," Colin said as if he hadn't spoken, "registers every significant financial transaction in the Pacific Rim, every banking operation on the West Coast goes through it."

"I'm talking about *emergency services*," Caute said. He was gripping the coffee cup in front of him with both hands. Somebody at the next table was looking up. Somebody was turning around. Fuck them. "You put out that switchboard this whole toilet of a city won't flush, you know that? Every ambulance call, every fire truck, every cop car—they *all* go through the Parker Center."

"What we want—" Fadhil began.

"What you want is L.A. on its hands and knees waiting to be buggered."

Outside a guy in a black vest was suddenly revving his motorcycle, right by the window, straddling the saddle and looking in, making the whole room shake.

"What we want," Colin said over the din, "is *international* headlines."

"Our eyes are on Europe," Fadhil said.

"But your dick's up L.A.," Caute told him.

They looked at each other, then back at Caute. He was getting too excited, he knew that, out of control, he should watch his language, stick to Colin's wavelength. To be doing something he used his tongue to lap up coffee and cream from the bottom of his cup. Abruptly the motorcycle stopped and the room shook itself back to normal. Caute wiped his lips with the back of his hand and looked around. It was a twenty-four-hour coffee house, burger place, dope-dealer club, a rambling brown-shingled building half an acre deep, thirty yards wide, the glass-enclosed porch facing the beach; only the beach was blocked off first by the sidewalk, then by palm trees, then by a kind of metal cage where later on the weight lifters worked out and the hot mammas did gymnastics on parallel bars and leather horses that Caute wouldn't have touched with two sets of rubber gloves. Their eyes were on Europe, right.

Reality had them by their little pearly balls and they wanted to take out 'significant financial transactions.'

"We can supply all the guns you want to get into the Federal Reserve Bank," Fadhil said coaxingly. "It's on Ninth and Olympic, in the middle of downtown."

"I know where it is."

"You're upset," Colin said.

"I'm not upset." Caute reached a hand into each of his jacket pockets. He had known it would be cold by the beach this time of day, so he had worn his Marks and Spencer anorak over a sweater. Colin of course had his Scottish tweed that they wove out of iron sheep. Only Fadhil was dressed as if he didn't care. The reason they all went to England, Caute thought, was because of the rain, the rain and the cold. Get out of the fucking sand and desert, go where it rains every day, the only color you see is green. He used his right hand to place the Semtex by his coffee cup, a lump of hard white doughy material that looked like a spongy rock. Colin was saying something else in one of his long British sentences that went on forever. Fadhil was watching his hands.

"You're quite right about Vandenberg and the oil refinery," Colin said. "We do see that. Impossible to get close enough to where we would want to be. But the Reserve computer is part of a busy office block that people go in and out of constantly, and granted that although the computer itself is well guarded, we think you should at least look."

"International headlines," Fadhil said. "For our purposes enormous prestige, leverage."

Caute pulled the other packet from his left pocket and placed it on the table. Colin knew what it was at once. Fadhil looked back and forth at them, raising his head. Caute spilled out half a dozen of the little pellets, about the size of rabbit food, but colored bright pink and yellow by the manufacturers, God knew why. Designer chemicals. Bill Blast. There was a splash of liquid on the Formica table top, below his coffee cup, between the two chemicals, and Caute used his paper napkin to mop it up. Water would start a chemical reaction. Copper would. Also some kinds of brass.

Colin was sitting very calmly. The waitress squeezed by without a glance. In Venice Beach you could tattoo your dick on the sidewalk, swap Uzis for cotton candy, nobody would look twice. Two derelicts outside wore jackets with exploded pockets.

"I can get you any kind of gun you need," Fadhil said in a wary voice.

"I can push these together and pour your water on them and blow this fucking room into orbit," Caute said. He smiled at him, imitating his polite razor-sharp insincere little camel-kicking smile. "This isn't a gun culture anymore," Caute said in a Colin kind of voice. "It's a bomb culture."

Colin had all the breeding you would expect, the cool, to the manner born. He wasn't thirty yet, but he'd been around difficult people all his life. The Arab had finally understood and he was sweating like bacon, ready to fall out of his chair. Colin simply reached out one long pale hand and pushed the Semtex six more inches away.

"We'll pay you five thousand pounds extra," he said calmly, "if you do as we say."

19

DASEIN. EXISTENCE. ONE OF THOSE COLD, DENSE GERMAN words, heavy as lead. Renner had read somewhere that the first question you ask about your existence is, why me? The second, why *here*?

He strapped on the digital watch and for a long blank minute studied without seeing them the fidgeting numbers on the dial. *Help*. Pure English, not German. It was past ten o'clock and the fog was smothering the motel like a huge gray blanket and he should have been up hours ago. He had called Jillian's apartment until three, fallen asleep finally by four. What the hell had he been thinking to let her go? What had he been *doing*? Watching while she grasped the handle of the shopping cart and rolled it away from him, around the corner of the aisle. Controlling himself, being distant, a professional. Act deliberate, he had thought; hold back, go slow. So that when he had reached the front of the store she was gone, vanished. The cart was standing alone by a turnstile, Cinderella's silver cage on four black wheels, empty.

He rubbed both hands hard across his face.

What you want to do now, he told himself, *is work, is question Keith Kassabian, the punk kid that built a three-stage bomb and set it off by magic. What you want to do is break the goddamn puzzle and stop the bombs.*

What he wanted to do was see her again.

He traced a careful path through the books scattered on the floor and the five little empty bottles of vodka, toward the bathroom door. Fifteen minutes later, wet-haired, balancing a roll and a Styrofoam cup of coffee in one hand, he opened his car door and slid in.

By the time he reached Artesia Boulevard east of the airport it was almost eleven-thirty. He stopped twice to check his street map and pulled into the Miramar apartment complex just before twelve.

There was nobody in sight. Here the seaside fog had long ago burned off, leaving the three square buildings of the complex naked, blistering in the sun on their flat lot. To the west stood another apartment complex, older than the Miramar, built of chalky brown Depression stucco around a circular flower bed and a dry fountain. To the east a huge metal pylon dangled high-tension wires from each shoulder.

Renner locked the car in a section marked "Guests" and walked toward the pool, checking numbers. There were plenty of cars in the parking lot, but nobody in the pool, nobody anywhere on the grounds, nothing but still, desiccated palm trees and a yellow eyeball of sky slowly closing. Across the street a young derelict in a T-shirt sprawled on a bench, arms spread out, baseball cap tilted down over his face. Renner's mother had told him that her first idea of California came from orange crate labels in her girlhood, pictures of bungalows and doves and Spanish dancers beside blue rivers. Renner walked around the laundry room with its huge red soft-drink machines like tongues coming out of the wall, and looked for number 63. Then, on impulse, he backtracked quickly and looked for Kestler's apartment, upstairs, 224, but even here there was nothing to see—a new unpainted plywood door wearing a sash of police tapes, a stench of wet plaster and cordite, black smoky patches along one panel of plasterboard.

Musso's revised report, the one that had cleared her as a potential witness, said that Jillian lived in number 63—but with a roommate? Alone? Musso hadn't asked, or it wasn't in the report. Renner frowned as he came out on the ground floor again and tried to remember exactly the wording, but his mind was distracted, worm-holed by vodka. He shook his head in disgust. The derelict lifted his cap and watched as he turned a corner.

Number 63 had a three-by-five index card tacked in the middle of the door and two names printed in bluish dark ink with an italic pen and underneath the names a tiny daisy drawn curving upward toward the sun: J. Speirs; J. Spelding.

He knocked twice on the door, loudly, and waited. Nothing. He tried the handle and found that it was locked. Glancing up the corridor, he dropped his hand into his sport coat pocket and felt for the metal bomb tool. Then slapped the pocket in frustration as he suddenly remembered it sitting on the nightstand in the motel, next to the telephone.

With another glance down the corridor he knelt and examined the lock. It was a standard Kwikset, cheap and tinny like the rest of the building, push-buttoned on the inside, no deadbolt, not even a guard-bolt. Renner took out his car key, pressed his left shoulder high against the door, and worked the point of the key past the frame plate and lifted. The wood tore a fraction, making a sound like paper ripping, but the door swung inward smoothly and nobody spoke, nobody shouted. Nobody pulled a gun. He closed it behind him and stood for a moment, blinking.

His instinct was to move quickly, push fast through each room and satisfy his curiosity—then get the hell out, go look for Kassabian. But he forced himself to slow down, to move cautiously into the center of the narrow hallway. When you search for a bomb, they had been taught over and over in Alabama, you divide the room into thirds, horizontally. You stand in one place, as if you were looking down into a swimming pool, and you study the whole floor up to knee level. Then you study the room again from knee to shoulder, then shoulder to ceiling. You *never* turn on the light switch—remember the poor bastard in London.

Renner walked farther in, stopped. The apartment was hot, stifling, the curtains all drawn, the air soupy and flecked with drifting motes. The corridor outside had been silent, but now inside he could hear the faint chatter of a radio somewhere downstairs, distant creakings, distant life.

He glanced at the kitchen and registered Formica surfaces, glass reflections, a sink full of plastic dishes, somebody's newspaper clipping taped like a sideburn to the refrigerator's pale face. A poster of Bon Jovi. The living room held a couch, a stereo, cardboard stereo packing boxes, two canvas sling chairs that must have materialized in a time warp from the fifties. Standing there he could see into both bedrooms at the same time; he had no idea which was Jillian's. The nearer one looked out on the parking lot. From the rumpled bed, he thought, you could roll over and see the cars as they pulled up to the curb, see Kestler's car, see Kestler stroll up the sidewalk to his stairway. Renner took two steps toward the bed. Women's clothes scattered on a bureau, a full-length mirror, a tiny three-inch television, its screen raised at an angle by some kind of wedge, wearing the cheerful blank expression of a family dog. Where was the personality? The individual touch? Was this the girl's room who had picked her up in the car? J. Spelding? Was it Jillian's?

He backed out and turned toward the other bedroom.

There was a bathroom next to it, and he paused first, glancing at the brown-mouthed sink, the cracked green linoleum by the tub. Plastic jars of all sizes lined the shelf above the faucets, unlabeled receptacles for female pills, creams, lotions. They taught you very well how to search a space at bomb school, and fear made you sharp, alert, *fear kept you alive*, the unofficial school motto. But nobody taught you how to *feel* about it, this. Intruding, for no good reason except curiosity, wavering suspicion. *I am not a cop.* He rubbed sweat from his forehead and looked at the jars again, mysterious signs of Eve, signatures; Vicki could produce them at will, like rabbits out of a hat. Suspicious

of what? She had talked to an unidentified man in the
parking lot; come back later. Lied about Joseph Picton.

The second bedroom was hers. He felt the tension, the
difference at once. Light streamed in through the open
window, setting the shaggy white carpet on fire. There
was a glazed mirror on the closet door, a scowling poster
of Mick Jagger. Dried-out paperbacks leaned in an uncer-
tain little stack by the foot of the bed. Renner waited for a
moment, listening to sounds far away, the slam of a door,
a car's engine starting. His mind jumped, refused to focus.
His ears thumped. He had two hundred and seventy-
nine dollars in his wallet; he needed to find a cheaper
motel, he needed to call in at Sacramento, at least make a
gesture before they fired him. There were clean clothes
piled on the floor, a few dresses in the closet. Across the
bureau top she had carelessly tossed underwear. A white
bra, a black bra. He resisted the impulse to pick them up,
handle them. Next, he thought, he would go to his knees
and feel for the place under the bed where his father hid
Playboy. He turned slowly and saw that the whole wall
adjoining the door was covered with masks.

African masks, he thought at first, exotic tribal masks
that you might buy at an art gallery, long-faced, warped,
surreal, more than a dozen of them in crooked lines of
three and four up and down the wall. But a second look
showed that they were homemade, constructed skillfully
out of papier-mâché and each one painted to a smooth,
glossy finish. A mask of a bull, with bright red horns. A
clown's face, dotted, weeping. A pig, a phantom, a princess
with real hair.

Four princesses.

Jillian's own face. The center of the wall held four
lifelike masks of her own face—grotesque but unmistakable self-portraits. She had used blond wigs, white papier-
mâché for the skin, painted mascara and lipstick. One
mask was wildly distorted, elongated in the gaunt, hollow-
cheeked style of an El Greco martyr. Another was rounder,
with full cheeks, closed eyes, lips opened in sleepy sensu-
ality. He stepped closer, astonished. The central mask had
Jillian's nose and wide, generous mouth precisely, but the

eyes and brow had been left unformed, a smooth band of white like a blindfold on a mask.

An actress would have masks, he thought, half desperately. There was another German word, *Maskenfreiheit*.

He knelt to look at the mask nearest the floor, his hands suddenly trembling again. From an angle it looked to him like Vicki.

No.

He shook his head. What kind of pain would create such images? In the next apartment there were murmuring sounds now, people cooing, a bedroom. But the masks didn't repulse him, they drew him closer, they fascinated. It took a moment for him to realize that in between the masks of her face was a rubber disc, pinned to the wall by a big nail driven right through its center. It took him another moment to realize that it was a rubber diaphragm.

"You son of a bitch!"

Renner ducked and fell at the same instant, tumbling left. The tire iron smashed into the carpet, bounced. He rolled back in a ball, grasping at a shoe, and the iron came swinging just past his head, a blur, and blew the nearest mask into fragments.

"Son'bitch!"

Another mask exploded; the air was full of exploding faces. As Renner dodged to the right they burst and sprayed from the wall one after the other. He staggered and rose, as the bull flew apart by his ears with a shattering sound, a bombshell of color. Blindly he drove his fist high, falling into the punch and felt cloth, leather coming free, bones and fat.

"Son'bitch!" The derelict gasped in pain, bent double and spun, spun again, losing the tire iron, banging into the far wall.

By the time Renner was upright and reaching for the tire iron himself, he had stumbled round once more, yelling, both hands holding his belly.

"I seen you, man!"

He weaved left and right as if he would fall and bobbed his head hard at Renner. "I watched you come in here, you don't live in this place!"

Renner glanced at the window, the open room beyond the derelict's bobbing head.

"Two girls," the guy panted, slowing down, quieter.

"What's your name?"

"Fuck you."

Renner raised his fist.

"*Tony.*" He pulled the filthy T-shirt up and peered down at his belly. Then he lifted his head, slack-jawed. When Renner made no other move, he slowly straightened the rest of his body and stretched one arm to pick up his cap from the floor.

Over the drumbeat of his own ears Renner was listening for voices through the wall, hearing nothing. A telephone had started to ring. If somebody had called the manager about the noise, if the manager had called the cops. His hand was shaking as he lowered the tire iron, sweat was rolling down his nose, his cheeks.

"Two girls," Tony repeated. He had a rasping, whiskey-throated voice and his teeth were broken off at the stumps in a black uneven row.

"Get the hell out of here," Renner said.

"I need work, man," Tony said abruptly, shaking his head, the rasp turning into a whine. "Any kind of work." He was in his late twenties, Renner guessed, but already weathered and ageless mouse-gray under the dirt. Up close he smelled of booze and sweat and bad grease and he swayed a little as Renner took his arm and jerked him forward. The telephone was still ringing somewhere. The voices next door hadn't resumed. Renner shoved him into the hall, past the kitchen, through the open front door.

Outside in the sunlight a middle-aged man was standing by the manager's office now, holding the screen door and watching as they passed. The derelict nodded sagely.

"*He* didn't see you, I did."

"You followed me up there?"

"I need work, man. I need something. I tried everything, you know?"

"You were watching their place?"

"I come from Texas, I'm in fucking L.A. eight months, man. There's nothing I can *do.*"

They had stopped by Renner's car, in the full sunlight, and Tony blinked, close to tears. He was skinny under the T-shirt, knobby-necked, round-shouldered. The Levis he wore were stained almost black with dirt and oil and his hair made a frizzy cloud of brown and blond, floating under the baseball cap. Renner rubbed sweat from his eyes and thought he had never seen so many derelicts as he had seen since coming back from England, so many lives and families cracked open and tossed into doorways, alleyways, grassy parks. It was a rich country, one part of his mind was thinking, to throw away so many people.

"What is it, Tony?" Renner said. "You're a peeper?"

"No!"

"But you're watching the blonde?"

"Maybe she's blond." Tony's face had changed, gone shrewd. His features were small and crowded together, dots drawn on a dirty brown bag. Renner could hear the high-tension wires buzzing in the next lot, feel his body begin to tremble in delayed reaction. Be professional, aloof, hold back. *Maskenfreiheit*: the freedom conferred by wearing a mask.

Then he was taking a furious step toward Tony, out of control, bunching his fist, making Tony repeat it. "The *guy*," Tony said. He backed away, nodding his head fast in fear and surprise. "That's what I said, what I said—this guy set me up to watch them. He said, 'Let me know what you see, *who* you see.' Twenty bucks when he comes by, *if* he comes by, that's it, that's all."

20

Keith Kassabian sat up straighter at the table and watched the tall guy work up and down the sidewalk.

It was what? Seven-thirty? Eight? He held up his wrist and clicked the little button that lit up the numbers. Eight-twenty-two.

Keith shook his head in an exaggerated motion, thinking he might catch somebody's eye, somebody might see him, see his face, think here's a guy with troubles. Comfort him. Like the waitress going by with the huge boobs, the thighs like big drumsticks. Like the punk-haired girl by herself at the next table reading her book. He shook his head again, but she didn't look up, the waitress kept on talking to the busboy, so Keith bent his head lower and looked over the top of his glass at the man on the sidewalk.

Just go there, Francis had said. *Just go there and sit the fuck down and wait.*

Why?

Francis had made his stone chief face. *Don't ask questions.*

Keith tasted his beer and pushed it aside. He had drunk

so much watery beer his head was like a washtub. Now the tall guy was standing under the nearest streetlight, rubbing his hand back through his hair, then squinting at his watch. He looked tired, his clothes looked like Goodwill, like he'd slept all night in them, but he moved fast when he worked. In the five minutes since Francis had made his signal the man must have stopped half a dozen people. He stopped them on the sidewalk almost at random, flipped open a notebook, showed them something.

What?

When I point him out, Francis had said, *if you know him, put down your beer and go in the backroom or the john. If you don't know him, wait till I go by and signal again. Then get up and walk straight to the Horse/Cow.*

To see the guy? The *other* guy?

Nothing. Not even a flicker. When Francis was pissed about something, he was harder than anybody, harder than his brother, harder than the stiff-faced Armenian lawyers who sat down behind their big desks and stared at him for half an hour before they spoke. Pricks, Keith thought. His mind made another disjointed leap of association, which was the meth working. But lawyers were exactly that, pricks. They were pricks in seersucker suits. And for once, for the first time in three days almost, he laughed. He pulled a paper napkin out of the metal dispenser and tried to draw a picture on it with his ballpoint, two huge dorks coming out of a collar, wearing fancy coats and ties. Two condoms for top hats.

He put it to one side of the table where the waitress could see it. But a moment later it wasn't funny, it was a terrible picture, it looked like a crazy design for a rug and he heard his goddamn brother's voice telling him to shape up, grow up, and then it was Francis's voice, snarling behind him and saying plans were changed, walk out to the beach, along the new bike path.

And Keith was frightened enough of Francis, his knees and hands trembled enough so that he stood up quickly, at once, fluttering dollar bills onto the beer-stained table, a scared tree shitting leaves. He half slapped, half rubbed his face with one hand, then he started out the door.

"Stop under the streetlight," Francis hissed. "Let him see you."

Renner turned almost at the instant Keith stepped into the light.

Even at fifty yards there was no mistaking the slump of the shoulders that the mug shot had captured, the sprayed hair and pale mustache, the slack O of the mouth. But Renner flicked one glance at the photograph in his palm to be sure. Then he slipped it into his jacket and started to follow.

There was something called "rough shadow" that the English liked to do to the IRA: Instead of concealing yourself from the target you followed out in the open, blatantly, letting him look back and see you and making him panic.

But this one—Kassabian walked like a man with one foot in a ditch, stumbling, coked to the gills or simply drunk. Would he notice if you rolled up behind him in a bus?

Renner slowed his pace to match Kassabian's. On the crowded asphalt strip that was Venice Beach's version of a boardwalk they wound north through a moving freak show of hucksters and exhibitionists, all ages, colors, and sexes, parading in and out of store fronts and streetlights. Every few feet there seemed to be small boys with drums or ghetto blasters, knots of dancers lurching in a circle. Renner shoved through a trio of sailors, a wheelchair dance. Under an awning a man was showing a monkey, a woman was changing T-shirts.

Kassabian turned left toward the darkness, between two open enclosures where teenage Goliaths grunted and clanged barbells in monotonous rhythm. What you couldn't smell over the dope and the cigarettes, Renner thought, was the ocean itself, couldn't hear the surf over the clash of metal and whine of music. Kassabian disappeared, reappeared farther out, where the line of palm trees started in the sand and an incongruous black asphalt path was being constructed.

He was moving faster now, well out of the crowd, as if

he had a purpose. Renner hung back. The police saw everything separately, he thought. They didn't see links between bombs, didn't guess at submerged connections, faces. What faces? What connections? The derelict Tony had handed back the mugshot of Keith Kassabian, shaking his head. Not the guy who had hired him to watch Jillian. Six separate bombs, fragments of spinning light, a girl with a starburst face. What connections?

Kassabian was gone again, swallowed by the black space past the palm trees, before the distant white line of the waves. Renner paused, scanning. In and out of the darkness, the round pools of light—it was like tracking a fish in a pond. He stepped slowly along the new path— why build a goddamn path on a beach?—and let his eyes adjust. Straight ahead, as if there were a dotted line drawn down the sand, the backdrop changed. Venice Beach simply ended and Santa Monica began, throwing up its walls of high rises and hotels.

When Kassabian reappeared this time he was much closer, no more than twenty yards away. Renner stopped beside a line of wooden sawhorses and a circular chain fence. Behind it he saw construction trailers, a bulldozer, stacked triangles of sewer pipes. He turned and looked away casually toward the ocean. From Jillian's apartment to Pasadena, to Kassabian's apartment. To Venice Beach where Kassabian had bought the cordite.

He heard the arm swinging before he saw it.

A huge fist thumping off his chest like a ball and sending him staggering backward. Falling, he grabbed at air, a sleeve. On the flying sand he tried to scramble and roll and the palm trees spun.

Then a shoe, not a fist, short hard kicks in his side, his hip, his shoulder, methodical as a hammer. When the fist came down again he was moving feebly to his left and he felt bones flatten against his ear, smelled leather and oil, rolled one more time to his hands and knees.

Not Kassabian—the last turn had brought the trees right side up, and Kassabian was ten yards away staring. The man in the leather jacket was reaching for Renner's shoulders and starting to lift. Renner punched him once in the belly, round and hard as a fender.

The man hit him again with professional efficiency, twice under the heart.

As his breath rushed out a hand dug for his wallet, ripping the fabric of his jacket. At a spot two feet over his ears, as if in hallucination, Renner heard air rasping in his own windpipe, the slap of the man's fist against his jaw, his neck.

A mugging, he thought, going down to one knee. A Venice Beach transfer of wealth. But Kassabian was still watching, and the man with the fists like a pair of shovels was standing flat-footed, his back to the fence, a black stump against the distant lights of the boardwalk.

Renner pulled himself up and lunged.

For one instant the man's face was caught in the lights, his features blazed up like a match in a dark room. Then Renner was swinging his own left hand, far too high and missing everything but hair. When he turned again Kassabian had vanished, and the man in the leather jacket was running north, off the asphalt path.

The beach pitched toward the ocean. Renner ran clumsily. He stumbled in the sand, dipped, tried to find some sort of rhythm.

Not a mugging. Ahead of him the man was running steadily on the hard packed sand just above the line of the waves. Renner felt his side stitching, his right shoulder jarred with every step. The man jumped over something, a mound. Renner stumbled, balanced with one waving hand, closed the gap.

There were streetlights, signs, car headlights not more than a hundred yards ahead, where the beach suddenly curved. Beyond a lifeguard's chair Renner saw the neon oval of his own motel. As the next wave boomed toward them he stretched full-length and caught heels and an ankle and they rolled like schoolboys into the surf. A wave exploded around their heads, churning white manes of foam and sand. Water stung his mouth and eyes. The man with the leather jacket, impassive, was knee-deep in water and drawing back his fist. Twisted in his jacket, half blinded by water and hair, Renner was a defenseless target, open to the huge blows coming.

> *At bomb school they learned to put improvised cordite caps under soup bowls and cover them with dirt. The explosion could drive a crater four feet into the road, lift an M5 tank on its side—like strapping a bomb to your fist, the instructor marveled . . . .*

Renner crawled gagging out of the clamorous water. Waves foamed around his legs, a white crest of dry sand rose above him. When he reached the asphalt path again he could see Venice Beach to his right, a wide strip of colored lights and movement. To his left the beach climbed a few more yards and stopped at an embankment just below Ocean Avenue. Near the point where his motel sign blinked blue and orange, a giant Californian mask, a heavy figure was running.

Renner reached the embankment and started to sprint along the sidewalk, cursing the vodka, the middle-aged legs that rose and fell in jolts of pain. The man was on the other side of the street. They were running parallel to each other when he glanced left, saw Renner, and turned right.

Into a pandemonium of horns, lights, and brakes Renner dodged and ducked. On the other side he started to run again, up the sidewalk, toward an alley.

A drugstore, a restaurant—halfway down the alley he caught up swinging and the two of them crashed sideways into a row of empty boxes and rolling trash cans. Renner slipped on cardboard and grease. When he came to his knees the man was already standing again. A dazzling antitheft spotlight hung from an alley door just behind his head. Out of its corona the fists dove in bursts, three to the face, three more to the heart. Sagging, Renner tried to block them, but his hands dropped, his head dropped. In the eerie center of the spotlight he saw a distinct square face, a man in his forties with stringy black hair, skin pockmarked and scarred. The man he had been chasing? Renner's mouth was filling with blood. What connections?

The face in the light divided. On the gritty concrete he scratched for something to hit back with, a board, a rock, felt his wet clothes tangle again, saw the point of a boot rising. His head flew apart in soup bowls.

21

RENNER CAME TO SITTING IN THE BACK OF A CAR.

He moved his arms gingerly, blinked once very carefully, sat up with a groan. His car.

"You throw up again," Musso said, "I'll book you for littering."

"Man's hurt," a woman's voice protested.

"Man *should* of been hurt," Musso mimicked, "but they only hit him in the head."

Renner raised his hands and spread his fingers wide, grasping the top of the seat in front. In the back of his own car. At his elbow the right-hand door was propped open. A streetlight was shining a few feet away and behind it, behind Musso's bulk were white steps, another circle of white light, a rising cone of darkness.

"You all right now, Colonel?" Rosalie Garbutt asked.

"Colonel," Musso snorted.

"I feel wonderful," Renner said.

"You at the Parker Center, Colonel Renner."

Now he could see her face. He nodded once and pictured his skull, alone, without a body, floating through black space, the planet Krypton exploding. He felt his damp matted hair, crusts of blood on his jaws and lips. He smelled wet clothes and something else indefinable and fetid from the boxes and cans he had knocked over in the alley.

"How'd I get to the Parker Center?"

"You drove here."

"You drove right up the curb," Musso said, pushing aside Rosalie Garbutt's heavy brown face and peering in. He smelled of little cigars and onions and for a moment Renner's belly and throat tried to clutch and squeeze. "Before that you strolled into Gold's Gym down off Venice Beach, threw up on the pay phone, and bled all over the towels."

"Musso."

"Let me drive you home, Colonel. My shift's just ended."

"The reason they let you walk out, Renner, is the blood. In Los Angeles we don't mess with somebody bleeding anymore. The boys down at Gold's took one look at the blood and covered up their steroid cocktails and let you stroll right back out on the street again. And blood or no blood you got back in your car and drove to the Parker Center just in time to jump the sidewalk and pass out."

Rosalie stood up with her hands on her hips and glared at Musso. "Man's hurt," she said. "I don't care who you are."

"This is Lieutenant Frank Musso," Renner said. "Homicide."

"Lieutenant Asshole," she said.

For a moment Renner grinned, then the cuts along his face began to split again and fissures of pain started to open everywhere. He slid three inches across the seat to the open door and leaned over the gutter heaving, feeling nothing come up. His left ear pulsed in a violent drumbeat. He balanced his head on three fingers like a plate.

"All right," Rosalie was saying furiously above him. "You got the rank. I hear you. But what I'm telling you is you *better* take care of him, that's all." Renner lifted his head and stretched his neck and shoulders. "That's all I'm saying." She bent down, a great dark sea of warmth coming close to his face. He felt a soft hand on his ear, his shoulder. Then she slipped a thick folded sheet of paper into the soggy jacket pocket and stepped back.

When she had gone, Musso sighed and pushed him, not gently, back into the car. He closed the door and walked around to the driver's side and got in. Watching, Renner felt his energy coming back, a false boost of adrenaline that fell away as sharply as it had come.

"USC Med Center," Musso said. "That's the closest."

"I'm all right."

"That's right. You feel wonderful."

Lights spiraled toward them; in slow, silent motion burst like globes on the windshield.

"Renner?"

"Yeah."

"You remember going into Gold's Gym?"

"Some. A little." He saw stacks of white towels, a boy in a jockstrap with muscles like a brontosaurus.

"Renner, you can dial nine one one without a quarter. You say the word, anybody in the gym would have called you the cops." Musso twisted to look back at him, an angry tangle of eyebrows and hair. "So who the hell were you trying to call?"

Renner sat back against the cushions and watched the freeway tilt and roll ahead of them, a concrete beach curving into the darkness.

At the Medical Center he sat in a green cubicle curtained off from an examining room. A harried young doctor with a tiny moustache and a limp wrote down his name, his various numbers, and left. Musso leaned against a NO SMOKING sign and lit one of his Dutch cigars, staring impassively at the next doctor, a Chinese woman wearing rubber gloves who dressed the cuts and scrapes on Renner's face, held up her fingers for him to count, and checked his torso for broken ribs. Outside the curtain, over the groans of somebody on an invisible gurney, she argued briefly with the mustached doctor, then strode back in with a vial of yellow pills and wrote out an order for an X ray, chest and skull.

When they reached the main corridor of the hospital, Renner swallowed three of the pills straight from his palm and tore up the order for the X ray.

Musso watched balefully.

Then Renner sat down abruptly in one of the plastic spoon-bottomed chairs by the door and closed his eyes. Half an hour later he blinked himself awake to find Musso holding the car door open in front of his motel.

"What's your room number?" Musso said.

"Two-sixteen."

"You got a mild concussion, Renner. It's not a bright idea to sleep any more for a couple of hours. You want me to bring you some coffee? Turn on the shower?"

Renner brushed past him and started up the outside stairs to his room. At the landing he paused and shivered in the gray sea breeze, feeling the whole city sway gently around him. Occiput bone. The back of the skull. The hardest part of the head. A mild concussion can actually leave you light-headed, more alert than usual, clear. He saw double because he had two eyes.

"Maybe I'll come up and tell you funny cop stories," Musso said just beneath him on the stairs. "Gold's Gym, for instance. We got a bunch of Vietnamese gangs working out of Torrance and Irvine now, ripping off Gold's Gyms and all the other yuppie health clubs. One of them goes into the locker room with an empty gym bag, the other one hangs around outside—and you know what they use? They use beepers, like doctors and drug dealers, beepers to let the one inside know when somebody's coming."

"High tech," Renner said, fumbling for the key in his jacket and not finding it. "A land of opportunity."

"Gretzsky says you could beep off a bomb like that."

Renner stood back while Musso worked something small and bright like a pipe reamer in his big hands and then pushed open the door to the room.

"Go home, Musso," Renner said. "Thanks for the ride. Bugger off."

But when he came out of the shower Musso was

propped in one of the two chairs, legs stretched out, Mexican boots crossed, putting down the telephone.

"You look better, Renner. You ought to get mugged more often. You gonna tell me what happened now?"

He had stopped fiddling with whatever he held in his left hand and placed it on the bedside table, beside the telephone. Renner stared for another two seconds before he remembered the flash of something bright at the door. "That's my bomb tool."

Musso looked at it in mock surprise.

"You broke into my room."

Musso folded his hands over his belly. "Another good cop story," he said, "was the time I arrested the color-blind counterfeiter, back in 1968. Guy printed up half a million bucks worth of blue twenty-dollar bills."

"How'd you know where I was staying?" Even to his own ears Renner's voice sounded forced, play-acting. What else did he expect of Musso?

"Renner, Renner—I followed the trail of little empty vodka bottles right up to the door, like Hansel and fucking Gretel in the woods. I'm a cop. That your daughter?" He pointed toward the photograph on Renner's bureau.

Renner nodded.

"She's what, thirteen? Fourteen? I got three daughters myself, three daughters and three ex-wives. Now I've joined Sex Without Partners."

"Get out of here, Musso. Let me go to sleep."

"The other thing, Renner, how come you got all these books about Thomas Jefferson?" He flopped one white hand toward the books scattered on the floor.

Renner stooped and picked up the nearest book, one of the middle volumes of Dumas Malone's biography. He had read them all twice through because Jefferson baffled him: a man apparently without passion, cool, controlled, utterly rational. Humanly impossible. Whenever Renner thought of him he thought of the coal fires in western Virginia that had burned underground for years in the 1920's, in an unreachable network of caverns.

"Jefferson had the black girlfriend, right?" Musso said.

Renner placed the book on the bureau next to his daughter's picture.

"Read this," Musso said. He pulled a crumpled blue sheet of paper from an inner pocket and smoothed it against his necktie.

"What is it?"

"It's a fax that Echeverria and I kind of liberated."

"You read it to me." To Renner's amazement, in the Parker Center they faxed memos and reports from floor to floor rather than walk them—one more luxury unheard of in England.

Musso cocked his head and looked at him for a moment, then held up the paper to the light. "'Blond, short hair, five six to five eight, slender'"—he broke off to stretch for his tiny Dutch cigar smoking on a plastic motel ashtray. "'Slender,'" he grunted. "They recruited some English major last year from UCLA and he writes up reports like Sir Walter Scott. 'Slender.' Next time it'll be 'willowy, eyes like limpid pools.'"

Renner was standing stiff, the pain in his head pulsing. "Go on."

Musso tossed the sheet of paper on the bed. "Seen walking near Kassabian Brothers about eleven, eleven-fifteen night before last. *Before* you made your little unauthorized visit, right? Early enough to plant a bomb. The guy in the black-and-white thought she might be a hooker, so he slowed down, but she disappeared. Sound familiar? The other report was from some homeless guy rooting in the dumpster, tried to talk to her."

Musso heaved himself out of the chair and hitched his belt higher around his belly. "She was there, Renner."

Simply to be moving, to be doing something, Renner started to walk through the clutter of books and dirty clothes toward the window. Musso moved beside him, almost bumping him with his big belly.

"The way I finally got it, Renner," he said, "you went to Harvard on a scholarship, right? Straight out of some jerkwater town in Virginia, one traffic light, one Flying A station with the flying red horse, ten black guys by the pumps singing 'Old Black Joe.'"

"Hometown of Little Richard," Renner said, moving away again, making for the bigger window that dominated the right-hand side of the room and opened onto the ocean. "Finney, Virginia. Ty Cobb spent a winter there once. It's supposed to be mentioned in *Finnegans Wake*."

Musso moved with him, bumping. "Your father was the town intellectual, taught science in the high school; your mother ran off with some lawyer who lives in Connecticut now and you bounced off to Harvard and then the service and then you got hooked on bombs and you turned up ten years ago doing security work in England, checking out all the European embassies for bad guys." Musso bumped closer. "What's-his-name in P.R. dug all this up."

"Vincent Brodie."

"Could of been. Like it was a big deal because there's no real police assignment in your record, just building security and guards, and Gretzsky still thinks you don't know shit about bombs."

"I went over to her apartment this morning," Renner said, "but she wasn't there." His ear was pulsing harder than ever. But he was still clearheaded, strangely alert. "Then I went to Pasadena to look for Keith Kassabian, and when I didn't find him there I went to Venice Beach."

"Where he bought the cordite," Musso said.

Renner pulled the curtain to one side. Off to the left Ocean Avenue turned into a freeway ramp. Above the ramp rose a hillside, black against the misty night sky, winking with thousands of orange and white lights like a tree full of birds. Darker hills rose behind it, smaller lights, receding toward the San Fernando Valley, the mountains, the long burning path to Sacramento.

What he actually remembered from the South—almost all that he remembered, all that he hadn't repressed, flattened, broken for scrap—was mornings. Early mornings, already hot; the first flower whose name he ever learned, the white morning glory, motionless as a photograph in his father's shadow. The motel had the thin air of all California buildings, scrubbed and rinsed by unseen buffeting machines above and below. Renner had gone to

France on an official trip once, resetting photoelectric
devices in the consulate at Caen, and afterwards drove to
the American Cemetery at Omaha Beach, where his father
had had his one day of wild, uncontrolled frenzy; heroism.
He had known the instant he stepped out of the car that he
was no longer in France—the cut of the shrubbery, the
grass, the designs of the few custodial buildings, everything in sight was subtly but unmistakably American and
he had experienced a mute, spiraling sensation of love,
drawn out of some reservoir of feeling he had known
nothing about.

Musso was watching him, pulling at the little Dutch
cigar.

California was as foreign as France. All of it was
displaced Virginia.

He ran his hand across the windowsill, feeling the ridges
and whorls of the paint, the rubbery pellets of gray dust,
the thin aluminum strip that clasped the cold glass like
fingers. Yes and no. In England, he thought, without
knowing it he was starved for American shapes, American
colors.

"Renner," Musso said.

What middle age does, Renner thought, is expand your
range of loving.

"Lieutenant?"

Both of them turned to face Echeverria, who had
shoved open the door of the room.

"Love is blond," Musso said.

"Lieutenant, we got another bomb."

22

But they didn't.

When Echeverria bounced the patrol car to a halt in the middle of a crowd they had a media circus instead—they were surrounded by news vans and television cameras. Generator trucks lined the street, humming. Huge portable spotlights were mounted on wheeled frames, their beams crisscrossed by microphone booms, antennae, ladders. There were uniformed cops everywhere, milling reporters, sightseers, neighbors come out of their houses in pajamas and bathrobes. On every side were squad cars with blue and red top lights flashing, civilian cars, fire trucks, ambulances, every engine running, every door open, every radio squawking, and all of it, everything drawn up in a semicircle around the driveway of an elegant two-story house, spotlit, set apart from the crowd by its sloping lawn and a barrier of wooden sawhorses and crime scene tape. At the center of the driveway, where spotlights, cameras and mikes all converged, sat a dark green BMW sedan, its horn blaring steadily, motionless except for a thin stream

of very fine purple smoke that rose from the right side of
the open hood.

"Where are we?" Renner asked.

"San Vicente Boulevard," Echeverria shouted over the
noise of the horn. Musso was already sliding out of the car,
letting it bump upward free of his weight, hitching his belt
and motioning his big hands toward somebody pushing
through the crowd.

Renner opened the rear passenger door and started to
make his way after him through a tangle of wires and cops.
They were fifty yards down from the edge of the lawn—
far too close, he thought, far closer than he would have
permitted in England. One hundred yards was the limit for
an ordinary one-pound TNT explosion on a firing range:
fifty yards on a residential street was wildly dangerous,
wonderful for TV cameras, suicidal for flesh and blood.

He worked to the right, along the line of sawhorses,
toward the biggest concentration of squad cars where the
command post and the bomb truck ought to be.

You set up a command post first, he thought, making
his pounding head slow down and ignore the horn, going
over the familiar steps—it was your automatic, first reaction: find a calm separate space to think. Then you look for
the civilians who have to do the initial search, because in a
building, in an inhabited structure of any kind the bomb
technician never searches. He sends in the people familiar
with the rooms, the furniture, the equipment—a stranger
would take hours trying to figure out what might be out of
place in a room, what didn't belong; a resident would see
at once. Even with a car bomb that was already discovered
like this one, you would send the owner up close for a
moment if you could, to see if there were packages or
bundles on the seat that shouldn't be there, packages that
might blow up in an instant if the bomb tech tried to touch
them.

What explosive gave off purple smoke? Without detonation?

In the crowd of people now there were fewer blue
uniforms, more dark business suits, bare heads. Musso's
head was just visible over the top of a civilian car, a shaggy

half-moon of black hair. Renner edged left, circling toward him, then came to a halt in front of somebody's warning palm. Ten feet away, furiously spotlit, by a trick of his watery eyes beginning to blaze at the shoulders and cheeks, a woman had begun to speak to a camera.

Her first words were lost in a grinding of gears nearby. Behind her Renner saw the outline of something like a flatbed truck moving through the other vehicles, loaded high with teetering boxes. The black man who had held up his hand dropped it and cursed, the woman let her eyes roll upward. When Renner glanced at the nearest television monitor he saw an aerial shot of the scene where they stood, a chaotic field of shadows and lights around the still bright center of the driveway. As he watched the aerial shot disappeared and the photo of a white man in a business suit replaced it, smile frozen in smug athletic assurance.

"Poor horny bastard," the black man told Renner.

Then the woman was suddenly speaking again and the warning palm had shot back up. She looked directly into the lens, turning slightly with it as the camera trolley moved, letting her free hand drift in a gesture. This time Renner heard her voice clearly through the background noise and the unending blare of the horn, inflectionless, earnest, telling her viewers that more than twenty police units had arrived by now, the expensive executive houses up and down the blocks were all evacuated. The bomb in the car was still not disarmed.

Renner stumbled behind the camera, over more wires and around more people. Two small boys in pajamas scampered past him on their hands and knees. When he could see again the reporter was extending her arm full-length and holding out her microphone to the deputy chief.

"Renner!" Musso shouted.

The deputy chief was dressed in a light tan suit, crisp as a taco, but he wore a red knit polo shirt underneath instead of a tie. The monitor at Renner's elbow showed his polished black gunbelt, puckered little dog face nodding. Patton in front of his troops, Renner thought.

"Renner's with the goddamn task force," Musso was saying to a cop in a Santa Monica bomb squad uniform, gripping his upper arm. "He's your fucking expert!"

"I thought it was Gretzsky. I trained with Gretzsky."

"You see Gretzsky right now?"

The Santa Monica cop wiped his brow. "What about jurisdiction? What about the bomb rule?"

Musso rocked with impatience. "What about the fucking *bomb*? What about two hundred people out of control? It's too complicated for you, this is the guy!"

The Santa Monica cop took a step to one side, grimaced at the noise, the television lights. "Fuck it," he said. "Bring him over here."

And as Renner let himself be led around the news van, toward the blue police truck nearest the sawhorses, the Santa Monica bomb cop started to spread out Polaroid snapshots on a car hood.

"Just like the first one," Musso shouted over the horn. The flatbed truck started a nerve-shredding change of gears.

"This civilian," the bomb cop said. He pointed to somebody near the truck, surrounded by cops. "The victim. He comes out of the house, gets in the car in the driveway."

Renner rubbed his face hard with both hands, feeling the pain roll through his head like a wave, burst in his eyes. Bales of yellow hay were triple-stacked on the truck, and uniformed cops started to unload them.

"Just like the first bomb," Musso shouted again, bending closer to look at the photos, sharp-breathed, pungent. "Another stud. He's leaving his girlfriend's house before the husband comes home. He's going to drive his new BMW back over the hill to Westwood and the wife and kiddies, nobody knows the difference. He turns on the engine, goes three feet in reverse, and the whole front end goes up in purple smoke. The horn goes off. You know what's under the hood? Six sticks of TNT."

"The bomb misfired?"

"You know what?" the bomb cop shouted. "Without Gretzsky here I'm putting hay bales around the whole fucking thing." Walden, Walton—up close, the name tag was fuzzy; the face above it was heavyset, fair-skinned, a Scandinavian face scattershot with dozens of black and brown moles. The giddiness came and went in Renner's head, in little flickers of hallucination. For one instant everybody in sight seemed to be wearing giant paper masks painted like clowns, the wall of Jillian's room come alive. What started the horn? What kind of bomb made purple smoke?

"Then I'm going to blast the car with the water cannon," Walton yelled, "and set the fucker off."

"You're going to blow up the car?" Musso was scribbling on his notepad.

"Why not? There's too many tricky fucking bombs these days for me."

Musso swiveled to look again.

"Hey," Walton said. "The guy's on the TV news, the girlfriend's on it—he's already blown two marriages to pieces. What's a car?"

Renner held up one of the photos. "Where's the blasting cap?"

Walton frowned. The photo had been taken by someone scooting on his back under the engine mount, without a flash. You didn't use a flashbulb on a bomb, for the same reason you didn't use a standard wide-beam flashlight-explosive chemicals were by their nature unstable, hypersensitive even to beams of light. Renner looked in disgust at the spotlights, the television floods. Los Angeles. Hollywood.

"You got a wire here," Walton said, tapping the Polaroid. The horn faltered, stuttered, started again. "Hanging straight down from the TNT charge. You can't miss it. Over here's a six-volt battery, maybe a timer—you can't really tell because of this smoke. Here's the fusebox for the engine."

"The blasting cap's gonna be in the center of the sticks," somebody shouted at their elbow. A new bomb technician, young, wearing a windbreaker over his jumpsuit. Renner hardly bothered to glance at him. The State Department gave you six days of grueling psychological tests, before and after bomb school, including one full day of self-assessment tests. He knew his own mind's weaknesses and strengths. Even with ears ringing, eyes blurred, even with a mugging and three yellow pills, the part of his intelligence that fastened on bombs, that was obsessed with stopping them, still functioned. He had tunnel vision for bombs, extraordinary focus, nearly flawless recall. Musso was wrong. This wasn't like the first bomb in the series, which had taken its detonation power from the car battery and gone off when the ignition key turned and completed the circuit. Turned *twice*. Renner knew dozens of ways to make white smoke from chemical combinations. No explosive he'd ever heard of gave off purple smoke.

"Where's Gretzsky?" the new man asked.

"Off duty, not on call."

Renner slipped the photos into his pocket and used both hands to lever himself around Musso's back.

"What the hell are you doing?" Walton shouted. At the line of sawhorses he caught up and pulled Renner back half a step, then stood with hands on hips and listened, nodding his head slowly as Renner spoke. When he finally turned and signaled, somebody ran forward to hand them both tool belts and padded bomb vests. Two more bomb techs rolled out a portable waist-high screen made of thick white fiberglass and metal like a bomb blanket, but folding at three different points. Renner started to walk toward the hay bales that had already been stacked around the rear of the BMW.

"You got wrapped packages on the back seat!" Walton shouted into his ear.

Renner nodded. It was like walking into the center of the brass horn itself, a demonic high-pitched wail that battered your head, your skull, that shook your ears and brain like a slow-motion bomb. The horn took its power from the car battery—what could have set it off?

"There they are." Walton was next to him, waving one hand to indicate the packages. His bomb vest was dark blue, ripped in many places and stained by patches of crusty fluid. Like all bomb techs he wore no gloves. In the intense white brilliance of the spotlights his long face was disappearing, moles and all, wax melting into light. His lips moved silently, pointlessly against the blare of the horn.

Renner looked away. He wasn't interested in the packages. The owner had identified them, there was no sign of tampering. Both he and Walton knew that the simplest way to rig a parcel was to use a mercury switch, a tiny ball of liquid mercury in an adapted carpenter's level. One touch or bump or sudden movement and the mercury simply rolled in its plastic tube, completed a circuit, detonated the explosive. Finis. But you needed a certain bulk to conceal the level. These packages were jewel-box size, too small, not dangerous.

The TNT, on the other hand, was.

Behind Walton he could hear the bomb techs rolling the heavy screen up the driveway. Standard but useless, he thought. No protection at all against six sticks of halfway decent explosive—if he made a mistake no shield in the world would slow down the blast wave for an instant. He and Walton would be torn apart before a single brain cell could fire its synapse, before an eye could blink, flung into eternity in a thousand smoking pieces of gristle and bone. To his right Walton had now put on his face mask as well, a clumsy multilayered hood straight out of science fiction. Renner shifted his arms and felt the constrictions of his own bomb vest over his sportcoat and shirt. They were standing beside the open hood, staring down into the nightmarish shriek of the horn. Renner leaned forward.

The purple smoke was still thick across the top of the engine. Through it he could just see on the far side the pale red sticks of TNT, nestled against the lower engine block. The horn was directly under his chin, shaking the purple air into fragments.

He lowered himself to his knees and twisted forward until he could see under the engine. Here the noise was even worse, the whole engine cavity transformed into an echo chamber. Just as in the photograph there was a long loop of electrical wire hanging from the TNT, impossible to miss, dangling almost to the pavement. But up close you could tell that while one end disappeared into the red sticks and presumably into a blasting cap, the other end curled around a pipe of some kind, then climbed up toward the carburetor.

Why?

If the wire wasn't properly connected to the battery, that would explain the misfire. But the battery was almost a yard away, to Renner's left, just behind the left headlight, nowhere near the carburetor. The wire was looped in the wrong direction.

The horn stuttered again, seemed to take a breath and grow louder.

The hand Renner saw stretching in front of him was pale, dripping with sweat, starting to tremble. He let his fingers come within an inch of the wire, stop. Walton grunted or coughed, said something. There was a rustle of cloth as he moved.

Renner stretched his hand another half inch. Touch the wire. Complete the connection.

He shifted, leaned. His arm already ached. His eyes burned from the residue of purple smoke—he registered an incongruous mixture of smells: the dry horsey smell of the hay, the bitter acid of ammonium, found in half the chemical explosives you could buy.

When he moved again his left shoulder touched something wet—water or oil. He lowered his head and squinted. Water. Dripping from the water pump.

The horn was intolerable now. He had slipped into the center of its sound, his head was packed in sound, swaddled and squeezed, beginning to burst. Renner held out his hand and grasped the double wires at the back.

Unending, unbearable noise.

He closed his fist and yanked.

23

THE SILENCE WAS MORE ASTONISHING THAN THE SOUND.

For a long moment Renner simply lay on his side under the engine, listening to nothing at all. When he finally lowered his arm, pulling the wire completely into view, it was as if he were watching someone else's hand in a silent film: black and white, unreal. Gradually he became aware of the other noises around him—his own rasping breath, voices, police car motors, generators. Somewhere far out of sight he heard the flap-flap rotors of a helicopter, clucking like a gigantic hen.

The horn had been deliberately wired to go off, but not connected to the explosive. A joke. A joker. For the first time Renner began to think of the mind that had rigged the bomb. The wife's husband? The cuckold? A fine old English word. He released the wire. His hand was as stiff as a claw. Walton thought so, Musso assumed it; the jealous husband. Renner closed his eyes and saw gray-green London, the carpeted steps leading up to their unfashionable fourth-floor flat in Belgravia. In his mind's theater he saw Edward, round-shouldered, gray-haired cuckolding Edward mounting the stairs to Vicki.

He shifted, felt the puddle of water again, and slid farther under the engine. Walton had come down on his hands and knees and was saying something, muffled by the mask, but Renner was moving away from him anyhow. You would set the horn going for a joke, a literate joke—the horned husband, the cuckold. In certain moments, certain blood red patches of anger he would have imagined setting a bomb for Edward. The wire leading to the sticks of dynamite now dangled an inch from his cheek. To his right, where the strange purple smoke was thickest, a flat plastic pan of something ran backwards toward the water pump.

White smoke was easy. Purple smoke was funnier, unmistakable. If you wanted to make purple smoke without a fire, without an explosion, you would line a tray with something like ammonium nitrate. Then a layer of zinc powder. Then a top sprinkling of iodine crystals for the color. What would ignite it?

Water.

He extended his right arm sideways and let his hand climb up the water pump until he found where the hole had been drilled. When you turned on the engine the water pump churned, water spewed out, smoke started up.

Then police arrived. Cameras arrived. Your marriage blew up.

Renner craned his head to look at the dynamite sticks. Next to him now Walton extended his arm, holding out a tiny flashlight similar to Renner's Tigar, a round lens less than an inch across, hooded to reduce the focus still more. In its beam Renner could follow the wire up. He could read the printing on the nearest stick, not quite a foot from his eyes. There was a manufacturer's code number first, telling the batch, the date, the type: sixty-percent strength nitro-glycerine gel dynamite, with a detonation speed of thirteen thousand feet per second. Strong enough to wreck a house. Strong enough to drive the peach pulp of their skulls ten feet deep into the driveway. Next to the code numbers was a little gold crown with the letter P drawn inside, standing for "Permitted Explosive." In blue lettering the brand name Driftex.

Which was the name of a British commercial explosive.

The wire went up, looped again through the cotton cord that held the sticks together, then disappeared.

It was the same guy.

The dynamite wire did what the horn wire did. What Renner's wire at bomb school had done. A joke, a decoy. Renner held up the blade of his bomb tool, twice the length of a finger. The length of a cuckold's horn. The blade followed the wire. Poor sap of a jealous husband. Renner floated on his back in a sea of concentration. Walton had vanished, the noise had vanished. There was only his blade going blindly into the light. Hire the guy to bomb her lover. How could he guess how the guy's mind worked? Blow them all to pieces with a bomb that wouldn't go off.

Renner twisted the blade through the loop of wire and pulled hard and as Walton gasped the wire dropped through the flashlight beam and coiled across Renner's face, a noose of light.

After a bomb is disarmed comes the high. Sheer serotonin pleasure, the State Department psychologist had explained, sniffing. A rush of the enzyme serotonin through the nerve cells of the cerebral cortex, like sexual orgasm, except prolonged, hilarious. Renner had seen bomb techs walk out of a bomb site grinning like apes, then start to stagger and shout incoherently and fall to the ground as if they were drunk—you defeat a bomb, you explode with laughter.

Pleasure and dominance are linked experiences for men, the psychologist said.

This time Renner felt nothing. He staggered away from the car, toward the lights, but not with pleasure. He barely heard the ripples of applause from the crowd. He shook away microphones, notebooks, bright inquiring faces, grasped instead at Walton's sleeve to steady his legs. The yellow pills had worn off, his bruises had blossomed up and down his chest and across the back of his head, burning circles of nonpleasure.

At a distance he heard his voice telling Walton something about the BMW's wiring system. By the time he turned painfully to look again, two techs had already removed the dynamite sticks and laid them out on a tarpaulin. From the other side of the bomb truck plainclothes cops were beginning to bring up their bags of equipment.

Renner's mind lurched, refused to move. Somebody— Musso? Echeverria?—was leading him by the elbow past a television van, dipping him into a squad car and closing the door. When he lifted his head again, they were pulling up in front of his motel in Santa Monica. At the stairway landing he remembered that he wanted to look at the sea, but Musso was opening the door and motioning.

In bed he rose for a moment on one elbow to stare at Musso's enormous wide back.

His last thought before sleep was a question.

Where the hell did the guy get British explosives in California?

THREE

24

June 14

IN GEOLOGICAL TIME, MOST OF SOUTHERN CALIFORNIA IS YOUNG and disorderly. The coastal mountains that stretch from Malibu to Santa Barbara are unstable layers of brittle rock, liable to shift or crack without warning. Inward from the coastal range, slightly older mountains sprawl across a vast network of underground faults, created by the uneven movement of ocean plates and mountain plates colliding and sliding past each other. Apart from the wet winter months, the topsoil everywhere is sandy and crumbling. The lower elevations are furzed with spiny dead grass, like a thin beard. Mountains, valleys, canyons; formless expanses of sediment. From an airplane the landscape looks deceptively like the vast tawny ocean it actually was some few million years ago—long furrowed ridges of mountains roll west and south from the desert like waves, converging in endless lines just above the arid plains of the Los Angeles basin. There they crest and hold.

Inside the basin, Renner thought ironically, drawing the window curtain back, the goddamn land rushes down to the ocean like a demented lover.

"If you have a theater that seats fewer than ninety-nine people, you don't have to pay Equity wages," Jillian said briskly behind him. "It's that simple."

Renner let the curtain edge drop and refocused on the dusty stacks of extra chairs lining the far wall of the dressing room. Who would build a dressing room on the top floor of a theater? What bomb had blown California upside down? Jillian pulled the bathrobe tighter around her waist. As she leaned against the dressing table six feet away, she was framed by the rectangle of frosted round makeup lights that outlined the mirror. Always light, radiance. Her face was an oval of sheer white. She had pulled her hair back into a bun, a little puff of blond. From where Renner stood the hollow at the base of her throat was shiny with sweat, the size of a tongue. Despite the heat of the room she was as cool, as neutral as if she had never spoken to him in the drugstore aisle, never seen him before. *Help.*

"Any other questions?" she said. "Or do you want a guided tour of the palace?" Her hand flipped casually to indicate the rest of the dingy room.

His mind was still not under control, he thought. The bruises across his ribs throbbed in an irregular distracting pulse, his head took sudden dips of viscous inattention. He rubbed his face hard and paced two steps across the crowded floor. There were the stacks of excess chairs in front of him that the management had dismantled and stored to save money. There was the dressing table, the show-biz mirror. Bottles and disks of makeup and powder. An old coffee can filled with pencils, feathers, junk. A narrow couch with sprung upholstery. Dirty linoleum. A footlocker. A loop of plastic cord with clothes hangers dangling from it. No posters. No homemade masks. His mind lurched again. Where the hell had the guy come up with sticks of British dynamite?

"He got them from a British citizen," Musso had said sarcastically. "Right? Not a British *company,* because British companies don't build squat in Los Angeles and what they do build they use American dynamite on."

He had paused and glowered at Renner.

"Met any British citizens lately, Renner?"

Renner stopped in front of her, barely a foot away now, conscious of the smallness of her body wrapped inside the thick robe, smelling her powder, wet hair. But a kick in the head had done wonders for his sense of smell, he thought.

"You really went to Cambridge?" he asked for lack of a better question. Foolish, spacy. There was no way he could mention her apartment, his witless, obsessive break-in.

She cocked her head. "I went to Trinity College, Cambridge," she said, watching him. "One of the first of the ladies' brigade. I read history for three years and I had a room in the chapel courtyard, where Lord Byron used to keep his bear. Anything else?"

Renner picked up a paperback from the table, the complete poems of Emily Dickinson.

"You were arrested at Cambridge," he said. "I saw Musso's files."

She took the book from his hand and replaced it on the table. "I chained myself to the fence at the Mildenhall Air Force Base," she said. "And it took a blow torch to cut me loose. I was demonstrating unpeacefully for peace."

"You were arrested *six* times. Musso pulled in your whole visa record."

"You know what," she said dryly. "You make a terrible cop. You're much too polite. Your friend Musso has the act down better—the manliest man's man since Attila the Hun, which is how a cop should be."

"You don't know why I'm here?"

"I haven't the slightest idea. You want to put me in the movies. You want to buy me a condo in Malibu."

Renner glanced at his watch. "You don't know about the bomb last night?" Had it been last night? Not even twenty-four hours ago? The pills had thrown his sense of time into a strange wavelike rhythm. He had awakened at noon, seen Musso at two, sat at Musso's office until—when? He looked again. It was seven o'clock now, ten minutes past.

"I don't have a television," Jillian said in a new tone. Renner frowned and looked up. Folded arms. High chin. An actress's instant summation of impatience.

"And I don't have time to read the papers." She held out her wrist and touched it with one finger. "Two more minutes," she told him. "You're a puzzler, Mr. Renner. You have a lopsided smile and a sympathetic manner and you must have talked a right line of chatter to get past Cerberus the doorman. But you also have a one-track mind. I give you two minutes and then I go straight downstairs to rehearsal."

"Listen," he said. "Jillian."

"First turn around, please." Brisker, cooler. Receding. With a shrug of her right shoulder she let the robe fall. In the mirror Renner saw a flash of skin, glass on fire.

"There was another bomb last night," he said, trying to drive authority into his voice, force. "Number *eight*. And this one was made with a British brand of restricted commercial dynamite. Nobody could buy it in this country. But somebody could buy it there and put it in a suitcase and fly it over from London, no problem."

She wore a flesh-colored bra and bikini panties, and male authority, force meant nothing to her. Ignoring him, she walked across the room and opened the footlocker.

"I don't understand what you're talking about," she said. "Not a bloody word. I was an innocent bystander once, just once."

"I'm talking about the L.A. police, damn it, the L.A. bomb squad." He flexed his hands in his jacket pockets, smelling ammonium now, purple smoke, hay, sweat, shampoo. "And not just once."

"I don't know bombs. I don't know police."

She bent to take out a checked lumberjack's shirt from the footlocker. Renner watched the muscles of her back scallop as she stretched. When she held out a sleeve to put on the shirt her nipples were stiff and pink under the bra.

"Listen." His mind veered, thrashed. Unreachable women. Pull a cord, disarm them. "Listen," he repeated. To his own ears his voice sounded ponderous, unconvincing. "You need help. Lieutenant Musso hasn't quit, he doesn't buy it. He's going to come and see you again. Musso, Echeverria, maybe the FBI—serious cops. And this time he's going to come with a legitimate warrant."

"Do you know what the author calls this play?" she said, looking away, looking at the idiotic extra chairs. She pulled on the shirt and fumbled in the breast pocket for cigarettes. "*A Lie of the Mind*. The first time I read it I said to myself, what other kind of lie is there?"

For a moment Renner's memory beat off the pills. She had a television. If he closed his eyes he could see it sitting on the shelf in her apartment.

"And then I figured out that it's supposed to be a play about the theater, about illusion, the old Hamlet theme, theater and life are the same thing, the world's a stage." To his amazement she was biting off her words in a clipped, angry accent. One hand held a cigarette trembling, the other was buttoning the shirt from the bottom. As always, he was two steps behind her change of mood.

"But now what I think it's really about is women. It's the girl in the play, my part, who starts out as an actress. 'Changed her hair and everything,'" she said in a hard mock-southern voice. "'Put a wig on. Changed her clothes. Changed everything. This acting shit is the real world for her.' You saw the rehearsal. You know why I spend half the play in a hospital gown? Because my lover's beat me senseless and left me for dead. The other half of the play I spend in a lie of the mind, that it's OK, that I'm not really hurt, that *he's* OK."

"Jillian."

"That's how women live with men," she said.

"Musso has a *witness*!" Renner hissed. He grabbed her wrist and squeezed as hard as he could. "He can place you at the goddamn rug store."

She flung his hand away.

From somewhere she had come up with a lighter. Her fingers shook as she held the flame just beneath the tip of the cigarette. In the mirror it seemed to waver and catch the light of her hair, light on light, flame on flame.

"There's a man outside your apartment who watches you."

Her look blazed, then vanished, fire in a vacuum.

"You're the only man I know who watches me," she said.

"He broke into your apartment." Renner's fingers closed on the slip of paper Rosalie Garbutt had given him with her address written on it. He was already late. Musso was waiting. Musso was furious. "And he smashed all the masks on your bedroom wall. I *saw* him, damn it."

She lit the cigarette. As she cupped her hand her gesture was like Vicki's, like his daughter's, alien, alluring.

"Listen to me—somebody *pays* him to do it."

"I don't have any masks," she said.

"You're late," Musso said. "You're forty fucking minutes late."

Renner took his receipt from the parking attendant and looked past Musso's angry face toward the street. At the bottom of the hill all he could see of the ocean was a vast encroaching island of black.

"I give you one fucking hour," Musso said.

Renner pushed past him and started up the steps of the Holiday Inn. Welcome to Bayview, Santa Monica. "You sound like fucking Gretzsky," he said.

Behind him Musso grunted. Renner shoved the door open and nodded at the bellman.

"Gretzsky went ballistic, you disarmed that bomb," Musso said, catching up. "*Then* he found out you snuck in and read his reports today." Together they stopped three steps inside the lobby and stared. Two stories high, California casual, a forest of ferns, potted trees, palm leaves. What Renner remembered from western movies in his boyhood was the sense of space and freedom they gave. What California cities and buildings did was shut out the horizon, squeeze down the space, clutter the big sky. He had driven as fast as he could from Jillian's theater—Los Angeles was a blur of signs, huge commercial signs on every street, every corner, meant for people who had trouble reading.

"Gretzsky writes shitty reports," Renner said. A posse of Japanese tourists was bearing down on them, elbows and cameras. Gretzsky had missed the car bomb episode completely—a cousin's wedding. Gretzsky was a very strange bomb cop. Renner stepped to one side and craned his neck to look up.

"When Keith Kassabian came here," he said, still looking, "what did he claim he was doing?"

"He was drinking brandy Alexanders," Musso said. He had his hands in his jacket pockets, turning from side to side. "Upstairs in the bar."

Renner started across the room toward the elevator rank.

"Which is not a punk kid's style," Musso said, close behind him. "Which is mouse-dick shrewd."

"Why is that?" He watched a red-haired woman in a manager's blue blazer walk deliberately by, studying them.

"Renner, Renner, the guy was making sure the bartender remembered him. He overtipped, he drank fancy cocktails, he bought drinks for the band. This is a guy setting up an alibi."

Renner stopped in front of the elevators and looked back toward the front doors, the long slope oceanward of Pico Boulevard. A lie of the groin. She had stood there in the dressing room glowering at him. Legs bare under the checked shirt, a triangle of white silk. His head was clearer every minute. He didn't understand a goddamn thing.

"If Keith Kassabian set off the bomb," he said, moving his gaze back to Musso, "he did it by remote control. All of these bombs have been remote control one way or the other, no timers. That's thing number one they have in common. If he did it from here, somebody saw him do it." He punched the UP button hard with his fist.

Musso rocked back on his heels, his bright cowboy boots. Musso's signature. "Lemme quote," he said. "'Fucking Kassabian didn't do it,' your words. 'No junkie asshole could make a three-stage bomb that worked from ten miles away.'"

Above their heads an UP disk appeared with a ping and a burst of red light, the controlled detonation of tungsten, Renner thought. Bang.

He entered the elevator and let Musso choose the floor. Two-Mezzanine.

"You got a theory," Musso said as the doors closed.

Renner's memory had been short-circuiting all day, all night, sparks of half-forgotten books, totally useless sayings. "'Theory is speculation by those unversed in practice,'" he said, letting the pompous syllables roll off his tongue. Samuel Johnson?

Musso grunted. The elevator bounced to a knee-shaking halt.

"You got a theory," Musso repeated as they stepped out. "You got a theory and a hard-on. Now do you want to stop this fucking bomber before more people get killed or you want to play head games and let him get off?"

"It's the same guy," Renner said. The mezzanine hallway was long and impractically narrow, a tunnel of green carpet and salmon-colored walls. On their left was a newsstand, closed; ahead on their right tall beveled windows that looked down on a swimming pool, dancing lights.

"It's the same guy with every bomb," Renner said. "I don't understand the desk at the rug store. I don't understand the wiring in the desk. But I understand him. He hires himself out and sets up people like Kassabian. He jokes, he uses different techniques."

"He pisses you off," Musso said.

"He blows up families."

Musso stopped and turned to face him.

"He blows up marriages," Renner said. "He free-lances out, he takes all kinds of jobs because he has to. But he always comes back to families. Brothers, cheating husbands. Families."

Musso pulled out one of his Dutch cigars and waited.

Renner moved his head. On the left, where the narrow hallway curved and opened up, he could see the wooden grillwork of a restaurant entrance, the gray shoulder of a cash register. "That's all," he said.

Musso waited.

"I asked you to bring Kassabian's mug shots," Renner said.

Musso patted his jacket pocket with one hand.

"And I want more than an hour."

How could he tell when Musso was really angry? The

big round face floated on a column of fat. The expression behind the black eyes was as distant, as unreachable as Jillian's. The voice habitually growled, pushed, sneered, a father's voice.

"You're not a cop, Renner," he said finally. Cold, far away. In the war. "Anybody shows mug shots, I do. Anybody says time's up, I do." He raised the little cigar to a point just in front of his lips but made no move to light it. "You let me know when you think I'm smart enough to understand your fucking theory."

The waitress behind the cash register was counting napkins. Otherwise the restaurant itself was completely empty. Renner glanced at his watch. Eight-twenty. It was a coffee shop rather than a restaurant. To their left rows of pale Formica tables circled a long counter lined with stools. A big picture window opened out onto the hillside. Through it he could just make out the lights and colored flags of the Santa Monica Pier.

Musso tapped his fingers impatiently on the top of the cash register. The waitress looked up quickly, then back down to her napkins.

"Where's somebody?" Musso said.

The waitress bent her head even closer to the napkins.

"Where's the manager usually on duty here?" Musso said. He opened a palm-size notebook and squinted. "Celso Perea?" He held out his ID wallet and waved his badge. "The manager."

"Dónde está el gerente? Fue lo que dijiste?"

"Speak English!" Musso roared and the waitress turned her head in terror, left and right. "Doesn't anybody speak English in this goddamn city?" He pushed his belly around the cash register and shouted at the empty room. Faces appeared over the coffee counter, vanished. The waitress trotted off toward the kitchen.

"This whole goddamn city," Musso said. "*Nobody* speaks English."

"Momentito," someone called from the back. "Moment."

"Musso," Renner said.

Musso stared defiantly back. He picked up a stack of napkins and put them down again. He took two steps onto the carpet, turned, reached into his jacket pocket and pulled out a manila envelope. When Renner opened it a contact sheet of black and white photographs slid out, twelve Keith Kassabians blinking owlishly up at the camera. Renner glanced at the top row, then looked away. In the State Department jargon for terrorist bombs there were Action Devices and Command Devices. Action Devices were like the car bomb last night—somebody or something made a mechanical motion that started ignition. But Command Devices worked only when a person told them to work—when somebody clicked a radio or pushed a plunger or closed a circuit. Or when one person told another person to do it. In Ireland the IRA liked to use a spotter—a child, a pretty girl by a door—somebody who signaled or telephoned when a soldier came by.

"Look at them," Musso said impatiently. He snapped the rim of the sheet with his thumb.

The Israelis were not so trusting. After the war they had invented the letter bomb for just that reason, avoid the middleman, let the guy blow himself up.

"This is a punk kid," Musso said, and he snapped the sheet of photographs again. Renner looked up to see his huge round face flushed, angry red, the controlled detonation of blood. Bang. "These are from last year," Musso said. "When Narcotics picked him up in some pathetic shooting gallery down in Venice Beach, trying to staple his veins together. You want to know why I'm here, Renner? Instead of downtown with Gretzsky? Because I think it had to be remote control too. Because a guy like this is too chicken shit to stand up close and do a job. He's got to be miles away, kidding himself."

"I want to ask what he was wearing when he was in the bar."

"He had a sandwich here first." Musso jerked his head toward the counter, a red sun coming loose, out of orbit. "Then he went upstairs."

"Whether he was carrying a walkman, whether he had on a heavy jacket, bulky. Whether he took it off."

"Study human nature, Renner."

Renner closed his eyes and saw a row of bombs going

off in black and white. Television film. Ambulances, foreign police carting away the injured.

"You know something, Renner? I actually like the Mexicans. I think they should learn English and tuck in their shirts, but I understand them. I came up the same way." Musso had moved completely around the cash register. His harsh voice was softer, mollifying. His pale white hand gestured in the darkness of the restaurant, against the black window, a fish flopping. "I was born two miles away from here in goddamn Venice Beach," he said. "Before the scumballs got it, when it had two piers and twenty little Jewish delicatessens and people rode out on the L.A. trolleys every Sunday to spend the day at the beach."

Renner leaned against the cash register, his head fuzzy with strain, tension. He felt in his pocket for the vial of pills.

"We were *poor,* Renner. The first phone call I ever made was when I was nineteen years old and came back from the army and they gave you one free call from the depot. I stood there in the booth wondering, Who do I know that even *has* a telephone?"

Behind them a thin middle-aged Hispanic in white shirt and gold vest came toward the register. He was wiping his hands on a cloth and he carried himself stiffly, on the balls of his feet, as if ready for insults.

"Yes?"

"You speak English?" Musso said.

"I speak English," he said. "It's OK."

"It's fucking wonderful," Musso said and showed him his badge. "This man here wants to ask you some questions."

But Renner was walking away from them, lowering himself into a chair beside the nearest table.

"Renner?"

"I get some water," the manager said.

"No." Renner waved his hand. English words, tortured out of shape in America. The first thing you noticed when you came back. "Device" meant bomb. "Surgical procedure" meant scalpel cutting through flesh. Two countries,

Jillian had said, divided by a common language. In England you hold your coin in a pay telephone until somebody answers on the other end. Then you press the coin in and complete the circuit. Action Device/Command Device.

The waitress had reappeared, placing a glass of water on the table in front of him, backing shyly away.

"I know how he did it," Renner told her.

25

"WATCH THIS," CAUTE SAID FROM HIS SEAT.

On the screen the man's face they had been watching vanished abruptly and they saw Caute instead, naked and shiny with sweat, moving on all fours like a wolf. Except where his ribs clawed at his skin, his muscles were pale, flat surfaces, far too white for California, grainy and toneless planes against a background of cheap red velvet curtains. He closed his eyes and raised himself higher on his bare knees.

"The big bang beat," he said from his chair.

Under his knees the bed sagged and squeaked. The woman, whose face was to the left and invisible, cried out softly and arched her back. With the fingers of one hand Caute slowly guided his penis down her belly, smiling what he called his drop-dead here-come-de-bomb smile, rubbing the head sensuously from side to side, hip to hip. "Here," he said on the screen. When she murmured again he inched forward on his knees. Grinned. Plunged. And then as her head came up with the force of the thrust Caute swung his other hand hard against her mouth and the camera tilted and started to fall—the next five seconds showed legs and arms tumbling, sheets, elbows, the woman's hair plastered with sweat, her bloody mouth, Caute's penis again, his hand, the camera lens suddenly smeared.

"This man is crazy," Fadhil said furiously and stood up.

In the seat next to him Colin stretched out one arm and grabbed him by the shoulder. Two rows away Caute laughed out loud.

"He's having his joke," Colin said, and added something in what Caute guessed to be Farsi.

"Tell him the next bit was shot at the zoo," Caute said, swinging his leg back and forth across the arm of the seat. "The elephant pen. Babar in heat. Got a wanker like a fire hose."

Fadhil glared at him, still standing. The most hypocritical people on earth, Caute thought. No booze, no porn, no pubic hair. Just drop kick a bomb, if you don't mind, right up Los Angeles' ass.

"You want to know my theory about movies?" Caute said. On the screen now there was nothing but clear white flickering light where Francis in the projection room had stopped the film.

"We want to see the footage on the Federal Reserve," Colin said in his lordly young-old voice. "We want to see the plan spelled out. We want to know who the man is you're talking about."

"No, listen," Caute said. He was interested in this. He sat up straight in the cushioned seat and waved one arm to take in the whole screening room. You could rent a screening room every other block in Los Angeles. You could show any goddamn thing you wanted. "Say this were a theater," he said, "a real theater with a stage. Then you'd see the actors in true proportion. If they were fifty feet away they'd *look* like they were fifty feet away. But movies play hell with your sense of proportion—in a movie everything's bigger than life, bigger than your eye thinks it should be."

"I don't have to listen to a madman," Fadhil said, but he slowly sat down again under the pressure of Colin's hand.

Colin himself looked at Caute without nodding, without blinking. Cambridge was better than Oxford, Caute thought. Oxford was excitable, Americanized, shaggy. Cambridge was cool, hibernal. Colin had learned to hate whatever it was he hated sucking at the ice tit of Mother Cambridge.

"Seeing a film on a big screen," Caute said. He stopped and cocked his head and thought about his voice for a moment. He was in his pompous mode, he decided; preachy, teachy. Snowman Colin affected him that way more and more. Colin with his idiotic plans, his grandstanding friends. "You sit in front of a movie screen," he said, starting over, "it's the closest thing in the world to being two years old again. When you're only thirty inches high and everybody else in the world is a monster."

"Giant," Colin said. "Surely."

"Giant." Caute waved it aside. "Movies are meant for fantasy regression, right? Which is what L.A. is all about, right? And the best way to use a movie is pornography—ten-foot dicks, cunts you can drive a car in. Just like childhood in true proportion, watching dear old mum and dad."

He held his grin for a long time, aiming it at the Arab. Then he turned around in his seat and punched the little relay switch he'd made from a garage door opener. In the booth behind them Francis let the film begin to run again.

"The Federal Reserve," Caute said. "Big as life."

This time the quality of the film was different, the colors truer, better focused. The camera panned slowly across the sidewalk in downtown Los Angeles, empty of pedestrians. On the other side of the street they saw flat dirt parking lots jammed with cars. Then a few stoic people, mostly black, stood waiting at a bus stop. A Texaco station appeared, its payment island armored in yellowing bulletproof glass. Then more parking lots, a homeless man pushing a shopping cart, a delivery truck turning in traffic, signals, a bright yellow dome of sulphurous sky.

Behind him Colin leaned forward and said quietly, "And television?"

"The reverse," Caute said without looking back. "Everything is smaller than it should be—elves, Dan Rather is an elf. Television's a puppet show. Waste of porn."

The camera meanwhile had moved slowly up the sidewalk, toward a persimmon-colored marble building. It paused once to frame two street signs—Ninth and Olympic—then again to show an imposing brass plaque on a cornerstone that read "United States Federal Reserve—Los Angeles Branch"; an armed security guard looked benevolently on.

"Francis took this," Caute said. "Francis dressed up like a tourist, rented some old lady and her kids, and walked right up and down the lobby with his camcorder going. In L.A. people video anything—ball games, car wrecks, Disneyland."

Fadhil was leaning forward in his seat and whispering something to Colin. When Caute looked around he lowered his head and started to write rapidly in a notebook, eyes flicking back and forth between screen and paper.

"The first floor's open to the public," Colin said.

Caute nodded. "And your computer's on the fifth floor. The very top."

The camera had stopped again, this time framing a mounted wall map that showed a vertical floor plan with fire exits marked in red, emergency phones circled in blue.

"A monster mainframe megabyte IBM," Caute said. "Five billion dirty RAMs per second."

"Every commercial check written in southern California is cleared through that computer," Colin said suddenly. When he started on his speeches, Caute thought, his voice went higher and higher, like a kid's. Why should he do what a kid said? "And every morning every business in Los Angeles that sends funds by wire to another business borrows the money from that bank and pays it back in the afternoon—blow it up in the middle of the day and all the records go up, all the backups go, a whole day of international commerce vanishes into a black hole."

The camera was scanning the lobby, a light airy room with walls of translucent marble. Tourists had come into view, up a ramp from the street, and were milling around a guide or drifting toward the far end where posters and bright signs advertised an exhibit, "The World of Economics." In the middle of the room, planted squarely in front of the elevator rank, another armed guard sat and stared at a television monitor.

"You can get through this?" Fadhil asked. "Upstairs?"

Caute nodded casually again. "Oh yeah, I can get through. I can lay my charge fifty feet from the actual fucking computer."

"How?" Skepticism in the Arab's voice. Colin had moved completely forward and sat now with long arms draped over the seat back next to Caute, eyes bright and intense.

"How will you do it?" Fadhil said.

Caute turned his back on him. The screen was showing an exterior view of the building, taken from a moving car. They passed the Federal Reserve sign again, the smiling guard; the camera zoomed to focus on a grill of windows and a spidery network of radio antennas rising above the rooftop edge. "Calling Mars," Caute said. And then abruptly, instantly the film changed again, from day to night, car to street—they were on a residential block crowded with vehicles and people, blinking lights roved the darkness, a glowing purple haze floated in the upper air. In the background an excited announcer began to speak. Toward the camera, leaning heavily on a policeman's shoulder, walked a thin man in his early forties, cheeks gaunt and streaked with bars of soot or grease like a badger's face.

"This is the same man again," Colin said. "The one you showed us before."

"David Renner." Caute pushed another of his relay switches and muted the television reporter's voice-over. Renner's hands came wearily up in total silence, waving aside the microphones pushed in his face.

"And you know him?"

The camera was pulling back from Renner, showing the whole circus, the whole media fandango. "David Renner used to work in England," Caute said. Like Colin he was now sitting up, no longer bouncing his leg across the chair arm. Even half whacked, he thought, Renner had an air of—what? Authority? Violence? "You remember the first little bomb I did for you? The Marine barracks in St. John's Wood?"

Colin nodded.

"This is the boy."

Fadhil thrust his head closer. "He's a policeman? In Los Angeles?"

Caute stopped the film with another flick of his home-made switch. "He's a good old bomb expert," he said in a mock-southern drawl he knew would irritate Colin and baffle the Arab. "He knows how European bombs work, which the L.A. redneck cops don't; he knows my little techniques."

"I warned you against other bombs," Colin said flatly. Frost, scorn, distance. There was nobody like the Brits.

Caute reached in his windbreaker pocket and pulled out a handful of tiny metal squares, none longer than an inch, all of them painted a glossy black. When he turned them in his palm for a side view, they all had tiny shelves at one end to make an L-shape. "Photovoltaic cells," he said. "Man-ufactured in Poland, shipped here and there, untraceable and unseen in the US of A so far. Solid-state, no glass envelope, no vacuum. Every single one of them works off the same equation, the electrical energy of an electron is proportional to the frequency of impinging radiant energy, multiplied by Planck's constant." He paused and looked at Colin. "You like that? You like a little erudition thrown in?"

"We know you understand your business," Colin said. "Explain Renner." Fadhil was extending a delicate finger toward Caute's palm.

"The Federal Reserve doesn't think much about bombs," Caute said. "They worry about computer glitches, power failures. They watch the cash like hawks. Otherwise, their idea of outside security is a passbook and a plastic badge. I only have two real problems. How to get the charge close enough to do the damage. Francis can handle that. And how to set it off. One of these cells handles *that*."

"Light shines on it?" Fadhil had picked up a cell between

two fingers and lifted it high enough to catch the pure white beam of the film projector overhead. On the screen fingers and cell made an elegant arched shadow.

"These are so sensitive," Caute said, watching the screen, "when I hook it up to a circuit you can start ignition with half a foot of candlepower. That's less than a triple-A battery penlight, less than a striking paper match. It takes about five seconds to build a charge, then it goes. They're going to set it off their own fucking selves."

"Where will you put it?" Colin asked. Cool monosyllables. Pissed at the car bomb, pissed at the idea of trouble.

"Where fucking Renner can't find it," Caute said.

Outside on the sidewalk Caute allowed himself to stand for a moment between the two men, feeling tense, caught in their space, an intruder. Colin wore sunglasses, a floppy Panama hat, a wrinkled white suit out of an old Alec Guinness movie. But he needed more fat on his bones to pull off the full colonial bwana effect. More suspicion. Fewer Arabs.

"All right then, three days," Colin told him. With a gesture of amazing casualness he reached in Fadhil's shirt pocket and pulled out a cigarette. Like best friends. Like one of the family. "Right? Correct? Our people in London are prepared to claim responsibility in three days. They're passing the word, standing out."

Caute sniffed. Bombs-R-Us. Babes-in-Bombland.

"You have no politics?" Fadhil said silkily. In the bright sunlight his features were paradoxically less distinct than in the dark screening room. He had a cap of flat black hair, no hips, no charm. What the hell did Colin see in him? Were they queer for each other? Caute stared at him with open dislike.

"I think the tallest candidate should always win," he said.

"But you left England to come to Los Angeles for us?" Fadhil persisted.

"I was born in Los Angeles," Caute told him. "I hate it." Get me out of here. He looked around for Francis, saw only traffic. What did you ever see?

Colin squeezed his face into a British lemon and started to talk idiot politics around the cigarette. He had been born here, Caute thought, and now he was more alone than he had ever been in England. The smell of American anger had greeted him as he stepped off the plane, and it had been building inside him ever since. He felt it in his guts, his balls. It came from somewhere way beyond him, like the weather, but it built up inside, up and up, pressure. Colin gestured with his useless pale hands. Not a lemon, Caute thought. A British embalmed face. Jokes would bounce off it like bullets.

"Fiat nox," Caute said, interrupting, turning away in disgust. Because they hadn't learned a goddamn thing from the movie.

But the Arab wasn't through yet. Colin had already dematerialized in the shimmering British manner, simply vanishing like a ghost into the parking lot. They pick it up from their butlers, Caute thought. But Fadhil—when you looked again, Fadhil was in fact a handsome man—Fadhil stood just where he was. He put a hand on Caute's sleeve and coughed discreetly.

"A moment, please." He hesitated and looked sideways. "Please." Caute followed his eyes, then jerked his chin once; Francis walked around to the front of the Mercedes and pretended to inspect a tire. Fadhil nodded and pulled out a little crocodile case for business cards.

Caute shook his sleeve free, as if the brown hand still held it. "You got something to say that Colin shouldn't hear?"

The Arab had a way of turning on one shoe when he talked, swiveling to present a smaller target. He coughed again into a tight fist. "Perhaps, maybe I am not always so political as my associate."

Caute rubbed his front teeth with the business card and then turned it over. It was in fact nothing more than the VIP check-in card for the Hotel Bonaventure, with a room number and the last name Bazan scribbled on it. "There's more than one of you, right?"

"There are three of us who are in Los Angeles."

Caute let his grin rise like a balloon out of his belly. Hypocritical as jackals. He *loved* it.

"You want to get laid."

Fadhil stared back at him coldly.

"Three nice-looking rich boys in a posh hotel," Caute said, making no effort to keep the mockery out of his voice. "You should be able to get what you want just by picking up the yellow pages—you call massage or escort or veterinarian, whatever you want."

Fadhil waved away the whole sentence, an angry gesture like a man pushing through a swarm of flies.

"It is not a difficulty," he said. He looked away, toward the street, speaking stiffly. "But one of us, I think, would be unusually interested in the girl in the picture."

"You think I'm a pimp, Fadhil?"

The Arab straightened his head with a snap. You can never tell with them, Caute thought; one minute abject as galley slaves, the next minute like they were princes of the realm. Mistah Caute, he dead. Why bother with it? With the Federal Reserve, for Christ's sake?

"My impression," Fadhil was saying with haughty precision, sounding exactly like Colin, "my impression was that you are a man who likes to make arrangements, all kinds of arrangements, any kind of arrangements."

"I surely do," Caute said, slipping the card into his windbreaker pocket. "You like American slang, Fadhil? You want to hear a joke? Hey, I like to arrange all *kinds* of bangs."

26

"YOU CAN SET OFF A BOMB BY TELEPHONE," RENNER SAID.

What did he expect? A bombshell?

Deputy Chief Linacre sat unmoved at the end of the long conference table with his hands folded over his notepad. To his left sat Musso, a slumped half-acre of blue shirt, blue jacket, mismatched tie. Next to him, in starched field uniform, Gretzsky leaned forward stiffly, his arms straight ahead of him on the polished wood like a pair of rails. Linacre turned his head slowly toward him. Gretzsky started to say something, then closed his mouth with a snap.

Renner began to pace again. "The technical term is 'initiation,'" he said. He rubbed his face, his jaw, squinted at the window. "A touch-tone telephone can initiate almost any kind of bomb. It can send a signal along the wires just like a transmitting radio. Or you can use a telephone to open a circuit, then send a signal with something else—a garage door opener, an answering machine remote control, even a tuning fork."

Linacre made a note on his pad. One word? Two? He

was the one to talk at, Musso had warned. Make your pitch to him. Short, fast, smart.

"It's a European technique," Renner said. "And it's almost never happened in this country. But it's starting. A year ago a hired arsonist in Florida blew up a furniture warehouse. He fit a microphone into a telephone receiver at the end of the business day on Friday—set to initiate a bomb when the bell rang. Then he called sometime during the weekend when nobody was there. Perfect alibi."

"They found the fucking microphone," Gretzsky said. "Right in the telephone."

Renner nodded. "He used a big clumsy microphone from someplace like Radio Shack and it stuck out in the wreckage like a flag. The IRA sometimes do that—they dismantle Japanese tape recorders because they're cheap and untraceable and plant the microphones in the telephone receivers. But they don't mind having the evidence found; they plan to claim responsibility."

Linacre made another note. Renner walked the length of the room, stepping around the clutter of filing cabinets and chairs, the overflow of *things* that was characteristic of the whole damn building, the whole damn state. He never holds meetings in his office, Musso had said of the deputy chief. People who go in there say it's immaculate, neat, nothing but books and rugs.

"In Northern Ireland they also rig phones in British Army barracks. But in that case they use a much more sophisticated element, because they want to wait for a full building, they don't want to waste a bomb on an empty structure. That means the phone has to be answered by somebody for the bomb to go off. Somebody has to actually pick it up and say hello. Just ringing the bell isn't enough. Even then they have variations. People can answer a rigged telephone harmlessly all day long, until a spotter signals a maximum target. Then they call. And when somebody answers they press a paging beeper at their end."

"There was no goddamn microphone at Kassabian Rugs," Gretzsky said, but his belligerence was curiously muted. He looked at the deputy chief after he spoke, got no reaction; looked at Musso, looked at the touch-tone telephone on the bookcase behind him.

"Theoretically," Renner said, still pacing, moving. "Theoretically you could do it long distance. Theoretically you could do it around the world, you could walk into a phone booth in Rome and blow up a house in Seattle. Libyan terrorists did it to a U.S. consulate in Wiesbaden, calling from Benghazi. You could do it with a cellular car phone on Mulholland Drive. You could do it with an in-flight telephone on an airliner, call Pan Am one hundred, bring it down."

He had them now, he thought. Linacre was sitting up straight, staring at him. Musso had flung one big hand back over his scalp, making the black hair jump. Even Gretzsky was watching warily, hunching his shoulders, turning his stiffness into visible tension. *Welcome to my world*, Renner thought.

"It's coming," he said. "European techniques are coming here, Middle Eastern terrorism. This is already a bomb culture and most people don't know it—the smallest backwater police department in California has somebody that's spent six weeks at Huntsville. Every major university has a bomb expert on its campus police. Berkeley has four of them, full-time. Foreign students, foreign quarrels, new electronics, the world's best phone system. Call Wiesbaden from Libya, you may or may not get through; either way you can be damn sure there's a record of the call in a government phone office. Call Los Angeles from New York, from a phone booth. Use MCI, transfer to Sprint—"

"Where's the evidence?" Gretzsky said.

Linacre pulled a cigarette from his suit jacket and lit it with a silver Ronson the size of his hand.

Renner looked at his watch, focused, looked again. Was it worth ignoring Gretzsky? "It's a hard bomb to rig," he said to Linacre. "In the first place, you need access to the telephone at the bomb end so that you can gimmick the receiver and plant the charge. Then you have to know how to connect the detonator in the bomb with the receiver and run the wires. For an amateur it's not worth the trouble even to try."

"Where's the evidence?" Gretzsky repeated, pushing back his chair. "Forget the fucking Libyans. You got no microphone, no double circuits, nothing in Kassabian's phone that wasn't supposed to be there."

"You had one leftover coil of wire," Linacre drawled softly. He held his cigarette straight up beside his cheek, like a little torch, a candle.

"From the guy's computer," Gretzsky said. "From the guy's brand-new desktop Apple computer." He paced down the other side of the long table and stopped opposite Renner, facing him. Renner shook his head.

"We're a long way from Wiesbaden," Linacre said more sharply, Maine coolness creeping into his voice. "It's an interesting speech, Doctor Renner, but we're not talking about terrorists in Los Angeles yet and I have to go along with my own staff experts." He shifted the cigarette from one hand to the other, still holding it straight up.

A British gesture, Renner thought, glancing at his watch again. An affectation, like the grafted-on Orange County accent. The deputy chief was another chameleon just like himself. Be theatrical for him, Musso had said. He likes the theater.

"You can't do it without a fucking microphone," Gretzsky said and leaned forward, bracing his fists on the table.

On the bookcase behind him the telephone rang.

For a long moment Gretzsky simply stared at it.

On the third ring he looked at Renner.

"My secretary never interrupts my meetings," Linacre said. He inhaled smoke and let his eyes travel from Musso to Gretzsky to Renner. "Standing orders."

Musso nodded. The telephone rang again.

"These rooms are swept for microphones once a week," Linacre said.

Renner crossed his arms over his chest and leaned back against the window sill. The glass pressing his back was warm, even through the madras jacket. In the corner of his eye he could see the freeway traffic far below, motionless in rush hour. At this distance the cars were like bright metal thumbtacks stuck into ribbons.

"Answer it," Linacre ordered.

Gretzsky straightened and picked up the phone.

The explosion that followed was no louder than a cap, the smoke no thicker than that of a cigarette, but Gretzsky howled in anger and surprise and threw the telephone half the length of the room before the cord jerked it short and wires and parts spilled in a rattle of flying plastic across the table.

"You son of a bitch!" Gretzsky shouted.

Musso was reaching forward, feeling in the base of the receiver, pulling loose a coil of thin gray wire.

"Musso." Linacre stood up and moved around the table with the sudden, energetic decisiveness Renner remembered from the task force. Bulldog face, air-chopping fist. Incongruously the other hand still held the foppish cigarette straight up. "Musso, you had something else," he barked. "A witness?"

Musso sat back and stretched the coil of wire between his index fingers. "We got a girl in the hotel bar who saw Kassabian walking toward the pay phones, just about ten-forty-five. She thinks."

Gretzsky turned the telephone upside down and probed the base with one thick finger. "A grandstand trick," he said over his shoulder. "Circus tricks."

"But no microphone, right?" Linacre walked briskly in the other direction. "Musso, tell Carnochan downstairs—Bliss Carnochan, not the other lawyer—tell him to write out a grand jury subpoena. Tell him we want the Message Unit Detail—" He paused. "You know which telephone?"

"No, sir. There were three in a row. She didn't pay attention."

"MUD on all of them." He stopped six feet from Renner and looked up at him. "Message Unit Detail. *If* the computer isn't down and *if* the phone he used was on the monitor list, we can check your theory. But this isn't Libya. I can't push a button and pull out a list of numbers a private citizen called. It's a grand jury matter. Routine but absolutely required."

Renner nodded.

"No microphones," Linacre said.

"I bought a call-forwarding attachment at a Pacific Bell shop this morning," Renner said. "Thirty-nine ninety-five. And I asked your secretary to call my motel extension at four-thirty and let it ring. She reached an empty room, but the call was forwarded automatically, untraceably to this phone."

"You made your point," Linacre said, starting to turn away. "I'll have the indictment redrawn and Musso will see if we can bring in Kassabian tonight."

"No." Renner was walking quickly himself, around the other end of the table, toward Gretzsky.

"No," he said angrily, squeezing between filing cabinets and folding chairs. "I didn't make my point at all. Kassabian didn't rig a bomb like this. Look at his background, look at his character. He couldn't begin to set up a three-stage bomb with a phone rig."

"Renner," Musso said.

"Look at that," Renner said, taking the phone from Gretzsky and holding it up, shaking it. "You people have tunnel vision, you see one case at a time, unrelated. What's the use of a goddamn task force? The *same guy* did all of the bombs, every one of them is a joke, a hidden gag of some kind. Kassabian is a stooge. The same guy did it."

Linacre had stopped at the door. "Who the hell do you think you're talking to?" he said.

"It's the same guy," Renner said.

Linacre took one step toward the table and ground out the cigarette in an ashtray. "You know who this building was named for, Doctor Renner? You know who William Parker was?"

Renner glanced at the window, rubbed his jaw. "He was the former Chief of Police."

"He was the most rational, superlogical man I ever knew," Linacre said. His voice had gone all Maine now, cold, clipped; the bulldog face was stiff with controlled indignation. "Some scriptwriter thought he was a perfect logical machine and drew Mister Spock in *Star Trek* after him. The first time you talked in here I thought you had a lot of Parker in you. I thought your mind was first-rate, professional, orderly. But you're not really logical, Doctor Renner, you're obsessive. You're not logical, you're one of those slouched Romanticists who dreams up black plots and enemies. The only joker I see in this room is you."

Renner took the coil from Musso and laid it carefully on the table in front of him. One part of his mind registered with disgust that his fingers trembled. Fear was one thing; anger was another. He picked up the flat telephone base and placed it over the coil.

"Every one of these last five bombs has blown up a family somehow," he said. "Check that out—wives, cheating husbands, brothers. That's part of his signature, clear as purple smoke. That's the kind of job he takes. He *looks for*. The other part is the little piece of irony, the bomb over the condoms, the husband on TV. Irony."

Linacre worked his jaw and said nothing.

"The British dynamite," Musso began.

Renner interrupted him, leaning forward, gripping the table. "You put two electrical conductors side by side and pass a current through one of them—the telephone bell, for instance—what happens, Gretzsky?"

Gretzsky wiped one hand across the front of his field uniform. His knuckles were the color of ham. After a moment he looked at Linacre. "You induce a weak current in the second conductor," he said. "Which could theoretically initiate a bomb. Without a microphone."

"Kassabian hated his own brother," Renner said, still holding the telephone over the coil. "Hated him." He glanced back at Gretzsky. "You know the other name for the electrical process?"

Gretzsky shoved his hands in his pockets. "Sympathetic induction," he said.

27

THE BEST ACTRESS DOESN'T FEEL A THING, JILLIAN THOUGHT. SHE imitates emotion. She controls.

She crossed the street with artificial briskness, arms swinging, the only pedestrian within four hundred miles. In British theater lore, when you walk across a stage you should lift your arms as if you were swinging a mouse by the tail—energy, briskness, a little jiggle; it looks good in a girl. She passed a doughnut shop, then a nail boutique and salon. Every Vietnamese immigrant in Los Angeles had opened a nail boutique or a restaurant, she thought. She formed her face into a perfect mirror. The men who couldn't cook had put on square paper hats and opened doughnut shops with three Formica tables, a refrigerated mausoleum of soda cans, a family of studious children hunched over books in one corner. Passing, she glanced at the plaster hands in the boutique window, the hands of warrior princesses, studded with bright red and gold nails and arching out of crepe paper lakes.

Help.

Inside the house she bustled for five minutes, making

herself a drink, closing doors and drawers, holding her
mind at a distance. Then she sank back carefully into the
leather recliner that always reminded her of a man's huge
brown wallet bent halfway open at the fold. Underneath
her the socket snapped into the base with its usual bonelike
crack. She placed her arms on the flat armstraps and closed
her eyes. After a long moment she let herself hear the ocean
tumbling in harness outside.

A foolish obsession is the hobgoblin of little minds, she
thought.

Obsession is how the mind makes a punching bag of
itself.

Hoping is dying.

All compulsive behavior springs from anger.

She recited her formulas behind closed eyes, her man-
tras, her slips of wisdom clutched tightly by stiffening
fingers. Then the pictures started to run just as if she had
done nothing. This is what it's like to be blind, she told
herself in a sideways spiraling thought; the same dead film
showing forever on a black wall of bone. And just as if she
had done nothing, London appeared.

She was home in bright, pitiless clarity, walking downstairs into an English street and an English rain. It must
have been winter and a cold rain, she thought, because she
could feel her scalp begin to itch from too much dye, too
many months of harsh shampoo and flaking makeup. But
winter or summer, England was just as she had left it,
London. She smelled exhaust fumes from jostling cars and
lorries, blacker than Los Angeles fumes, more pungent and
heavier, but not foreign. Nothing was foreign, nothing
English was alien to her.

As always the film jumped.

She was a white body, lying on her back.

She walked mirrorlike between fountains of anger.

She stood at a phone box on Regent's Park Road,
between the zoo and Primrose Hill, positioned to see a
triangle of three landmarks. To the west was Lord's
Cricket Ground, which she had never entered. To the east
was the soaring bird cage that Lord Snowden had designed

for the zoo, a three-story silver theater for royal thoughts. To the north, at the apex of the triangle, though hidden from view by a block of flats, was the other cage, the four-story barracks for American Marines, which she had also never entered.

The best actress feels nothing. She controls her gestures, her accent, walk, pitch. What fills a hollow place better than love? Anger does. Under her left arm, as a signal, she was to carry her paperback volume of Emily Dickinson. Later, amazed at her own prescience, she would discover that the book had been cracked open at a single page.

> *The soul has moments of escape*
> *When bursting all the doors*
> *She dances like a bomb abroad.*

Jillian squeezed her eyes even more tightly closed, squeezing until she felt pain. In the utter darkness of her head she saw a brilliant explosion of light, nothing but light, a fireball like the first day of creation, the birds all rising like flecks of light into Snowden's steel sky, the sun itself bursting up through the green crust of Primrose Hill.

When the door slammed shut behind her she leaped up in panic, spilling her drink, ruining her skirt. On the porch, in the kitchen, running like a maniac from room to room and switching on the lights, Caute waved to her and gestured, hauling her in.

28

June 18

AT ELEVEN–FIFTEEN THE LAST CLERK IN THE PAN AM HIERARCHY looked at the Visa card, turned it over, compared the signature with the one in the passport, sniffed faintly, and handed them both back to Renner. Then with a princely tilt of his head he nodded toward the boarding gate.

At eleven-forty-two they were airborne, Pan Am 120, the last flight of the day from Los Angeles to London, the first flight Renner could get on after the disaster of the deputy chief's meeting. He twisted in the seat and grimaced as the plane banked and the battered muscles of his chest and neck tightened in protest. Outside the window California was falling away like the inside of a black bowl. He closed his eyes and saw little sparks of pain. Meteor showers inside his skull. Bootprints on his scalp. He made himself count, an old childhood trick when his feelings started to flood and panic and the world came undone. He had a three-thousand-dollar credit limit with Visa. Subtract the motel bill. Subtract the open Pan Am ticket that, even with a government discount, came to nine hundred dollars. A hotel would cost eighty pounds. He squeezed his eyes and drifted. He had five clean socks, one clean shirt. He would buy a razor in London. He would buy dynamite from the stewardess.

When he shook himself straight and sat up again they were already far above the clouds, droning over the mountains of Nevada, and he was buying little bullets of vodka, not dynamite, from the traveling cart. Dynamite. Musso was hipped on dynamite. In England just as in the United States every stick was numbered, labeled, elaborately coded by the manufacturer. If you knew how to read its signature, you could tell the place of origin, the date, the discard date, the chemical composition, the solvent, the rate of detonation. Legitimate buyers—mines, quarries, construction firms—all kept meticulous records, but sticks and cartons disappeared anyway, just as rifles, rockets, bullets, even the occasional tank disappeared from army bases. The world was a great flat table. Inanimate things roamed chaotically across it with wills of their own. Given luck and an open phone line Musso could trace the British dynamite back all the way to the original manufacturer, then forward to the purchaser, the warehouse, the shelf, the police report when it was discovered missing.

Then what?

Then Musso would start over again. Musso and the British cops would follow the theft step by step to a dead end, an airplane ramp going up to nowhere, a forged manifest, an unknown courier. While the bombs went on in a steady tattoo.

Renner shifted in the seat, trying to find the place where his head would stop throbbing, his mind would slow down. There were better signatures than dynamite. Someone who used a phone. Give me a man with an obsession, his father liked to say, wind him up, stand back.

His eyes felt sandbagged with sleep. He peered through the window and caught a glimpse of stars over mountains. Human bodies were made of elements cooked up eons ago in the cores of stars, hydrogen and helium fusing together, high school physics. What was the point? He closed his eyes once more, drifting deeper. There wasn't chaos. That was the point. If you held your mind steady there was always coherence, connection. Our small, miserable lives. The great vast heroic lives of stars. Explosion, combustion, a slow, insensible sinking to darkness.

Then what?

He dreamed of Vicki, pregnant, swimming in a pool. A bomb that went off with a phone call, over and over and over. Jillian's skin, wet with light.

They landed at Heathrow forty-five minutes ahead of schedule. In the terminal there were armed guards everywhere searching for bombs. On the runway, around a Pakistan Airways 737 a ring of soldiers in camouflage suits carried assault rifles at the ready. Renner changed money at the first Barclays he saw, then caught the underground to Green Park, where he mounted the stairs two at a time, swinging his little overnight bag, blinking at the afternoon sunlight. By four-fifteen he was going upstairs at the address on Old Bond Street, past the diamond store still going bankrupt, over the famous haircutters' shop, by appointment to the prince, down the plush carpeted hall to the raised face of the guard, the sliding doors, and the set of rooms he knew by heart.

Inside the third rank of doors, behind a thickly curtained partition, Billy Finley was sitting at a Chippendale desk, sorting photographs.

When he saw Renner he put down his photographs and leaned back in his chair, not grinning or smiling, but nodding in a self-satisfied way that instantly reminded Renner of Musso. The young man who had escorted him from the guard's desk handed Finley a visitor's pass to sign. Renner glanced to the right, remembering the expensive, contrived casualness of the room as Finley had put it together, its odd mixture of English men's club and American pop. Two walls were lined entirely with bookcases, row after row of polished leather-bound volumes interrupted only by a VCR and its monitor and occasional tapes. The wall directly behind Finley contained a six-foot-high metal cabinet, four long horizontal doors open to double layers of manila files; above it there was a shelf, figurines and knickknacks, then three gilt-framed paintings

of famous dead British horses. To Finley's right, beside a
curtained window, was the inevitable computer station. In
the corner beside it Finley had installed a Naugahyde chair
shaped like a baseball glove. In the other corner a waist-
high soft sculpture that Renner recognized as an Oldenburg copy, a blue leather ice bag that slowly twisted atop
an electric motor.

"You know this guy?" Finley asked the young man with
a jerk of his head.

The young man frowned and unfolded the visitor's
pass. "He's the one who called you, right? Yesterday from
L.A.?"

"He was head of ESR till a year ago, that's who he is."
Finley rocked in his chair and looked up at Renner
deadpan—Musso completely, Renner thought. Chop
Musso down to about five eight, cut forty pounds and trim
his hair to a federal length, Finley was an uncannily older,
paler version of Musso.

"Embassy Security," the young man said. "European
Sector. You must have done bombs."

Finley grinned and pulled a red coffee thermos across
the desk, over his photos. "Never, never, never," he said.
He snapped three Styrofoam cups from a drawer and
started to pour coffee for them. "Bomb guys are engineers,
correct? They study physics, chemistry, they look at the
world like a big machine, vectors, planes, forces, they talk
about capacitors and relays and resistance ohms. Renner
here kept *poetry* all over his office. Am I right, Renner? I'd
go in his office down the other end of the hall, John
Bender's now. He always had four books of poetry right
there on his desk where the bomb kit should be, the *same*
four books."

"Blake, Keats, Rilke, and Plath," Renner said. "The
Four Horsepersons of the Apocalypse. How are you,
Billy?"

"Listen to that," Billy grinned. "All that horseshit and
he still figured out bombs like he was the guy that invented
them. A couple of years ago, before you ever got here,
Miller, every slimeball in England was trying to dream up
a bomb Renner couldn't bust. He was a famous man."

"Did they ever do it?" Miller asked.

Finley widened his eyes in mock amazement at the question and shook his head. And then because, as Renner remembered, he could never do just one thing, he pushed back his chair and started to wander the little room.

"So how's your wife, Renner?"

"I'll leave you two," the young man said.

"Renner's wife walked out on him, what was it, last May?"

Renner lifted his Styrofoam cup and closed his eyes for a moment. When he opened them again the kid was backing apologetically toward the door.

"I'll take you out front when you're ready, Colonel Renner."

"Colonel," Finley said, watching him close the door and leave. "I love it. Titles, formality—they're contagious over here, that's why I stay. It'd drive me crazy to be in California like you, twenty-five million people on a first-name basis. One of these days in L.A. they're going to publish the phone book like that, nothing but first names—Bruce, Bonnie, Balthazar."

"She's fine, Billy. My wife and daughter are fine."

Finley put his own cup down on the shelf with the knickknacks and figurines and took off his green Savile Row sports jacket, revealing a short-sleeved shirt, two sweat moons, and a protruding belly like a swallowed cannonball. Musso to the inch. He tossed the jacket underhand into the baseball glove.

"Good. You know what I think you should have done? You should have stuck a bomb up the guy's ass, popped his kneecaps. What was he, some college professor on sabbatical?" Finley gripped both hands behind his neck and stretched. "Okay then, Colonel. Welcome back to the cradle of democracy, the heart of progressive capitalism, the art museum and bomb-manufacturing capital of the world. What the hell can I do for you?"

Renner made himself walk casually to the desk and sit down in Finley's chair. On second thought, not a bit like Musso, he decided. "I want to take a look at the Face File for one thing. Four years, five years back. Whatever you've still got on demonstrations at Mildenhall or Cambridge."

Finley paced a few steps in a half-circle, stopped, and touched the Oldenburg ice bag with a stubby finger, making an exaggerated scowl of disapproval. Then he shook his head. "Off limits, even to an old trooper. What else?"

Renner pinched his nose and watched Finley start to wander again. The Face File was something the FBI liaison had dreamed up in the late sixties, Finley's first year with them—a photo collection of serious British militants, Oxbridge political crazies, subversive anti-Americans in general. During the Vietnam war they had meant it to be Englandwide, but over the years since it had dwindled to embassy and consulate level, a rogues' gallery of British and Irish citizens who dropped dead animals in the mail slot at Grosvenor Square, overheated marchers who set off bombs, cut telephone wires, shit on the steps, chained themselves to fences. Like most good security ideas it was completely illegal.

"What else?" Finley said.

"The Signature File."

"Ah." Finley had reached the shelf of figurines in his wandering now. He studied a tiny, hand-carved piano on the shelf, no more than ten inches long, and hit a single note with his finger. "Now here's a great signature idea, I just thought of it. Guy puts a bomb in a Baldwin, right? Sets up a little plastique, sticks in a blasting cap, rigs it to go off when James Mason plays 'Chopsticks.' Good Hitchcock effect. Alfred, thou shouldst be living at this hour."

"Telephone bombs," Renner said, leaning forward. "I want to see bombs detonated by calls or beepers through calls. And switchboard bombs."

"I shouldn't."

"Billy, I *authorized* the goddamn file, I put it together."

The miniature piano had an octave of actual keys. Finley let his right hand play a sudden ripple of melody that filled the little room with sound, then abruptly stopped.

"I know you put it together," he said. "You remember what's-his-name Broadbent?"

"Milton Broadbent."

"Right. Huge Jewish guy in the Special Reaction, five six or seven at least, loves to play bridge and spook Arabs. After you set that file up Milton comes into my office, lies down in my baseball glove, and says he wants to unburden himself of a secret."

"Billy."

"He said he thought you were 'unsound.' You drank too much. Also your file was too 'intuitive.' This is an official request, right? This is something to do with whatever dustball outfit you ended up with back there?"

"I don't have a letter, if that's what you mean."

"You wouldn't," Finley said, and he shook his head slowly, not smiling at all anymore. "Not you. You know something, Renner? If I set bombs I wouldn't want you after my case. Like a fucking buzz saw."

Renner stared back at him, seeing nothing, no warmth, no friendliness, no message. In the old days Finley had liked to sit around their living room on Primrose Hill, grousing in companionable drunkenness about the state of the world, spinning endless war stories about the embassy bureaucracy. He was a self-educated man, with the self-educated man's overstated confidence, and his war stories invariably ended up as dramatized debates between himself and goggle-eyed colleagues imitated with a tilt of his head and a falsetto voice aimed at the ceiling. Billy Finley was the hero of his own life, Vicki had caustically observed.

"You have the files right here," Renner said. "In this office."

There was a knock at the door and the young man named Miller leaned in, looking warily at each of them in turn. He slid a small shoe-box-size canvas sack onto Finley's desk, made a vague gesture with one hand, and closed the door again.

Renner pushed the sack to one side, against Finley's red thermos, and swiveled back. "The file's right there, under the famous dead horses, Billy."

Finley finished his coffee in one head-tossing gulp and crossed the carpet. He took the sack and dropped it into the bottom drawer of the desk, which he locked with a flat metal key shaped like a butter knife. "I might have to go out and do some business," he said carefully, straightening, placing a flat hand against the small of his back.

"Buy yourself some diamonds."

"So I'd be back in about an hour and a half. About seven." He paused and picked up his jacket. "Which is about when we close up the office, as you no doubt remember. British banking hours, right?"

When he had gone Renner looked at the lock on the drawer. A double-serrated special-order Yale lock that you couldn't buy in a store and that Thomas Chippendale had never heard of. You wouldn't open it with a bomb, you'd have to tear down the desk around it. And there was no reason to do that at all. The canvas sack was a standard embassy mail pouch container, lined with flexible lead sheets and demagnetized nylon fabric to keep the film inside safe from X rays up to and including the strength of a medical CAT scanner. The only thing on the outside was the courier label stamped "Los Angeles. Pan Am 120."

Finley returned at quarter till seven, smelling of scotch.

He closed the door firmly behind him and came directly up to the desk, where he bent forward and stared over Renner's shoulder.

"So who do you like?"

Renner moved a small stack of manila folders to one side with a frustrated motion. "They're all Irish."

"Of course they are," Finely said, nodding, reaching past him to poke at the folders. "If it can be done by just bloody talking the Irish are the boys to do it. Not to mention, half the linemen for British Telephone are IRA."

"This one," Renner said, tapping the top folder on his pile. He pushed the chair back and stood up and Finley sank into it like a collapsing balloon.

"You want a guy who dings bombs through the blower," Finley muttered. He opened the folder and began to pick his way expertly through the clips and labels. "A guy who obviously popped up like a fucking gopher in the golden soil of California. This one?"

He held up a black-and-white surveillance photograph

of a tiny, dark-haired man, birdlike in his features, no more than twenty or twenty-five. He was emerging from a restaurant with window signs in German, wrapping an oversize greatcoat around him, dipping his chin into his scarf.

"He studied electronics for three years at Tübingen," Renner said. "You marked him down for half a dozen attempted phone bombings at the Siemens AG, 1987–89. Now he's gone."

"Now he's in a state sanitarium in Amsterdam," Finley said. "You squeeze our Dieter Sammel these days, he's like a sponge full of heroin. I love the fucking Dutch. This file ought to be pulled."

"And this one."

Miller knocked on the door and entered and Finley swiveled the other way and frowned, still holding in his lap the second folder Renner had given him.

"We're closing," Miller said.

"This one is in Frankfurt," Finley said. "Eight thousand nautical miles from California." He snapped the manila cover with his stubby finger and looked up, first at Renner, then at Miller.

"You're sure?"

"My personal word. Would I lie? Guy hangs around with Arabs. He's got an apartment on the Gutleutstrasse, three ex-Abwehr watchers on him right this minute. Look at him, Miller."

Renner watched as Miller reluctantly slid the photograph out of its plastic holder and twisted it slightly under the light. "Miller's an economist," Finley said, exhaling scotch. "But he's trying to overcome it."

"This looks like somewhere in London," Miller said, still frowning.

"We took it here, he *lives* there. The mighty colonel can tell you, Miller, the two great centers for slimeball activists in Europe are Frankfurt and London—Paris used to be, but I don't know. Something happens when they get to Paris. They get sulky and fat or else they start reading Lacan and Derrida and Nietzsche and they get so confused they never figure out what to do next. Besides that, Renner, the phones don't work."

Renner walked around the baseball glove and retrieved the rest of the folder, smelling Finley's scotch, his spiced deodorant. You can set up a screen of talkative stupidity with alcohol. Nobody knew that better.

"You gave him the wrong picture," Renner said softly. Miller looked up quizzically and tilted the photograph so that Renner saw it again, a tall sandy-haired man lounging in a wooden pub chair. No more than thirty, horse-faced, all bones and flannel. Behind him rose blossoms exploded in puffs of brilliant color.

"No, that's our boy. That's Colin DeVere," Finley said, standing up, puffing, pulling out his keys ostentatiously. "DeVere, just like the captain in *Billy Budd*. Marine Barracks, Marylebone, 1988. Nice little phone bomb from a call box, remember it? Now he lives in Frankfurt in a state of spiritual malaise."

"He never set a bomb himself," Renner said. "According to the workup he read history at Cambridge. No scientific education. He can't change a light bulb."

Finley cocked his head at Miller and shrugged.

Renner turned on his heel, walked to the idiotic ice bag, turned again and stared at a row of titles on Finley's bookcase. The works of Rudyard Kipling in twenty-four volumes. The bomber would be scruffier, leaner. He would be obsessed, crazy, even in a photograph. Sexual. Renner touched his face with one hand. His skin was like marble. How did he *know* that?

When he turned back Finley was still standing by the incongruous antique desk and buttoning the blazer over his pot belly. "He's sharp," he told Miller. "Didn't I say so?" He rounded his mouth in pantomimed admiration and waved a pasty hand at Renner. "The mind of a poet, right? Remember his desk? All intuition. OK. So Colin's a goony bird, not a bomber. Colin's dad was in on the Brit giveaway of Palestine in '47, which is how Colin sees it—the poor horny old man was only a junior pen wiper in '47—but now that he's dead Colin's got a mission to straighten out that little mess, clean up after Dad. And thanks to higher education and a trust fund he's worked out a whole program. Stage one, give Israel back to the Palestinians the way God wants it to be, unless of course you think God's wandered off to look at some other planet and doesn't give a shit about Palestine. Stage two, world disarmament through bombs. Stage three, peace and white suits and tea." Finley paused to grin. "But he's still in Frankfurt."

"This is a bomber," Renner said, and he pulled out the second photograph in the folder.

29

"SIMON CAUTE," RENNER SAID.

Finley took the photograph that Renner held out to him. He studied it for a moment, then extended it between two fingers for Miller to see.

"Simon Caute," he said. "Right. Simon Caute, who used to be in our air force, which trained him to near genius-level in military ordnance and disposal and paid him eleven hundred and fifty-seven dollars a month before taxes. Miller's an economist—they give courses in greed where you studied economics, Miller? We see this four or five times a year in Europe, some twenty-year-old kid stationed in the boondocks, dying of boredom, no money, no attention. The Soviets come around, the Poles come around, the IRA, the Israelis—they all line up outside the barracks with their pockets stuffed full of cash and their sports cars loaded with redheaded extras and before you know it the ship of state has sprung another leak. Typical recruitment. Am I right, David? Is this how it happens?"

Renner took the photograph from Miller's hand and looked at it again before he dropped it back into the manila folder. Finley was saying something else, but Renner heard only oily jargon, unconnected syllables. In the photograph he saw a man nearly his own height, thinner, fifteen years younger, standing in a swimsuit at the edge of a rocky beach. Except from this angle, under fluorescent bulbs, the face was gone, or not there yet, or rising just out of reach. What did he see? The photograph had been taken with a telephoto lens, and its focus was badly blurred. The whole upper left side of the print was dissolved in streaks of bright, exploding sunlight, as if Caute's face were vanishing into a fireball, his right hand slinging flame.

"All his air force pictures have been removed from his file," Finley said, grinning with only one side of his mouth. "Funny thing."

"It's way past seven," Miller said. "Sir."

"It says he's a free-lancer." Renner ran his thumb down the thick folder, then snapped it shut with a plastic clip.

Finley shrugged. "Whatever that means. He bombs what he wants to bomb. *If* he feels like it and you pay him first. *If* it turns him on. He's a borderline sociopath. You get the feeling Miller wants us out of here?"

"He's in DeVere's file," Renner said, staying where he was. He placed the manila folder on top of the VCR in Finley's bookcase. A shiny new machine with a German brand name that he had never heard of. Billy Finley was notorious in London for two things, his love of high-tech gadgetry and his taste for low porn.

"He's in the file because these days he mainly bombs for our boy Colin." Finley crossed the room and took the folder from the VCR. "It's Colin's only ace in the business." He dropped the folder on the desk with all the others and rubbed his hands quickly together like a man building a fire. "Don't worry about the mess. Security puts them back as soon as I leave, right, Miller? The fact is, everybody wants Colin's bomber—he's very good, he's very ruthless. He's probably in half a dozen folders, cross-referenced. He worked for at least two years while he was in the air force—we think—we *think* the IRA liked a couple of his things very much. God knows why Colin turns him on, incompetent little la-de-da snob, but it's the truth; right now Colin's the only political bozo Caute will work for."

"Sirs."

"Is he homosexual?" Renner asked. Miller opened the door and held it wide for them, glancing again at his watch.

Finley hitched his belly under the green blazer and shook his head. "He likes girls. Girls like him. Some girls like him a lot."

"He could run a bomb through a phone."

Finley grinned. "He could run a bomb through a gym shoe. But if you want him in California you're out of luck. He's in Frankfurt too."

At the deserted guard desk Miller took Renner's security pass and slipped it into a wooden box by the entrance, like a ballot. He turned stiffly, as if to say good-bye, but Finley was still talking, still in his teacher-to-protégé mode.

"Frankfurt," he said wonderingly. "Why Frankfurt, Miller? They all love the Frankfurt airport. We know slimeballs who live there weeks at a time, camping out, they're like one of those Pakistani families you see that missed their plane home."

"It's a business," Miller started to say.

"It's *show* business," Finley said. "Ask the colonel. Somebody like Colin DeVere, we're not talking old-fashioned national bombers anymore—Greeks that bomb Turks, Serbs that bomb Croats—we're talking the *other* kind of terrorist, the existentialists, the *spiritual* bombers. These are the guys that give malaise a bad name. They don't know what the hell they want, except modern life sucks, capitalism sucks. I hate, therefore I bomb. They're in show biz, Miller, and what you do in show biz is make headlines."

Miller nodded and started to edge down the stairs. Finley watched him for a moment, then put out an arm and caught him by the shoulder. Sandbags, Renner thought. He's surrounding himself with sandbags, people and words, to keep me out. The three of them walked lockstep down the stairs, Finley still talking, rolling his shoulders under the elegant jacket as he moved, in a boxer's shrug-

ging mannerism. On the sidewalk next to the barber shop
he turned it into a clownish little lecture.

"You make headlines in their little world the same way
you do in any other," he said, wagging his finger, exhaling
scotch again.

Miller looked down at his shoes.

"You make headlines," Finley said, "by dislodging the
competition. You ought to know this, Miller. You introduce a new Ford car that runs on smog. You make a tiny
radio that people can carry with them when they walk or
sleep or just make the beast with two backs, so Americans
will never ever have to be without the sound of electronic
entertainment. And your competition is either the old guys
leading your group, the ones too sluggish and *old* to go out
and plant more bombs, or else the group down the street
in Amsterdam that's come up with a sexier theme and
started getting all that good Syrian money you used to get.
Am I right, mighty colonel?"

Renner rubbed his eyes. He was too old himself, too
tired to listen to Finley. He stepped forward, forcing Miller
to one side. In California it would still be morning, light
would still be rolling over the dry, brown mountains.
Musso would be up, in his office, working the phones,
chasing the dynamite back. Jillian would be on the edge of
her bed, staring at masks.

"I need to see more files tomorrow, Billy."

Finley's round face went hard. The clownish note
dropped out of his voice and he sounded like a different
man. "Not a chance. You're out of the service, my friend.
You did it yourself and you're all the way out. I'm busy
tomorrow. I'm busy every day after this. You just got the
Finley wisdom and the Finley favor auld-lang-syne-wise,
all there is of it. All there's gonna be. Say hello to your
wife."

"I ought to leave you people now," Miller said, raising
his cuff and gesturing vaguely toward the street.

"Billy—"

"Miller," Finley said. He held him by the elbow and
rocked back on his heels, staring at Renner, suddenly
grinning again. "Miller, Miller, did you ever hear about

the day Renner built a test bomb for the Royal Army Bomb School?" Miller shook his head. "*Famous* bomb, Miller. Nobody could disarm it, nobody in the whole goddamn school. It was a hostage exercise, a free-the-hostage game, so he attached the bomb to a dummy hostage's body with a handcuff. The gimmick was, he made it out of something called a collapsing circuit. Not two different bombs, two different *circuits* leading to the same detonator. When you disconnected circuit number one, it automatically collapsed into circuit number two and set it off. You disarmed one part, the other part blew up. Perfect."

"Billy."

"My absolute favorite clipping in the world, from *The New York Times*—I used to carry it around in my wallet," Finley said. "See if you can figure why I thought of it now. One day a bunch of police in Bangkok disguised as bandits arrested a bunch of *bandits* disguised as *police*."

It took Renner twenty minutes to find the pub he was thinking of.

He walked down Curzon Street, past the Heywood Hill Bookshop, still open for customers behind its dusty, paper-littered windows. At Half Moon Street he made a wrong turn and ended up briefly in a swirling crowd of Danish tourists going to see the Olde England show off Picadilly. Somewhere just east of the Dorchester he stepped down an alley, past one of the three working gas stations he had ever seen in central London, and sat down in the courtyard of the pub.

He sat by himself at a white metal table and drank two pints of soapy beer while he waited for a plate of sausage and potatoes—"bangers and mash," he thought wryly, the British blitz, bombs everywhere. He had no reaction at all to England. His mind was first on the photographs, then on Finley's office. When the waitress took away his plate he leaned back and pictured it all over again, starting with the VCR.

There were genuinely secret people in London—Renner remembered a dapper little embassy man with a tooth-

brush moustache like the Great Gildersleeve who worked
"an hour and a half from here." There was a navy
climatologist whose computer program was so sensitive
that he worked in a bank vault, then later in an underground room adjoining the silversmiths' chambers sixty
feet beneath Chancery Lane. But Finley—Finley ran a tiny
liaison staff for the FBI, an ordinary white-collar office. He
had only a guard at the desk who quit at seven. He had a
security crew that put away files and probably drank tea
the rest of the night in the basement. He had a shredder
somewhere, a scrambler maybe, but Renner doubted it.
He had an unbreakable lock on his antique desk.

The pub's telephone was too noisy. The gas station's red
call box, in the great British tradition, was big enough for
two people, a massive phone and a rack of books, and a
polished walnut writing ledge. At nine forty-five Renner
dialed Finley's home number and waited.

It took Finley less than fifteen minutes to pull up in a cab
outside the barber shop. Renner turned and watched while
he paid off the driver, then he stepped out of the shadows,
shrugging apologetically, and fell into step behind him.

On the stairs Finley jerked his keys free from his
raincoat and let them both into the corridor where the
guard's reception desk stood. A janitor slipped by, carrying
an empty trash can, nodded at Finley, and disappeared.
Each of them filled out a pass from the supply on the desk
and dropped them into the box.

"It fucking well better be there," Finley said.

"I left it right next to your desk, a little Pan Am bag.
You saw it. I don't know why I forgot it."

"I keep my fucking passport in my jacket," Finley told
him. "And my credit cards."

Renner shrugged again and watched him unlock the
door to his office. Then he took one step forward,
wrenched Finley's arm back and up in a fierce grip and
spun him around like a flapping brown top.

"Oh shit!"

Renner switched his grip and shoved and the pistol was
right where it should be, holstered under the blazer. He

jammed it barrel first into the carotid artery under the jaw and twisted.

Finley rose on his toes, eyes bulging, and tried to lift his chin.

"Open the desk."

Finley shook his head and Renner jammed the gun higher, stepping him backward, belly to belly, two bears dancing. With his left hand he slapped the raincoat, high, low, the blazer. The keys were on a leather thong six inches wide. He pulled them free in a single motion, ripping fabric, scattering coins, and he shoved again, punching with the flat of his hand, punching dough until Finley tripped, wobbled, and dropped onto the edge of the baseball chair.

When was the last time he'd held a gun? Adrenaline burned in a film on his skin, his mouth seemed to fill with cotton. He backed to the desk, feeling behind him, hand like a torch, and knelt. One part of his mind was still watching Finley the way he would watch a bomb, a small, distant, untouchable screen, blue and white. The other part was diving in loops, like a terrified bird, in and out of fire. He felt for the double-serrated key and fumbled it into the lock. His mind saw Musso sitting on the chair, Vicki on the sling chair, Jillian, tissue-thin faces superimposed on Finley's.

"Renner." Finley lowered his hands carefully to the sides of the chair, gripping the vinyl or leather, whatever it was. "Renner, I can yell like a fucking banshee."

"Yell then."

The desk drawer slid open.

"Renner, I can put you away for twenty years, right now. Before you ever touch that drawer."

There were two videocassettes in the drawer and the little canvas courier sack. Nobody bothers with locks in the embassy mail sack, he thought, not in the age of fax. He yanked at the zipper and pulled out a third cassette.

"The man's in Frankfurt," Renner said, watching Finley's cannonball belly rise and fall, a green buoy on a sea of fat. In twenty years he'd be sixty-two. Mature. Free of obsession. "You're watching a bomber in Frankfurt, but you're getting film from L.A. On my flight. That's one thing wrong."

He rose slowly, hearing his knees crack, following Finley's expression. Pig-eyed, fat-cheeked. A born bureaucrat.

"The minute you leave," Finley said and stopped.

Renner walked to the VCR, turning the pistol in his hand, and snapped on the power. The first cassette was labeled "London. Bio."

"You signed me in, Billy." He switched on the television monitor above it. "You're fifty-six years old, with the softest job in the world—you tell them you signed me in. Twice. You tell them you showed me the Signature File without a letter." Finley moved his hand to his jaw. "What's going to happen to you then, Billy?"

The tape had started to run immediately, a flickering parade of code numbers, test patterns, government junk. Under the shelf of knickknacks the blue ice bag turned its head like a dog. Renner's mind jumped one more step.

"This is DeVere," he said, watching the patterns. "Right, Billy? Colin DeVere and Simon Caute are in L.A., not Frankfurt."

Finley's voice was almost normal. He worked his mouth and leaned back in the chair, sighing, and just as the first human figures appeared on the screen he started to grin and Renner, an instant before he spoke, straightened as if he'd been shot.

"This is Jillian," Finley said. "Meet Jilly."

It was a terrible videotape, overexposed, bloodshot with threads and wriggling lines.

"You're so fucking smart," Finley said. "Sit down."

But he didn't sit down.

Renner shifted the pistol, aimed it at Finley's middle, and cocked the hammer. Finley stopped, arms stiff on each side of the chair.

On the screen Jillian's face was a blurred oval of white. She wore a dark costume of indeterminate style, she moved in front of plaster columns, the overpainted canvas backdrop of an ancient city.

"You don't need a tape for a bio," Renner said. His finger on the trigger was as big as a scythe. "Backgrounds are on file, on paper. That's another thing wrong."

"Look at her," Finley said. "She's hot."

She was Juliet, Renner suddenly recognized. Her voice came scratching out of the monitor's speaker, reciting a speech early in the play, before Romeo appears. The camera caught her as she walked upstage, lithe, swinging her arms, hips turning. The camera crept toward her face. Close up the dark costume was frayed and shiny; sweat trickled in beads down her throat, over her collarbone, into the high space between her breasts.

"She curls iron, she's so hot," Finley said from the chair.

Renner took a step backward, looked at him.

"This is the Cambridge Footlights Club," Finley said. "Amateur tape. Five, six years ago. Somebody sent us a copy."

"She doesn't set bombs."

"She does bad things," Finley said. On the monitor the tape had hit blank white, filled by the sheer beam of the projection bulb. Renner's finger tightened on the gun. What he wanted to do was shoot the wall down, books, knickknacks, paintings, drive holes the size of stoplights through Finley's fat face. "You're watching the bomber," he said. "Simon Caute."

Finley shook his big head Musso-fashion, in contemptuous admiration. "I told them," he said, "the day they passed along your report from Huntsville, I told them to keep you out, move you to Arizona, anywhere, back to Virginia. You spotted it twenty miles before anybody else—Caute's a *super* bomber, he uses tech we want to know about, he studied bombs one-oh-one with the sainted Arab masters. There's people in London would give their left ball to know what he knows, who he knows."

"You worked me off the task force."

"Renner—you drink like a swamp. You break rules, you wave guns at old men. You got domestic problems. You *quit*. We're gonna tell you secrets?"

Renner closed his eyes for a moment, remembering

Gretzsky, Musso, the long table where the task force met.
When he opened them again Finley was standing, watching him, extending his left arm tentatively toward the
monitor.

"I forgot how you are," Finley said. "I thought I could
kid you along, send you home." Next to the harsh light on
the monitor screen his face looked old, drained of blood,
hanging in dried sacks of flesh from gray bones.

"L.A. doesn't know he's the bomber. They don't even
know he's there."

Finley nodded slowly. "We tell L.A., we never get to
touch the fucking bombs, the evidence. State law, you
know it as well as I do. They're assholes in L.A. They'll
never catch him in the first place—you can hide in that city
forever, it's like Calcutta. Or if they do find him they'll
fuck it up, they'll keep everything in court for two
hundred years. We want Caute here, in Europe, where we
can use him."

Renner shifted the pistol to his left hand. His right hand
was shaking, cramped from the cold weight of the metal.
Office politics on a grand scale. A community of greed, the
deputy chief said. "And the bombs?"

"The bombs are foreplay. If L.A. goes up like popcorn,
that's not our jurisdiction. Our priority is national defense,
right? *Europe*."

"She's in a play in L.A."

Finley nodded again. "That's why we're watching.
Nobody's actually seen her with Caute, ever, here or there.
But we're right, we can smell it. Caute's walked out of
traps in six cities already when we couldn't see him. He's
brilliant at staying out of the way. He hides like some
bloody chameleon."

"If nobody's seen them, you don't know she's in-
volved."

"Renner." Finley reached forward and pushed the eject
button on the VCR and the white screen went dark. "Till
yesterday you were right as a rabbit. We were just guessing
smart. But they faxed me already that this was coming.
They said I'd like it. Special treat." He inserted the new
cassette. "You wait five minutes to shoot me and you can

see it too. We took it from a tame screening room in Glendale, except the idiots chopped off the second half and ruined it, and they developed what's left like movie film, with the wrong kind of solution."

Finley touched the play button and the government codes began to run, handwritten this time, childishly large. Renner took a step closer, his skin suddenly cold, pumping fear from every pore.

And then Caute was in front of them, on hands and knees, naked. The tape's transparency of colors was so extreme that the image of his face was still unfinished, unresolved, a circle of wriggling white lines, a mask of snakes. Beneath it his chest muscles were moving shadows, the background a washed-out red, nearly pink. As he lowered one hand to his penis the camera seemed to move hungrily up, licking the sheets, the bedspread, the long white legs and rising curve of belly and hip that had started to sway under his weight. Jillian's breasts came into view, the bright exploding star of her face. The terrible quality of the tape had almost lost their features completely. Their figures were wildly distorted by intense white light, broken into moving blurs, flame people, fire lovers, unreal. Real. Renner's hand shot forward and plunged the screen into darkness.

30

THE PAN AM FLIGHT LANDED FIRST IN NEW YORK. RENNER dozed in his seat while the customs officer passed through the plane and the cabin crew made its pickup rounds. He barely noticed the takeoff again and awoke only as they started to circle Los Angeles, drifting down through a sea of yellow cloud, dropping under at the last minute, into brilliant afternoon sun. His only thought as he stared through the window was its incoherence. After London, after any other city—if he were a bomber he would choose Los Angeles too, out of instinct, kindred spirits.

At the Avis desk he picked up a new rental car, mentally calculating that he now had less than four hundred dollars left on his Visa line, enough for a day, two days at most of car and motel. Then hitchhike to Sacramento.

By four o'clock he was driving up Santa Monica Boulevard, sixteen miles from the airport, pulling to a furious halt outside the Pinero Theater.

She wasn't there.

There were handwritten signs taped to the glass doors—no rehearsals on Thursdays, cast's day off, tech rehearsal only on Friday. He walked down the alley, pulling at doors, shaking handles. In another half hour he was creeping down Artesia Boulevard toward Gardena, sliding through a chaos of fast-food restaurants, lumberyards, car wreckers, warehouses. Everything was made of cinder block and sheet metal junk, he thought, pressing the accelerator, everything had the self-canceling Los Angeles feeling of clutter and space together.

Tony wasn't there. Nobody anywhere in sight who might be watching. The shabby Miramar apartments stood in their flat lot, shoulders hunched against the fog beginning to blow in, roofs just ducking under the power lines. At Jillian's apartment he knocked hard until the door was answered by a woman he recognized at once as the one driving the car days ago, to pick up Jillian at the theater. Jillian was gone, she said, pulling her wrap about her. Gone for the weekend. Behind her, in the dark apartment, Renner could hear noises, smell beery masculine odors. Jillian was almost never there, she told him, closing the door.

What could he do?

He was suddenly dog tired and a hundred years old. He telephoned his motel in Santa Monica and drove back slowly, through endless traffic. As he crossed the ridge east of the airport and came down again the sun was scorching the long hills red. Headlights bobbed in the black valley in front of him, pearls on water.

They would never catch Caute.

He checked into his motel, left his bag, and returned to move the car. They'd never lay a finger on him. Before he had left Finley's office, in the treaty of Old Bond Street as Finley called it, he had gone through every page of Caute's own file—a dozen bombs in England at least, technically brilliant, vicious, virtually without a pattern except for the advanced technology. The jokes had come in Los Angeles, the game-playing bombs that tore families apart—not families so much, Renner thought, as the illusion of families, the illusion of order and warmth, coherence.

He sat in the car, eyes closed. Upstairs in his room was vodka, Thomas Jefferson, television. Oblivion. He would pick up the telephone and call Vicki, his own incoherent family; he would wash the film out of his brain with Vicki.

Instead he pushed open the car door and started to walk toward the beach.

If he called Musso? What for? A games-playing bear. The deputy chief? Nothing. Finley had made it clear. The federal side would wait, the Los Angeles police would bumble. If he interfered again, Finley said, there would be no second chance.

He stepped over a low fence and wound down a spiraling concrete walkway.

What could he do?

Think. Decide. Act.

If you know what you want you can act in the blink of a star, his father used to say—one of his father's impenetrable sayings. He hadn't understood it then, he didn't understand it now. How long was the blink of a star? A thousand years? A millisecond? How could you calculate fuse time for a star?

He lowered his head and walked along the beach, indifferent to the sliding sand, the curious glance of a slowing jogger. For the first time in twenty hours he let his mind swing round again, like the mad needle of a compass.

How long had Caute known Jillian?

How did he *hold* her?

There was nothing in the files—they never appeared together—but Renner knew obsession when he saw it. In his mind her face turned again and again to the camera, and Caute's face met her, but his arm swung at the same time to drive her away. Love frees. Obsession shackles. *I want her. I don't want her.*

He slowed almost to a stop. Overhead the fog blew clear, in one round spot, to reveal a swath of stars and the long, thin-boned shank of Orion.

What Caute loved was fragments, not order. Not Jillian.

At the edge of the surf Renner stopped completely and blew on his chilled hands. His shoes sank heel first into wet sand. Far to his left the fog had to roll lower, covering the lights strung along Santa Monica pier, swallowing whole hillsides behind it. To Renner's eye now every object, every light in the long dim landscape seemed to be struggling into existence, dependent on him to see them, to bring them by an act of willed consciousness into being. *Dasein.* The opposite of fragments, bombs, destruction. The whole country was falling into fragments, he thought, his whole life was in fragments—Vicki, Casey, splintering lengths of time crashing into the surf and tumbling away—and all he wanted to do was hold it together, stop the collapse. That made him no different from anyone else. Human. Not like a bomber.

Overhead in the rolling fog a few cold stars began to blink themselves out.

Somebody had parked a camper van directly in front of his staircase to the second floor. Renner walked cautiously past it and stopped to study its dark tinted windows. To his right, along the parking lot border, shoulder-high bushes and shrubs swayed with the wind, heaving great silver billows of fog from their crowns. *You hate California,* he thought; *it's cold and it's damp*—the tune dropped in and out of his head. He climbed the next set of stairs conscious of shadows behind curtains, voices behind walls.

In front of his door he hesitated for thirty seconds, staring over his shoulder.

Inside the room he had advanced halfway across the carpet, his jacket was halfway to the floor when he stopped, frozen in midstride, hearing the knock a heartbeat before it came, in the blink of a star.

He stood for a long indecisive second, counting.

Musso would be louder, harder, shouting.

Jillian opened the door herself—he looked down in surprise at the key still in his palm—and stepped softly in.

He registered macintosh, blond hair, fog steaming up from the walkway behind her.

"I think," she said calmly, but her face was strained and her voice was almost too soft to hear. "I think that I told you some lies."

Renner had moved no more than a step toward her when Echeverria appeared in the doorway. In slow motion

she turned to see, astonished—Echeverria shoved her
staggering forward with one broad hand in the back. The
other hand waved a police badge. Behind it somebody
else—a man, not Musso?—materialized in the fog.

Jillian took a step backwards and the palm closed, the
badge winked. The new cop held up its twin—and started
to circle. Renner saw leather jacket, sloping forehead, bits
of face in a kaleidoscope. Echeverria turned slowly on one
foot and his partner stalked her with the jaws of his
handcuffs open.

She shot a glance of fury at Renner.

"You want to pat her down, Renner?" Echeverria said,
grinning wickedly, moving, taking the cuffs.

"Where's Musso?"

"You got a hard-on like a bazooka for Jilly, am I right?"

"Did Musso send you?"

"Renner, Renner"—one part of his mind picked up the
imitation, Echeverria as Musso, down to the last weary
put-upon syllable. "Renner, are we idiots? Musso told you
we cleared her. We've been watching like buzzards. We're
on a surveillance of Jilly's theater, Jilly's apartment—hold
still!—we're staked out twelve different ways from Mon-
day, waiting for Jilly."

He had never paid real attention to Echeverria, Renner
thought, a forgettably handsome face in Musso's big wake.
Slick black hair, cut daringly long for a cop; taut shoulders,
an air of secret tension. His English was perfect, unac-
cented. His eyes were flat with resentment. What did
Echeverria want that he couldn't have?

Renner swung his right fist as hard as he could and
Echeverria sailed backwards grunting and into the wall.
Jilly spun, dropped to her knees. The other cop yelled and
dodged left. She was scrambling for the open door. Renner
hit him twice, left jabs that drove his head sideways, set
him up for the right hand again. The little room was
tilting, brown arms and legs, flapping cloth. Renner
punched with both hands, feeling the back of his skull open
up, his giant bruise storming to life.

Echeverria pushed to a kneeling position, swaying, and
Renner hit him with one long endless punch that began in

England and crossed Los Angeles like a rocket. As he went down Renner's hands were fumbling in his coat—pistol first, sliding out of the holster, keys for the handcuffs.

Down the stairs Jillian was running and stumbling, crossing the lot and weaving through parked cars. Beside the high shrubs the fog parted to take her. Renner leapt and sprinted. The stairs flew, huge shapes rose in the shadows. At the edge of the sidewalk, close to the corner, his hand caught up with hers. She glanced once, a flash of white, and together they vanished into the fog.

31

THE OLDER L.A. FREEWAYS WERE BUILT TO FOLLOW THE CONTOUR of the land, like a river, curving gently around the hills, seeking the valleys. The new ones, built with a new generation of superheavy equipment, simply blasted in a straight line from point to point, bombing the landscape flat. If he looked at her, Renner thought, he would lose control of the car and all idea of what he was doing.

Oncoming headlights appeared in the fog, near and far, glowing white balls shot from ghostly cannons. Not that he had the slightest idea what he was doing.

"You're bleeding," Jillian said from light years away.

It was true. In the rearview mirror he could see a bright worm of red crawling down his cheek. Who the hell had hit him? Echeverria? Renner touched the blood with one finger, then locked his mind on the road and concentrated with a will. He was on the San Diego Freeway going south. In three miles the Harbor Freeway crossed and ran north, then the Santa Monica curled through the loop they made, heading downtown. It was her car, not his. Would

Echeverria have its license? Would every patrol car in Los
Angeles already be looking?

Oh yes. And for the rented car. And at her apartment.
And his apartment in Sacramento. Renner blinked at the
fog, seeing double lights. His brain flicked right to left,
back again, the quick bright patter of consciousness. His
mind was flying with adrenaline. His heart banged like a
pump.

If he went to Vicki's apartment, all the way to San
Francisco?

If he went to San Francisco there would be roadblocks
on every highway, he wouldn't make it past Santa Barbara.
And if he did, if he walked into Vicki's apartment with
Jillian on his arm—

Jillian stirred in the seat. Renner started to speak and the
left front wheel struck a line of cat's-eye lane dividers,
rattling the little car's joints and banging a rear door shut.

"Who got in?" he said, making it a joke.

She smoothed her hair back with stiff fingers. Even
without looking he could tell that the back of her head was
pressed against the window, her full gaze was turned on
him. He took one hand from the wheel to push the defrost
lever higher.

"The minute the fat cop said your name in the restaurant," she said softly. Over the whine of the tires her voice
was barely audible, it had the low burr of the north of
England. "As soon as he said it I knew I'd heard it before."

Renner squinted and leaned forward until his brow
touched the clammy glass of the windshield. Signs for the
Harbor Freeway swam toward him, green and white flat
surfaces. He had a brief surrealistic vision of giant playing
cards, green and white, spinning through the gray fog. In
London, all those years, he had never seen fog as restless,
as sinister as California coastal fog. His foot found the
brake pedal and the car slowed almost to a halt. They
inched their way down a ramp, turning until he lost all
sense of north, south, up, down.

"David L. Renner," she said.

"L for lost." Now there were signs for Artesia Boule-

vard, the Compton Airport. A milk white gull came out of
the fog with an angry squawk, just above the windshield.

"Do you know what you're doing?"

"The Santa Monica Freeway runs downtown. There's a
bus station on Sixth Street. Or you can catch a train at the
SP depot."

"Where I heard your name was London," Jillian said.
"Some people there said you were the top bomb policeman
in England, the absolute smartest. I have no intention of
getting on a bus. Do you know how far I'd get?"

Like a line on a map, the fog simply stopped. They
drove through it and into brilliant, clear blackness. Ahead
of them the freeway rose toward a field of stars. To their
left the curtain of fog pulled away hissing and cut at a sharp
angle north, half a mile high, a wall of billowing cotton.
Renner stepped on the accelerator. His right hand brushed
hers as he reached again for the defrost lever. When he
trusted himself to look, she was just as he had pictured,
back to the window, facing him squarely, stiff fingers once
more smoothing her hair.

"You warned me. You said they were coming."

Renner nodded.

"I didn't set a bomb. I've never set a bomb."

"I was in London yesterday," Renner said. Yesterday?
An hour ago? He touched the brake again, pumping. "I
saw films."

He was steering for the first exit ramp he saw—
Manchester, Imperial Boulevard, he couldn't be sure because he was glancing from the road to her face, back and
forth. As the car slowed the streetlights seemed to flash on
and off behind her, backlighting the pale oval of her hair
and face, the interval between them growing longer and
longer until he could just catch the tiny lines around her
eyes, the crow's-feet that were a sign of reality, of age, not
impulse or imagination, not film. The lights slowed to a
flicker.

"I'm an actress," she said finally. Then lowering her
voice to a whisper, sinking into the corner, sardonic and
tearful at once. *"Help."*

He had exited on Manchester. Disoriented for a moment, Renner wound the little car at random along numbered side streets, working his way west through rows of pale bungalows and double-parked cars until he came to a wide, desolate boulevard that announced itself as Normandie Avenue.

It was the south-central, he remembered, L.A.'s ghetto, and it was like driving through a shipwreck. Overhead a canopy of empty black sky, on either side buildings like broken ribs, snapped off, boarded up, jagged, collapsing by stages into the street. There was almost no traffic, no pedestrians, only unearthly palm trees bathed in the lurid underwater glow of the street lamps. On corners, in front of flashing neon beer signs, young black men in sleeveless shirts paused to look up. Jillian shivered and folded her arms. Renner moved to the middle lane. At the first traffic signal he slowed for a yellow light and then, as shadows began to detach themselves from the buildings, he kicked the accelerator again and sailed through the intersection.

"You *are* lost," she said, sitting up straight.

He punched the car through another changing light, glancing reflexively at the gas gauge, looking left and right for signs of a patrol car. He was Dis, she was Proserpine. If he let the fear and adrenaline come together he would rip the steering wheel off the column, he would burst out of the car like a human bomb.

"Renner—"

Just ahead the street had miraculously begun to change—more cars, brightly dressed people; the sidewalks shook with color. In another two minutes they had entered an Oriental section, one of the block-long strips of twenty-four-hour Asian commerce that punctuated every Los Angeles neighborhood south of Beverly Hills. Korean, Philippine? The street was blazing with lights, red and yellow dragon script, crowds and banners; from the palm trees plastic lanterns dangled in bunches like firecracker flowers.

By now the highway patrol would have joined Echeverria, cops would be fanning out across the city, thick as thieves, a wolf pack—searching for what? He angled northeast, off the boulevard, holding the needle at thirty-five. On Pico six blocks ahead they would be looking for small blue cars, they would stop a tall, wired-looking white male, a blond bombshell. He wrenched the car hard right again, through another residential neighborhood, and then abruptly, without warning they passed under the giant crisscrossing veins of a freeway and into a wasteland even emptier than Normandie Boulevard. In the sudden eerie darkness they could have been driving through downtown Beirut, through blitzed-out Warsaw. There were brick warehouses instead of bungalows, crumbling stucco offices from another era, storefront windows braced with iron mesh. Jillian shuddered. To the left, in the distance, Renner saw the grinning marquee of a porno house. He turned the wheel and a new street flashed into view and Jillian twisted sharply in her seat to see it.

"Absolutely crazy," she breathed.

For what seemed like a dozen blocks straight ahead, right through the middle of the darkness, the sidewalks were lined and crowded with hundreds and hundreds of dressmakers' mannequins. They stood along the curbs, against the doors, halfway into the street, most of them with arms akimbo, nude, shiny white, and cartoonishly human. Some were bald; many had rakish blond wigs clamped to their skulls. As Renner crossed up one block and down another he was forced to slow down again and again for the pedestrian traffic. Late-night shoppers streamed through the intersections; husky men trundled dress racks and packages in all directions. Overhead was a forest of hand-painted signs in Spanish, English, Chinese, all advertising wholesale clothes, used clothes, retail clothes, *telas al por mayor*—"rags" in five different languages. The mannequins themselves were held by bicycle chains to doorframes and parking meters; they waited stoically, tilted at every angle, while straggling customers picked at their sleeves or hurrying owners stripped the last few items of clothing into baskets.

"Here?" Jillian said, twisting again toward him.

Renner shook his head.

The city was a film strip, jumping from frame to frame. As abruptly as they had appeared, the rag shops and people disappeared, vanished and the car seemed to plunge downhill on buckling asphalt, coiling around and down, into the third and darkest ghetto yet, toward bottom in California.

Now the only figures on the street were black men again, drifting, shadowy against brick walls and alley mouths.

"I hate this country," Jillian whispered.

A homeless family, wrapped in multiple layers of clothes, looked up from their supermarket cart. In the south, Renner thought, when he was a boy—then he broke off the thought. He had stopped at a crosswalk to peer at street numbers. From nowhere at all men were materializing around the car.

Jillian looked at him, then half stood in her seat to reach for the back door lock. Renner touched the accelerator, but two men walked, trotted directly in front of the hood, holding him to a crawl. Another man rapped on Jillian's window with his fist. Renner saw faces lowering, palms and fingertips spread. The car was lurching to the right, to the curb, and swaying under their weight.

"*Go!*" Jillian hissed.

He swung the wheel hard to the right and pulled up under a street lamp. Except for the men, silent, grinning, who swam out of the darkness, the whole street seemed deserted. They sat alone in an island of light. Jillian's hand gripped his arm; he felt her fingers digging and one part of his mind heard her voice. With his left hand he yanked the emergency brake, then cut off the motor.

"*No!*"

Renner opened the door, forcing them back. How many? Six, eight, all ages, more coming, souls swarming aboard a barge.

"You lost, man."

"You made a wrong turn, man."

"Spare change, man. Gimme some cigarettes, gimme some change."

He pushed forward between them, parting them with his shoulders, rounding the car, pulling her out by one limp arm. What showed in his face? A wild man, wrecking his life? The asphalt was river black, littered with trash and sticks. What lies had she really told him? What lies did she mean to explain? By a mad trick of shadow the nearest figure, tall, thin, dressed in army fatigues looked to him for an instant like Simon Caute. The adrenaline surged back, higher than ever. In the glass of the windshield his face was a wheel of fire.

They walked like two white ghosts, surrounded by a mob.

With a fierce grip on her wrist Renner led, dragged Jillian half a block down the sidewalk, craning his head back and forth as they moved, scanning numbers. At the entrance to a sagging brick apartment building on the nearest corner he stopped and the circle of men around them suddenly pressed forward.

Renner turned to stare them back. Somebody's hand probed at his jacket. Another hand rose toward Jillian's hair. With one arm he pushed her behind him, into the doorway. How long would the car last anyway, between the cops and the street? With his free hand he lifted the ignition keys shoulder high, waved them, and threw. They sailed through a cone of light, silver fish, and skidded on concrete twenty yards away. While the crowd broke and scrambled after them, he jammed his shoulder against the locked door and drove it open. At the top of the first flight of stairs, he stooped to read a name card, then knocked twice, twice again.

When the door jumped open, Rosalie Garbutt, still in her dark police blazer and skirt, was already waving them in.

32

"LIKE *RATS*," ROSALIE SAID OVER HER SHOULDER. "DIRTY BLACK rats on the street."

One room away from the end of the hall she stopped and with a huge frown waved them into her kitchen. Then she squeezed herself in after them and bustled to the stove.

"Daylight comes," she muttered, "and all the junkies and muggers and *rats* are gone, nothing on the street but cars and homeless." She clattered a red metal coffee pot across the burners and looked hard at Jillian. "Two years ago—a year and a *half* ago—it wasn't too bad at all, not in daytime. Now it's all *drugs*. Crack, smack, cocaine, something new they call ice, guaranteed to make your eyes pop out, your brain flip, your ears turn round on the stem. Six more weeks I'm gonna be walking out the door and stepping on *ice* men as far as you can see."

Jillian had lowered herself into a painted wooden chair by the window. Her head was back, her chin up; her eyes were closed and the hands in her lap gripped and regripped each other with convulsive force. "Why live here?" she said, her eyes still closed. From the other side of the little room Renner watched her hands in motion.

"I mean, you have a job, you make a salary?"

Rosalie snorted. She dropped the lid on the pot with a bang. "Honey, you want to try living in L.A. on twelve thousand eight hundred dollars a year? You want to pay car insurance, you want to buy *groceries*? Besides that, I got a husband with a stroke—Colonel Renner knows—right down the hall, can't work. And his mother, born not two miles from here, eighty-three years old. She was a little girl, she worked for D.W. Griffith on Spring and Second, in a movie studio. That's three blocks from the Parker Center now. She was a grown woman, this was all *downtown*, with street cars, night clubs, jazz clubs—she still goes every Sunday to the church she got married in. Some people loyal to people. Some people loyal to places."

"You heard it on the radio?" Renner asked. "In the EOC?"

Rosalie slipped her blue duty blazer from her mountainous shoulders and dropped it on a second chair, never taking her eyes from Jillian. "I'm not religious," she said, "but I go out the door, I walk down Main Street to the Parker Center, stepping over junkies, and I can't help thinking about Pharaoh and the plagues of Egypt. In school you read about the Black Death back in England— white powder means black death in this country. You want to call somebody, Colonel? You want to call your wife?"

"No."

"I didn't think so." Her eyes took in the stained macintosh, and she made a clucking sound in her throat.

"What did they say?" Renner asked.

"I heard it on ATO just as I was going off shift. That sergeant you wanted me to find the other day, Echeverria—Echeverria calls in yelling like a maniac. The woman they watching got away, David Renner beat up all the cops in Santa Monica. They had your car license, your clothes. The way Echeverria tells it you left a bloody trail all over L.A. County. He wants the FBI, the CIA, the army after you two." She lifted the lid of the pot and peered in. "This coffee might float a crowbar, Colonel. I made it too strong. But you put a few drops on the lady's wrist, the handcuff come right off."

Jillian lifted her right wrist.

"You got the other one tucked up your sleeve, is that right, honey?" She thumped a green ceramic mug of coffee on the crowded breakfast table beside Jillian's chair. "Ladylike."

Jillian looked from Rosalie to Renner, back again. "I insulted you," she said softly. "I'm sorry."

Rosalie handed a second mug to Renner, nodding. "You under stress," she told Jillian.

Renner lifted the cup and tasted. Even stronger than she had said. Southern-style coffee, pungent and laced with chicory, smelling of earth and roots and kitchen tables in small rooms before dawn. Rosalie had poured her own cup and now stood, back to the stove, facing them.

"When Colonel Renner gets under stress," she said, "he just says less and less. At the embassy in London we always knew when the bombs were bad. Usually he came by every morning to say hello, the only officer that would. Charm the birds out of the trees, in the right mood, happy with his family."

"Rosalie, we can't stay here."

"That's right," she agreed. "You gonna have to go upstairs." She turned her face toward Jillian again and worked her lips in and out, frowning. "There's twelve apartments in this building, two on each floor, and the top four are all empty. You can't stay here 'cause I don't have beds and I don't have rooms and I *do* have a social worker nurse that comes in every morning to look after Milton."

"I meant—"

"I know what you meant." She put down her cup and started to go past him into the hallway, lifting her broad, flat face to study him. "You in trouble, Colonel Renner." She paused and jerked her head once toward Jillian, still sitting in the chair. "I guess I see why. I wouldn't give you my address if I didn't know something was coming."

"We'll leave in the morning—I promise."

"Leave to go where?"

Renner rubbed his jaw with one hand. In the kitchen

Jillian had closed her eyes again; her neck was stretched taut with weariness. She seemed asleep, exhausted, but on her lap her fingers worked ceaselessly around the handcuff. Renner's gaze traveled across her face. The bleak fluorescent light of the kitchen sculpted her skin, digging lines, hollowing spaces. In her gaunt cheekbones he could see the coming look of middle age and beyond—his mind flicked to one of Vicki's quotations, the skull beneath the skin.

"We've got to help her," he said.

"Now I learned something new," Rosalie said. "I learned love can blow up something just as bad as hate can. You could put love in a bomb."

"In the morning I'll call Musso and tell him what happened."

"What for? He already knows. Man's got a radio in his car, right? Mister Lieutenant Whale Rat Musso."

Renner kept his eyes on Jillian's face and didn't answer.

"You one of the ones loyal to people, Colonel. It breaks you in two."

The apartment she led them to was on the top floor, three dusty unheated rooms, looking down on an air shaft. Only one window revealed the battle-scarred street below, completely black now, and behind it a pale hump of California hillside.

Rosalie had the key. She muttered apologies like a fussy hostess as she opened doors for them, tried lights, pulled a sad rack of red curtains tighter. Twice she labored up the stairs from her own apartment, waving Renner back, hauling towels and linen enough for a month. The apartment was vacant like so many others, she explained, because nobody wanted to live surrounded by junkies—the landlord kept the building decent, or almost decent, but he was losing money, losing tenants. She ran brown-stained water for them until the pipes rattled in protest behind the walls. There was no furniture except the curtains—the junkies had broken in and stolen everything else. She padded away and came back carrying two wooden chairs from her kitchen and a box of cups and saucers. With Renner's help she foraged in a second empty apartment and turned up a pair of thin mattresses and plopped them onto the dusty floor.

"You want food?" she asked, hands on hips, standing in the middle of the room. "Sandwiches, chicken, scrambled eggs? You must be hungry—it's ten o'clock."

Jillian shook her head.

"You want whiskey? Colonel Renner likes vodka and there's one thing we're not short of on this street, it's liquor." Without waiting for an answer, she reached in her skirt pocket and pulled out a clear half-pint bottle. "You got three locks on the front door," she said. She handed Renner the bottle. "Better use them *all*. The windows got locks too, in case some of the junkies learn to fly. You saw the front door. No fire escape. No phone. You marooned up here like Robinson Crusoe." She frowned at the bare linoleum floor and poked at dust or a crack with the toe of her shoe. "No broom."

"In the morning," Renner began.

"In the morning, there's gonna be a racket outside like an army moving in, Colonel. That's the wholesale clothes people bringing in their trucks. They start unloading about six-thirty or seven, two blocks up on Broadway, and after that there's nothing but traffic and dirty Spanish." She hesitated, with her hand on the doorknob. "Any other building on this block," she said, "the stairs are a toilet, everything's covered with trash and filth, the junkies sleep on the floor and the homeless camp out on the roof. Don't go out. Don't go *anywhere*."

She pulled the door open and let her frown drift from the corners of the room inward, until she was staring angrily at Renner. "You a decent man, Colonel R.," she said. "Without a doubt brave." She puffed her cheeks in and out, then shook her head with the air of not having said what she wanted to say. After a moment she closed the door without a sound.

Even in a place like this, Renner thought, she gravitated toward the light.

In the main room where Rosalie had left them there was only a single dim overhead bulb screwed into a ceiling fixture. Jillian paced back and forth beneath it, three steps each way, staying in its pale glow as if she were an animal trapped in a cage.

Renner stood by a wall and watched her in silence. At each left-hand turn she tossed her head and brushed aside a strand of blond hair stuck to her cheek. When she lifted her arm, under the frayed sleeve of her macintosh he could see the handcuff flash.

He reached in his pocket for the bomb tool. "I can get that off for you."

She stopped and held up her wrist.

"My knight," she said sardonically. "What can you do? Set a bomb on it? Bomb man? Never mind. I'm used to props."

Renner pushed away from the wall and took her wrist in both hands. The bomb tool, as complicated as a Swiss Army knife, had two sets of pointed levers at one end, awls that doubled as blades, and he fit the smaller one into the keyhole on the flange of the cuff. Her pulse drummed under his thumb.

"Or I could gnaw it off with my teeth," she said and raised her eyes to him. "Like all the other street rats." Her eyes were red and wet—with what? anger? fear?—he could almost taste their salt. "Your hand's shaking," she said.

"It always shakes."

"You were crazy to do this. You could have let them take me, you could *still* let them."

"You came to the motel," Renner said and for an instant didn't recognize his own voice. Rosalie's voice was deep and southern, so rich and syrupy that he could dive in it and swim away like a boy. Where had his own southern-ness gone? What had absorbed it? "You came to see me in the motel to explain about lies."

"I came to find you," she said. "I was like my poor cracked mother suddenly seeing a policeman. I thought you could help me. I thought—I don't know what I thought."

"You lied about having a television. Big lie." The handcuff was heavier than he had imagined, and the chain to the second bracelet kept slipping against his knuckles.

When he looked up again she had forced a wry, ironic smile, a new mood.

"'If I tell thee a lie, spit in my face; call me horse.'"

"And you lied about bombs. You lied about bombs in England, bombs here. You lied about the man who builds them here."

For a moment he thought she would pull her wrist away and jerk loose. But she only clenched and unclenched her fist and swallowed.

"When I was in school," she said finally, a clipped, neutral accent, "Marshall McLuhan was a friend of the headmistress and came to deliver a talk."

The Medium is the Message, Renner said. The keyhole was far too small and he flipped the tool around to the screwdriver end.

"And I was head girl, so I got to sit with him all through lunch. We were in our new hall, right in front of a huge new picture window, and he looked out and spread his arms and said that the great thing about modern life was that technology had removed all artificial boundaries between us and nature—instead of being walled in by the room, we were continuous with the lawn and the sky, we were all unified by the open window."

Renner pressed the tool with his thumb as hard as he dared and slipped the ratchet of the handcuff one notch. In the gray light of the bulb the veins of her wrist were shadows of shadows.

"But it was a long lunch, two shifts of admiring girls and teachers, and when the second group sat down he waved his hand at the window and said in exactly the same tone that the trouble with modern life was that technology had removed all the natural boundaries between us and the outside and instead of being *cut off* from the lawn and sky as we really were, the open window made us believe in a false unity with them."

Renner held his breath, head down, eyes on the ratchet, and squeezed. When the cuff dropped free, she sprang back from him and into the light. He stood with the chain in his right hand, then tossed it into a corner.

"Lies of the mind," he said.

Jillian paced to the distant edge of the light.

"Whatever you want it to be," she said.

Renner sat down on one of the wooden chairs and poured vodka into a plastic cup from Rosalie's carton.

Under the bulb Jillian stood with her arms folded, just as she had on the stage, and brushed hair away from her cheek again. She had opened the buttons of the macintosh and even from the chair Renner could see the pressure of her breasts lifted against the stiff raincoat, the gray-blue curve of her dress against her thighs. "He made me call the Marine barracks from a phone box on Regent's Park Road," she said defiantly. Under the flickering bulb, although she stood perfectly still she appeared to sway. "I was supposed to dial the number and ask for you in an American accent—I'm good at accents, that's why I was chosen. 'Who does accents better than our Jilly?' He knew you weren't there, you worked at the embassy, but he wanted to make it a joke, a public challenge—everybody in Colin's group had heard of the American bomb wizard who couldn't be fooled."

She drained the vodka in one gulp. "He told me it was a miniature transistor bomb that would set fire to the building when the phone rang but not kill the soldiers and you'd never figure out how he did it. And I was such a puddle-brained little socialist street-marching radical I believed him. I can close my eyes now and see the explosion, the top of the street just suddenly blowing apart. I believed anything he told me. He could tell me the sky was falling and I'd cry myself to sleep. He still could."

"Where is he?"

She kicked the empty cup clattering toward one of the mattresses.

"So," she said, turning away.

In his own veins the vodka burned like a fuse.

With his back propped against a wall Renner sat on a mattress and listened to sirens racing up a faraway street. In the bathroom he could hear the shower pattering and the pipes shaking. Automatically he held up his watch and squinted. Past midnight. Do we repeat our parents' lives? His father was the most conservative man he had ever known—cautious, wary, distrustful to a fault; his mother had left him because he was too dull, too cautious. But in the war there was the one wild instant of uncontrolled and murderous action that had always seemed to Renner the key to his character. What had brought it on? Youth? Fury? Love?

Love, his father had said, on the single surprising occasion that Renner had worked up the nerve to ask him—love for his comrades falling and dying in bloody rags around him. Hate for the unseen Germans hunched on the hill and spewing fire.

On a coin, he told Renner, the closest thing to heads is tails.

Jillian came out of the shower and stood framed in the doorway watching him. She had dried herself with one of Rosalie's innumerable towels and put back on her cotton dress, but not the macintosh. In the faint glow of the bulb she seemed to be far away and under water, drifting toward a gray surface. The dress clung in damp patches to her breasts and thighs.

"In three or four hours," Renner said and showed her his watch, "the trucks should start arriving downstairs. When it's crowded enough I can get to the street without anybody noticing and make a call to Musso. I won't ask Rosalie. If I turn myself in—if I promise to bring you with me—I can stall them until tonight at least and you can be over the border by then, into Mexico. If you made it fast enough you could probably catch a flight straight to London."

While he was talking she had crossed the room. She knelt on the mattress beside him and lit a cigarette.

"Is this in exchange for Simon Caute?"

Renner sat for a long moment, then shook his head slowly. "In exchange for nothing." He tried to imitate her sardonic accent but found that he was a poor mimic. "Think of it as a gentlemanly, chivalrous gesture. A compliment."

"You'd go to jail."

He shook his head again.

Her bare feet had left dark outlines in the dust where she had walked. He concentrated first on the soles of her feet, black and white, divided by an invisible line. The room was so still that he could hear the siren miles away, a thin, high aubade. He could hear the indignant pipes shake on the floor miles below. He could hear the cigarette burning, miles from his face.

"It would only buy you time," he said. "They want Caute first, but they'd still come after you eventually."

"Your southern accent's stronger. You're starting to sound like your black friend downstairs."

Renner stretched his right hand toward her face, cupping her cheek with his palm. Her lips opened. Her face and hair made an oval of light.

Why did he see her always in terms of light?

He leaned forward through the infinite darkness. Light was simultaneous order and destruction, the orderly waves of luminescence that bind the chaotic things of the world to each other, the silent, unending explosion of surfaces. When he touched her breasts the dress fell away from her shoulders. His hands were like gloves of fire. Caute was a lie, the film was a lie, the bombs were a lie. Lies were spinning away in fragments. She stood and he pulled the thin cotton dress down slowly, over her hips, then she lowered herself again to her knees. Renner kicked away his trousers and shoes. Skin against skin. He touched her waist, thighs. As she lay back against the mattress, the long soft curve of her belly arched under his fingers. He rolled on top. With the first thrust of his hips her eyes opened to him completely, her face had the radiant look of a mask.

"For a long time," she said, "I suppose deep down I hated any man. I said I'd die before I ended up like my mother."

She stretched across on the mattress and felt in the crumpled dress for another cigarette. Renner held her hand as she turned, unwilling to let her pull a fraction away. Her breasts were small and soft. He bent his head to kiss her.

"He's like a drug," she said. "He's like your friend's *ice* man. I tried to run away from him. I grew up, I left

Cambridge, I stopped marching in the street. I had a job in London, in a repertory company, that would have led to the West End, no question. I did Juliet, I was already cast for Hedda Gabler."

"And?"

She made her voice caustically self-mocking. "I like to be hurt. I have a poor self-image, the headshrinkers said. He found me. He hated himself for coming after me, he said. And I hated myself for going back. I cashed in all my money, all my savings, and bought a ticket to Los Angeles and he found me again in a bloody week."

In the darkness Renner could see the glow of her cigarette but not her face.

"You know my favorite line in Shakespeare, the craziest line in the world?" she said. "'Love may transform me to an oyster, my lord.'"

"Where is he?"

"In London he set bombs for political groups, even though he laughed at them. Here he sets bombs out of pure hate. I think he even hates me. He has people he hires, manipulates."

She stabbed out her cigarette in one of the plastic cups. "I tried to live with a girl in an apartment, like a normal person. He said he'd go to the police and send me to prison, because of London. But I've never done any of his bombs here. I hate them." She turned toward him again, brushing his shoulder in the darkness. "What we have in common is hate," she said softly. "Hate makes us come alive."

Renner touched her wrist with his fingers.

"You took off the handcuff," she said. "But I still feel it."

They finished the vodka, measuring it off in their plastic cups, and then sat down on the mattresses again, far apart. Renner remembered a phrase from school, in pompous Latin: *Post coitum omne animal triste est.* After love, every animal is sad.

Six feet away, cross-legged, knees and bare feet in the light, Jillian leaned back in shadow. "He's not like you," she said in a voice harder than Renner had ever heard her use. "He doesn't look like you. He doesn't talk like you. He has no moral code, no beliefs, no wife, no family. He's brilliant."

Her moods were an actress's disguises, he decided, removable at will.

"Tell me where he is."

"No."

"You left him. You came to me, you changed sides."

"On stage," she said, "if you walk from left to right it's called a downhill cross. An easy cross. But if you go right to left it's harder to watch somehow, so you call it an uphill cross, a long cross."

"Where is he?"

Her face disappeared completely in shadow. "He's exactly like you," she said.

When they made love again she moved with slow, melancholy tenderness, murmuring his name, rising and brightening at his climax, as if he rode on a pale, golden sea.

"If I showed you where he is," she said, "would you kill him?"

she said in a voice harder than Renner had ever heard b

33

"WHAT DID HE SAY?" CAUTE ASKED.

"He said to give you this."

Francis reached into his leather cyclist's jacket and pulled out a beige letter-size envelope.

Caute ripped it open with one quick movement of his thumb, read the single folded page, and dropped them both on the table beside his coffee cup.

"You know what this letter is, Francis?" He made himself look around the restaurant—Cindy's, Denny's, who knew what the hell it was called. Then he looked back at Francis who was still standing like a small block of solid leather, some slicked-down two-legged stud bull with acne scars and zipper pockets. Fucking Francis.

"He just said to give it to you. I didn't read it."

"Was he packing his suitcase? Did he have his streamer trunk out, his white bwana suit, his little stack of pamphlets on how the West is sliding down the sewer?"

Francis stood with his hands in his pockets and his sullen red-necked pose of not being able to hear you. Words ricocheted off Francis. Talking to Francis was like shooting a pistol at a rock.

Caute pushed his chair back and slipped the letter and envelope into his anorak. Through the nearest picture window you could see the Pinero Theater across the street, you could see the headlights and the traffic, you could even see the Mexican hookers with their fine sagging tits and their fat hips as big as truck wheels. What you couldn't see was any blond English actresses with little tits and hips like a snake.

At the door Caute paused and looked back at the nearly-deserted restaurant. Plastic and neon. Orange and brown.

"You want me to go somewhere with you?" Francis asked.

"It's one o'clock in the California morning," Caute said. They decorated the walls and booths in orange and brown for earth colors. You walk in, you think you're in an orange and brown farm, you grin and spend your money. "Where the hell do you think I want to go?"

Francis didn't even shrug. Behind him Caute could see a black guy working the grill, a Mexican teenager cleaning the silverware, in the far corner an old man with a filthy gray beard sitting in a wheelchair and staring at the floor. He'd been there when Caute walked in at ten o'clock, he'd be there till the black guy threw him out. When he first came back to America, Caute thought, after four years in England, the first thing he noticed was the junked cars everywhere—you could go to the bottom of the Grand Canyon and find junked cars—now it was junked people. Colin had the right idea, blow it all to fucking pieces. Colin just didn't have the King Billy bomb balls the fucking job needed.

Beside the double door was a stainless steel cart they kept their coffee pots on, and their extra cups and saucers and napkins, and an orange-brown water jug surrounded by orange-brown plastic tumblers. Caute put his right hand under the edge of the cart and suddenly lifted it as hard as he could, filling the air with flying shit, making a noise like a little bomb.

On the sidewalk he glanced back at the window, the Mexican guy still yelling. Francis walked quickly along the curb two steps ahead, in and out of streetlights, not looking back but frowning, unhappy. Francis had no imagination, zero, but he was deeper into money every day; forty years old, he liked money now so much he would stick, he would stick as long as the money lasted. Francis was the age now, Caute thought, without money he could suddenly see himself as one more American junked car.

The Arab was with him, right?" Caute said.

"Two Arabs."

"They say anything?"

"They told the Englishman they'd see him tomorrow, he should come see them tomorrow night at their hotel. Then they look around and I'm still there, so they tell me to get out."

Caute stopped in front of his parked car and looked down the block toward the restaurant. Denny's. "They were all arm in arm, right? A love feast. Family." Francis made no answer. "Come in the morning to the beach house," Caute said. "Come about ten o'clock."

He opened his wallet and counted out six one-hundred-dollar bills, right into Francis's palm. Colin's money. Colin the baby British banker.

"On the way, stop and get me two cheap briefcases at some all-night twenty-four-hour mall shop like K Mart. Cheap cases, I don't care what they look like as long as they open at the top with a snap like a suitcase lock. You keep the rest of the money for your hope chest."

Francis had delicate hands for a biker. Caute had always thought so. It was one of the reasons when he was setting up he had hired Francis—thin white fingers, quick sure motions. Good with wires, good with locks. Francis's hand scurried away with the bills like a mouse.

At Beverly Boulevard, Caute swung left on squealing tires, crossing three lanes, and headed due east, downtown. Each time he had to stop for a traffic signal he spread Colin's letter on the dashboard and read it again. Spidery handwriting. No date, no signature. Written in constipated prose like a fucking telegram from fucking Hemingway, Colin's idea of being tough. *Project canceled. Federal agents here. Payments stopped.* It was the Arab, Caute thought, Fadhil Bazan. He turned off Beverly Boulevard and into a tunnel that had billboards and ads plastered on every wall—in California the undertakers would put an ad in your coffin, somebody paid them. The Arab had taken one look at the movie—taken one look at the Federal Reserve building, for Christ's sake—and seen it was a scam, it couldn't be done, Caute's little joke, Caute's little double cross. The Arab was too smart by half. Except he was still in town. If Francis was right, he was still in his hotel making up lists, watching porno movies, hoping to score some blond-haired English action.

At Fourth Street he drove slowly up the right lane, sticking to the speed limit, careful not to call attention to himself. Just before the Parker Center there was a double-deck garage with a sign that said "For Official Business Only," but there couldn't have been more than twenty cars in it and Caute turned smoothly in with his turn signal blinking and chose the first open parking slip. When he switched off the engine his ears popped, as if he had climbed a great altitude. He put his hand on the door and spoke out loud. "Jillian." He opened the door and spat on the concrete. "Cunt."

The Parker Center is always open, he thought, pacing up the front walk, twenty-four hours a day just like K Mart, just like Exxon. To his left was another parking lot, this one filled with big police vans and black-and-white patrol cars and uniformed cops milling around, changing shifts. Straight in front of him was the main entrance, two guards inside, a long desk, metal detectors like an airport, more guards behind *that*. Then elevators, sawhorses, stacks of furniture being moved. All over the lobby, even from the outside walkway, he could see people standing and talking, civilians, cops in business suits, lawyers fastened onto the walls like leeches on skin, holding their briefcases.

Caute turned abruptly on his heel and walked back to the sidewalk. On the other side of the street was a nondescript modern building, a septic tank with elevators, Caute thought. He entered the deserted lobby and studied the elevators, two ranks facing each other, then stood by the nearest one on the left, where a light was rising. When the doors opened a woman in a blue police blazer stepped out, clutching a gigantic purse to her chest and reading a *Cosmo* magazine. Caute slapped his anorak pockets in pantomime and smiled and she looked up, nodded, and stuck her key back in the slot. When the doors closed he punched the lowest button on the panel.

On the sixth level down there was only one direction to go. Caute let the elevator close behind him and started down the corridor, smiling, following the arrows toward the guard's booth. He could see the locked double doors on the right, he could see the walls, the engineering. There was no way he could get past the doors and into the main switchboard rooms.

"You got business down here?" the guard said.

Caute looked left, right, feeling his anger deflate, his *reason* take over. There was no way a bomb down here would do anything except crunch some walls, bend some girders, scare some cops. He remembered how he'd described it to Colin and Fadhil—take out the 911, he'd said, L.A. goes right to its knees, screaming for help—but the place, now he saw it again, was built to withstand an earthquake. You'd have to take a bomb all the way in and stick it under the switchboards. Otherwise it was just a symbolic bang, and he wasn't like Colin. He didn't care about symbols or capitalist oppression or revolution by headline. He liked bombs that worked, victims he could see.

"I'm looking for a guy," Caute said, smiling, taking his hands out of his pockets and smoothing back his hair in an apologetic, nice-guy gesture. "They told me in the Parker he's probably working temporarily in the EOC."

"Who is he?" The guard hoisted a clipboard up to his lap.

And besides, Francis wouldn't carry a bomb down here. Nobody in his right mind would. He hated this fucking city. For his own reasons he'd like to stick a bomb under its nuts, go right down Colin's list, blowing one-two-three, but what made him different from the others was discipline, restraint, *intelligence*. Inside he was still shaking, he hated California so much, but the guard was looking out through his plastic window like a ticket seller in a movie and seeing only a guy that was probably a night-shift clerk from some horseshit office across the street, tilting his head and smiling. He would find a better target, he would find it to-fucking-morrow. He would blow somebody's happy world to garbage.

"I just remembered he's not going to be over here till the day shift starts," Caute said.

"We can look him up anyway. What's his name?"

Caute kept on smiling. "David Renner."

34

RENNER AWOKE JUST AFTER DAWN AND TURNED ON HIS SIDE TO touch her.

During the night they had pushed the two mattresses together and covered them with Rosalie's sheets and blankets. On Jillian's side the blankets were pulled back in a loose, open pile and the sheet underneath was cool.

He sat up and looked at the bleak room. The bathroom door was open. The kitchen was clear and open. Her dress and shoes were gone; the macintosh still lay in a pile beneath the faded red curtains.

She would be downstairs, with Rosalie.

She would be on the street, checking the car.

He stood up carefully, like a man held together with strings or stitches, and walked across the dusty linoleum to peer down into the street. In the distance he could hear motors and voices. Directly below, he could see faintly a stretch of potholed asphalt and the open jaw of a dumpster.

Suddenly he pulled on his trousers and shoes and yanked the front door open and started to run, shirtless, sockless, down the black stairs.

The street was filled with Jillians.

Renner jogged to a halt on the corner, panting, and turned left, right. Up and down the block smoke-belching trucks and vans were unloading, double-parked all the way into the center of the chaotic street; and up and down the sidewalks, between the racks of clothing and crates of clothing and hurrying, hustling shirtsleeved dealers, the mannequins stood in their blond wigs and bright dresses, row after row of them, an army of Jillians, staring serenely back at him.

He took three pointless steps into the crowd.

In front of him a dozen burly Hispanic men were lifting new mannequins, tilting them headfirst out of a truck; the early sun was already blazing down on them over the rooftops. Their blond hair flamed, their painted faces vanished.

"I went out to make a call," she said, and tossed her hair in the same defiant gesture as before.

"You could have used Rosalie's phone."

"She was sleeping."

Renner squinted at his watch. Six-fifteen. She had been gone for over an hour. In the pale light he couldn't make out the tiny date on the dial. Was today the longest day of the year? June twenty-first? Every year until now, in a funny little father-and-daughter game he and Casey had awakened themselves at dawn on the longest day and looked at the sunrise together. He raised his head and saw Jillian standing by the window, staring down at the street, opening a new pack of cigarettes. Some protective, irrelevant padding of memory reminded him that Vicki smoked too; he liked women who smoked, do you smoke after sex, I don't know, I never looked. He braced his weight on one palm and rose slowly from the mattress where he had been sitting.

Everything was different in the daylight. She was another person. When he approached her, she moved away. When he reached out a hand to touch her, she was gone.

"They'll never catch him," she said. Renner stretched out his hand again and she walked to the end of the window, turned, and watched a pickup truck full of broken boards pass under them. "He'll keep on setting bombs," she said, "and the bloody stupid police will *never* catch him."

"Where is he then?"

"I'm going back to buy clothes on that street. A black wig, some false boobs. Heels."

"Tell me where he is."

"Then I'm going to do what you said. I'm going to take the bus to San Diego. After that, Mexico, Mexico City. Canada. Canada or London."

"Jillian—"

She moved away in a sweeping gesture, gathering the macintosh from the floor, kicking aside the mattresses as she reached for her purse.

"He says he's a truth teller," she said, straightening again. Her hair already seemed darker, streaked with black. "He says people like you are fools to work for the government. He says this whole horrible country's in ruins, just collapsing minute by minute, the immigrants, the stinking education, the obscene politicians."

"He's wrong."

"He hates you, you know that—what you stand for?"

"I'll come to Mexico City. Call me from there. Call Rosalie."

She was already at the door. Every move he made drove her farther away. He thought of Casey again, her two toy magnets in the shape of black and white dogs that clasped each other, then reversed and repelled.

She pulled the door open and stared at him. Her mood had changed utterly again. Her voice was as bitter, as mocking as it had been to Musso the night she turned on her heels and walked out of the restaurant.

"He's so smart and he hates you so much," she said, beginning to close the door. Her face was cold and white and small. "How do you know he didn't send me just to find you?"

"Good riddance," Rosalie told him emphatically. She poured another cup of the poisonous sweet coffee that she kept brewing constantly on her stove, then sat down on the other side of the tiny kitchen table. "You *sure* she's gone?"

"I'm sure."

"I saw you going down the stairs and out on the street, arguing, her stomping away."

Renner rubbed his jaw with his palm and stood up, carrying his cup. "She's supposed to call tomorrow. Here. But she won't."

"Extra good riddance," Rosalie said, watching him. "I knew you in London, Colonel, don't you forget that. Everybody in the embassy knew you, because you were *there* every time some English twerphead called up with a bomb threat and because you were *decent*. I meant what I said. Get on back with your wife."

"Things change, Rosalie."

"She went off with another man?"

Renner nodded and threaded his way between chairs to the other end of the kitchen, balancing the coffee. Rosalie had spread her morning paper across a plastic cutting board and the front page had a new bomb story—Gretzsky's grim photo, the deputy chief's—under a sarcastic headline: "Can the Police Do Anything at All?"

"But you're not divorced?"

Renner folded the paper so that Gretzsky's photo was out of sight, then took another step. The glare of the sun against concrete was terrific; the building across the street bled streaks of light. He was not a cop, not a vigilante. You could set bombs for him, she said, if I showed you where. *I don't set bombs. I disarm them.* He picked up the green cotton sweater that was the only thing she'd left behind. "Not divorced," he said. "I'm too stubborn. I keep hoping she'll change her mind."

"Start over with your wife," Rosalie said. "Forgiveness is the way." Through the thin plasterboard walls they could hear the growl of her husband's television in the next room. "Do the right thing."

Renner pinched the bridge of his nose and closed his eyes.

"I got a good look at that girl's face last night," Rosalie

said. "She's beautiful. She could give my old boy another stroke just walking in the room. But you know what, Colonel?"

Renner looked up.

"That's the saddest girl I ever saw," she said. After a moment she reached across the table with both massive arms and readjusted slightly the coffee cup and the plate of eggs she'd fixed for him, now a cold gelatinous mass. "Where's a beautiful girl like that gone?" she said.

Renner shook his head and sat down at the table again, folding the green sweater in his lap.

"They'll be watching the airports," Rosalie said. "The buses, the car rentals, all that good police routine."

"She's an actress. She'll go in disguise." His tone just missed being light, his mind was veering off toward Jillian's apartment, the masks on her wall.

He turned the sweater over, emptying the pockets automatically. In the first one he found an unopened pack of cigarettes and a crumpled page of script from her play. I want her, I don't want her. *I want him, I don't want him.*

"I don't really know where she's gone," he said.

Rosalie looked at him steadily. "Humph," she said and stood slowly, working her lips in and out in a disbelieving frown. She put her cup on the sink rack and reached for the blue duty blazer she had hung on the back of her chair.

"Can I ask you another favor, Rosalie?"

"Does a chicken have lips?"

"I need a car, just for today."

She shrugged on the blazer and stood buttoning it. "I can probably let you use my cousin's old Ford," she said, "but I have to go down the hall and get the key."

When she was gone, Renner picked up the cup of coffee and tasted it again, then closed his eyes and sat back in the chair. *Why do you do it?* she had asked in the night with sudden fierceness—*Why stop bombs? Why stop bloody bombs?*

Renner opened his eyes. Because for as long as he could remember his world, his life seemed on the point of flying apart. Because he grew up in order and lived in disorder.

"It's down in the garage, waiting for you," Rosalie said.

"Door number four-D, off on the left. Now *I'm* going to walk. I always walk to the Parker Center."

"You're going to work?" He glanced at his watch, glanced again. It was nearly nine.

"Overtime on the ATO switchboard. There's FBI people all over L.A. all of a sudden, burning up the radios. Big hush-mush. There's even a man you used to know from London. Mr. William O. Finley."

Renner rubbed his face with one hand, feeling his skin tighten, grow stiff. His face was a lump of ice.

"Drive that car to a lawyer," she said. "This is the garage key, this is the ignition. A lawyer can still get you off."

He fumbled with the second pocket of the sweater.

"You dropped something," Rosalie told him.

She stooped to retrieve a tiny broken horseshoe of silver wire that had fallen skittering to the floor.

"I'm due at work," she said, placing it beside his cup. "That looks like one of her hairpins. You don't want that. You want to go call yourself a lawyer. *Then* call Whale Musso."

Renner held the wire up so that the sunlight from the window cast a tiny prismatic rainbow onto the bare wall.

"That's not a hairpin," Rosalie said, frowning.

"That's a photovoltaic cell," Renner said.

35

June 21

FRANCIS EYED THE PACKAGE ON THE TABLE WITH DISTASTE.

"It's a movie film?"

"It's a box of Delft china," Caute said. "It's a cattle prod. It's the long lost Hope Diamond. Pick it up and put it in the briefcase."

Francis hitched his belt buckle and looked around the room. The television was going in the corner, as always, with the sound off. Some idiot game show this time. The curtains were open to show the morning sun on the waves, but it was still foggy outside and the ocean had a gray metallic look to it, like waves made out of tin or sheet metal instead of water. He had never thought before that the beach could be ugly, but this morning it was, this morning it was ugly and it perfectly matched Caute's mood.

"You think it's going to blow up," Caute said sarcastically, "then what the fuck am I doing standing ten feet away?"

Francis grunted and bent down for the package.

"Good," Caute said. "Somebody actually does what I ask them to do. You know Tony?"

Francis turned the package carefully over. It was wrapped in waxy brown paper from a drugstore, tied with cheap cord, and it was the size and weight of a big book, a dictionary. Francis had once worked at Universal Studios delivering packages from one lot to the other on his motorcycle. This was absolutely the wrong size for movie film.

"I asked you," Caute said, "do you know fucking Tony?"

Francis looked up warily. "He's the bum, the kid you got out by Gardena, watching something."

"Watching somebody, Francis." Caute paced across the living room rug and stopped in front of his workbench. "I do more things than you think about, right? That's why I live in downhome California luxury by the beach, you live in some bikers' swamp up a canyon, right?"

The thing that was different inside, Francis thought, besides Caute's mood, which was horrible, which was much worse than last night even—the thing that was different was that all the doors were open. There were no closed-off rooms today, no showers running somewhere. He could stand by the big leather recliner chair and see into three different rooms, not counting the kitchen-bar behind the living room, not counting the stairs up to the second floor. The nearest room was some kind of study or den, but all he could see of it was an overturned bureau, with drawers sticking out, and the smashed shade of a Tiffany lamp on the floor. Behind Caute, on the sink and kitchen board, there were smashed cups and glasses raked together into a big colored pyramid.

"I want you to tell our friend Tony he's fired, right? You deliver this where I told you, then go out to Gardena and break his dick off and tell him he's fired."

Francis held up the package, read the address, and frowned. A room number at the Bonaventure Hotel. A room and a color code, because the Bonaventure had four different towers and each one was named after a color. If he walked into the Bonaventure Hotel in his leather and his boots, he'd get twenty, maybe thirty feet into the lobby before three sides of beef detached themselves from the walls and helped him downstairs where the house security kept a soundproof bunker in the garage.

"Tony didn't do what I said," Caute told him, walking back across the rug. "He didn't do his fucking job." Now he had started looking, Francis noticed bits of broken glass on the white rug, fresh stains by the sofa and the TV; the rattan furniture looked half shredded from kicks or knives.

"Right. Off with his dick. You want me to deliver this to the Bonaventure, I'm gonna have to buy a suit, get a haircut. They'd like me to also scrape off my tattoo."

"There's a problem?"

"There's hotel cops. Plus, downtown right there is full of regular cops, special cops. Downtown is busy right now. And the Bonaventure is a supernervous hotel. You go in the Bonaventure looking like me, you'll never get this package delivered." He placed it gingerly back on the table and pushed the new briefcase aside with his foot. "You want the cops to open up the Hope Diamond?"

Caute laughed a lot, Francis thought, but rarely at anything that was funny. Now he laughed with his mouth shut and stared at the ocean through the big picture window. The man paid enormously well—but he was definitely getting crazier.

Caute finished his laugh and, just as if he hadn't heard a word, he took a position with his legs spread and his arms folded across his chest and watched two seagulls pick their way across the sand. The tide was way out and the sand was gray, the water was gray, the fog on top of the water was black and gray.

"You know who might do it better?" Francis said.

Caute didn't even look around. He was wearing pajama bottoms and a baggy white sweatshirt with the name of some English college on it and his shoulders were like two stiff boards inside it.

"Kassabian could do it," Francis said.

Caute did something Francis had never seen before. He spat on the picture window, not moving his head or his neck, not tensing or leaning, just doing it like a snake or an animal.

"Can you find him?"

"He comes down to Venice every day."

"Is he totally blind or wired or is he capable of driving downtown and parking his car and finding his way up to a hotel room?" Caute turned around slowly, with his arms still folded. Francis decided to look somewhere else. He had never realized the little beach house had so many rooms. From the outside it looked like a two-story shack, even though it was the last one on the frontage road before the public beach and had a prime location. Twelve, fifteen hundred square feet, beautifully furnished. With the little mother-in-law addition where you came in, it had to be worth at least a million and a half. Caute had to be paying three or four thousand a month in rent. And now he was apparently wrecking it room by room. Wrecking the house, wrecking his lease. You could see suitcases in the front of the den already packed. If you had half a brain, you could see the money train starting to pull out.

"He can drive. He thinks the cops are watching him all day long, so he stays about three-quarters clean."

"Are they?"

Francis shrugged. "You ask me, the cops got other things to do. I never see them. The point is, he can wear a coat and tie and walk right in."

"He could stay and watch the film after he delivered it," Caute said thoughtfully. He shoved a rattan chair out of his way, knocking the cushion onto the rug, and poked at one of the ceramic canisters lined up on his workbench. What Francis thought he smelled was kerosene, but he knew that it wasn't.

"He could do us both a favor," Caute said. He closed the canister and picked up one of the little surgical blades also lined up on the workbench.

"I'll tell him that."

"But you know what's a better idea?" Caute said slowly.

Francis followed his eyes to the table and the package on the table that was film.

"Our Arab friends ordered this film," Caute said,

turning the blade between his fingers. "They still want it. Do you believe that? The most two-faced people on earth, right? Now Kassabian goes to the hotel to deliver it, I don't really know how they like it, I don't see their reaction."

Outside, Francis thought, the wind had changed and you could hear waves crashing against the packed sand, like big fists thumping a door.

"So you find Kassabian now," Caute said, still slowly, still holding the blade and looking at the table. "You take him back to his house—I don't want him here. I'm doing things here. Stoke him up, keep him nodding. And forget the briefcase."

"Forget the briefcase," Francis said.

"Find out if he has a little knapsack in his house, like hikers wear. If he doesn't, stop and buy a new one."

Caute snapped his wrist and the blade sank quivering into the wooden table, an inch from the film.

"Buy a red one," he said.

36

From Rosalie's apartment Renner drove north, skirting downtown, then fell into the rush hour traffic stacked along one of the westbound freeways. He had no idea which freeway. He paid no attention. The cousin's Ford was twenty years old, had a corroded hood the size of a carrier deck, and groaned in protest at fourth gear. He knew lawyers in London. Lawyers in Washington. He could stop at any telephone booth and make a call and pull himself kicking and screaming back into the mainstream. Citizen Renner. A little stressed out, a little boozed up. Love had changed him into an oyster.

Where was she? Hitchhiking to Tijuana? Could he believe it? A picture came unbidden into his mind: Jillian on the side of the highway, hiking her skirt, cars braking to a halt. Who would he kill?

At the nearest on-ramp two black-and-white patrol cars rolled up with their racks flashing and Renner eased back, curved away, dropped down the exit ramp like a giant finned washboard.

Thirty minutes later, still long before noon, long before

a beach town came awake, he drove down a funky little street of crowded wooden houses, roof-high in thin fog, ankle-deep in litter, and entered the flat cracked asphalt square that the city of Venice Beach had slapped on the sand as a parking lot.

An old man sat on the ground, wrapped in burlap, and watched him lock the car. A cop came whirring down the sidewalk on a ten-speed bike. Renner walked past a row of closed shops, an apartment building with no curtains, a surfboard shop. It started with Kassabian and it all came round to Kassabian again. Kassabian had been arrested here, Kassabian had been spotted here, by him, by the cops. One advantage of a memory like flypaper, he remembered numbers, reports, phrases. Who, where, what. Slender, willowy, 'eyes like limpid pools.' He was a little man inside his own head, he thought, peering out through a grillwork of numbers and words. He was an eavesdropper listening to his own brain mumble.

The big brown-shingled coffeehouse-restaurant was open, it was always open, but there were only a few customers yet, bewildered-looking drifters sitting one to a table and staring out at the ocean. Renner walked past the window, found a row of telephones on the outside wall of the next building, and wedged himself into the first partition.

Next to the phone was a newspaper rack, Gretzsky's face glowering up.

When Vicki answered he could hardly distinguish her words over the motor of a passing truck, and then in rapid, excited tones she was repeating the name "Musso" and spelling it out.

"Musso's in San Francisco? Frank Musso?"

"No, he *called* me. He called last night and then this morning, from Los Angeles. How did he get my number? How does he know me?"

"He's a cop."

"He's very worried about you, he's concerned." She paused. He heard a nearly imperceptible intake of breath and saw her in his mind, the long, elegant curve of her neck, the dark-rooted hair spilling into frizzy blond. "He told me you were in trouble," she said, "but it wasn't too bad yet and he thought you'd call here."

"Is that you, Daddy? I'm on the upstairs phone."

"Hi, goosey."

"Are you coming back from L.A.?"

"Does a chicken have lips?"

She laughed and said something to her mother that Renner lost in the motor again. The truck was backing into an alley, turning around. The tourists were marching out of the restaurant in single file, like a line of ducks in blue jackets, padding cautiously onto the sand. At the edge of the water the sunlight made a thin bright line of white just above the gray waves, just below the gray fog. Tijuana? Canada? England?

"A half-day," Vicki said, "every other Thursday. The teachers have it in their contract. We certainly didn't have it when I was in school. She's going to a party and talk to 'dudes.'" Another pause, longer than before, with an edge to it. Halfway up the block a kid was emptying a plastic bucket under a battered neon sign, "Horse-Cow."

"She misses you," Vicki said.

Renner watched the stream of dirty water fall from the bucket to the curb, over the curb, into the gutter, downhill toward the beach. "She has Edward," he said.

He imagined her twisting her head to one side, the way she did; looking away from the telephone toward the wall of antiquarian books or the French doors and the patio and the wide, pretty view of San Francisco Bay five hundred miles away.

"As a matter of fact," Vicki said, "Edward isn't staying here any more."

Renner waited.

"He's left us the apartment till the end of the month, then I think I'm moving out. Casey and I are. I think."

Renner hated the sound of his own voice. "Some new popsy for Edward?"

The pause was shorter, sharper. Cars were moving on the side street, looking for parking; more people were drifting along the sidewalk, slow dreamy groups blown down to the beach.

"You had a right to say that," Vicki told him, so softly that he almost missed it. "And the answer is yes, probably."

The first time they had made love, Renner thought, they were twenty-one years old, in Cambridge, Massachusetts, and dinner had started burning on the stove in her apartment. When the smoke reached the bedroom, Vicki had bobbed up, grinning, laughing, touching him *there* with a long, delicate, teasing finger. "Hold that thought," she had said.

"—this Musso," she was saying on the telephone. "David? I can't hear you. Will you call me? Please."

At the corner of the brown-shingled restaurant, wearing dark sunglasses, walking with a limp, stumbling through the sand and sitting down on a bench, was Keith Kassabian.

Before, he had moved too fast, he hadn't paid attention.

Renner had no idea what he said to Vicki or how he hung up the telephone. He walked in a long, slow circle past the concrete bench and across the sidewalk, thirty feet into the sand. From the point where he stopped he could see the back of Keith Kassabian's head, his half-dollar of bald spot, his white sleeves wing-spread on the top of the bench.

A doper, the police reports said, but just at this moment he seemed to be sober, sober and morose. Directly in front of the bench the coffeehouse jutted onto the sidewalk in the form of an octagonal bay window. In the slanted panes of glass he could see a dozen images of Kassabian's long horsey face staring straight ahead; after a moment he lifted one arm from the bench and studied his watch.

Renner took off his rumpled madras jacket and dropped it in a trash basket. Good riddance again, as Rosalie would have said. He should have done it hours ago. If you wanted to stay unnoticed, there was no point in looking like a Christmas tree planted in the sand. He walked farther to his left, making his circle, keeping his reflection out of the glass.

Kassabian would have come in a car—he lived in

Pasadena, San Marino, somewhere—and parking along
the side streets by the beach was limited to residents with
permits. Renner stopped in the foggy shadow of a palm
tree and glanced left toward the public parking lot. There
were a dozen cars in it now, and most of them were like
his, older American models, rusted, sagging, discouraged.
Yuppies went to Marina del Rey; families with money
went to Santa Monica. Cops and robbers came to Venice.
The only car in the lot that would belong to Kassabian was
a racing-blue Mazda, right by the gate, pointing up the
street, ready to go.

When he reached the sidewalk again, he bought a cup of
coffee from a takeout window and walked it carefully back
to his car. Then he turned it around and parked three slots
behind the Mazda and waited.

In thirty minutes, just as one part of his mind had
expected all along, the biker who had mugged him strolled
up to Kassabian and jerked his head.

Years ago Musso had visited a con in Atascadero, where
the state of California had built one of its unlovelier prison
facilities.

Musso lit a cigar and leaned against the door of Renner's
old office. Halfway down the corridor Billy Finley was
arguing loudly with a man in the navy blue uniform of the
Federal Protective Services.

Facility, Musso thought. The LAPD now had a deputy
administrator for facilities—in the army, in prison, anywhere normal people used English, a facility was what you
flushed when you were through with it. Across from the
Parker Center now there was a Security Pacific "banking
facility"—a bank? Echeverria had wanted to know.

Musso inhaled smoke and watched Billy Finley win the
argument. The FPS man walked away with a snap of his
head and a rolling, pissed-off macho gait that said somebody downstairs was going to listen to the whole thing all
over again, blow by blow. The con in Atascadero had shot
a gas station attendant during a robbery, then killed a CHP
who tried to stop him. When Musso had finally arrested
him, he was in the basement of a church off Normandie

Avenue, weeping like a loon. At Atascadero the guy kept busy every night writing letters of advice to his five children. They were solemn, repentant, born-again, damn nice letters—he showed Musso the copies he kept in his cell, filed by date in a dozen shoe boxes under his bunk. But there was no shoe box full of answers, because none of the five kids could read or write.

"You going to stand there and show off your boots, Musso, and let me do all the work?" Finley had on his Hoover-era FBI uniform, a lightweight blue suit, a white plain collar shirt, a green tie covered with jumping fish, but because of his potbelly he couldn't button the suit jacket and you could see his walkie-talkie looped on one hip and on the other his nonsnag Commanche holster. "Or are you going to let me have one of your fine twenty-cent cigars?"

The reason he had thought of the con in Atascadero, Musso decided, was that there was just about the same amount of communication going on here. "I'm in disguise," he said. "Camouflage. I'm laying down a smoke-screen. You're not supposed to notice me."

"Oh but you're one of the players," Finley said, grinning, clipping the ends of his words in his high east-coast English voice. "You're the liaison man. You heard the deputy chief say so. We're a team. This was his office?"

He squeezed past and entered the little cubicle. Musso turned like a door on its hinges to watch him. "Renner used it for two weeks, then the powers-that-be kicked him out."

"No books." Finley prowled to the filing cabinet at the far end of the desk and tugged at a drawer. "Locked." He lifted the shade on the window. "You know what Renner had on his desk in London? Poetry." He picked up a framed photograph that had been placed by the telephone, a woman and a young girl standing beside a tour boat on a river. "You like him?"

"I like him all right," Musso said.

"He's a strange guy to be a cop."

"He's not a cop."

"I went downstairs after our meeting this morning,"

Finley said, putting the photograph down again. "Gave my whole spiel all over to the BAFT. Then I read my London cables. Absolutely reliable sources, everything confirmed. This man's absolutely targeted one of your federal facilities downtown, one of the six biggies—probably a computer room, a computer auxiliary. Absolutely first-class information."

"Simon Caute," Musso said and put out his cigar.

Finley opened a notebook on the desk, turned a page, closed it. "As soon as we saw Huntsville's report, we called you, the very minute. Simon Caute is major, serious talent."

"You already know everything, what do you need me?" Musso growled. He looked down at their two protruding bellies; side by side, they looked like a human barbell. "You're having your conferences, your quality time with the deputy chief. The buildings are all on alert."

"Gretzsky." Finley started to follow him down the hall. "Gretzsky, for one thing. Your bomb squad colleague Gretzsky comes up to me twenty minutes ago, we're on the sixth floor, and he shoves his big face in mine—and he's big, he's enough to hunt—and he says do I want to go to Colorado Boulevard with him."

"And you say?"

"I say, 'Your logo or mine?'"

Musso grunted and stopped to look in the detective squad room, where Vincent Brodie was standing under the television again. Renner drank. Brodie let the television suck his brains out. Where the hell was Renner?

"I tell him, hold a meeting to decide on a meeting."

Musso moved down the hall again, away from him. They had fucked up the preparations so completely—the logo Finley meant was the police department Great Seal. If the FBI or the Fed Protective or the Bureau of Alcohol, Tobacco, and Firearms gave the press conference, any of them, they did it in front of their own logo, they showed the news film to the budget committee in Congress, they drowned in dollars. If L.A. gave the press conference, it was in front of *their* seal and they showed the film to *their* committees. And if Gretzsky did it, it was in front of a sign that said bomb squad and nobody, not even the deputy chief would get near the cameras. One big happy self-destructing family.

"Meanwhile your friend noble Renner," Finley said, following him again. "Your friend noble Renner is still at large."

"Pussy-whipped," Musso said, thinking if he were crude enough Finley would go away in disgust.

"Low priority, right? Nobody's even bothering to look for him? Take it easy on the stressed-out hero?"

"You people kind of reset priority," Musso said. What kind of point was Finley trying to make this time? Where was his motor-mouth going? "A bomb's going to blow up downtown in the next two days, you absolutely guarantee it."

"He'll be back in England in a week," Finley said. They were forced aside for a moment, into a recess bounded by old cabinets and benches, while a maid pushed a coffee trolley by. "Noble Renner's stuck on England—the man thinks England's the Golden Age."

Musso looked down on him with distaste and thought no, no chance at all Renner would split for England. Renner would stay in Los Angeles like everybody else in the world, as long as the bomber was here and breathing. Renner's obsession was all for the bomber.

"Renner," Finley was saying, shaking his head, "Renner and the actress. You want a play Renner and the girl should act in, try *Troilus and Cressida,* right? And remind me to tell you about his wife."

Musso hunched his shoulders like a fullback and bumped back into the corridor, toward the elevators, and Finley stepped in front of him, blocking him, and came to his point at last. "Gretzsky still says we can't touch the fucking bomb."

"You can't."

"We want that bomb. When it comes."

"The law says only a PD bomb squad can touch an unexploded device. No federales."

"We want that bomb and that evidence."

Musso walked around him.

"We want that evidence in *our* lab," Finley said, grabbing his sleeve. "Not in some L.A. cinder block outhouse halfway to the San Fernando Valley. You know what we're talking about? We're talking about reciprocity. You know how much we've already given you?" Musso pushed him aside with one arm and lumbered toward the elevators. "What about the factory worker bomb, the wig we found in the girl's apartment, the goddamn British dynamite she smuggled in?" Finley jig-stepped alongside him, bouncing. "She's an accessory—we did half your work!"

At the elevators Musso timed it just right. Finley was still talking, leaning his head in, growing red-faced, purple-veined. Musso shook him off and stepped all the way to the back before turning around to face him.

Renner was right. Renner was so obsessive and smart he was bound to be right, he was bound to be out of step with bureaucrats like Finley, cretins like Gretzsky. The guy was a joker. The guy bombed people—he couldn't care less about a computer or a federal building, downtown, uptown, anywhere. You could stay here, knee-deep in invisible bullshit, or you could act out a little, like Renner.

"Are you leaving, Musso? Are you walking on this? You're liaison-in-charge." Finley was incredulous. He stood in the hall, in front of the elevator, his mouth wide open, holding his potbelly between his hands like a man about to shoot a basket.

As the doors slid shut Musso lifted his middle finger.

37

Kassabian drove away in the Mazda.

Renner hunched forward, tensed over the wheel.

In another moment the biker appeared, trailing him, driving a silver-white Mercedes—where did a biker get a Mercedes?—that must have been parked illegally up one of the side streets, off the beach.

Renner jammed into gear and spun to the left. If they split—?

But they didn't split. They drove as a team, in tandem, straight along Ocean Avenue, decorous as grandmothers, under the speed limit, coasting until they reached the freeway. Then the Mercedes pulled sharply in front, taking charge, and Kassabian had to wobble and cling to its bumper, weaving from lane to lane like a drunk. At the first big curve Renner pushed the Ford hard enough to draw alongside him. Behind the wheel Kassabian was white-faced, unshaven, a sick calf; his mouth half open, he glanced to his left straight into the Ford and registered nothing.

Renner fell back slowly, letting his mind drift, juggle. A white Mercedes 300SE—a toothy, big-snouted, intimidating car, built for power trips. Where did a biker come up with a car like that?

He changed lanes and glanced at his watch. You're turning into a cop, Musso had said. Nobody looks at their watch as often as cops. Hookers do, Echeverria had sneered. Renner glanced at his watch again—it all came back to Kassabian and it didn't. How did a guy like Kassabian find a Simon Caute in the first place, a *bomber*—much less hire him to blow up his store?

They slowed at a curve, brake lights coming on in all directions. Change perspective, Renner thought. Take the other point of view. If you set up as a contract bomber, you didn't buy an ad in the paper. You would want a middleman, a sales rep, somebody who could spread the word where it counted and size up the clients and take the orders. Because bombers by nature like insulation, privacy. They like to keep their labs or workshops out of sight, where nobody can smell what's brewing and casually walk up to borrow a pound of plastic. By nature a bomber is manipulative and secret, a genius at staying out of sight.

Where would Kassabian go? In any big American city if you wanted to find a mugger for your boss, a gas-can tosser for your business, a kneecap man for whoever—in any American city there would be a district. In Los Angeles everybody knew where it was. In Los Angeles you would sit down in a bar in the south-central, the Pico-Union section, with a Mexican, a gang member, a black brother. If you wanted somebody safer—

Renner swerved to pull himself out of the Mercedes's mirror. They were climbing east over the dry bed of the Los Angeles river, a vast concrete gutter the width of a football field, that filled only in the winter when hundreds of miles away, far out of sight, the rains gathered on the mountains.

Caute stayed miles away, out of sight. Kassabian was a rabbit, a calf, a doper. Kassabian would never go into east

L.A. or Watts or Pico-Union. He was middle-class, milk-fed, media-formed. He would choose the illusion of menace, the shabby swagger of a beachfront town with a Holiday Inn, a freeway, lifelines back to the city. If you wanted somebody sharper and safer—

You might ask a tame biker.

The freeway unrolled like a scroll. In front of him downtown Los Angeles appeared, glass stalks rising out of brown smog, a bed of brown light. The Ford was no match for the Mercedes or the Mazda if traffic really opened. When the exit ramps suddenly peeled away to the right, Renner was half a mile out of position, fighting fourth gear.

At the Wilshire exit he lost them.

At Third and Cinnabar he saw them again, then lost them for good.

Twenty minutes later, a record for downtown to Pasadena at midday, a record anytime, Francis thought, he pulled into Kassabian's condo parking lot and waited for the kid to walk over.

"The guy's not mad?" Kassabian said when he reached the car window. The two hundredth time.

"Hand me the knapsack."

"He's not mad?"

"He's worried," Francis said. "All the cops, all the shit, he wants to see if you can do him a simple favor, a job." Francis balanced the knapsack between his belly and the steering wheel. He opened it and lifted out the packages one at a time, three videocassettes in dark brown plastic boxes, each one sealed with four strips of shipping tape. He turned them over in his hands, checking each seal, then dropped them in and closed the knapsack again.

"Just a minute." Kassabian watched silently while he picked up the electronic garage door opener from the seat beside him and put it in his jacket pocket.

"Now show me your goddamn place."

They wound through a complex of carports and stairways and little enclosed yards the size of henhouses, jammed with barbecue grills and bicycle wheels, until just past the pool Kassabian said something squeaky and high-pitched and they went up a flight of outside stairs to his apartment.

Inside, before he said a word, Francis walked to each window and looked out. Cars. Tennis courts. A kidney-shaped swimming pool, a woman in a two-piece bathing suit, oiling her thighs, reading a book.

"You can have these," Francis said. "The guy knows you're under pressure." Kassabian held the two little plastic pill bags in his palm and looked up, good dog, knowing there was more. "And you can have two beers, that's all. Whatever you want to eat."

"Then we leave?"

He lifted his face to the kid, making his face all stone, knowing the kid was afraid of stone faces, stone disapproving faces. "Then we sit here and watch the swimming pool and the carport and the goddamn color TV and we leave for the place at midnight, not a minute before."

"To deliver the film."

"To sit at the table and see if they want the film," Francis said. "These are Arabs. They like kinky stuff. The guy makes money on the side this way sometimes. He gives them a sample, maybe they buy more, maybe they don't. He sells but he doesn't carry himself."

The kid nodded as if he'd said something that made sense. Francis stared at him, then turned and walked across the expensive carpet, nicer even than Caute's, thicker, softer. Like walking on some person, he thought. Like walking on layers of soft white fat.

"You've been in the coffeehouse a thousand times," he said, sitting down in a chair. "Nobody's gonna look twice."

"And he gives me a signal."

"*If* he wants the extra film. Otherwise, sit. Wait."

"I need to see him—you don't know. My lawyer says—"

"You do this," Francis said, turning on the television, "you can see him. I promise."

When the kid had snorted the first bag and gone back into his bedroom, Francis stood up and went into the kitchen to find the extension phone. The "guy" would pay extra to hear this, he thought, and he rehearsed it in his mind before he dialed, thinking how to say it—Caute was so jumpy, crazy, *bitchy*; you wanted to say it right, to jar the dollar bills loose.

Caute picked up at the first ring and Francis waited three beats before he said, "Who do you think I saw on Venice Beach watching the kid?"

Renner punched the heel of his hand against the steering wheel twice and then pushed the door open with his knee. In the full sun he swayed for an instant, feeling the heat and smelling the woozy, chemical-loaded air. Exxon self-serve. Made-up words, saying nothing at all in English. He slipped on his sunglasses and hurried across the pavement, past the pumps, toward a vandalized phone booth, which was tilting at an angle and stuck in the asphalt like a sinking boat. Neon palms, neon sky.

"Yo," Rosalie Garbutt answered.

"Rosalie."

She hesitated no more than an instant, then punched buttons, faded into static and returned.

"Colonel, I can't talk."

"Does that computer you drive keep a record of car licenses and home addresses?"

"You're not at a lawyer's, are you?"

"I'm downtown, in a booth."

"I can see where you are, right on this screen. You crazy to be so close. You sound sick. Are you all right?"

Renner pinched the bridge of his nose, squinted at his watch.

"You drank all that vodka. You didn't eat a *thing* this morning."

"I need this license," Renner said. He closed his eyes and recited the Mercedes's number from memory. It was true. His veins and arteries were dry beds, wide as the Los Angeles river; he depended on storms of vodka, far away in the mountains. When had he eaten last? When had he drunk anything except vodka and coffee? In his trousers pocket his fingers closed on the little photovoltaic cell.

"You don't *ever* give up," Rosalie grumbled. "It's going to take me an hour at least to get this license. You call me back at four."

38

WHEN JILLIAN OPENED THE DOOR CAUTE WAS PUTTING THE telephone down.

She dropped the key in her purse and snapped it shut. Then tossed her head as if she belonged, as if she hadn't been out all day in the worst city in the world, looking for help, finding nothing. Caute slid his hands into his back trousers pockets and watched as she pushed the door closed and walked down the hallway toward him, careful not to wobble, careful not to show fear, not to show pain, not to show any emotion at all that he could turn against her.

As always, she thought, one part of her mind was rising away from the present moment, circling at a distance as if to evaluate her performance. She reached the couch in the middle of the living room and dropped her purse carelessly onto it. In England actors always seem to collect in families—not in America, but in England they do; it goes with the national personalities, somebody had told her. American actors are loners, solitaries; English actors live in groups, work in groups, travel in groups. Outside of groups they hardly exist.

Caute pushed an overturned chair out of the way and folded his arms on his chest, in front of the big picture window, more pleased with himself than she could explain.

"The return," he said, "of the prodigal fucking princess."

"I wrote you a note."

"Hey, I get notes from all over. Lists, notes, letters, phone calls. You didn't like him, right? No big bang beat."

"I need money."

"Right."

"Because I need to leave." Her voice sounded too shrill, starting to climb. She fumbled in her macintosh pocket for cigarettes. "We *both* need to leave, before the city police—"

"And the FBI and the CIA and all the tribes of Shem—right. Time to go." He walked around the couch, keeping his arms folded, staring at her. "You change plans, I change plans," he said. "For instance, if I get a phone call, maybe everything changes."

Her pocket was loaded with junk—bus stubs, more keys, tissues, cough drops because of the smog and her throat. She found the cigarettes and the lighter.

"How about," Caute said, "how about I get the money, Jill-Jill-Jilly, and we leave together?"

"No."

"When the bank opens at nine. Drive right to Canada, fly straight to the merry isle."

She raised her lighter in hands that wouldn't hold still and watched him pace. He was tense but not angry, not at all what she'd expected, prowling like a cat in his Levis and Oxford sweatshirt, smirking, self-satisfied. Something had happened, she told herself; something was about to happen. He was a maniac and a genius and she was back again, handcuffed, drowning.

She exhaled a ragged breath and made him vanish in a puff of smoke. Where else could she go? Who else would have her?

"It's a nice plan," Caute said. He stopped by the door to the patio and grinned. Then he pulled the string that ran the big curtains and they started to close in quick, jerky

movements, so that the gray ocean behind the window
seemed to jump and somersault backwards. In the pale
half-darkness of the room she saw him step over litter,
broken china, a broken chair leg on the carpet. When he
reached her he stopped and spread his legs apart and
grabbed the lapels of her coat.

Because of her life, Jillian thought. Because of her
cracked, vulnerable life. His hands roamed from her face to
her neck. She felt their heat and smelled the faint scent of
dangerous chemicals that went with him. His mouth was
thin, his lips scissored her skin.

"Stop."

He pinched her nipples through the thin cloth of her
dress, lifted her dress. "Jack and Jill," he said, pressing her
hips to his.

"Stop it."

"You made me angry, Jill-Jilly, *furious*." His fingers
were skates, blades, sliding higher. Against her will her
thighs parted, her lips parted.

"I wrecked half the house when I found your note,"
Caute said. "Look—like a fucking bomb hit it. But I
should have known." He wrenched her head back. She
tasted blood in her mouth, salt in her mouth. "Was he
better than me? Was he *good*?"

She let him walk her backwards to the edge of the couch
and then sit down. On the worktable by the curtained
windows he was making something out of long pieces of
wire, tapes, a box, two flashlight batteries. When she
looked up he was standing over her, unbuttoning his shirt
with one hand, holding in the other a black eyeless sleep
mask, a black mask exactly like Renner's.

"Right, this is his," Caute said, dangling it, grinning
again. "I stole it. I went to his motel room last night and
walked right past the sleeping cops and stole it. Now
everybody gets to be an actor."

"I'm leaving. I'm going back to England alone—if he
doesn't kill you, the police will, the Arabs will."

He sank to his knees, holding the mask by the string and
trailing it slowly down her belly. "Was he big? Bigger?
Biggest? How many times did he do it?" His voice was

insinuating, horrible. He crawled over her whispering. He put on the mask and lowered his face to hers, a black ghost filling her vision, and his voice went hypnotically on and on—was Renner long? thick? as thick as *this*?

She flung his hand away. "He *hates* you."

He smiled and shook his head under the mask.

"He loves me," Caute said.

Then he unsnapped the mask from his own face and, straddling her, leaned forward to fasten it on her. For a moment she twisted violently away, then his weight carried her down and the mask stuck and she lay on her back in the darkness, breathing loudly and hearing the rustle of cloth like wings. His voice began again in her ear, her invisible, cankering lover. The best actress feels nothing, she thought; is empty. His thumb pressed her hipbones and dug. His fingers lifted her buttocks and pushed her legs. Then from stomach to throat, unseen, his hands began to squeeze and touch. Her breasts were traitors, stiffening to the very tips. She was wet, dissolving. Tears rolled under the mask and his tongue carried them away. He drove her head back and bent her wrists until she cried out and he exploded with a huge moan, but to please herself she kept moving long after he had finished. Inside the mask her eyes were open and she saw the light that appears when light goes away, false light, she told herself, gripping him harder, lifting—lies of the mind. Jill came tumbling after.

39

"You know what David Renner was famous for in England?" Caute asked.

Through the peephole in the door he watched Francis come back from locking the Mercedes and let himself into the little front grandmother addition, just as they'd planned. If he opened the door and stepped outside he'd be able to see Kassabian sitting in his piece-of-tin Mazda under the streetlight, doped out as promised, semi-California-conscious, waiting to help out the "guy." Five more minutes.

"Fantastic bomb." He looked at his watch again. Twelve-thirty-two. "Collapsing circuits. You know about circuits?"

Jillian didn't raise her head.

Always the same, he thought, leaving the door, starting to pace the room again. Even slumped like a rag doll on the couch and wrapped up in her grubby raincoat she was amazing. To a certain type of susceptible man she would be like—like what? Like catnip? Like a blowtorch? Caute ran his fingers up the back of her neck and she shook him away. He stared down for a moment, then crossed the carpet to his worktable. The surgical blades were lined up in a row, six little silver minnows taking a nap. He picked up a coil of wire and cut it in half with the longest blade.

"So. Did he tell you you were beautiful?"

"Yes." Sullen. Pissed.

"Surefire. Then he takes you home to look at his etchings."

"I'm leaving," Jillian said. "I'm not going to wait." But she made no move to go, and Caute felt her eyes on him as he stood at the table. What was it about sex between them? Like a drug, like an addiction. He could just walk away from any other woman he'd ever met; but here they still were, him working, her watching—domestic as Dagwood, domestic as kids. Would she be so hot if he, for instance, were a carpenter, if he built hatracks instead of bombs?

"So he said you were beautiful, right? He'd run away with you, right? He'd make it all OK, every little thing stop hurting?"

"He has a wife. He's still married."

"Hey, I looked into that. His wife left him. Ran away with some college professor in San Francisco. His family— splat."

Jillian looked at the picture window and the ocean, the carpet of bright starlight floating on top of the black water.

"So he said you have great tits, good legs, nice hair, right?" His voice sounded good, Caute thought, mocking, cool, unconcerned. He looked at his watch. He could keep the edge out of his voice whenever he wanted to, he could make it sound however he liked. When you came right down to it, he thought, feeling himself beginning to smile, he was a better actor than she was.

"He said I was like light to him, in fact, if you really want to know. He said I was like a tide of light."

The voice was still lethargic, but there was a rising note of defiance that interested him. Caute put down the coil of electrical wires. He cocked his head at her. "'Like light'? Mama. What does that mean?"

"He's not like you. He doesn't talk like you. And he's still married, he's married for good."

"What did he say about me?"

She tossed her head and said nothing.

"Did he say I was wicked?" Caute asked. He rationed himself one more look at the watch. "Meganasty? Hey. Did he say I was 'brilliant'?—the L.A. word, the yuppie word. 'Brilliant.'"

She finished her wine with a jerky motion of the wrist and stood up without answering.

"You know, the funny thing is," Caute said, still keeping his voice cool and unconcerned, but feeling it slip away a little. A voice was a mask, his mask was slipping down over his eyes. "The funny thing is, I had three photovoltaic cells I showed you—right here on this table, in this box, special imported goods. Now I've only got two."

"I'm leaving," Jillian said. She glanced around the room, looking for something.

"Somebody else might think a person took the little bugger to Renner, said 'Here, make a nice bomb for me, stuff it up Caute's kazoo.'" He pinched one of the tiny cells between his thumb and forefinger and held it up to cast a shadow on her face. "'Like light.' I really like that."

Jillian pulled her purse from under a cushion on the floor, next to one of the shattered chairs, in a hurry now.

"The black's name is Rosalie Garbutt, right? She works the old nine one one?"

"I'm not telling you anything else. I'm leaving."

"No."

It was twelve-forty-five. Caute spread his hands wide on the worktable, pressed an electric button, and leaned back. "If you went out," he said, "and the L.A. cops picked you up and asked you questions, where would that put me?"

"I'm leaving."

He felt his grin detaching itself from his face, floating lopsided in the air like a kite. He picked up the long surgical blade again. It was fine enough and sharp enough to slice paper edgewise. He held it straight out, pressed lightly against the ball of his thumb, like a painter studying a model. The blade was a line of silver light vertical between her eyes, her breasts, her hips, down, down. If he closed one eye and squinted, the optical illusion cut her in two, two Jillians, one for each of them. King Solomon Caute. Where had he read that men who shared the same woman were queer for each other? Bullshit, of course.

The front door opened and Francis came in, holding a rope taut between his fists. Jillian wavered on the end of the blade.

"This is Francis," Caute said. He looked at his watch and stood up and nodded to Francis. "You can't leave," he said.

Collapsing circuits.

Caute shifted in the narrow little bucket seat and watched Francis turn down the brightly-lit street that led to the beach. In the backseat of the Mazda, six inches behind him, Kassabian was folded up like a yardstick and trying pathetically not to talk to him, trying to follow orders.

A brilliant bomb. Hostage dummy, handcuffs, briefcase with a little one-gram charge of Semtex because the Brits like to train realistic. Two interlocking collapsing circuits connected to a blasting cap. Break the positive relay, the negative relay switches on instantly, and vice versa; it goes off instantaneously, in a microsecond, fuse time zero. Renner the great.

"Stop here."

Francis pulled to the curb and Caute levered himself carefully out of the tiny car, putting the knapsack back on the seat. Then he watched as they drove on, downhill, toward the coffeehouse.

How do you know he'll come? Francis had asked when they were tying up the girl. Stupid Francis. Good riddance, Francis. Because he saw the car, because he saw the goddamn license plate. It's leased, Francis said, he can't get your address from the license. He's smarter than you are, Francis. Because I made a little phone call, too. *Because he'll do exactly what I would do.*

Caute walked down the rough pavement under the streetlights, stepping over puddles, breathing the chilly wet air, making sure they had time to go in ahead of him, sit down, order their coffee.

At the Horse-Cow with its bright flashing sign he paused and looked at his watch. He had the tethered lamb. He had the time. So where could he put the trap? Where could he put the fucking Semtex? On her dress? Between her legs? To disarm it Renner would have to reach up her legs, up her skirt—Caute jammed his right fist into the pocket of his anorak and stared straight ahead. Concrete path. Sand. Suicidal waves throwing themselves at the beach, exploding. Beyond them, in the deep California night, the bog-black ocean. Put it where the sun don't shine.

Like light.

He turned and looked into the coffeehouse, where he could see the Arabs sitting by a window. The Arabs were history. Ten minutes from now the Arabs will be with their fathers. But for Renner, for the second bomb, he had to make a joke of it, something *clever*.

From his other pocket he pulled the length of spliced wire and the two supertiny photovoltaic cells. If he could build a collapsing circuit like the one that Renner had made. But *better*. Without using batteries for power. Make *him* pull the trigger. He watched the waves break along the sand. The two cells glittered in his dark palm like stars scooped up out of the water. You can reverse a photocell, he thought. It can go off either when light strikes it *or* when light is removed from it.

Light to light, dark to dark.

A collapsing circuit of light.

It was way too bright in the coffeehouse. Caute stopped at the door and blinked, looking left, right, feeling his eyes begin to water. Even at one-thirty in the morning the place was half full, the only café still open in Venice Beach where the underage bums, kids, hippies could congregate. He smelled coarse cigarette smoke, winced at the jukebox blaring something from the sound track of Armageddon.

Through the windows, under the palm trees on the sand, you could see the homeless lying rolled up in their bags.

There were two Arabs. Fadhil and Fadhil junior, both of them dressed in the silver windbreakers that were this week's L.A. fashion, hunched over bottles of Coke at a big round wooden table. They watched all the way as he went to the counter and got his own coffee. No waitress after midnight, he remembered. Who would work in a toilet like this late at night?

Did he have time? he thought as he sat down. Francis was gone, back to the car. Kassabian was sitting at a table not twenty feet away, smelling the back of his hand. *Did he have time not to?*

"You kept us waiting."

"I'm right on fucking time." He put the tape box down in the middle of the table and watched as they stiffened and looked around the room. Nobody gave them a second glance. The jukebox crashed and thundered to a halt, the end of the world in A flat, and in the sudden silence his voice started out too loud and he had to adjust almost at once.

"Colin's gone home, right? You scared him off?"

"Colin has backed away. The project is canceled." Fadhil was the older of the two, handsomer, the definite spokesman. The other one was thinner, lighter-skinned, constantly craning his neck to see behind him, nervous as a cat.

"Because of the heat," Caute said. They frowned at each other. "The federal cops," he said, "the wonderful FBI." They nodded slowly. "You speak French?" he asked the younger one. He looked at Fadhil, then nodded all by himself. "*C'est la vie sportive*, right?" Caute said. "Colin baby's gone and you guys are a team, family. Is this your brother?"

"We are together," Fadhil said carefully.

"You're together and I'm not and I still need money. You're in the market, that's what you told me?" He pointed at the tape box. "A full hour of her. You take the tape home, watch it for free. If you still want her, call me the same way I told you. The price is five thousand dollars for a night."

"Don't be absurd," Fadhil said.

"Take the tape. Call me."

Fadhil pushed the box delicately back toward him, two inches over the slick, gunk-covered table. Caute's palms were slippery with sweat. Under the anorak his armpits were soaking wet. Despite himself he looked at his watch.

"We don't take anything home from you, Mr. Caute, until we know what it is. You are a too ingenious man."

Caute looked from one face to the other. Somebody started the jukebox again, Bon Jovi this time. He wiped his palms on his trousers and picked up the box. Then he opened it and pulled out the videocassette. He jammed one finger in and spun a loop of tape free, showing them the transparent plastic, the absolutely ordinary box. "OK?"

"We don't want tape," Fadhil said. "We can make our own tape. We want to see the girl in person."

Caute hesitated, held the tape and the box in the air, one in each hand, and looked back and forth as if he were snookered. Brilliant. Laurence fucking Olivier.

"Did you bring her?" Fadhil said.

He snapped the tape back in the box and slipped it under his anorak. "She's out in my car."

The younger one stirred and said something in Arabic and Caute put out his hand, palm up. "You don't trust me, Fadhil baby, I don't trust you. I'll bring her in. Maybe I'll let her sit down at the table. If you're nice boys she can run her little fingers in and out of your fly, play with your mouse. Then we're gonna talk five thousand dollars."

He stood up and jerked down his anorak.

Why wait? Why look back? There was nothing else to see. He walked stiffly between the tables, past the jukebox, past Kassabian. The kid faced the other way, just as he was supposed to, and drew the knapsack in with his feet.

Outside the door Caute stopped, letting them see his back. Then he strode off up the street, moving deliberately, not running, going ten feet, twenty feet before he started grinning. On the other side of the street there was a row of pay telephones, an alley, the Horse-Cow. The

Mazda was pulled around, pointing up the street. He opened the passenger door and slid in. Francis shoved the car into first gear. Caute took a deep breath. Smiled. Pressed the garage door opener.

40

IN THE DELIBERATE, HALF–TRANCE–LIKE MOVEMENTS HE USED TO take apart a bomb Renner shook the last bits of ammonium nitrate into his palm and forced his hands to funnel them into the plastic tube on his lap. What was it called? A biker's bottle. Casey had showed him one in San Francisco a lifetime ago—you filled it with water or juice and strapped it to your waist for a long-distance ride, or you filled it with homemade explosives and stuffed an improvised blasting cap in it, a wire, a photovoltaic cell.

He held up the cell and watched it glint under the streetlight. Polish or East German manufacture, ultrahigh-tech. Virtually unknown in this country. He had seen them coming out in London just before he left, cells so sensitive that they could generate blasting power with less than a candle-foot of illumination falling on them. Their only disadvantage was a three-second delay in building up energy, but who could act in three seconds of fuse time? Who would know where to reach? The IRA had placed one in a telephone switchboard in Wolverhampton outside

London and blasted a two-story building into eternity. Call the selected number and let the bulb go on. Or wait until someone else called it at random. Either way, the light went on, the cell warmed, the circuit ignited.

The steering wheel got in his way. He slid to his right on the bench that served the old Ford as a front seat and picked up the binoculars on the dashboard. "Night-scopers," bought at eight o'clock that evening, right out of the Santa Monica Sears showroom. Perfect for voyeurs and Green Berets and hunters with insomnia.

Half a mile away, at the other end of the little state park, through low brambly bushes, he could see Caute's clapboard beach house. No lights. The Mercedes still parked by the front door, no other car in sight. He'd arrived at two, just past two, after half a night of sitting and staring at the ocean, dying by inches inside, and the house had been just that way for more than an hour.

Half a mile away and out of reach.

They'd never catch him. Finley said it. Jillian said it. Incompetent police, squabbling bureaucrats—how would they come close? They would catch *her* first.

Renner replaced the binoculars on the dashboard. With the same deliberate movements as before he attached one thin wire to the L-shaped bottom of the cell and left the other end dangling while he added two ounces of vodka to the ammonium nitrate.

If you could disarm a bomb you could build one. You could walk into any drugstore in America and come out with the chemicals. Walk into True Value Hardware and come out primed to explode. His mind was as hard as a stone, he thought, quartz hard, fused into decision.

He pushed the car door open and stepped out onto the parking lot and caught one last glimpse of his face before the car door closed and carried it away. The truth was, he had imagined Caute for so long, he had brought him to life in some sense. He had willed him into focus. He had made him up in the dark workshop of his own bomb-obsessive self.

If you could make him up, you could destroy him.

■

From the bluff at the end of the parking lot he was able to see much more than he could from the car. South lay the condominiums and streetlights of Santa Monica, crowding down to the water's edge, then a long snake of moving lights crawling over the horizon toward Los Angeles. When he faced north the lights disappeared, replaced by the dark strip of undeveloped state park. On the right the park was bordered by widely spaced street lamps, on the left by the curving black-and-white collar of the beach, then the endless black body of the ocean. At the top of the strip the lights began again, a straight row of beachfront houses unbroken as far north as Malibu.

Renner felt in the pocket of his new jacket—the ammonium nitrate had cost eleven dollars at a garden supply store on Wilshire, the wires, extra chemicals, and crimping pliers another thirty. The binoculars he had charged to Visa—still his and Vicki's Visa—and also the jacket, in order to look presentable to the Sheffield Auto Leasing Company, who knew Caute's address and didn't know it. The little six-pack of vodka he had bought with cash.

Wooden steps led down to the flat sand.

Renner took them two at a time and then turned north, walking with his arms out, his flashlight on. Even then, even at almost three in the morning there were people on the beach. Against the bluff to his right, in the shadows, he could see forms moving gently. Between waves, over the hiss of the fading surf, he could hear somebody's boom box playing music. He veered to the left, closer to the water, and walked through shoulder-high patches of wet gray fog that left him with nothing to see for yards at a time, only the squelching sound of his shoes on sand and the boom box of the surf to hear.

He drove his heels into the sand and pushed through the fog into clear air again. Out of nowhere a big dog came scrambling' toward him and then skidded away on two legs, spraying sand and running toward somebody's whistle. Renner looked at his watch.

She was gone by now. Intuition over intelligence, just as Finley had said. The truth was, she was gone to England,

gone out of his life. You couldn't misread her character—
you couldn't misread the fear in her voice or the hate. By
now she was halfway to England—there was nobody left
but Caute. Caute and his biker.

He looked at his watch again. He hadn't seen a goddamn
thing on the dial.

Abruptly he reached the border of the park. More
wooden stairs climbed fifty or sixty feet up the sloping
bluff to a cyclone fence. And just to the left of the fence, on
the rim of the bluff, was the parking space for the first of
the beachfront houses.

If you were two selves, he thought, one self was turning
around, inside, toward Vicki, but the other was leading
him up the stairs, toward the houses. His hand felt for the
railing. A collapsing circuit of selves.

The truth was—he paused on the first step. How many
times had he said that to himself today? *The truth was,* love
was a screen for hate. Jillian was a screen for Caute.

Behind her face, in his mind's eye he saw Caute's face.

Behind Caute's face he looked into a mirror.

At the top of the steps he found the Mercedes parked by
itself in an asphalt turnaround twenty yards from the
house.

He crept forward in the dim glow of the street lamp and
checked the windows of the car for burglar alarm tape; he
found none. Confident Caute. In front of the hood he
pulled the bomb tool out of his right pocket. Carefully,
silently, he levered the hood latch with the flat edge of the
tool and lifted the hood until he could reach in and
disconnect the battery. Then he lowered the hood and
crept to the driver's door.

All Mercedeses have a courtesy light under the right-
hand side of the dashboard. It goes on when you open any
door, at the same time as the overhead interior light.
Renner jimmied the door lock with the flat edge again and
opened it. No light. No battery, no light. He slipped into
the driver's seat and began to take out the biker's bottle, the
sets of wires, the other tools, and finally the photovoltaic
cell.

He looked at his watch. Four o'clock. June twenty-first, the longest day of the year. Except for an occasional porchlight and the retreating line of street lamps, he could see only dark, sleeping houses and below them on the beach low gray clouds and the phosphorescent lips of the surf, curling in with the tide.

He wedged the biker's bottle between the dashboard and the floor mat and felt for the bulb of the courtesy light. Then he pressed the photovoltaic cell to the bulb and secured it firmly with two short lengths of electrical tape. When the door opened and the bulb went on it would shine on the cell in a little cocoon of tape, shine on the cell and nothing else. A live bomb, a dead-certain explosion. He took the one remaining wire from the top of the bottle and held it an inch from the cell.

You hear it said of a person: She just blew up, he just flew apart. Renner closed his eyes for a moment. Emotions under pressure blew up. But how about a slow-motion explosion, a slow deliberate blowing apart of what you stood for, what you did? *Did you ever set a bomb in Europe, Renner?* Musso with his huge belly, his cop's sneer. Bomb experts don't set bombs. He let the little Tigar flashlight run down his wrist to somebody else's trembling fingers pinching the coiled end of the wire. Somebody else set bombs. He glanced over the dashboard at the huge, gray, impersonal ocean. He wound the wire into place.

On the sand outside he knelt and repeated the jimmying motions to lift the hood. With one hand he reconnected the battery cables and then let the hood fall back into place.

As he straightened and looked toward the house his hands passed through the glow of the street lamp on the other side of the little roadway. He had had the slight tremor in his hands for years. There was no medical problem, no difficulty with his work. His hands simply trembled night and day, he thought, as if shaken by a thousand invisible, unheard explosions.

A schoolboy phrase came flying out of his memory. *Jactata est.* The die was cast. He pocketed his bomb tool.

Twenty yards away, suddenly, the lights on the lower floor of Caute's house flashed on and off, on and off.

41

"HE CALLED YOU TWICE," MUSSO SAID AS LOUDLY AS HE COULD, trying to make himself heard over the goddamn police radio on the desk. "According to my information."

The voice on the radio rose again, calling for a backup fire unit, asking for the ETA of the other ambulances.

Musso cursed and worked his hands in his pockets and swiveled on one foot. He paced, turned, lowered his face, and glowered. From her chair Rosalie Garbutt looked up defiantly and recrossed her arms over her chest. Beside her the EOC supervisor started to scribble again.

"You want to turn that down?" Musso shouted. "You want to turn it down from ear-split to deafen?"

"This is a major bomb, Musso," the supervisor said, and he wrote another sentence on his pad, not looking up, looking miserable, Musso thought, looking like he didn't know which one of these shit-eaters he wanted out of his office faster. "You listening? This is a whole restaurant in Venice Beach—eight, ten people dead at least, two buildings on fire—"

Musso leaned forward and snapped the radio off. Rosalie Garbutt stared back at him. She didn't look miserable, Musso thought, straightening, rolling his shoulders in the sudden silence. She looked ready to come up swinging out of her chair and whack off his head. Renner had something, all right—the girl had run off with him, the black lady had taken him in, his wife or ex-wife or recycled wife was calling every half hour from San Francisco. And here he was, old enough to know better, fat enough to hate risking his pension, here he was standing in the goddamn EOC six floors underground and trying to figure out what an over-the-line guy like Renner would do.

"Twice," Musso said in a normal voice. "He called you twice, Rosalie."

"Maybe he did, maybe he didn't."

Musso sighed. The supervisor had put down his pencil and swiveled to look through the one-way mirror into the 911 area. Directly behind Rosalie's broad back were two lines of identical blue-and-white telephone consoles just like the one in the supervisor's office, half blurred by the glass and the weird indirect lighting that Musso still hadn't figured out. With the radio down, the office was totally soundproofed, so that the dim figures hurrying up the aisles and talking urgently into their consoles all looked like half-focused actors in a silent movie. The Mole Cops. Musso and the Mole Cops.

"Show her," he said.

The supervisor swiveled back, studied Musso's face for a moment, then popped a series of buttons on his machine. For thirty seconds or more there was only the sound of Musso's raspy breath in the room. The console made a loud clicking sound and they could abruptly hear Rosalie's voice on the radio speaker, talking in a stage whisper, while Renner answered against a background of traffic.

"All right," Rosalie said, shrugging her big shoulders in her blazer. "That's the first time he called me, that was early afternoon. You show me a law against somebody taking a call at work."

"The man's asking you to run down a license, for God's sake," the supervisor said wearily. He hitched his belt and pointed his chin at Musso. "How long you think I'm going to sit here and play social secretary for your fun and games, Musso? I've got my own ass to cover—that's a huge bomb."

Musso squinted at the name tag the supervisor wore on his shirt pocket just above his badge.

"Scudder, right? Didn't I know your father?"

Scudder swiveled in his chair and glanced sideways at Rosalie Garbutt.

"Rampart Station in the sixties," Musso said. "Arthur C. Scudder. A hell of a cop."

"He's retired," Scudder said.

"I'm two years and five months off golden retirement myself," Musso said. "You let me alone for another ten minutes, Scudder, and you can do whatever you want to do. Just remember, I'm the one who came in here and suggested you do a little review of your tapes. I'm the one pointed out your problem." He pulled a Dutch cigar from the tin packet in his coat pocket and felt for a match. "I'm the one trying to stop *another* goddamn bomb. Ask your father about the time we chased three guys into the duck pond in MacArthur Park."

Scudder swiveled from side to side. Then he turned and shoved another button with the heel of his hand.

"This is the second call," Musso said.

Rosalie bunched her fists on the arms of her chair. "I can't fight with a whale," she said. "A lieutenant whale rat that knows every cop in L.A."

From the console speaker her own voice was coming quickly, in the same stage whisper: "It's not licensed to a person," she said. "It's a leased car. Leased from a British company in Westwood that's called the Sheffield Auto something. Auto Registry. I can give you their number and that's *it*."

Renner's answer was lost in static and then they heard the clunk of his receiver being replaced.

"That was four o'clock today?" Musso said.

"About four."

"Four-eleven," the supervisor said without turning around.

"And the last call came when you were already off shift and still just hanging around the building?"

"She stayed for overtime, on the ATO," Scudder said, and picked up a tape cassette from his cluttered desk.

Musso nodded. It was human nature to stay where the action was. A man as obsessive and loyal as Renner would have loyal, obsessive friends. He tapped ash off the end of the cigar and shifted his boot. So. Bomber number nine. Four o'clock on a Thursday morning in the goddamn EOC, burning the rule book. Did that make him Renner's friend too?

Suddenly the new tape started to run and a different operator's voice came on. Rosalie sat forward in her chair. Scudder frowned.

> "Nine one one Emergency. Los Angeles Police. How may I help you?"
>
> "I'm calling for one of your operators."
>
> "Sir?"
>
> "Pass along a message to Rosalie Garbutt, right?"
>
> "Sir, this is nine one one Police Emergency. What is your emergency?"
>
> "Rosalie Garbutt. Tell her to tell David Renner it's open house, right? Come to the party. I'm betting he knows where. Got that?"
>
> "Sir—"

The click of the receiver on the tape was nearly inaudible. The line simply went dead.

"He was calling from where?"

"On your way out," Scudder said sarcastically. He stood up, shook his trouser legs, and ejected the cassette. "On your way out, ask yourself how many people actually know when you call nine one one the number and the address go up on the screen?"

"This guy would know," Musso said, thinking that he sounded for all the world like Renner, making pronouncements about the bomber, somebody he'd never seen in his life.

"Yeah. Well, he called from a public phone booth

halfway up Pico in Santa Monica, in the Safeway mall.
Lots of luck."

Musso turned his head slightly to see Rosalie, who sat
stubbornly with both hands now on her lap, holding her
purse. When she caught his look her nostrils flared.

"You're not getting into trouble," Musso said. "I'll take
care of it."

"I'm not the one in trouble. Colonel Renner is."

Musso nodded slowly, as if she had answered a question.

"That man that called," she said, "has got a voice like a
snake. I've heard people talk like that before. In London we
got calls like that all the time on the embassy switchboard,
they were people calling about bombs."

"Scuddy, do me one more favor."

"No more favors."

"You have a business directory in here? Out in the big
room? Look up the home number of somebody for me."
Musso clenched and unclenched the fists in his pockets. He
was too old and too tired for this. He needed to sleep. His
eyes felt like fried eggs and his mouth tasted like an owl
had slept in it. Rosalie Garbutt was rising at last from her
chair, clutching the purse, as tall as he was and nearly as
heavy.

"You know what I'm doing?" Musso asked her.

"I might be female and black, my friend, but I'm not
stupid."

"I never thought you were."

"You like him as much as I do," she said. "It's three
o'clock in the morning and you're *long* off your shift. But
you're getting ready to call the man at Sheffield Auto and
wake him up and find the address of whoever leased that
car."

"I like one Renner fine," Musso said, pushing for the
door. "I like the sad-faced guy that reads poetry in his
office. The other one scares me to death."

42

ON AND OFF.

Like a signal.

At the third repetition the lights in Caute's house went black again. Renner held up his watch to catch the street lamp and waited. Five minutes passed with no sign of motion or life.

He crept forward, bearing to the left along the grassy rim of the bluff. Stairs, car hood, cyclone fence. He swung around the end of the fence, still holding the bomb tool in his left hand, and came up beside wax-leaved shrubs that ran in a border the length of the house. On the other side of the shrubs lay a narrow path, garbage cans, a fuse box.

Renner crouched on the path and listened to the surf. To his right was the end of the street, the beginning of the parking turnaround. To his left the path stopped at a waist-high wooden gate onto the patio. Down the patio to the beach. Across the patio to a neighbor's fence, more parked cars. In the flicker of the lights on and off what had he actually seen? He pinched the bridge of his nose and closed his eyes, bringing the boom of the waves suddenly nearer. Brown was what he had seen. A brown shape like a raincoat.

He stepped over the gate and onto Caute's patio deck. Beach chairs, umbrella—more wooden stairs ran down to the sand ten feet below the deck, where he could see the surf clearly, the changed tide turning back toward shore, sniffing him out.

Your eyes play tricks. Lies of the mind. She was gone to England. The lights could have come from the next house over, or from passing clouds. He padded silently across the deck to the row of curtained sliding doors that opened into the house. No movement, no lights behind the curtains. He knelt and inserted the bomb tool, flat edge first, into the lock on the sliding door.

In the distance a dog barked, a single sharp, explosive sound.

Renner twisted the bomb tool between the door frame and the latch bolt and felt it give. Then he slipped the tool back into his pocket and listened. There was only the rhythmical crash of the surf, dragging the ocean closer. Slowly he allowed his left foot to press the door sideways in its rollers. He had brought the bomb tool with all its edges and blades, the Tigar flashlight, assorted small pliers and wires. Not the little .32 government-issue automatic, which he'd left in the motel years ago. No weapon at all. *She had gone to England.* He leaned forward, letting his eyes adjust. The house was deceptively large, two stories high, backed up against the neighbors. As far as he could tell, the interior was gray, murky air, black fan-shaped ribs of furniture. The walls creaked in the sea wind. The posts holding the deck over the beach shook with a wave.

He slid the door shut behind him.

The bomb in the car was a mistake. With abrupt, belly-wrenching certainty he saw that it was a mistake. For a long moment he stood with his back pressed against the glass door, breathing deeply. Fear squeezed his eyes shut. He listened to the waves beneath him. When he opened his eyes everything was changed. If he disconnected the bomb, he thought, he could still call Musso. Caute was upstairs sleeping. There were hours yet. *There was time.* He

let out his breath and started to turn, stretching his left
hand toward the door handle. On the other side of the
room, through a partially opened window, wind moved a
curtain. A faint circle of light drifted from point to point.
A kitchen wall, a countertop, the back of a chair. A
worktable covered with wires and knives.

Renner's hand stopped an inch from the door. You think
in images, not words, he told himself. Light turned on the
wall like a wheel. He lowered his hand and took a step
forward. A human presence was in the room, sharper than
the sea air or the musty smell of damp furniture. He leaned
toward the window. He took a second step and bumped
into the leather arm of a chair. On his right he could see
now a doorway and a half-opened door. Beyond the
doorframe, in another patch of gray floating light, he could
see the triangular corner of what looked like a coat.

By the time he reached the doorway the breeze had
stopped and the patch of light from the window had faded.
He braced one hand high on the doorframe and tried to
peer into the darkness. Impossible to see. He slid his left
shoe forward and touched the ridge of a carpet and
stopped. The house vibrated with the thump of waves
against pilings. His breath brought the smell of chemicals
from somewhere behind him—the worktable?

If Caute were here?

Renner shook his head and slipped both feet onto the
carpet, straining to see. Bumps in the carpet, odd lines. He
hesitated and shook his head. His mind seemed broken into
independent, unattached thoughts. If he felt Caute's
presence—now and for so many weeks—what did Caute
feel? If he were Caute, what would he do?

The thought burst in his head at the same moment his
shoe touched the pressure switch under the carpet: He
would set a bomb. Three feet to his right a small beam of
light came on instantaneously, cutting across him at the
knees.

Renner froze. The beam was in fact two beams, two
small pocket flashlights mounted six inches apart on a box.
Their beams joined and ran across the doorway, across his
knees, like the photoelectric beam in an automatic door.

He raised his eyes. On his left, out of reach, the joined beams hit a sheet of plywood covered with a maze of wires and circuit relays, topped with a small photovoltaic cell exactly like the one in the Mercedes.

He took a tentative half-step.

The beam wavered on the plywood.

Against the wall, in the shaky glow of the flashlights, he could see the edge of a bed or a cot. *Ignore it.*

The wires led in a rolling tangle toward a briefcase turned on its side by the bed. Too dark to see inside. Light enough at the mouth to see the crimped end of a blasting cap and a puttylike mound of plastic.

Renner looked down again. His shoe clearly rested on a circular pressure switch under the carpet. If he stepped off, the plunger in the center would rise, breaking the circuit, the light would go off. If he moved forward or backward with either leg he would block the light for a second or more and the photovoltaic cells on the plywood would be in the dark, then in the light again.

How did it work?

Automatically he felt in his jacket pocket for his own flashlight. The bomb he had set in the Mercedes worked on light—light would strike the cell and power would flow to the blasting cap, boosted by the car battery, igniting the bomb in a ball of fire. Here the light struck the cell but there was no explosion. Why?

He extended the flashlight toward the plywood, but without turning it on. His hands were sweaty and trembling. His memory was tumbling down ladders. He heard the waves against the pilings, his own heartbeat, indistinguishable. In Europe they rigged traps for cops. *You're not a cop.* In Europe they rigged bombs with photovoltaic cells just as he had, light-to-power-to-charge. He closed his eyes. Light to dark.

The first rule of disarming a bomb is go to the power source.

He opened his eyes. The room was blacker than ever. He was a fisherman, wading in a tiny stream of light.

If he were Caute—if he reversed roles?

He swung his flashlight, still off, in a slow arc back and

forth above the plywood, a pantomime of action. If the light and dark reversed roles?

In London he'd made collapsing circuits for the Royal Army Bomb School, positive to negative, an "antidisturbance" device—notorious, unbreakable. Finley had remembered it. Caute would know all about it. Caute would know as much about him as he knew about Caute.

Renner positioned his thumb on the flashlight switch. A bomb was a logical, orderly construction. He forced his breath to slow down. He counted his pulse, exhaled. There were two sets of relay contacts that he could see, high and low on the plywood. The cell would generate the power; the relays would pass the power through the wires to the explosive. Why hadn't it worked? Because Caute did nothing the usual way. In his hands light yielded no further light. Renner moved the dark flashlight like a pointer. If you reversed the direction of the contacts, then darkness, not light would set off the bomb. Light would energize the top relay and close the circuit. When light went away the energy would fall, the bottom relay open.

He lowered his flashlight to the center of the plywood panel. In the corner of his eye the bed and the coat seemed to move with the rhythmical shaking of the house. Shadows rubbing against shadows. He waited, hearing nothing but the sea and the steady tom-tom of his ears. If he shone his own flashlight on the cell and stepped off the pressure switch, would the relay stay closed and harmless? Or had Caute built a second reversal into the circuit? Two lights make a dark. You think by images, you act by instinct. You choose. He could stand on the switch for hours, wondering.

He straightened and took a long, slow breath.

He extended the Tigar flashlight again until it pointed directly at the cell, then slid his thumb once more up its barrel. Count to three, point. Jump to the left, through the open door. Pray for the three-second delay. He pressed his thumb. One. Two—and at the last instant, obeying some impulse deeper than logic, he jerked his arm to the right, toward the bed, and saw at the end of his beam a woman's face impossibly white, made out of paste, crowned with blond hair, turned toward him in a macabre smile.

His foot came off the switch.

The lights overhead flashed on and off, on and off.

"It doesn't work," Caute said from the doorway.

Renner whirled and saw him, behind him the biker, and back of them both the swaying blond hair of Jillian. He looked at the mask on the bed, back at Caute, who was grinning and holding a pistol aimed at his chest.

"It doesn't work," Caute repeated. Still grinning, he lowered himself to one knee and felt with his left hand for the plywood. "Because I didn't have time to finish the good old circuits. Collapse city, right? Look at this."

Renner took one step and slung his fist like a rock into Caute's head, as hard as he could, hanging onto the flashlight barrel despite the pain, swinging again.

They went down in a rolling tangle of arms and legs, tumbling into the living room, out of the light. The flashlight skidded from his hand. He punched at shadows, half stood somehow, went down again under the biker's thick arms. Lights were coming on everywhere. Caute was staggering sideways toward the deck and the ocean. The biker hit Renner again with the same big fists, fists as big as houses, driving him back.

What he wanted was Caute. He dove past a toppling couch and the biker caught him by the shoulders and heaved him around. Together they waltzed, crashed into the worktable, spun, and came down in a cascade of wire, blades, pieces of wood. Renner's hands were slippery with oil or sweat. They skated on the floor. Blades skittered away. The biker raised an enormous fist, filling the air, preparing to swing, and Renner punched by reflex at the center of his chest. When his hand came away the blade remained. For an instant, frozen, they both stared at the circle of bright arterial blood beginning to pump. Then more blood spilled from the biker's mouth.

Renner inched backwards. The biker sat on both knees, hands at his sides, watching his chest as his shirt filled with blood like a sail.

At the door to the deck Renner glimpsed Jillian's hair

and shoulders. He lurched to his feet. The curtain where he had entered the house was ripped completely away. Through the glass the gray ocean rose and fell under a brow of fog. He stumbled forward.

On the deck itself the sky was growing lighter. He heard voices far to his right. To his left, by the steps leading down to the beach, he saw her again—a white dress, a face turned and lifted, as if she were looking back for him. His mind made a second leap. His memory seemed to collapse like a wave, in a spray of images— Jillian's face, her face lit from within as she walked out of the restaurant, her face on the bed, on his arm, in the dark, a starburst of faces. And then he was tripping like a drunk and starting to fall down the steps.

Foam rode up the sand and over his legs. Caute stepped out from between the pilings with a piece of wood in his hands and swung it like a baseball bat into his ribs and Jillian appeared behind one post, then another, receding by strobic flashes into the darkness. The next wave reached all the way to the pilings and rolled him over and over like a log. He bounced against wood, rebounded against concrete and wet sand.

Jillian, not Caute. On hands and knees he crawled, fell, crawled again. A new wave caught him in its arm and flung him sideways. He burrowed to the surface and dragged himself higher. Beyond the last piling he could see them both, two ghostly shapes but running in the same direction, floating over the sand as if they could rise and fly. Jillian, not Caute was what he wanted—he had misread his own mind, misread every face. With a huge thrust of his arms he tore free from the surf and started up the beach after them, calling her name.

The part of his mind that saw the Mercedes went blank, dead.

Caute was already halfway up the sloping wooden steps to the rim of the bluff. With one arm he was pulling— pulling or helping—Jillian climb in her dress.

He was fifty yards away when he could first hear her voice. Then Caute's voice overrode it, taunting.

A last wave clawed at the sand under his feet and sent

Renner falling forward, wrenching his ribs where Caute had hit him. His eyes went black, his mouth filled with the ocean. By the time he reached the foot of the steps he was on his hands and knees again, unable to move any farther. Caute's face hung just over the rim of the bluff, like a crazed moon. He could see Jillian's hair, her green eyes, her wide, beautiful mouth calling something to him that the wind swooped and carried away.

"No!" Renner cried. "Get away from the car! Get away from the car!"

"You want her—take her!" Caute shouted.

"Get away from the car!"

"Let *her* choose, right?" Then Caute stopped. "The car?"

From the bottom of the steps Jillian's hand was just visible as it reached toward the car door. Caute stood ten feet away, poised for an instant, motionless. *Come down!* Renner was shouting again, but her face was turning away from him, choosing, her eyes were lifting toward Caute as she stooped and pulled open the door.

Three seconds.

Against the clearing sky, in her white dress, she looked just as she had looked the first time he had seen her in the theater, alone on the stage. Naked. Luminous. Bathed in light. And then for a heartbeat dark against light, and the bomb exploded.

For Musso, far down the beach, running, the noise of the blast came second. First he saw the girl in tall, bright silhouette on the top of the bluff. The car, Simon Caute bending. Then the flash, then the sound. Then beneath them, on his knees in the waves, staring at the vanished bodies, Renner.

The fireball covered the bluff with incredible speed. Behind it the sun rose burning and orange over the Santa Monica hills and the hills themselves metamorphosed into shadows, like black waves rolling westward, bearing a sea of light.

Acknowledgments

The following people very generously took time to talk with me about police work and bombs. I am deeply grateful to them—Nick Concolino, Police Department, Davis, California; Don Hansen, San Francisco Police Department; Ron Howell, Sacramento Sheriff's Department; Ron Marley, formerly of the U. S. Air Force; David Weller, Los Angeles Police Department. Needless to say, this is entirely a work of fiction: none of my characters (and especially Gretzsky) resembles these dedicated officers.

For other conversations I am indebted to Vicki Riskin, who shared with me her knowledge of the psychology of bombers and sociopaths, and William Corson and David Kramer, who let me glimpse the world of counterintelligence. David Miller and Geoffrey Cowan are semper praesentes. Diana Dulaney typed and encouraged with unfailing generosity.

About the Author

MAX BYRD is the author of four other thrillers, all published by Bantam Books. *California Thriller* won the Shamus Award of the Private Eye Writers of America. *Target of Opportunity* was a Featured Selection of the Book-of-the-Month Club. He makes his home in northern California.